COUNTER STRIKE

A PJ Carpenter Thriller

Michael Monahan

COUNTER STRIKE Copyright © 2019 by Michael Monahan. All Rights Reserved.

All rights reserved. No part of this book may be reproduced in any form or by any electronic or mechanical means including information storage and retrieval systems, without permission in writing from the author. The only exception is by a reviewer, who may quote short excerpts in a review.

COVER DESIGNED BY ROBIN KEYS
www.robinkeys2.com

This book is a work of fiction. Names, characters, places, and incidents either are products of the author's imagination or are used fictitiously. Any resemblance to actual persons, living or dead, events, or locales is entirely coincidental.

Michael Monahan
Visit my website at www.michaelrmonahan.com

Printed in the United States of America

First Printing: Jan 2019

ISBN- 9781728826899

Other books by
Michael Monahan

The Bringer of Death

ACKNOWLEGMENTS

I have often been asked: *What led you to decide to write a book?* It's a great question and one I am sure many writers have been asked, especially ones with no background in creative writing. The answer is rooted in a recommendation from many years ago. Just before high school graduation, one of my favorite teachers, Richard Joyce—apparently sensing some modicum of ability—suggested I might consider writing or journalism as a career. Of course, I ultimately dismissed the idea, choosing instead to pursue a degree in business and international relations before securing a juris doctor degree.

Nevertheless, writing has proven to be an integral aspect of my vocations, whether as an attorney, investment banker, or corporate strategist. As such, I developed an awareness of and appreciation for quality writing, which motivated me to improve my own abilities. I found that I liked the challenge of writing effectively and even occasionally managed to put together a legal brief, white paper, or offering document that garnered strong praise. However, while the roles I have held throughout my professional career require at least some facility with the written word, cogency is the aim, leaving little room for artistic license in the work product.

It was not until I became an avid recreational reader that I began to consider trying my hand at authorship. Over time, I discovered that the seed first planted by a well-intentioned and thoughtful teacher had taken root in my subconscious. As I read more and more, the prospect of writing a novel increasingly entered my thoughts. Indeed, on one or two occasions over the years, I actually sat down and tried to start the process, but each time other priorities and ineptitude conspired to stymie the effort. Finally, in early 2017, I decided to give it a concerted shot. By that point in time, it was more a personal challenge than anything. Since I had no idea what I was doing, I simply started typing. I began with nothing more than a premise and a general idea for an ending.

I admit to feeling a sense of accomplishment when I released *The Bringer of Death* in December 2017, but I had no expectations about how the book would be received. While I allowed myself to romanticize that readers would find the novel a worthwhile and fun read, I certainly did not anticipate the effusive feedback it has received. The response has been truly humbling, and it encouraged me to give it another try.

As in any journey in life, I have received invaluable assistance and encouragement from family and friends—old and new—during my ventures, including those as an author. I am truly fortunate and blessed to be surrounded with loving family and friends. And I would be remiss if I did not extend my gratitude to those who have helped me, not just with my writing, but in so many ways. Hopefully I have regularly expressed my gratitude adequately so that you realize your importance to me. That said, there are a few particularly special people I would like to mention here, each of whom I admire and attempt to emulate, yet often fail to live up to their examples.

To my wife, Julie, you are truly everything to me and our family. Besides your boundless love and patience, you inspire me to believe anything is possible. To my Mom and Dad, one cannot ask for more loving and nurturing parents. To my sister, Melissa, thank you for your always timely advice and encouragement. To my cousins, Matt Jones and Robin Keys, distance will never diminish the special bonds we share—in fact, it probably works in my favor! To my dear friends and brothers, Christopher Bellini, Michael Fitzgibbons, Vincent Gallucci, and John Madden, I cherish the bonds we share and am grateful for your always sagacious counsel and relentless support. To Father John Bauer, thank you for your friendship and spiritual guidance; I am a stronger and an aspiring better person for both.

I want to also include a special thank you to the aforementioned Ms. Robin Keys, who designed the cover for *Counter Strike*. I hope the book approaches the quality of its cover. More information about my wonderfully talented cousin and a portfolio of her brilliant work can be found at: www.robinkeys2.com

Not least of all, thank you to my readers for your willingness to give a budding author an opportunity. Without your feedback and encouragement, I may have simply checked writing a novel off the bucket list and not continued to pursue this passion. With each of my novels, I endeavored to provide you with an eagerly anticipated and entertaining escape. It is my sincere hope *Counter Strike* at least approaches that standard. Please know your continued support and recommendations of my books to your families and friends is very much appreciated. And please always feel free to send comments and questions to me at: michaelrmonahan@gmail.com

Again, thank you and I hope you enjoy *Counter Strike.*
Michael Monahan
January, 2019

To
Julie, Sam, and Gabby

Chapter 1
Chaambi Mountains, Tunisian-Algerian Border

Preston James Carpenter slipped from the trees and carefully weaved around the muddy puddles that were growing by the second along his path to the edge of the cliff. He and his team had been in Tunisia for less than seven hours. In that short time, they had experienced two seasons. When they landed in Tunis shortly after midday, the skies were mostly clear and Carpenter was comfortable in short sleeves. But on their drive south, away from the capital, the nasty storm that had been forecast started rolling in from the west. The first drops of rain started to fall just as the men began their stealthy ascent through the alpine forest. Now, slightly more than thirty minutes before the shrouded sun was scheduled to officially set, the temperature had fallen at least twenty degrees and the low black clouds overhead were dispensing a cold steady rain. To add to the misery, a gale had preceded the darkening skies and the winds were showing no signs of abating. Although the foul weather was to be expected, it still sucked. At least it wasn't snowing. Not yet, anyway.

Carpenter bit down his disappointment as he peered over the edge of the exposed cliff. The layer of fog and low clouds ushered in by the storm had settled into the wadi below and completely shrouded the five-thousand-foot peak looming above him. His new vantage point failed to offer any better insight than they had back in the forest, which was close to nothing. Between the fog, the howling wind, and the encroaching dimness, he could not see or hear any signs of life above or below. He crouched into a squat and waited, silently wishing for circumstances to change and thinking about the events that had led him here.

Chapter 2

Carpenter and his team were in Tunisia at the behest of the United States Central Intelligence Agency—more specifically, as members of a select group within the CIA that was specifically charged with preventing and disrupting terrorist threats. In the Agency's nomenclature, "center" was the formal term given to the group and, in this case, it referred to what was again known as the Counterterrorism Center or CTC. Comprised of both analytic and operational functions, the CTC represented a unique and particularly effective weapon against extremist threats.

Carpenter and his teammates spent the majority of their time on the operational side of the ledger. As highly-trained paramilitary officers, they were tasked with denying terrorists safe harbor. In simpler terms, they took the bad guys off the playing field. Men like these were called on when a greater degree of precision than a laser-guided weapon was necessary or desired. This required that they infiltrate and operate in hostile territory. Adding to the peril, these covert operations were, more often than not, executed without official US government sanction. And all of this was true in this case.

On this occasion, PJ Carpenter and his men were hunting one of the perpetrators of the coordinated attacks at the Super Bowl and the Great American Mall two months earlier. Only weeks before those attacks, Carpenter had raised concerns that al Qaeda might be ready to rear its ugly head again. While analysis was not his main function, the veteran operator had earned a reputation as one of the Agency's best critical thinkers, and his opinions carried significant weight up to the highest levels of the US government. At the time, his warning was based on little more than a hunch, but the theory later gained some steam through a report authored by Ella Rock, one of the CTC's rising stars. A team headed by another of the CTC's brightest and most capable analysts, Samantha Lane, was quickly assembled. In short order, some disturbing pieces of intelligence began to fall into place. Carpenter was dispatched to Cairo where he latched onto the trail of the two men who would ultimately lead the attacks in Minnesota. The information he gathered in Egypt took him to the unruly Tri Border Area in South America. Each time, Carpenter was a step behind his prey, but it soon became clear that a team of terrorists was in the United States and planning an imminent attack.

Over the course of the next three weeks, the full resources of the US government were brought to bear on the most serious matter. But those efforts failed to yield any information that even remotely suggested the whereabouts of the terrorists or their intended target. As time passed, one by one, potential targets were eliminated until the Super Bowl loomed on the calendar. The president's decision to send Carpenter and a paramilitary team to Minnesota was based on nothing more than Carpenter's educated guess. Despite the best efforts of the intelligence community and federal and state law enforcement, the US suffered the most devastating attacks on its soil since 2001.

The after-action review concluded that the attacks would have been far worse but for Carpenter's quick thinking and decisive actions. But Carpenter did not see things that way. He blamed himself for having failed to make the decision to take out the driver of first vehicular-borne improvised explosive device sooner than he did. The fact he and his team foiled the second VBIED attempt at the Super Bowl was a hollow consolation. By that point in time, dozens already lay dead and many more were injured. And Carpenter barely had time to rue his mistakes before another attack was underway at a second location.

The second attack at the Great American Mall commenced before the situation at the Super Bowl had even begun to stabilize. With an unsteady situation downtown at the stadium and no time to spare, Carpenter left his team in place headed off by himself to confront the second attack. When he arrived at the mall minutes later, three sides of the building and portions of the adjacent parking ramps had been completely destroyed by car bombs, killing everyone within a few hundred feet and closing off all but one exit from the massive building. And more terrorists were garrisoned inside, hunting down and shooting those who were unable to escape. With a massacre unfolding and no reinforcements in sight, Carpenter slipped inside the mall alone.

He was inside only seconds when he dropped the first terrorist in range, and he kept moving deeper into the mall to track down the rest. As he closed in on a pair of jihadists, he encountered a young man named Tyler Kennedy, who was looking for a way out for himself and his young cousins. Carpenter had no intention of putting the earnest young man in harm's way but circumstances left him no choice. By the time reinforcements finally arrived, he and Kennedy had killed the remaining five, heavily armed terrorists. More than three thousand terrified people were subsequently evacuated from the expansive building. Although it could not be known how many of those fortunate people Carpenter had saved from certain annihilation, the rosiest of estimates put the figure in the hundreds. The authorities ultimately recovered a cache of unspent rounds that could have killed the number of survivors more than twice over.

When Carpenter finally had time to reflect on the intelligence leading up to the attacks and the events of that day, he knew he had failed his fellow citizens. He believed he should have expected that the terrorists might strike multiple targets, and the Great American Mall and Super Bowl offered two highly attractive targets in one location at time when the Twin Cities would be at the center of the world's attention. In hindsight, it was all plain to see. Carpenter didn't care that everyone else had underestimated the ambitions of the planners; it only mattered that he had.

To compound his frustration, the attacks had been orchestrated by the man Carpenter had been pursuing for years. The al Qaeda bomb-maker was known only as Mumeet—the Bringer of Death. No Western intelligence agency had even one photograph of the terrorist. Rather, his identity was unmistakably connected to a trail of destructive devices that bore his unique signature. US intelligence had long since determined that Mumeet was responsible for more deaths than any other jihadist. This was more than enough to earn Mumeet a prominent place on anyone's most-wanted list, but Carpenter had a personal score to settle with the terrorist. And Carpenter had failed to stop him in Minnesota. He was even more irritated when it was later determined that Mumeet had, in all probability, been in the vicinity of the mall when Carpenter arrived on scene. Yet, despite the most intense manhunt in US history, Mumeet and the man they were hunting in Tunisia had somehow evaded capture.

At the time of the attacks, US intelligence had only poor-quality passport photos of two men, one of them suspected to be Mumeet. The second man was a complete unknown. Despite weeks of circulation prior to the attacks, the passport photos had failed to prompt any insight to their true identities. Even before the recovery operations were underway, a frenzied search to find better-quality images had become a top priority. Kevin Lingel of the CTC assembled a team of technology specialists to scrutinize video from both attack locations. One of Lingel's first additions to the team was Blake Palmer of the National Security Agency. Palmer had been the NSA's designee to the Interagency Incident Management Group the president convened to track down the terrorists after it became clear they were already in the country. Together, Lingel and Palmer supervised the team as it scoured every frame from more than seven hundred hours of footage from the ninety-four cameras interspersed throughout the security zones surrounding the stadium in downtown Minneapolis, as well as thousands more hours of video from scores of cameras inside and outside the mall.

Their first break came when the Honda Civic was discovered a day after the attacks. Once the area around the stadium had been deemed safe, people were instructed to retrieve their cars. The Civic, parked on the roof of a parking ramp where one of the terrorists had been spotted, was one of the few cars left unclaimed. The car was traced to Farmshire, a remote suburb about twenty-five miles southwest of the stadium. While information was gathered about the owners from government databases, a team was dispatched to the home. It didn't take long before they realized the terrorists had used the farmstead to stage the attacks. In addition to evidence of explosives, three bodies were discovered behind the barn. A short time later, the farmer's pickup was found in a hotel parking lot across the street from the mall.

The most apparent conclusion was that Mumeet had driven the pickup to the mall, where he monitored the attack from a safe distance, while the unidentified terrorist had driven the Civic to the stadium. Working on those assumptions, Lingel directed Palmer and the rest of the team to focus their efforts on determining the time of the compact car's arrival at the stadium. Palmer was the first to pinpoint the car's arrival, just before 10:00 a.m. on that fateful day. From there, the enterprising NSA analyst and the rest of the team scrutinized succeeding hours of activity at the parking ramp, looking for patterns among the tens of thousands of fans in the area. It was Palmer again who first identified the terrorist, having detected the same man exit and enter the parking ramp several times throughout that morning and early afternoon. But Palmer had only been able to identify the man by the football jersey and stocking cap he was wearing. There wasn't a single frame that clearly captured the man's face. So the search expanded beyond the parking ramp, zeroing in on men wearing the local team's colors from the time of the compact car's arrival to the first sixty minutes immediately following the first car bomb explosion. One by one, as suspects were eliminated, Palmer finally isolated the man. After nearly three days and operating on little more than a few hours of sleep, Palmer had captured what ultimately proved to be the one fleeting but well-defined image of the man's face they would find.

Palmer later located one additional image of the unidentified man. It was taken nine days before the attacks. The man had glanced up at one of the cameras positioned inside the mall just long enough to capture a grainy image of his face. But there was no question they were looking at the same man. And this time, the man was not alone. Despite the baseball hat covering his face, no one doubted that the other man was Mumeet, the shadowy mastermind of the attacks.

Lingel went to work on the captured images. Using the geometric data gleaned from the measurements of spatial relationships between facial features, the CTC technologist attempted to create face templates for both men. Unfortunately, the mall footage did not reveal enough of Mumeet's face to produce sufficient photometric data. Lingel tried but the algorithms failed to produce anything better than the poor-quality passport photo they already had for the Bringer of Death, so Mumeet's true identity remained a mystery. But Lingel had much better results with the images of the unidentified terrorist, particularly that captured at the Super Bowl site. The template Lingel constructed was compared to all domestic and international law enforcement databases. There were no positive hits but they had their first solid piece of evidence. And it was not long before it paid dividends.

Besides directing the full resources of the United States to identify and track down the terrorists involved and anyone else who even remotely supported them, President Daniel Madden made it clear that less than complete cooperation by any sovereign nation would be viewed as an act of aggression against the United States. He got the point across over the course of numerous private telephone calls and a passionate primetime press conference, for which he was ridiculed by the press and a cadre of pundits, both at home and abroad, for his uncompromising posture. According to the cognoscenti, that kind of bellicose diplomacy was unsuitable to the presidency and would only serve to isolate the United States. Undeterred, President Madden doubled down on his warning, telling allies and adversaries alike in a follow up press conference two days later, "You are either with us or against us. It is a simple, binary choice," he said.

A notable upsurge in cooperation from foreign intelligence agencies soon followed, including from some with a checkered past when it came to sharing sensitive information about radical Islamists. Almost immediately after circulating the captured image and Lingel's template of the man's face, he was identified by the Saudi General Intelligence Directorate, Al Mukhabarat Al A'amah. The man who had driven the Honda Civic to the stadium was a Saudi, and his name was Fahd al-Rasheed.

Acknowledging that fact had been particularly difficult for the Saudis. It was more troublesome when, a couple days later, al Qaeda publicly declared another Saudi, and a member of the extended royal family, as its co-leader. His name was Prince Sadiq bin Aziz. Aziz's confirmed role did not come as a surprise. Even before the public declaration, the US was reasonably certain Aziz was somehow tied to the attacks. In fact, President Madden had raised the Aziz issue with the Saudis when they acknowledged al-Rasheed as one of their own and before the al Qaeda statement. At that time, the Saudis dismissed Aziz's involvement as implausible. They claimed the highly successful businessman had no connections to extremism or al-Rasheed.

The public praise of Aziz dispensed with further denials and placed the Saudis in a precarious position that President Madden unabashedly leveraged to secure their full cooperation.

Yet, even with the concerted effort at home and nearly universal assistance from around the globe, the frantic search to find the three principals behind the attacks failed to yield any credible leads. No one, including the now fully-supportive Saudis, had any idea where Aziz, Mumeet, or al-Rasheed was hiding. It was widely assumed that Aziz was encamped with the rest of al Qaeda's senior leaders—known as the *shura*—somewhere in the Federally Administered Tribal Areas of Pakistan. The unsuccessful efforts to find them also dictated that Fahd al-Rasheed and Mumeet had probably slipped out of the United States and were likely with Aziz plotting future attacks.

It was two months after the attacks in Minnesota when the news arrived that Fahd al-Rasheed may have been spotted in Tunisia. For several reasons, Tunisia was as plausible as anywhere for al-Rasheed to have fled. North Africa had become a favored destination for terrorist groups seeking to avoid annihilation in places like Syria, Iraq, and Afghanistan. Adding to that, the newfound autonomies enjoyed by its overwhelmingly peaceful citizens of the smallest country on Africa's Mediterranean coast were equally attractive to extremists. The successful revolt against Tunisia's dictator had ushered in the Arab Spring in 2011 and, ever since, Tunisians had been enjoying the freedoms to organize, travel, and share information. And these liberties also worked in favor of jihadists by giving them freedom to operate as they worked to exploit the poverty and marginalization that stubbornly clung to certain parts of the population. For these reasons, Tunisia had become fertile grounds for the recruitment and training of new warriors. In fact, the percentage of Tunisians engaged in jihad outstripped that in every other nation.

Fortunately for Carpenter and his CTC colleagues, the Tunisian government had shown no tolerance for extremists and aggressively sought to eradicate them. Although the efforts produced some successes, the Tunisians quickly found that the escalating problem was too great for their limited resources. Realizing this, Tunisia was increasingly open to assistance from the United States, a country with whom it had a long, yet unsteady alliance. The number of Central Intelligence Agency officers operating out of the US embassy in Tunis was one indication of those warming relations. That number now stood at four, twice the figure it was only a year earlier in the former French colony.

One of those recent additions was veteran operations officer Dan O'Reilly. It was only fitting that O'Reilly was sent to Tunisia. Over the years, he had repeatedly found himself in whatever was considered at the time to be one of the most hostile regions on earth. Each time, he went willingly and, most importantly, he delivered the goods. The Irishman had indeed kissed the Blarney Stone and he could spin a yarn in six different languages. But as much as those tangible skills contributed to his success, O'Reilly was as highly regarded for his nerve. Legend in the Agency was that O'Reilly had both the balls and the talent to coax a lion away from a fresh kill. He was revered throughout the Agency, especially by those lucky enough to have worked alongside him. And, during his thirty-two-year career, six of his former colleagues who had gone on to become CIA directors. The most recent of them being Melissa Gonzalez. And one of the first things Director Gonzalez did after assuming the leadership role for the Agency was put O'Reilly to work in North Africa.

When he had arrived in Tunisia ten months earlier, O'Reilly didn't waste any time hitting the ground. He set his sights on the mountainous area around Kasserine. O'Reilly quickly found that despite the alarming number of Tunisians committed to jihad, the overwhelming majority were just as passionately opposed to extremism. They were not at all interested in substituting one merciless, dictatorial power for another. To fend off the threat to their freedoms, citizens had boldly taken to the streets in "no to terrorism" protests. Recognizing the potential intelligence value, O'Reilly paid particular attention to the demonstrations, attending every one he could. In no time, the gifted Agency veteran had a burgeoning stable of spies. And among his more recent recruits was a shepherd by the name of Tahar Kemiri.

When O'Reilly encountered him after a demonstration in the small village of Boulaaba a few months back, Kemiri had yet to fully recover from a shrapnel wound to his right leg. The injury resulted when one of his goats stepped on a mine that had been planted by one of many terrorist groups besieging the area. At sixty-two years old, Tahar Kemiri possessed the savvy that one acquires from decades of dealing with all sorts of people. So, when O'Reilly approached him, Kemiri already had a pretty good idea about what O'Reilly was peddling. When Kemiri called his bluff, O'Reilly, having a sixth sense of his own, came clean.

An immediate friendship was born and Kemiri willingly offered O'Reilly his assistance. But he didn't want any of the money O'Reilly was offering. Rather, he said that his only motivation was returning peace and security to his small village. While downplaying his own travails, Kemiri told O'Reilly about the horrors he had witnessed in and around Boulaaba at the hands of the jihadists. As a devout Muslim, Tahar Kemiri denounced the violence and evil these radicals perpetuated and he was committed to cleansing them from his country. Kemiri's only conditions were that he not be seen with O'Reilly and that the CIA man had better act on any relevant information he provided. Kemiri wasn't interested in risking his life without a direct benefit to his fellow citizens.

Four days before Carpenter and his team arrived in Tunisia, Tahar Kemiri phoned the number O'Reilly had given him. Unfortunately, O'Reilly was in the field on another recruiting op and unable to accept the call. Kemiri was forced to leave a coded message and a promise to try again in two days, when he next expected an opportunity to make the seven-mile walk to Kasserine. When Kemiri finally called late during that second evening, O'Reilly answered on the first ring. The skilled operations officer listened as Kemiri told him how he had seen a man bearing a strong resemblance to one of the men in the photos O'Reilly had showed him several weeks before. A few questions helped convince O'Reilly that Kemiri had, in fact, seen Fahd al-Rasheed.

From that point, things moved quickly. As soon as the call ended, O'Reilly reported the information to Kelly Bellini, the Tunis chief of station, and then immediately left for Kasserine. Even before O'Reilly was out of the embassy, Bellini was on the phone with CIA Director Gonzalez. Knowing O'Reilly and Bellini as she did, Gonzalez had enough confidence in the report to interrupt the president's brief holiday.

At the time, President Madden was in in the remote Chic-Choc Mountains on the Gaspé Peninsula in Quebec, backcountry skiing with the

Canadian prime minister. She was the first foreign head of state to visit the president, shortly after his inauguration. It was at that meeting that they realized their mutual affection for skiing, and the prime minister readily accepted the president's invitation for a day of skiing in the American Rockies. But her acceptance was given with one cheeky condition—that she be allowed to host the following year. Before leaving Colorado last year, they set the date and place for their second annual trip. The Canadian prime minister had promised him the best spring skiing in the world. And, after taking in the unspoiled views during a morning of skiing on top of more than ten feet of snow under bluebird skies, the president had absolutely no reason to argue otherwise.

The two leaders were enjoying a light lunch and charting plans for next year when they were approached by Travis Keys, the head of the president's security detail. Keys had partly earned the position by being the only person in the Secret Service able to keep up with the president on the slopes. With only enough time to apologize to the prime minister, the president followed the former University of Colorado All-American through trees and unbroken snow until they reached an old mining road and the rest of the security team. From there, the president was hustled to the nearby town of Murdochville, where his forethinking chief of staff had already established a makeshift secure communications facility.

While the president was being briefed by Director Gonzalez and Timothy Patrick—the director of the CTC and Carpenter's boss—Chief of Staff Bill Tackett was on another secure line prepping Secretary of State Julie Christensen and Secretary of Defense Michael Fitzgibbons. As soon as he hung up with his intelligence chiefs, the president was patched into Tackett's call with Secretaries Christensen and Fitzgibbons. Thanks to the lead-in provided by Tackett, the cabinet members were fully prepared when President Madden started peppering them with questions. Secretary Fitzgibbons first explained that a strong low-pressure system was predicted to be moving into and lingering over the northern part of the continent for the next seventy-two hours. Unless the forecast was wrong, Secretary Fitzgibbons said, a reconnaissance drone was unlikely to be of much use. In the secretary's opinion, having boots on the ground in the mountainous region was the better option for dealing with al-Rasheed, anyway. Secretary

Christensen also poured water on any plans to go after al-Rasheed with a drone. She counseled that it was not a foregone conclusion that the Tunisians would grant permission to their airspace. More than that unpredictability, Secretary Christensen had little faith that the Tunisians could fully contain the information the US government would be forced to share about the critical mission. His top advisors agreed that the only benefit to alerting the Tunisians would have been to gain access to their airspace. It just so happened that advice was consistent with the president's own preference. In truth, the president never entertained any thought to seek permission from the Tunisians to enter either their territory or their airspace. Although the president listened to the counsel of his advisors, he knew all along that he was going to send PJ Carpenter to handle things. In no time, President Madden was back on the phone with Gonzalez and Patrick.

Less than two hours had elapsed from the time Director Gonzalez received the call from COS Bellini when she and Patrick sat down with Carpenter to brief him in. As his bosses laid out the intelligence, Carpenter felt the adrenaline surge through him. He was aware of reports that al Qaeda had been suspected of assembling men and matériel in the remote mountains of southwestern Tunisia. It made sense to him that the terror group would be drawn by the rugged terrain on both sides of the border with Algeria, making the region difficult for authorities to monitor. It would also be appealing because the environment would be familiar to anyone who had previously served with al Qaeda in Central Asia. Although the climate was more temperate, the isolation and collection of caves and tunnels in this part of Tunisia would be reminiscent of the safe haven the terrorist group had once enjoyed and was attempting to reclaim in Afghanistan. Finally, there were reports that some Islamic State splinter groups operating in the Chaambi Mountains region were said to be switching allegiances to the reemergent al Qaeda. Carpenter recognized that all these factors supported the possibility that Fahd al-Rasheed was in Tunisia. As Gonzalez and Patrick filled in more details, Carpenter began to feel something he had no felt in weeks—a sense of purpose and a real opportunity for retribution.

After they finished relating how the intelligence had transpired, Carpenter listened as the two senior Agency officials moved onto tactics and objectives. He would be going in covertly, they told him. The president's orders were to capture al-Rasheed, if at all possible. Al-Rasheed was a big fish, but not the one the president most wanted, nor did Carpenter for that matter. Mumeet was the real prize they were after. If he could be captured, the US wanted any intelligence al-Rasheed could provide about the Bringer of Death. Even though there had been no sighting of Mumeet in Tunisia, the expectation was that he and al-Rasheed had plans to reunite at some point. However, the president made sure there was no confusion about the ultimate objective. Gonzalez and Patrick told him the president had said, "If capture is not possible or it even remotely imperils the team's safety, I want PJ to kill al-Rasheed and every last terrorist with him. Under no circumstances is Fahd al-Rasheed to get out of Tunisia alive."

Carpenter had no concerns about the clandestine nature of the operation or the objective, though he would have preferred a straight kill order. Based on experience, he was skeptical that someone like al-Rasheed would give up any useful information. But Carpenter had one demand of his own—he insisted that he be allowed to bring the men who had been with him in Minnesota. To begin with, he trusted the four men, having worked with each of them prior to their time together in Minnesota. Just as important in his mind, Carpenter had a sense of obligation to the men for they, too, had unfinished business.

Knowing Carpenter as well as he did, Patrick had anticipated this. No matter how many times Patrick tried to convince him otherwise, Carpenter refused to accept the reality that theirs was not a zero-sum world; that successfully stopping every terrorist attack was an impossible standard and complete victories were elusive. Patrick attributed this denial to Carpenter being the most stubbornly competitive person Patrick had ever known. Because of this, Patrick had a strong feeling Carpenter would want the men with him in Minnesota to have a shot at redemption. So, right before he and Director Gonzalez sat down with Carpenter to brief him on the operation, Patrick had issued instructions to round up Ben Doran, Terrance Wood, Dan Hofstad, and Seth Anderson.

Chapter 3

By the time Carpenter arrived at Dulles International Airport a few hours later, his team was already aboard the private plane. In other circumstances, Carpenter would have preferred to avoid entering through the capital, but insertion via a more direct and concealed route was ruled out. Despite a feeling that the team could probably slip into the country undetected by Tunisia's relatively poor air defense systems, Carpenter and Patrick agreed it was too risky to attempt a helicopter insertion from the *USS New York*, which was currently sailing in the Mediterranean. Besides the weather forecast, there was a good chance the bird would land right in the middle of several terrorist camps believed to exist in the area. Because the situation in the theater of operations was fluid and largely unknown, it meant the landing would have to be staged in a distant location, out of sight and earshot from any potential terrorist enclave. After factoring in the logistics and the nominal time they could potentially save, Carpenter agreed that arrival through Tunis made the most sense. His only concern was customs but Patrick assured him entry would not be a problem.

Given the time difference and distance, it was early afternoon the next day when the highly-skilled hunters arrived in the sunny North African coastal city. They stepped off the plane at the private hanger for Tunis-Carthage International, immaculately groomed and donning the smart attire of sophisticated diplomats. Dan O'Reilly was there to meet them and idling nearby were two large SUVs, each operated by one of O'Reilly's Agency colleagues. Standing alongside O'Reilly at the bottom of the plane's steps was a high-ranking Tunisian Customs official. The man was one of O'Reilly's first agents in Tunisia, and the modestly-compensated bureaucrat had come to greatly appreciate the pecuniary benefits of the relationship. Although his self-effacing nature kept him from saying it aloud, O'Reilly was convinced the official would allow him to bring a nuclear weapon into the country.

More than sufficiently motivated by the roll of hundred-dollar bills bulging in his pocket, the unctuous customs official merely feigned interest at the passports flashed by each of the five athletically built men as they stepped onto the tarmac. The official didn't even bother with the pretense of inspecting the several extra-large travel cases as they were loaded into the first Chevy Suburban under the keenly alert eyes of their owners. As soon as the luggage was aboard, O'Reilly dismissed the official and Carpenter directed his men into the two armored vehicles. Less than five minutes after stepping off the plane, the convoy was leaving the airport and heading straight for the embassy.

The team wasted no time once inside the secure compound. After organizing their own gear, Wood, Hofstad, and Anderson stuffed their muscled frames into a dented Toyota 4Runner and left the embassy wearing more casual attire. Minutes later, the Chevy Suburban followed, carrying Carpenter, Doran, O'Reilly, and all the equipment. When their occupants were certain they were not being tailed, the two vehicles hooked up on the outskirts of Tunis and headed south on the A1 Highway toward Sfax.

Some three hours later, they stopped in Subaytilah, not far from the ancient Roman ruins in Sbeitla. That placed them about an hour's drive from Kasserine and the nearby Chaambi Mountains. O'Reilly's same colleagues from the airport were waiting for them in Subaytilah with a new fleet of vehicles. The dust-caked Renault Symbol sedans were commonplace throughout Tunisia and far less-likely to garner attention when the caravan entered known terrorist territory. After the gear was transferred to the new vehicles and the men changed into tactical gear, the convoy left Subaytilah. There was little talk during the ensuing short drive, as Carpenter and the team concentrated on the task at hand. After silently rolling through mostly baked-out desert for an hour, Carpenter and his team entered Chaambi Mountain National Park.

Al-Rasheed had not been seen again in or around Kasserine since Tahar Kemiri had seen him four days earlier. If al-Rasheed was still in the area, he was believed to be hiding somewhere higher up in these mountains under the protection of a group of terrorists associated with al Qaeda in the Islamic Maghreb, or AQIM. To the uninitiated, it might seem almost worthless but the uncertainty of the intel was typical. And this was the best that had come their way in the past two months. The lack of specificity had no effect of the team's enthusiasm. The chance, even a slim one, to bag al-Rasheed was all the motivation they needed.

When they arrived at the base of the mountain, the convoy was stopped for only seconds, allowing the men to disembark with their gear and scurry into the trees. Once in the protection of the forest, the trained killers changed into weatherproof woodland digital camo and put the finishing touches on the dark camo face paint they had started applying as the cars approached the park. Less than five minutes later, Carpenter and his men slid into their rucksacks and started their stealthy journey up the mountain under darkening skies and freshening winds. The men did not know what to expect but they were prepared for anything. Among other gear, each man carried a Sig Sauer P226 semi-automatic pistol, a KA-BAR military and tactical knife, and a rifle. Carpenter's two best shooters, Wood and Doran, were equipped with sniper rifles, while the rest of the team hefted carbines; either an HK416 or, in the case of Anderson, the Colt M4A1 he grew up shooting on his family's farm in Vermont. Anybody foolish enough to confront them was going to regret that decision.

As Carpenter and his team picked their way through trees and rocks covering the mountainside, their senses were acutely engaged to detect the subtlest sign of trouble. Alert eyes scanned in every direction and darted toward the slightest sound. Every step was taken and measured in preparation for swift and maximum aggression that the team of assassins could dispense in any number of ways. Carpenter appreciated how the team's determination had been building since the plane touched down in Tunis. To him, this operation was personal and he sensed the men felt the same way.

Forty-five minutes into the journey, Hofstad broke the silence with a comment about the first sprinkles. When the first downpour came, they stopped to put on the rest of their snivel gear—the team's preferred term for inclement weather clothing. Since then, they had forged halfway up the mountain in a driving rain. Inside the weatherproof clothing, the men were dry and, for the most part, warm. Except for its effect on their pace and having to consciously adjust their senses to it, the weather was largely an afterthought. Every one of them would have marched up the mountain in their skivvies on the chance al-Rasheed was there.

Chapter 4

Now Carpenter was squatting at the edge of the cliff, gauging their next move, while absorbing thousands of blows from a cold, driving rain. He ignored the discomfort and waited expectantly for the slightest break in the weather that would yield a better perspective on the ground they still had to cover. They had some recent satellite photos but little else to guide them. They were in poorly-mapped and largely unknown territory, requiring them to proceed with extra vigilance. The journey to this point had been no picnic. And without the ability to see what lay ahead, Carpenter expected the rest of the trek would only get more difficult.

After a few minutes, he adjusted his position and tried hunching his shoulders to divert the rivulet of icy water dripping down the back of his Ops-Core ballistic helmet and onto his neck. The worsening weather was just another variable and he used this pause in their search to consider what modifications it required, if any. During similar operations around the globe for the better part of two decades, Carpenter had dealt with all kinds of elements. Given the rugged and unknown environment, he had already anticipated that they were going to have move in tight if they were going to identify Fahd al-Rasheed. Now, if these conditions persisted, they were going to have to move in even closer. But the weather and the timing potentially worked in their favor. For starters, the night was only beginning. The darkest hours were always best for his kind of work. The natural complacency that arrived a few hours after sunset tended to dull a person's senses. And that inattentiveness reached its zenith just before dawn. Even the most committed were not immune from this innate phenomenon, including the terrorists they were stalking. The nasty elements would only intensify this vulnerability. Carpenter knew from experience that no one really wanted to be outside in these conditions, especially when trouble was not expected. Anyone posted as a lookout would be more concerned with staying warm and dry. All things being equal, the inability to see or hear would work strongly in their favor. But to take advantage of the conditions, his team needed to cover the remaining ground and locate al-Rasheed and his friends before they improved.

His thoughts turned from situational analysis to the team's directives. A clean kill mission would have eliminated many of the problems created by the weather. Once the terrorist hideout was identified, they could have simply assaulted the location without regard for capturing anyone alive. Instead, they were supposed to try to capture Fahd al-Rasheed. The men had received the news about their orders to capture the al Qaeda terrorist with the same disappointment Carpenter was unable to hide when Patrick gave him the instructions back at Langley. The thought of al-Rasheed not having to pay for his offenses did not sit well with any of them. It was some consolation knowing that even if he was captured, al-Rasheed would not get off easy. The jihadist was coming out of these mountains with at least a few, carefully-chosen and painful broken bones. Carpenter would make sure of that.

After waiting a few more minutes for even the slimmest improvement, Carpenter finally relented. If anything, it seemed the conditions were getting worse. But the weather wasn't going to prevent him or his team from doing what they were here to do. And it was time to get moving. Carpenter carefully slid back from the edge of the cliff and stood up to shake out the rest of the water that had collected in the folds of the ultra-lightweight rain jacket. Then he made his way back to the others.

"Did you see anything, PJ?" Ben Doran asked.

"No, it was a complete waste of time. I couldn't see shit and didn't hear anything other than the howling wind," Carpenter said.

"You want to stay on this route or try something else?" Terrance Wood asked.

"As far as we know, this way is as good as any," Carpenter said. "According to the topo map, we have to go up at least another thousand feet in elevation to reach the caves where Tahar Kemiri thinks the terrorists are holed up. We need to keep pushing. I'd like to try to find their hideout while we still have the cover of this weather."

"We might have some issues before we reach the caves," said Doran. "So far, we've had plenty of cover, but the satellite photos show that as we get toward the summit, it's pretty much all exposed rock."

"Assuming the caves are up near the peak, we're going to have to traverse five or six hundred feet on exposed rock if we want to get close enough to see what we're dealing with," Seth Anderson said. "We're not going to be able to stay in the trees; we can barely see a hundred feet in these conditions."

"We could head over to this peak," Wood said, pointing to the topography map. "It's actually twenty-five feet higher in elevation according to the map. When the weather clears, we should be able to get eyes on their actual location and figure out the best way to approach."

"We'll be fine on this path as long as we hide behind your fat ass, T-Dub," said Dan Hofstad.

"Hey, Hof," Wood said, while flipping Hofstad the finger and laying a spittle of tobacco juice at his friend's feet.

"All right boys," Carpenter said. The two snake eaters had served together in Army Special Forces before joining the CTC and they were always needling each other. Carpenter knew the good-natured ribbing was just another sign his team was tension-free and ready. "We don't have a choice. If al-Rasheed is the area, we need to find him before he has a chance to slip out of here. I don't want to be sitting half a mile away where we can't see what the fuck is going on."

"As we were then?" asked Doran.

"Yup. We don't have any better options," Carpenter said. "Let's fan out, no more than twenty-five yards apart. We'll regroup after another five hundred feet in elevation." He allowed the men to check their altimeter watches before continuing. "T-Dub and Hof take the left flank, while Ese and Benny take the right. I'll split the middle."

Chapter 5

A few moments later, the men were in position, spread out in a line, and ready to move further up the mountain. "Comms check," Carpenter whispered into his in-ear microphone. All the men were equipped with the same lightweight tactical headsets that used push-to-talk technology. One-by-one, the men responded. "OK, let's move," he said.

As he and the men slowly moved higher, the mountains and the scrubby arid lands surrounding them reminded Carpenter of the Santa Rosa Mountains in southern Arizona. The Aleppo pines, holm oak and Juniper trees that were providing much-needed cover were similar to the species dotting the rocky mountainsides he had scaled many years ago just west of Tucson. There were differences, of course, most notably the olive trees they had traveled through when first starting out in the foothills and the lack of cacti here. In different circumstances, he might be able to enjoy the raw beauty of this place, an opportunity he had also denied himself during his time in Arizona. The Santa Rosa mountains had been one of the places Carpenter had gone to grieve following the murder of his fiancée in Pakistan a decade earlier. The natural resemblances served as a painful reminder, yet one he used as additional motivation. The bomb that had killed Lizzie had been assembled by Mumeet, and the possibility that her killer's close associate, or even Mumeet himself, might be in these mountains had his heart pounding.

Carpenter quickly recognized he needed to calm down. The difficult conditions and lurking dangers required his undivided attention and, after years of operations, he was easily able to put aside his emotions and refocus.

But it was becoming nearly impossible to see. Despite the spacing of the trees, the canopy overhead was still thick. The unseen sun had set only minutes before, but dusk was not going to be making an appearance. In the space of the last few minutes, there had been a quick fade to blackness. The wind rattled the branches above him and the rain continued to hammer down, obscuring his sense of hearing beyond a few feet. And the only thing he smelled was cold, damp air and wet foliage. He radioed instructions to the men before stopping briefly behind the trunk of a large oak tree to slip on his own night vision goggles. The sixty-five thousand-dollar NVGs provided a one hundred twenty-degree field of vision and allowed Carpenter and the team to operate in complete darkness.

When everyone was geared up and ready to move forward, Carpenter gave the order for the team to resume their quiet ascent up the north face of the mountain. Although the goggles restored their ability to see, the men still had to alternate between looking at the ground and up the mountain between steps on the uneven terrain. The risk of injury and causing a commotion by tripping over a rock or large stick was too great. The steepening of the slope further added to their slowed pace as the team quietly and cautiously navigated the rough mountainside.

Some thirty minutes later, Carpenter paused with his foot in midair. "Guys, hold up!" he urgently whispered. "I might've almost stepped on a mine!"

Hofstad quickly made his way over to Carpenter. Among the men, the Montanan held the most explosives expertise. Carpenter pointed to the slight protrusion that had barely caught his eye and the trip wire extending from it. Hofstad carefully dug around the bump and exposed the lower half of a quart-sized plastic storage container. After removing the remaining debris and carefully cutting the activator, Hofstad removed the top. "Look familiar?"

"Is that ammonium nitrate?" Carpenter asked. The fertilizer was a common ingredient used by terrorists and had indeed been the explosive in the vehicle-born bombs used at the Super Bowl and mall.

"Bingo."

"Son of a bitch."

"This would've sent parts of you about thirty feet in the air. And I'm sure there are more," Hofstad said.

"Boys, we must be getting closer," Carpenter said over the secure communications equipment. "There are confirmed mines in the area. We're going to have to take it extra slow from here. Watch every step and look for trip wires. We've got all night to get up there, if we need it. I don't want any of us leaving anything important behind."

When Hofstad was back in position, Carpenter gave the signal to move out. He and his team were well-experienced navigating minefields but the recent discovery was going to further slow their pace. To make matters worse, the rain had picked up in intensity, causing the men to have to stop every few feet to wipe drops of water from their goggles. It was painfully slow going but absolutely necessary. Along the way, two more mines were identified and defused. It took them more than an hour to move up five hundred feet in elevation. Carpenter called the men to his position behind several large boulders to reassess the plan.

"We should be almost to the edge of the trees," he said. "After that, it's mostly rock surface with a few alpine shrubs and stubby trees here and there for the last five hundred or so feet to the summit. The good news, I guess, is there won't be many places to bury a landmine. But we still need to be alert for tripwires. According to O'Reilly and Tahar Kemiri, the caves are located on this side the mountain somewhere between here and the top. I'm guessing the caves they are using will not be too far above the tree line. From there, they would be able to see anyone approaching, but still be close enough to sneak into the forest for an escape."

"There's a ravine on the map, not too far up, and slightly to our right," Doran said. "We should be pretty close to it. Should we split into groups and follow the ridges on either side?"

"No, I don't want us separated if we encounter trouble. Until we have a better idea where they are and what they have, we'll stick together," Carpenter said. "We'll all move up the left side of the ravine in a two-one-two formation. Ese and I will take the lead, T-Dub you follow us, and Hof and Benny will bring up the rear. Let's go."

After perhaps thirty minutes of wary stepping, the terrain suddenly steepened and became gravellier. Pockets of muddy soil could only be found around the few scrubby florae protruding from the rock-strewn surface. They had reached the tree line. Anderson signaled silently to the men behind, while Carpenter moved ahead a few more feet to recon the terrain above. He sensed the rain was beginning to lessen, but the wind was picking up in intensity as he edged closer to an expanse of exposed rock. Carpenter could make out what appeared to be cliffs, several hundred feet up the mountain. It was up there that Carpenter expected to find the caves. They needed to move higher in order to surveil the top of the cliffs, and he was thinking about how to make that happen when he heard one of his men's voices in his ear.

"Anybody smell that?" Doran asked.

"Yeah, I do now. Smells like a fire," Anderson said.

Carpenter looked up the mountain in search of the source. The lack of ambient light limited what he was able to see with his NVGs. He ripped the goggles off and grabbed the Leupold thermal imaging monocular from his rucksack. He scanned the mountainside where he thought he had seen the cliffs. On his second pass, he caught a glimpse of a figure, slightly to their left, and maybe a hundred-seventy yards away. He kept the device glued to the spot, anticipating another sighting. About twenty seconds later, the figure passed again. This time, Carpenter could clearly see the upper half of a man's body, suggesting he was walking a few steps back from the cliff's edge. After watching for a few more minutes, he moved back down to the others.

"It looks like there's one guy on watch," Carpenter said. "I didn't see anyone else or any fire. I think we have to assume there's at least one cave up there and there is more than just that one guy. They're probably inside keeping dry and feeling pretty secure right now, given this location, the darkness, and the shitty weather. Now is our chance to get a closer look."

Carpenter motioned for the men to follow him back down the mountain and further into the trees. When he found a good spot, they regrouped and huddled over the topography map and the satellite photos. Carpenter realized they were going to have to take some chances. It was unlikely al-Rasheed would stick around very long before moving to another hidey-hole. The intel was already days old. If he had not left yet, there was a strong possibility al-Rasheed would be leaving soon. And Carpenter was concerned that the conditions might allow al-Rasheed to creep right past them. In these conditions, he was going to get right on top of the cave to surveil the area and come up with a plan to move in on al-Rasheed and whoever else was with him.

As Carpenter reviewed the map and satellite photos, he considered their options. There were no apparent places close to the caves where they could set up observation posts. Between their current position and the base of the cliff was a hundred-foot wide, fairly steep rockslide, covering the length of a football field. A direct approach would surely expose them before they could reach the base of the cliff. They were going to have to find other paths to follow up the domed summit. Carpenter elected to split the group, sending Doran and Anderson left, toward the west side of the mountain. Of the men, Carpenter was most familiar with Doran. He had long since lost count of the number of operations they had worked together. Although Anderson had proven himself on two prior occasions, he had only been with the CTC for a couple years. It was only because he was less familiar with the youngest member of the team, that Carpenter decided to pair Anderson with Doran and his experience. While those two were heading west, he, Wood, and Hofstad would work their way east.

After dropping down a hundred or so feet in elevation, Doran and Anderson swiftly picked their way through the forest. The cover was excellent and the terrain was easily navigable, much more so than the path the team had followed on the ascent. Less than twenty minutes after leaving the others, the two former SEALS were situated on a rocky bluff, partially encircled by the upper branches of several pine trees. A gap in the branches gave them a clear view of the cliff, while a larger one on the opposite side of the bluff provided what, in better conditions, would have been an unobstructed view of the valley below. It was an ideal spot. For that reason, they were not surprised to find signs it had been used recently. Several crushed cigarette butts littered the surface and the pungent smell of urine clung to the damp air.

"I can see why they've been using this lookout," Doran said. "We'll stay here for now and wait to hear from PJ. I've got a feeling they're not going to have it so easy. They're going to have to circumvent that ravine."

The two men settled in and waited. After a few minutes, Anderson broke the silence. "I can't make sense of that dude," he said.

"Who, PJ?"

"Yeah. I rode in the car with him from Subaytilah. I tried to chat him up but he pretty much shut me down. Is it me or is he like that with everybody?"

"It's not you," Doran said. "PJ is not the talkative type to begin with and, once he gets in operational mode, he's even more reticent. He is constantly thinking about possible scenarios, planning for eventualities, staying two steps ahead of the enemy."

"I just got a sense he might prefer someone else on his team."

"Believe me, you wouldn't be here if he didn't want you here. PJ gets to pick his teams. You don't work with PJ Carpenter unless he trusts and respects you. How many times have you worked with him?"

"This is my third operation with him," Anderson said.

"So the Super Bowl was the second. What was the first one?"

"That was in Mosul, not long after I came over to the CTC. There were four of us, including PJ. We had intel about an ISIS safehouse in a real nasty part of town. A week before, a Marine patrol was shot up pretty badly in the same neighborhood. Heading in, everybody on the team was wired, figuring we were going be in for a real brawl. Anyway, we jump out of the Humvee five blocks away from the target house and make our way over. After some quick recon, PJ positions us to provide cover and tells us he's going in alone. We all look at each other dumfounded; we can't believe it. But off he goes and we just sit there and watch. Anyway, he saunters down this badass street and marches right up to the front door, like he's going home. Next thing we know, he's inside. Two minutes later, he calls us in. I eventually count four dead hostiles throughout the house. It was like we were there just in case something went bad. All we ended up doing was humping a few boxes of documents and two computers. Then he did the same thing in Minnesota, taking off by himself to the mall."

"I could tell you similar stories. PJ is always the first guy in and he won't risk anyone else if he thinks he can do it alone. But Minnesota was different. When he left in the chopper, no one knew if there would be more attempts at the stadium or what was going on at the mall. He's not crazy by any stretch. He's definitely fearless and confident, but he's not arrogant, if that makes sense."

"I guess it does," Anderson said. After further considering the implications for a few moments, he asked, "You ever hang out with him?"

"Only to have a few beers on a handful of occasions."

"What did you guys talk about?"

"Like I said, he doesn't say much and he never talks about himself. He tends to ask a lot of questions about you and he's a very good listener. More than once, he's brought something up that I forgot even mentioning to him."

"Do you feel like you even know him?"

"Only from what I am able to glean from working with him but that's okay. You know exactly who you're dealing with every time and that's someone who sees the big picture and covers every angle. Going into an operation with PJ, you know he's going to make the right decisions. He has an uncanny ability to cut through the clutter and know exactly what to do. He's just a really smart dude who's very cool under pressure. I've worked with a lot of guys and PJ is by far the best at what we do."

"Everyone I've worked with says the same things about him. It's like we're working with a mythical legend," Anderson said.

"Don't get caught up in the hype. PJ may have some supernatural abilities, but he's still just a regular guy. And he's got the scars to prove it."

"I've heard he's had some tough times."

"I've never heard him talk about it, but I know that he lost both his parents when he was still pretty young. I've also heard he got into a lot of trouble before he got his act together and went off to college. And his fiancée was killed in Pakistan. I guess that was about ten years ago. That was the only time I ever saw him go off the rails—I think anyone would have."

"You ever talk to him about his fiancée? I've heard that story too."

"Nope. Not once. But I know that's why he's ultra-switched on now. It was personal even before the attacks back home. Mumeet should have never stepped from the shadows. PJ Carpenter is the last person on this planet you want chasing you."

"No shit," Anderson agreed.

"I'll just say that when the time comes, you'll know when he's ready to shoot the shit. And, if it does, baseball is always a good bet with PJ. He loves the game. Apparently, he was quite good. Patrick told me PJ was drafted out of high school but had no interest in pursuing it as a career. Besides not signing as a draft pick, he had multiple scholarship offers but didn't even want to play in college."

"Thanks, I'll try that," Anderson said.

"And one more thing, don't force it with PJ. If I didn't know better, I'd think he hates ass-kissers more than terrorists."

"I've already been warned about that. Is it true he made a guy literally walk away from an op?"

"It is true. We were running an operation out of Camp Shorab in Helmand Province. Patrick had sent this guy over to join our unit; I think his name was Moreland or something. From the minute he arrived in Afghanistan, Moreland was all over PJ, agreeing with and echoing everything PJ said—kind of like the Andy character on *The Office*, if you've ever seen it. Anyway, we get our orders and head out for the mission. The entire time, Moreland is ingratiating himself with PJ, until PJ's finally had enough. We're probably thirty klicks from Shorab, in the middle of East Bumfuck, when PJ orders the Humvee to stop and tells Moreland to get out and start walking back to camp."

"Holy shit! So the guy did actually have to walk back?"

"You bet your ass he did. PJ caught shit from Patrick but Moreland never worked with us again."

"Damn, that's awesome!"

"We all thought so too. The moral of the story is to follow his example and just do the job. That's what he's all about. If you do that, you'll stay on his good side."

Throughout the entire hushed conversation, the two men kept their eyes fixated on the cliffs and paused periodically to listen for signs of anyone approaching their lofted post. Eventually, they moved on from Carpenter to other subjects. They talked about Doran's young family and what it was like to grow up on a five-thousand-acre farm in southern Illinois. Farming was another common thread the two frogmen shared. Anderson was raised on a small dairy farm and his family's cheddar cheese was famous throughout New England. Later, they were arguing about who made the best pickup trucks when Carpenter's voice sounded in their ears.

"Benny, Ese, sitrep," Carpenter said. He, Wood, and Hofstad were hiding underneath a strand of Aleppo pines, with a clear view to the cliffs. It took them much longer to get into position because they were forced to keep dropping further down the mountain until they found a suitable place to traverse the ravine. After heading back up toward the summit, their position put them slightly below the level of the terrorists' hideout.

Before responding, Doran glanced at his watch. "We're on an outcrop surrounded by some pine trees looking slightly down on the target area from eight o'clock from where we split up, about a hundred, hundred-twenty yards out," he said. "It's a good spot. Problem is, it smells like piss. Someone else has been using it."

"Use your judgment whether to stay there," Carpenter said. "We're in the trees to your east, about four o'clock from the cliffs. I'd guess we're maybe two hundred yards out from the cliff. We haven't been here long and we've only seen the one guard. What have you been seeing?"

"We've been here exactly forty-four minutes now and we've only seen that one lookout," Doran said. "Can't tell if it's the same guy or they're rotating. I'm also picking up a faint heat signal from inside the cave. That must be the fire we were smelling."

Carpenter thought it over for a moment. There had to be more than one man up there. He still thought it likely that the others were staying warm and dry inside the cave but he couldn't count on that being true. He and whoever went in with him were going to need cover as they moved in on the cave. He wanted his two snipers emplaced in positions that offered wide and clear shot angles. "Benny, you maintain that position and keep eyes on. Ese, find and secure the trail they are using to get to your perch but don't push too close to the cliff. We don't want to draw them out yet but if they do come your way, take them down."

"Roger that," Anderson said.

"T-Dub will stay here," Carpenter continued, as he pointed up at one of the pine trees. "He's got a good field of view of this side of the mountain. Hof and I are going to circle around to the south side of the mountain and see if we can come over from the backside."

When Wood was halfway up the tree, Carpenter and Hofstad started out. To reduce the chances of stepping on a mine, they stayed close to the outer edge of the forest as it meandered up and down the rocky slope. It was well past midnight when they settled in the trees on the south face of the mountain. Carpenter guessed the cave was directly in front of them on the other side of the summit. From their position, he didn't see anyone on the peak or anywhere around it, but they would have to cover several hundred yards over the rock-strewn face to reach it. Despite the risks, it was the best option to figure out what he was dealing with. If they could reach the summit, they'd be looking down on the cliffs. "Hof and I are in position and ready to move in. It's quiet on this side of the mountain. What are you guys seeing?" he asked.

"All's quiet on the western front," said Doran. "The guard ducks back in the cave every few minutes, but I haven't seen anyone else."

"Ditto here," said Wood.

"Sounds good," Carpenter said. "Benny and Ese, Hof will be working his way to your side of the mountain, and I'll be working slightly back toward T-Dub. Let us know if anything changes."

Less than an hour later, Carpenter checked in with his men. He was nearly to the summit, where he expected to be able to look down on the cliff. Hofstad was on the west side of the mountain and reported that he was prone in a small fissure in the rocky surface. From there, he had a limited view of the cliff and said he should be close enough to hear voices. Doran was still watching the cliff and said he had Hofstad in his sights. Anderson was dug in, ready for anyone making his way to Doran's nest. He could also look up and see the entire bottom edge of the cliff from his position. Wood was secured in a tree fork, resting against a large branch, twenty-five feet off the ground. Like Doran, Wood could see anyone stepping out of the cave and onto the cliff. He could also see Carpenter's thermal image, huddled behind an alpine shrub.

The rain had almost stopped, and the wind was beginning to subside. Sunrise was still four hours away, enough time for the reconnaissance Carpenter needed to formulate a plan to either grab or kill Fahd al-Rasheed. "Get comfy, boys. Hopefully, we can figure out what we're dealing with before the hornets start to leave the nest."

Chapter 6

"PJ, it's T-Dub. You got him?" Wood asked. It was the first anyone had spoken in more than an hour. Up to that point, nothing had changed, except the weather. After a short downpour a few minutes before, the rain had stopped completely.

"Yeah, I see him," Carpenter answered. He had moved up to the summit and was looking down on the near side of the cliff. Two boulders protected his rear flank. He had heard rocks crunching before he peered around one of the boulders and saw the man approaching from below. He had no idea how the man got there. Nobody had reported seeing the man moving toward his position. And, despite being close enough to hear movement on the cliff below, neither he nor Hofstad had heard anything. Carpenter figured the man must have come up from the trees, like he and Hofstad had. He carefully adjusted his position for a better view, seeing that the man was now no more than fifty yards away and continuing to lumber up the slope toward him.

Just then, Anderson said, "I've got some movement coming down the trail."

Damn it! Carpenter quickly realized there must be other ways out of the cave besides the cliffs Wood and Doran were watching. There was another, and potentially worse scenario. It was also possible that more terrorists were coming in from another location. Either way, he and Hofstad were stuck. There was no way to pull back now. The only way out was forward, and they would have to do it without the benefit of knowing exactly what they were up against. But the first step was to take care of the most immediate threats.

"Make it quiet, Ese," he whispered to Anderson. "Everyone else, don't give away your positions unless you have to."

Carpenter used the darkness to his advantage. While he had the benefit of his night-vision googles, the man was traversing the rugged terrain with nothing more than a penlight. Carpenter would remain hidden until the man was almost on top of him. He crawled from behind the boulder and risked a cleaner look down the slope. He could tell the man was large, probably three inches taller than his own six-foot frame, and, based on his thick neck, thirty or more pounds heavier. The man was casually holding an AK-47 in his left hand as he zagged around the rocks. Carpenter pulled the straight edge KA-BAR knife from the sheath on his calf and waited for the man to move in closer. But when the terrorist was no more than twenty feet from Carpenter, he suddenly stopped. Carpenter remained perfectly still as the man turned and faced down the slope of the mountain. It seemed as if he was looking directly at Wood. Carpenter slowed his breathing, while deciding what to do. He had no idea why the man was just standing there, looking into the forest. There was no way he could have spotted Wood in the tree, hundreds of feet away. A moment later, Carpenter had his answer. He heard the unmistakable sound of liquid splashing on rock—the man was pissing.

While the man was preoccupied, Carpenter silently shifted onto his feet and inched toward the terrorist. As Carpenter closed in, the man stayed focused on his urine stream and showed no signs he was at all aware of Carpenter's menacing presence. When he was almost within reach, Carpenter took one last, quick step before slamming his left hand over the terrorist's mouth and, with synchronized precision, violently jerked the man's head to the side and plunged the six-inch blade in his right hand squarely into the terrorist's subclavian artery. He swiftly moved the blade back and forth twice before removing it and ripping it across the man's neck. Carpenter hastily threw the blade down behind him and wrapped the stunned man in a bear hug, while keeping his left hand tightly clamped over the man's mouth. Carpenter knew he wouldn't have to hold on long before the man bled out. At least, he hoped so. The man was larger than Carpenter had estimated, and he was strong. He attempted to wriggle free by smashing several crushing elbows into Carpenter's torso. When that didn't work, the man resorted to a few feeble swats in the general direction of Carpenter's head. Within seconds, the man stopped struggling. Carpenter released his grip when he felt the man's body go limp. Carpenter put his hands on his knees and took in several deep breaths before he started rolling the corpse to the edge of the slope. He gave it a final stiff kick and watched it tumble down the hill until it came to rest against some rocks fifty feet below.

Carpenter listened intently for more trouble. The exertion from the battle and moving dead weight had left him laboring to restore his breath. But he realized the clock was ticking. He had to keep moving. He allowed himself one last long inhale and then bent down and picked up the knife before making his way down the mountain in the direction from which the man had come. He heard Anderson's hushed voice in his earpiece.

"Muj is down," Anderson said, using the slang term they sometimes used for a terrorist. "All clear."

"Copy and same here," Carpenter said without stopping. After a few more steps, he discovered how the terrorist had been able to surprise him. "I found a tunnel not too far down from the summit. My guy must have come out it. What's going on out front?"

"I've got two hajis pacing the cliff," Wood said.

"I've got eyes on the same two guys," Doran said. "And a third guy just came out of the cave."

"I can't see them from my position, but I can hear them," Hofstad said. "Sounds like their day is getting started."

Things were escalating quickly. It would not be long before they discovered that their two buddies were missing. Once they did, all hell would break loose. Unless Carpenter could get inside the cave before that happened, the chances of capturing al-Rasheed without an all-out fight were diminishing. "Benny, could any of the three guys be al-Rasheed?" Carpenter asked.

"Not unless he shrunk half a foot," Doran said.

"Roger that," Carpenter said. "T-Dub, can you take the guys on the cliff?" In this case, his concern was stealth. The suppressors would not eliminate all sound from the rifles but because Wood was nearly twice as far away, there would be less noise if he could execute the shots. If Wood did not have a clear shot or he missed, Doran could easily clean up the mess but the sound would almost certainly carry the much shorter distance to the cave.

"Won't be a problem," Wood replied. Before Carpenter called, he had already adjusted his position atop the large branch and scoped the targets. Now, he began a breathing exercise while placing his eye on the scope of the MK 12 SPR Mod 1 sniper rifle. Once again, he brought the closest man clearly into his sights and then moved to the other two. Wood was ready. For someone with Wood's skills, these shots were like tap-in putts for a professional golfer.

"All right, wait for my call, T-Dub. Benny you stay put in case T-Dub loses the line of fire. But once those guys are down, I want you to join Ese where the trail meets the cliffs. Hof and I are going into the rat tunnel. Hof, meet me on the backside."

Several minutes later, Hofstad joined Carpenter outside the tunnel entrance. Shortly after, Anderson reported he was in position. It was time to go. "Ese, sit tight and be prepared to move on anyone else coming out of the cave. If you can help it, don't take down anyone remotely looking like al-Rasheed. Pop him in the shoulder or leg, but don't drop him. We need him alive, if possible. T-Dub, give us sixty seconds to work our way into the tunnel. On my count. Three, two, one."

Carpenter entered the tunnel on his knees, with Hofstad right behind him. It was just wider than his shoulders and no more than three feet high at the entrance. The floor was covered with gravel, and jagged edges protruded from the ceiling and both sides as the tunnel sloped gently downward. After crawling twenty or so feet on the uneven floor, Carpenter could see light ahead. He signaled back to Hofstad. They ripped off their NVGs to give their eyes an opportunity to adjust to the burgeoning light and kept moving. In his head, twenty-five seconds had elapsed. He pressed their pace slightly but without compromising stealth in favor of speed. All the sudden, the ceiling of the tunnel heightened so that both men were able to shift onto their feet, albeit in a crouch. A few feet later, it was wide enough for Hofstad to squeeze in alongside. Now able to make full strides, their progress accelerated further. Carpenter sensed they were more than halfway down the tunnel when he heard Wood's voice in his ear.

"Bogeys down," Wood said.

Carpenter clicked confirmation and kept moving. He and Hofstad stepped into a slow jog. They had to get to the cave before anyone inside realized the carnage on the cliff. They synchronized and carefully placed their steps as they continued down the brightening channel. Up ahead, there was a sharp bend, decorated in flickering beams of light cast by the fire both men could now clearly smell. Other than a few crackles from the fire, there was no sound coming from what had to be the cave and the end of the tunnel. Carpenter looked at Hofstad, and nodded. Nothing more had to be said. Just before they reached the bend, Carpenter leapt to the far side of the tunnel while Hofstad, leading with the barrel of his HK416 assault rifle, peered around the corner on the near side.

Carpenter could see blankets scattered all over the ground, surrounding the fire burning in the center of the spacious cavern. Three men were sleeping on the far side of the fire pit. None of them was al-Rasheed. A fourth man, his back to Carpenter, was creeping toward the cave's entrance from the cliffs, cradling what appeared to be a rifle in front of his stooped frame. Carpenter flashed a hand signal before they stepped into the cave. As soon as they did, the lone upright terrorist at the mouth of the cave swung around. A split second was all Hofstad needed to confirm the man wasn't al-Rasheed, but it wasn't enough for the terrorist to save himself. Before the terrorist even had a chance to raise his rifle, he was chest was riddled with four rounds from Hofstad's carbine.

The echoes from the suppressed rounds caused two of the other three men to stir. Just as the man closest to him raised his groggy head, Carpenter rushed forward and slammed the butt of his rifle into the man's temple, instantly knocking him back to the ground. He followed his momentum over toward the second awakening man. Before Carpenter reached him, the man jolted up and wildly swung a knife, but Carpenter saw the move coming and easily dodged it. As the man was bringing the blade around for a backhanded attempt, Carpenter put him down with a double-tap to the face. Carpenter looked over and saw that the third man was lying flat on the floor with the end of Hofstad's rifle pressed against his forehead. He guessed Hofstad's prisoner was probably no older than twenty. He reached down and ripped the blanket off to check for weapons. He and Hofstad both wretched at the awful odor.

"Aw, man. This guy shit his pants!" Hofstad said.

"Please, do not kill me," the young man said in French.

"Sitrep," Carpenter barked.

"I'm with Ese on the trail. No movement over here," said Doran.

"Ditto," said Wood.

"You two guys stay put. Ese, move around to the back side and guard that tunnel entrance while Hof and I take some inventory in here."

The rounded cave was approximately fourteen feet in diameter and had a ceiling height of ten feet or more. The smoke from the fire filtered along the ceiling toward the cliffs, though it was unable to mask the undercurrent of fresh feces and overpowering body odor. Several wooden boxes were stacked along the circular wall on the rear side of the cavern. Carpenter began ripping them open. Inside four of them he found nine-millimeter rounds, another held grenades, and the remaining two held rocket propelled grenade launchers. A dozen automatic rifles rested against the boxes, and next to them were several cases of canned food and bottles of water. Missing, however, was Fahd al-Rasheed and any sign of him.

Carpenter pulled the picture from his thigh pocket and shoved it into the man's face. "Have you seen this man?" he asked in French.

"Yes, yes, but he is no longer here."

"When did he leave?"

"He has not been here for days."

"Where is he now?" Carpenter asked.

"I—I do not know."

"Do you understand that if you don't have any helpful information, you are no use to me?"

"Please, sir. I am not mujahideen. These men forced me to join them. They said they would kill my sister if I did not help them."

He told Carpenter his name was Ridha, and he was sixteen years old. He lived in one of the small villages at the base of the mountains with his mother and twelve-year-old sister. He said that several weeks prior, a group calling itself *Hafaza*—the Keepers—moved into the area to establish a training camp. Ridha claimed the dead man at the mouth of the cave was named Hammad Dhib, and he was the group's leader. He told Carpenter four men showed up at his home one day looking for food. The men forced him to watch as they raped his mother and his sister. For good measure, they took the family's three sheep and demanded that Ridha join Hafaza. He had been living with them in the mountains since.

As Ridha was finishing his story, the man who Carpenter had smashed in the head with the butt of his rifle began to groan. Carpenter grabbed Ridha and pulled him out to the cliff to continue the interrogation while Hofstad turned his attention to the wounded terrorist. Ridha said that al-Rasheed arrived with two other men he had never seen before. The three men stayed only two nights before leaving. While al-Rasheed was there, he never saw him speak to anyone except his two companions and the group's leader, Hammad Dhib. Ridha claimed that he was not allowed to speak to the three travelers. Right before al-Rasheed and his companions left, Ridha overheard Dhib say to him, "We wish you well and hope to hear good news from across the sea." Carpenter pulled out the crappy passport photo of Mumeet. As expected, Ridha said he had never seen the man.

Carpenter asked more about Hafaza, its members, and its plans. Ridha claimed there were at least twenty men in the group, but he was not aware where the rest of them were posted now. He had only been to this location. The other men came here from time to time, usually in sets of three or four, he said. They, too, ignored him and spoke only with the group's leader. Ridha was not aware of any plans Hafaza might have. The only thing he ever did was stand guard outside the cave or in the trees below. When it was clear Ridha had nothing more to offer, Carpenter bound his hands and feet with plastic zip ties and told the shaking teenager to stay put.

"If this guy so much as moves, drop him," Carpenter said to Wood through his headset.

"You got it," Wood said from his position in the trees.

Carpenter then went back into the cave to check on the other prisoner. Hofstad looked up as he approached. "Does he have anything to say?"

"Not much. But I found out he does know how to say 'fuck you' in English."

"Is that why he's bleeding from his nose and mouth?"

"Could be."

"Anything else noteworthy?"

Hofstad reported that the man said he was Algerian and his name was Kashif. "He asked to see Hammad Dhib, whoever that is," Hofstad said.

"He's the guy you whacked near the mouth of the cave. Supposedly, he was the leader of this group called Hafaza."

"Well, Kashif here claims he's been in cahoots with Hammad Dhib for years. Other than that, he didn't give up anything. Oh, he did say that 'you infidels will soon pay a heavy price.' He spat on my leg right after he said that."

Carpenter moved over to Kashif to try his hand at getting some information. But the terrorist simply refused to talk. Carpenter considered employing some more aggressive tactics but those would take time, something he didn't have. They needed to get out of there. Carpenter didn't know if there were any reinforcements in the immediate area, but if Ridha was telling the truth, they might show up any minute. Besides, there was nothing further to gain by staying. Al-Rasheed was gone and all except two men were dead. There was no other intelligence to gather. The only things of value were some weapons and ammunition.

Carpenter told Hofstad they were leaving and then shared the news with the rest of the team. He told Wood and Anderson to remain in place, guarding the front and rear entrances to the cave. He called Doran up to the cave. While they waited for Doran, Carpenter laid out the plans for Hofstad. He wanted Hofstad and Doran to trash the rifles and dump the ammunition down the cliff. They would take the grenades and the launchers with them, he said. He did not yet know what the plans were for the prisoners, but he told Hofstad to make sure Kashif was bound tightly before he took care of the weapons and ammunition. When Doran arrived, Carpenter had him bring Ridha in from the cliff. Then he told his men he was going outside to make two calls.

Chapter 7

Carpenter went out onto the cliff and pulled the satellite phone from his ancient ALICE rucksack. Once the phone was powered up and locked onto the signal, he called Dan O'Reilly, telling the operations officer to meet him and the team at the extraction point in three hours. Before signing off, he added they might have extra cargo. He next called his boss, CTC Director Timothy Patrick.

"We missed al-Rasheed," he said to the CTC chief. "He was here, but he apparently left several days ago. We took out seven men, including the leader of this group, calling itself Hafaza. Two men are still alive. Well, a man and a boy, really. The man isn't saying shit. Only been able to get his first name, which he says is Kashif, and that he's Algerian. According to Kashif, we should expect to pay a 'heavy price' sometime soon. Not sure if that's the same old bullshit or it means something this time. Other than that, he's not talking.

"The kid is named Ridha, and he says he was forced into service with this Hafaza group. The leader of the group was a guy called Hammad Dhib. Ridha told me al-Rasheed was here for only a few days. He arrived and left with two others the kid didn't know and hasn't seen since. Ridha did overhear the group's leader say something to al-Rasheed just before he left about hoping to hear 'good news from across the sea.' That might be related to the Algerian's threat, but Ridha claims not to know anything about any operation."

"You believe the kid, that al-Rasheed was there?"

"Yeah, I do. He's scared shitless. Literally. Either he's not a hard ass terrorist or he's a damn great actor. Unless you tell me otherwise, I'm planning to let him go back to his mother and sister."

"No sign of Mumeet?"

"None."

"Any chance al-Rasheed is still in those mountains somewhere?"

"I don't get that sense. Do you want us to nose around?"

After a few seconds, Patrick said, "No. If there's no sign of him, you guys better get out of there. We can't risk the Tunisians catching wind of this."

"You hesitated a bit there. Why?"

"We picked up some chatter in the last twenty-four hours. The analysts are convinced something is about to go down."

"What's the chatter?"

"Nothing concrete but a lot of repetition of what we think are code words for one or more attacks. No indications about timing or location."

"You think what we learned here is related to Aziz's statement?" Carpenter was referring to the statement Aziz released through Al Jazeera eight days earlier. It was interpreted as a follow up to his claims shortly after the attacks in Minnesota that al Qaeda would continue to strike the West.

"I'm thinking it could be. But it's odd that we've only heard from Aziz and no one else at AQ. I would have expected to hear from other members of the shura." Patrick was referring to the senior leaders who approved and often commented publicly on all large-scale operations undertaken in the terror group's name. "Usually they put out several messages to boast about their success and to show the group is strong and well. I'm starting to wonder if Aziz has gone rogue and, if so, whether he has the support to follow up on his claims for more attacks?"

"That's tough for me to say. What do the analysts think is going on?"

"I don't know yet. I have a meeting with them tomorrow. They've been working up some analysis of potential next moves by Aziz and AQ."

"Well, we now know for certain that al-Rasheed got out of the US," Carpenter said. "The same is probably true for Mumeet. Still no word on where Aziz might be?"

"Nothing. I was hoping we'd get al-Rasheed there and he'd lead us to Mumeet and maybe Aziz too. We take Aziz out and the whole thing starts to fall apart."

"I kind of doubt Aziz is trusting anyone these days with his whereabouts, especially a guy on our radar like al-Rasheed. You sure you don't want us to poke around here, try to see if we can figure out where al-Rasheed went?"

"No. He's gone; get out of there. But let the kid go."

"What about the Algerian?"

"Since he's alive, bring him with you if you can."

"We can change his status."

"No, he might have some intelligence value. We'll put the professionals on him for a few days; maybe they can get something out of him. I'll send a separate plane for the Algerian. Call me when you're back in Tunis," Patrick said.

Chapter 8
Luxembourg City, Luxembourg

The woman smiled as she accepted money from the outstretched hand of the nattily dressed man. She was almost sure that she had seen this man in the market before but she could be mistaken. She found that appearances were often blurred in this ethnically and culturally diverse city. She was sure of one thing, however; if she had seen the man before, it was more recently. As she processed these thoughts, she decided that it must be his refined manner that she recalled. There was a sense of aristocracy about the man, an aura that suggested confidence and power. Perhaps, more than anything, it was his clothes that gave her that impression. His attire was impeccable and noteworthy, even here among the well-healed. But as the woman handed the man his change and thanked him for his business, she couldn't shake the feeling that there was something else about him that had unleashed these thoughts. The woman was further impressed when the elegant man spoke to her in flawless French to both acknowledge her gratitude and wish her a pleasant day. As the man walked away, the encounter and the sense of familiarity lingered in the woman's thoughts. But before she was able to finish probing her memory, another customer was standing before her and in need of her attention. And soon, her regal customer no longer occupied her thoughts.

Prince Sadiq bin Aziz left Place Guillaume and approached Rue Notre Dame. In each gloved hand, he held a shopping bag containing the fresh produce he had just purchased at the farmer's market. While he waited for the pedestrian crossing signal to change, he reflected how fortunate it was that he had no need for an umbrella. After six days of intermittent rain, the skies had finally cleared, producing a fine mid-April morning, albeit an unseasonably cool one. He looked skyward under the brim of his buffed wool fedora, relishing the warmth of the sun on his recently modified face. Just then, a bus passed by, ushering in an added chill to the thirty-eight-degree temperature. In a reflexive response, he shook slightly, burrowing his core deeper beneath the tri-colored cashmere scarf and dark gray, glen plaid Alpaca overcoat he was wearing. At that moment, he embraced the rare sense of normalcy he was experiencing. For weeks, he had largely been confined to his home. And the dreary weather had only been exacerbating his anxiety. The chance to finally be outside was improving his mood, as was his recent visit to the semi-weekly farmer's market. It was one of the very few occasions he left the house for, and he looked forward to making the short stroll to the town square in the heart of Luxembourg's historic Ville Haute quarter each Wednesday and Sunday.

As soon as the signal changed, Aziz crossed the busy street with a handful of other pedestrians and ventured onto Place de Clairefontaine. After a few steps, the bustle of the city and the farmer's market was behind him. As he passed the bronze statue honoring Grand Duchess Charlotte, he settled into a more leisurely pace, enjoying the stroll and feeling secure in his anonymity in what was reputed to be one of the safest cities in the world. Although this route was not the shortest to his home, he preferred it. He typically encountered only the occasional passerby during this short stretch of the journey, a fact pleasing to his longtime bodyguard, Faraj. These forays to the farmer's market were the only times Faraj was not within a few hurried steps of his master. Aziz appreciated that venturing outside, let alone by himself, was not without risk, but he enjoyed the solitude. Walking along the quiet cobbled streets offered him an opportunity to clear his mind and reflect on important matters. And it was here, on Place de Clairefontaine, that he often began his best thinking. Today, Aziz's thoughts turned to the circumstances that had brought him to this exquisite European capital in his quest to usher in a new world order.

It was several decades earlier that Aziz had his first taste of jihad. He worked in Pakistan alongside his distant cousin, Osama bin Laden, securing financing for the mujahedeen during the Soviet conflict across the border in Afghanistan. After the Soviets capitulated, Aziz left Peshawar. He wasn't home in Saudi Arabia for long before he left for London. He enrolled in university there and studied economics. Within days of graduation, he started an investment firm with his own money. Almost from the start, he found success and was named a rising star on the London investment scene. But all the while he was earning fortune and acclaim in the world of finance, Aziz maintained his ties to jihad. He continued to support al Qaeda and its founder, largely through substantial donations that ultimately totaled tens of millions of dollars. He also shared his views on how to strengthen and guide al Qaeda into the future, only to see that advice go unheeded time after time. His frustration climaxed when, after his cousin's death, the once-dominant terror group began a hastened slide into irrelevance.

In 2012, Aziz abruptly sold his private equity firm. He walked away with hundreds of millions of dollars and a portfolio of discreet investments; assets he intended to use to restore al Qaeda, while still leaving him with more wealth than he would ever need. After several months, Aziz had reconnected with the council of al Qaeda senior leaders. In the first meeting, he told the shura that al Qaeda was broken and in need of change. Since the Planes Operation in 2001, the terror group's leaders had largely been content to merely stay alive. He chastised the senior leaders that they no longer had the means or courage to lead the global jihad movement. Instead, they chose to cede operations to affiliated groups, whose focus was on regional conflicts and interests that did little to advance al Qaeda's cause. The shura listened impassively and then dismissed him without making any commitment to change.

Over the succeeding years, he continued to press the shura to change course. He had warned them throughout about the emerging threat of al Qaeda's one-time affiliate in Iraq—the terror group now operating as the Islamic State—only to see it replace al Qaeda as the vanguard of the jihad movement. One-time fertile sources of financing were shunning al Qaeda in favor of the Islamic State, and more and more fighters were defecting to the former associate. As a result, the allegiances of other affiliated groups were becoming increasingly tenuous. Al Qaeda had lost its grip on global jihad. Still, the shura refused his entreaties for change.

While the shura continued to rebuff him, Aziz started to reconsider his objectives. Although he remained fully committed to jihad and restoring al Qaeda as the leader of the movement, pure altruism was no longer his sole motivation. Perhaps due to the shura's indifference and the passage of time, Aziz had discovered that he was no longer able to suppress his own ambitions. As he became increasingly frustrated with their indecisiveness, he began to envision a legacy for himself, one that granted him the same reverence as that bestowed on his distant cousin. And, like his cousin, he intended to secure that by leading the faithful in violent jihad. No longer willing to wait, Aziz began to make plans to achieve his goals independent of the shura and al Qaeda.

Roughly a year ago, the shura finally agreed to hear his proposal. Aziz anticipated the meeting with steeled determination. By that time, core al Qaeda's situation had only worsened. Most members of the council had accepted that the terror group was at a crossroads and on the brink of obsolescence. It was almost impossible for Aziz to feel overconfident when he sat down with the senior al Qaeda leaders. The shura needed his assistance if al Qaeda was to be saved, and he was emboldened by the progress he had made on his alternate plans. Yet, he knew that moving forward with the aegis of the shura and al Qaeda would make things easier. Despite its demise, the terror group had at least the framework of a working infrastructure and the name still carried considerable value. Going alone would require more time to recruit additional followers and acquire necessary resources. Of course, that path would also require more money. Ideally, the need for more time could be avoided. The money was not an issue. But Aziz was determined not to concede any ground to the shura. They would accept his demands or he would go on without them.

Aziz had two objectives going into the meeting: to obtain the shura's approval for his bold strategy to restore al Qaeda to its rightful place as the leader of global jihad and, in the process, to put himself in position to create the legacy he coveted. As soon as he was yielded the floor, Aziz outlined his strategy. Al Qaeda would return to jihad operations, using experienced commanders to renew attacks against the West. The first attack under the new strategy would take place in the United States. Like his cousin bin Laden, Aziz viewed the United States as the greatest obstacle to al Qaeda's objectives. Attempting to liberate Muslim lands from non-Muslim and apostate leaders was futile so long as the United States was in the game; any victories would only be temporary. In order to establish a caliphate and impose its vision of *sharia*—Islamic law—the United States would have to be defeated. Aziz knew that could only happen if all the believers were unified. And the best way to realize common cause was an attack on the Great Satan. Before the senior leaders had even resolved to approve his new strategy and the initial attacks in the United States to implement it, Aziz told them he also expected to be named the group's new leader. It was essentially a take-it or leave-it offer. Perhaps in an attempt to save face, the shura had insisted on one condition—that the attacks in the United States be led by the terror group's most prolific jihadist. Aziz welcomed the stipulation; he had intended to ask for the man's involvement, anyway.

Aziz emerged from the meeting with new leadership status in the terror group and authorization to implement his strategy. Better still, he also had his own burgeoning network up his sleeve. What's more, he had al Qaeda's most capable and lethal commander to lead the first attacks in the United States. It really was the best possible outcome, but Aziz did not stop there. Aziz was determined that his iteration of al Qaeda would not suffer the same fate as its predecessor. Aziz pursued parallel paths, continuing to construct his own terror group while gradually molding al Qaeda into his image. In the short term, he would operate under the al Qaeda brand, but his longer-term plans envisioned a rebranding he could call his own.

Until then, he would use his new control of al Qaeda to enhance the capabilities of his own growing group of loyalists. These men were all highly committed and elite fighters. They were alumni of the 055 Brigade, a group of ruthless and highly skilled mercenaries first assembled by bin Laden just before the turn of the century. Soon after the US invaded Afghanistan, these capable warriors dispersed around the globe, where they honed their skills and led many of the attacks carried out by al Qaeda associated groups. Recruiting these men had been the foundation of Aziz's plan to seize control of the jihad movement. And thanks to handsome up-front bonuses, regular payments, and a commitment to return to jihad against the West, he had earned their sworn fidelity. In return, Aziz acquired a steady supply of loyal commanders to lead the various attacks that he alone would direct. Over time, he would merge what remained of al Qaeda into his own group, resulting in a consolidated jihadist organization under his exclusive control.

But as much fortune as Aziz left that meeting with, those profits were merely prerequisites to his destiny. He understood that his goals would not be achieved overnight. He appreciated that the timeline was much longer. He had no intention of pursuing the gradualist approach toward a caliphate that was favored by the shura. Instead, Aziz intended to execute in a relentlessly aggressive and speedy manner. His stratagem to do this called for coordinated, purposeful, and noteworthy attacks. Those military exploits would, in turn, build his following and allow him to incorporate the political components of his plan. As more supporters joined or rejoined the fold, Aziz's organization would become a political force by embedding with local groups to accomplish regional objectives. Aziz would use his new status to convert those local groups, and, eventually, the entire Muslim world, to his own radical views and global agenda. But Aziz was a pragmatic man. Because he knew the Americans would hunt him until he was dead, he put succession plans in place. Until then, he intended to accomplish as much as possible. He hoped that whatever he was able to achieve during his lifetime would be more than enough to earn the legacy he coveted.

So far, his approach was paying dividends. It had been only a year since he sold the shura on his proposal. In that time, al Qaeda had once again conducted successful operations on US soil, a claim no other terror organization could make. Although the death toll fell short of his optimistic estimates, the audacious attacks at the Super Bowl and Great American Mall had electrified the global jihadist movement and cemented his status among the believers. They had also restored confidence in al Qaeda's capabilities and reach. But al Qaeda existed in name only. Aziz judged that he could rightly claim responsibility for the money and new recruits that were again flowing into the organization. Regional terror groups that were once feared to be spurning al Qaeda, were expressing renewed pledges of loyalty to the group and, specifically, to Aziz. Still others, who were previously hostile toward al Qaeda, were signaling genuine interest in joining the fold. Control of the terror group and the jihadist movement was shifting in his favor.

Beyond these gains, his own group of loyal commanders were strategically stationed around the world and he had a steady supply of warriors ready to serve under them. As a result, Aziz had most of the pieces in place to execute the next stages of his campaign against the Crusaders and Jews. And it was only a matter of time before he would truly be regarded as the undisputed leader of global jihad and its righteous cause.

When Aziz approached the Chemin de la Corniche, his thoughts turned to his most lethal operator. As much as he wanted to convince himself that his improving fortunes were due solely to his own cunning and careful planning, Aziz recognized those gains would not have been possible without the contributions of one man. Hamid Fahkoury had secretly been his choice all along and he was more than pleased when the shura insisted that Fahkoury be allowed to lead the operation in the American heartland. Those successful attacks were, however, just the opening salvo in what Aziz had planned. He was fully aware that he would have to demonstrate a sustained ability to hit the West if momentum was to be carried forward. For that reason, even before he met Fahkoury and his companion Fahd al-Rasheed in the Arabian Desert, Aziz began making preparations for the next phase of his strategy. Now everything was in place. Once he addressed a minor threat to his power, he would initiate a series of preliminary attacks that would set the trap for another spectacular attack. And it would once again be led by Fahkoury.

Aziz stopped on one of the wider portions of the Corniche to rest his aching hands and arms. A respite here on the promenade was unlikely to draw any attention. The Corniche was commonly referred to as "Europe's most beautiful balcony" and many tourists and even locals often stopped to take in the view. But on this brisk morning there were surprisingly only a handful of others, including a newly arrived couple that had taken up position on the far side of a freshly-bloomed maple tree. Aziz casually glanced at his fellow sightseers and calculated that none were within thirty feet of him. He assumed they were all tourists, as almost every one of them was taking or posing for pictures, and some held the cheap canvas bags typically handed out by tour companies. He marveled at how, when given a choice, humans elected to maintain a respectful distance from strangers. None of them gave any indication that they even knew he was there. He was happy for the privacy, especially here among the nonbelievers, but he still found it strange that in more confined circumstances, these same people would be apt to smile or otherwise acknowledge his presence. It didn't really matter. He wasn't there to make any friends. In fact, he took a great measure of joy in the possibility that when these infidels returned to their own countries, they might become casualties in the next round of attacks.

After he completed his scan, Aziz looked down at the picturesque Grund neighborhood, whose seawalls and the attractive dwellings sitting atop them defined the meandering River Alzette. His eyes settled on Stierchen—the stone footbridge crossing the Alzette—before moving onto the Neumünster Abbey on the far side of the river. The complex of seventeenth century buildings was originally a Benedictine cloister, before later serving as a military barracks and prison. Currently functioning as a public meeting place and cultural center, Aziz could see more tourists scattered about its wide courtyard. Between the tourists frolicking below and those gleefully posing for pictures alongside him on the Corniche, there seemed to be no consideration for the attacks in America and how they might foreshadow threats to their own fragile and unworthy lives. *If they only knew*, he thought.

His gaze shifted and continued southward, following the sun-sparkled river until they came to rest on his own beautiful home. He wondered if today would be the day that he would hear again from Hamid Fahkoury, the man the rest of the world knew only as Mumeet—the Bringer of Death. It was only yesterday that he received confirmation that Fahd al-Rasheed was in place and preparing for his attack. Al-Rasheed would be ready in a matter of days and Aziz didn't want to risk that operation by delaying it indefinitely. He could not wait much longer to hear back from Fahkoury.

During their last exchange several weeks earlier, Aziz had reluctantly agreed to Fahkoury's request. The deviation presented considerable risk but Fahkoury had been both persuasive and insistent. When Fahkoury first proposed the idea, Fahkoury assured him that he would not do anything that would compromise the primary objective there, or the greater plans Aziz had for him later. In addition to the potential pitfalls, Fahkoury's scheme would require some alterations to the original plans. But as he thought more about it, Aziz began to see the brilliance of the scheme. After a short deliberation, Aziz agreed to Fahkoury's proposal.

But now, as he awaited word from Fahkoury before initiating the action, Aziz was having doubts about putting his best commander in harm's way for the sake of vengeance. Satisfying his top commander's thirst for revenge was secondary to cementing his grip on power. Still, the potential of the proposed twist continued to intrigue him. Because of that, Aziz decided right then that he was inclined to wait a bit longer. Not only would this step strengthen his position, it would further guarantee the Bringer of Death's undying loyalty. And once it was done, the path for him to implement the second phase of his war on the West would be clear. It was all coming together and, once it started, there would be no respite for the infidels. That thought brought a smile to Aziz's thin lips.

Reassured and rested, Aziz gave one more casual look around before stooping down and picking up his bags of groceries. He moved to the center of the promenade and resumed walking at an unhurried pace, feeling pleased enough with himself to feign a polite nod at the young couple when they turned toward him as he passed. He continued down the Corniche, edging closer to his home and the day of his fulfilled destiny.

Chapter 9
Langley, Virginia

A day later, PJ Carpenter opened the door into Timothy Patrick's sixth floor office. He had spent the better part of the day catching up on his reading after having arrived back from Tunis in the early morning hours. He had expected to be elsewhere, but when he and his team showed up with their prisoner at the airport in Tunis, Patrick said he needed him at headquarters. Patrick had three planes waiting in Tunis and told Carpenter to return alone on one of them. The other paramilitary officers jumped on another plane bound for Afghanistan, where extremists were once again making inroads. The final plane was for the prisoner. Over Carpenter's objection, it was Dan O'Reilly who accompanied the prisoner to the interrogation site. Even though it was unlikely, Patrick was concerned the Tunisians would inspect the plane before allowing it to takeoff. Patrick did not want his best man in the middle of what was sure to be a shit show. Plus, he wanted Carpenter, with all his experience and smarts, back at Langley so that they could assess their next moves.

When Carpenter walked through the doorway, the CTC chief was listening intently to whomever was on the other end of the phone. Patrick grimaced and quickly pointed to a chair on the other side of his desk. By the look on Patrick's face, it was clear to Carpenter that the conversation was not going well. After a few minutes, he rose from the chair and headed to the small refrigerator tucked under the credenza, several feet behind Patrick's desk. He opened the door and looked at his watch. It was almost four o'clock in the afternoon. Carpenter pushed aside some bottles of diet soda until he found what he was looking for. He had turned Patrick into a craft beer aficionado a few years earlier, and his boss usually kept a few of the better locally-brewed beers in his office. He popped open the ice-cold can and was making his way back to the chair when Patrick raised his eyebrows and motioned for Carpenter to grab one for him. As he placed Patrick's beer on the desk, he heard Patrick speak for the first time.

"Thank you, Mr. President. I'll be sure to tell PJ when he arrives. Thank you, sir."

Patrick replaced the receiver and took a deep breath before taking a long swig from the can. He looked away before turning to face Carpenter. When Patrick finally looked him in the eyes, Carpenter was shocked by his appearance. It had been only three days since he had last seen his boss. Carpenter assumed the short stint away was the reason he was only now noticing the striking change. Before the excursion to Tunisia, he had seen Patrick nearly every day for the better part of the past three months. Patrick's youthful countenance had always belied his sixty-three years but looking at him now, it seemed like Patrick had aged ten years.

Patrick had started a diet in the days before the attacks in Minnesota. He attributed his decision to Carpenter's constant pestering about his burgeoning middle section, but they both knew something needed to be done. After a rough start, the benefits had gradually started to materialize. But what Carpenter was now seeing was not the result of any diet. He guessed that Patrick had lost more than twenty pounds and only a small portion of it from his still too-round belly. The weight loss did not make Patrick look healthy at all. Carpenter even thought he could detect some hair loss. The full head of wavy peppered hair was one of the main reasons people often mistook Patrick for a man a decade younger. The stress was clearly getting to his close friend.

"I just realized, you look like shit," Carpenter said.

"Well, fuck you too," Patrick said. "Been a little stressful around here."

"How pissed is he?"

"From my sense of that call, I'd say more disappointed than pissed. Though he wasn't too happy when Director Gonzalez and I first told him we whiffed on al-Rasheed in Tunisia. Since then, he's calmed down a bit. He understands it was a long shot and one we had to take. But he's the president, and he expects results. And he's getting tired of waiting."

"I don't know him like you do, but he seemed reasonable and fair the few times I've been with him. He understands how hard it is to find one, two, or three people in a world of more than seven billion, doesn't he?"

"He absolutely does. But he's taking hell from his political opponents and their media stooges for the attacks in Minnesota. And they continue to ramp up the rhetoric, saying he's unfit to lead during a national security crisis."

"They're still pissed he won in the first place. They aren't about to do him any favors; he should know that."

"I'm sure he does. Elinore Wilson and her colleague in the House, Allen Schmidt, are on the news every day blasting him. I'm pretty sure he writes that off as just playing politics. But reading between the lines, I think he's most upset about the former intelligence folks ripping him. I think he's concerned they are undermining his credibility with the intelligence community."

Carpenter mostly avoided watching and reading the news. He long ago considered fact-based journalism to be dead. In his mind, most in the media were partisan hacks who slanted their reporting to their own political views or to those belonging to the people who signed their checks. And that included those ordained as national security pundits. He had seen a few former colleagues feeding the echo chamber on cable news in recent weeks, so he had an idea about what was frustrating the president. "They're nothing more than mouthpieces singing for their supper. None of the ones I have seen on television were ever worth a damn, anyway."

"One jackass in particular. He's always quick to criticize," Patrick said.

Carpenter knew exactly who Patrick was talking about. And he knew how to shut the man up. "Maybe you should suggest to the president that he declassify the report about how that guy almost got his colleagues killed." Carpenter was referring to the man's capture by the Taliban in the first months of the Afghan invasion. His initial captors were not hardcore jihadists but, rather, regular Afghans forced into service by the hardliners. In what was essentially being questioned by farmers at the end of a pitchfork, the man had blurted out the location of Carpenter's team on the Shomali Plains. Only the random fortune of intercepting a radio communication saved Carpenter and his teammates from being overrun. When they rescued him later, Carpenter briefly considered leaving the since turned-television pundit to the real Taliban wolves, but duty ultimately prevailed. In another example of a good deed never going unpunished, the ungrateful coward had been a devout critic ever since his discharge from the Central Intelligence Agency days later.

"I wish he could do that. But that's not all of it. In addition to the hammering he is getting at home, there are whispers from our so-called allies that we've brought this on ourselves."

"Oh yeah, how so?"

Patrick explained that Secretary of State Julie Christensen reported this development just days before. Apparently, as time moved further from the recent tragedy, representatives from certain countries had become more comfortable intimating in private conversations with the secretary that the president's rhetoric may have been the motivation for the attacks in Minnesota. Several of these diplomats chastised Secretary Christensen about the words the president used to define the threat from Islamic extremism and his repeated promises to the American people to eradicate it. During the campaign, the president had been harshly critical of his predecessor's apathetic approach to terrorism. He vowed that, if he were elected, his administration would acknowledge it for what it was and employ every means possible to defeat the threat. In addition to referring to the threat by name, he had received nearly universal condemnation for his views on border security and immigration controls from political and media elites at home and abroad. Now those critics were pouncing on the opportunity to prove themselves correct.

"That's exactly why I don't trust any of them, with the probable exceptions of the British and the Israelis," Carpenter said. "When are the rest of those idiots going to wake up and realize extremism threatens their values and very way of life? This problem is not going away until we can get rid of the guys at the top."

Carpenter correctly understood that information and opportunity were the keys to take away the oxygen that fueled radical views. The people in power and directing the violent jihad movement had vested interests to distort information and deny opportunity. By exploiting their fellow Muslims in this way, these leaders were able to foment the hatred necessary to convert otherwise peaceful people to their radical views. The people running the show did everything they could to make joining the fight the only option. In turn, they secured the power and influence needed to perpetuate violent jihad. Carpenter recognized that a long-term solution incorporating diplomatic, educational, and economic efforts was necessary to counter the efforts of the terror leaders and bring about an end to Islamic extremism. But that process of democratization and empowerment was a long one. In the interim, it was critical that those leading the efforts to propagate radical views be dealt with, and dealt with harshly. And the kinetic solution was Carpenter's primary focus.

"Sorry, I thought we would have time to catch up, but I can't right now. Tomorrow we are meeting with the team before I head over to the White House," Patrick said. "The president wants us to tell him our thinking about what is likely to come next and our plans to stop it. Meet me back here at eight tomorrow morning. We can catch up before we meet with the team at nine o'clock. Now, get your ass out of here so I can get back to work."

Chapter 10

Carpenter popped out of his bed and headed straight for the shower. He had rented the studio apartment in Falls Church, Virginia a few weeks after the attacks in Minnesota. Patrick had made it clear that he wanted him around and ready to deploy on a moment's notice, just as he had for Tunisia. Patrick also relied on Carpenter's insight and assistance interpreting sketchy information, which was typically the only sustenance in the intelligence world. His boss was disappointed when he told him about the apartment. The CTC chief had hoped his friend would continue to stay with him and his wife across the river in Bethesda. Although he appreciated Patrick's offer, Carpenter had more or less been living alone since his mother passed away when he was fourteen and he liked it that way.

The monochromatic apartment wasn't much but it was close to headquarters. The walls, doors, linoleum floors, Formica countertops in the galley kitchen and bath, and the carpet were one shade of white or another when he moved in eight weeks earlier and little color had been added since. Other than a bed, a small blue sofa, and a coffee machine, Carpenter had made no additions to the place. In fact, with the exception of a few items hanging in the closet, most of his clothes were in neat piles on the bedroom floor. In the fridge, there was only bottled water and craft beer. He ate most of his meals out or brought them in, using whatever utensils were provided by the restaurant. He had, however, used the in-unit washer and dryer a few times. But the only thing he cared about was the coffee machine. While staying with the Patrick's in Bethesda, he had grown extremely fond of their

Nespresso machine. When Carpenter said he was looking for his own place, Patrick's wife Suzanne ordered him one as a housewarming gift.

The spartan apartment was more than adequate for his needs and ensured he could come and go as he pleased without question. More than freedom, he was really more concerned about being a disruption to the normal ebb and flow of the Patrick household. After years of operations, he knew his sleeping habits were abnormal by anyone else's standards. He functioned on short rests. It was rare that he slept longer than four hours at any one time. And when he was in town and wasn't napping or working out, the indefatigable Carpenter was usually at CIA headquarters the rest of any twenty-four-hour cycle.

For the most part, he had not been involved in the day-to-day analytical effort, preferring to let the experts do their jobs without his interference. But, besides the trip to Tunisia, he had kept himself busy with his own homework. Now he was looking forward to comparing notes with the rest of the team. After his shower, he dressed and made himself a coffee that he drank during the short drive to headquarters. He walked into Patrick's office a few minutes before eight o'clock.

"You look chipper this morning," Patrick said.

"Slept really well and ready to go."

"You love that coffee machine, don't you?"

"I do. I actually craved an Americano while I was in Tunisia. It's probably the best gift I've ever received and I'm not sure how I'm going to do without it. I hope you and Suzie know how much I appreciate it."

"Don't get mushy," Patrick joked. The Patrick's had no children of their own and Carpenter was like a son to them. When Carpenter entered their lives many years ago in Beirut, they were both immediately taken with him, in particular by his humility, determination, and values. And as they learned the detailed story of his troubled youth, their affection for Carpenter grew even more. Ever since, each time he put Carpenter in harm's way, Patrick had worried incessantly about his friend. And Suzie doted on Carpenter every chance she got. "I'll be sure to tell the missus."

They spent the next fifty minutes going over the operation in Tunisia. Both of them were convinced that al-Rasheed had been there, but neither of them could explain why. There was nothing of intelligence value in the remote hideout, and nothing to indicate that al-Rasheed had picked up anything important while there. And al-Rasheed had stayed only a short time. The only conclusion they could reach was that the Tunisian mountains were merely a way station on al-Rasheed's journey elsewhere. On that, they put the odds at even that al-Rasheed was either bound for an al Qaeda safe haven in Central Asia or on his way to carry out another attack, possibly with Mumeet. Carpenter said he was leaning one way but wanted to hear what the team had to say before sharing his take.

"It's almost nine. We should head down," Patrick said.

"Aren't we meeting in here?"

"No, we're meeting in the first-floor conference room."

A command post had been set up in the drab room to host the members of the Interagency Incident Management Group convened by the president in the days before the attacks. The IIMG was still a functioning group that continued to use the same conference room as its primary workspace. Carpenter had come to despise the interior room, more for the unpleasant memories than the stench of crappy food and stress that seemed to have permanently settled in the confined space. With only a few exceptions, he had been able to avoid it in recent weeks. "Super," Carpenter said sarcastically. "Since we still have a few minutes, let's grab some food in the cafeteria. The stink in that room kills my appetite."

"We don't have enough time for that. The cafeteria will be a zoo right now. Besides, I had some fresh fruit and coffee put out downstairs."

"Wow, you're taking this diet thing pretty seriously. You're going to waste away."

"Despite your insubordinate comments about my appearance, I'm feeling a lot better, at least physically. Mostly, I've noticed that I have more energy. And, you'll be happy to know, I'm walking two miles every day. And I haven't even touched a donut in sixty-four days. But who's counting?"

Carpenter laughed as he followed his boss out of the office and to the elevator. He half expected Patrick to tell him they were taking the stairs down six flights to the conference room. On the ride down the elevator, and for the first few steps on the short walk to the meeting room, Carpenter asked about Tyler Kennedy, the young man who had helped him take down the terrorists at the Great American Mall. Upon hearing Carpenter's glowing praise for the young man, President Madden had arranged to speak to Kennedy. After speaking with him, the president was even more impressed than he was following Carpenter's stellar assessment. Never one to allow a special talent to slip away, President Madden went into recruiting mode and asked Kennedy to come work for the government. After allowing himself some time to recover from the harrowing incident and reflect on the president's offer, Tyler accepted two days later. Kennedy was whisked through the background checks and was placed into an accelerated training program less than two weeks later. Carpenter checked with Patrick on Tyler's progress on an almost weekly basis.

"Tyler is doing extremely well," Patrick said. "I read all his training reports because the president also regularly asks about him. The training staff says he is handling everything they throw at him with aplomb. They think he'll finish the program and be ready for the field in less than a year."

The original plan had been to start Kennedy out as an operations officer, but his acceptance of the president's offer was conditioned on him being able to work alongside Carpenter in the CTC's paramilitary division. At Patrick's urging, Carpenter had tried to guide him down the intelligence gathering path but Kennedy was adamant. Carpenter did not see a need to press the issue. The job was demanding but Carpenter had seen enough to know that Kennedy was capable. His only concern was how Tyler would be able to handle the singular existence of a paramilitary officer. Although Kennedy's initial assessments strongly indicated he could, Carpenter knew that was something only time and experience could determine. "Please tell him I say hello next time you see him," Carpenter said.

"I do every time."

When they walked into the conference room, they were greeted by the usual suspects. Seated around the table were Samantha Lane, Ella Rock, and Dalton Jones, all colleagues from the Counterterrorism Center. They were joined by Paul Dunleavy from the FBI.

"Good morning everyone," Patrick said. "As you know, I will be heading to the White House later to brief the president and his staff. After missing Fahd al-Rasheed in Tunisia, the president wants to know our latest thinking and what we plan on doing to find Aziz and his band of devils. So what do you all have for us?"

"Thank you, sirs," Samantha Lane said. "Dalton, please start us off."

Carpenter liked the way Lane operated. He'd now been in enough meetings with her to recognize that she led by empowering her teammates. The senior counterterrorism analyst delegated assignments and stayed intimately involved each step of the way, discussing and helping her colleagues to refine their findings until she was satisfied. And rather than present the material herself, she called on her teammates to share their conclusions. Lane offered her own informed views as appropriate or to support her colleagues, but she mostly served as emcee to maintain the flow and order of the meetings. And she also knew how to pick a team. Carpenter settled into the uncomfortable chair as best he could and waited to hear what Dalton Jones had to say. Jones was a targeting officer and his job was to understand the relationships between key people and terrorist organizations. Quite often, it was the intelligence gathered by people like Jones that Carpenter relied upon to do his job. He liked Jones' thoroughness and determination. Plus, Jones' thick Georgia accent was reminiscent of his youth.

"At the outset, we have no new information indicating or even intimating the whereabouts of Sadiq bin Aziz, Fahd al-Rasheed, or Mumeet," Jones said. "We have been mapping Aziz's known and suspected associates. So far, we haven't uncovered anyone with potential jihadist ties, and we have not found any new faces or any new leads since the last update. It's becoming clear that Aziz took great pains to keep his business and jihad worlds separate.

"The same result is true for Fahd al-Rasheed, despite genuine assistance from the Saudis. His parents are dead and he has one brother who lives in Singapore. The brother claims not to have seen him in more than twenty years. Besides the family, the Saudis have interviewed anyone even thought to know al-Rasheed, and they have allowed our case officers in the Kingdom to assist with those interviews. He's been described universally as a pleasant person, but it's clear he is also secretive. No two interviews revealed the same information. It appears al-Rasheed told a different story about himself to every friend and acquaintance.

"That brings me to Mumeet. Of course, we still don't know his true identity so we haven't been able to go through the same exercise with his associates. We continue to question every extremist in US custody. We haven't found anyone who knows his real name. The guy is an enigma. And none of our allies has any better information on the Bringer of Death than we do. But we are still digging on all three," Jones said. Then he looked to Lane to indicate that he was finished.

"Thank you, Dalton," Lane said. "At the same time, we've been attempting to understand al Qaeda's new operational strategy under Sadiq bin Aziz. Using what we have pieced together, we now believe we have an idea how Aziz intends to operate. But, before we go into that, a review of the incidents in Minnesota and the events leading up to them will help contextualize our current thinking. Paul?"

"I'm going to first address the time frame for those attacks," Dunleavy said. "In summary, the time the terrorists were in the country, for what were pretty sophisticated and coordinated mass-scale attacks, was remarkably short. To date, the FBI and local law enforcement have conducted one hundred-twenty-three interviews in Dearborn, Michigan. Based on those interviews, we have been able to pin down the arrival of the first wave of terrorists in Dearborn to sometime in mid-December, approximately six or seven weeks before the attacks."

"Sorry, but any update on the Syrians?" Carpenter asked. He was referring to three men arrested at the southern border in the same general timeframe. The men claimed to be from Syria and seeking asylum in the United States. They were released by the immigration judge with orders to return for a hearing several weeks later. They never showed up and had not been seen since.

"We have yet to locate them," Dunleavy said. "Law enforcement across the country has copies of the photos from their fake passports but there are no descriptions to go along with them. Customs and Border Protection records have no indication of age, height, weight, or any unique characteristics. Our best guess is that they are still here but there are no indications they are related in any way to the terror cell that carried out the attacks in Minnesota."

Carpenter wasn't so sure and that was something he had warned Patrick about previously. "I hope you're right because the alternative is no good. We need to continue to make finding them a priority. I'm afraid there's an equal chance they are a sleeper cell, here to carry out an attack," Carpenter said.

"I spoke with Chip last night and he assures me that finding them will remain a priority" Patrick said. He was referring to FBI Director Charles "Chip" Forti. The nation's top law man had admitted to Patrick that by directing resources to interviewing witnesses, accumulating forensic evidence at the attack scenes, and girding for more attacks, the Bureau's focus on the manhunt for the illegal aliens had taken a back seat. But Forti told Patrick that he understood his and Carpenter's unease. Forti had promised that finding the Syrians would be put back at the top of the FBI's list.

"Good to hear. Sorry again, Paul. You were talking about waves of terrorists coming into the country. How many waves are we talking about?" Carpenter asked.

"It's our best guess that the people who actually carried out the attacks—the warriors, if you will—entered the country weeks before the leaders, Mumeet and al-Rasheed did. Activity at the two homes in Dearborn was first detected in mid-December. We don't know how many occupied the homes, but we believe the warriors were all inserted into the country around the same general time."

"Do you know how they got into the country?" Carpenter asked.

"Again, we don't know definitively, but we think all the terrorists, including Mumeet and al-Rasheed, came across the southern border."

"And you base that on the possible connection between Mumeet and the killing of the civilian border guard in Texas just three weeks prior to the attacks?" Carpenter asked.

"In part we do, yes. But we were also able to trace three of the vehicles used in the attacks to the Houston area. We've been sorting through the rubble for weeks and it wasn't until a few days ago that we located a vehicle identification number for the third vehicle used at the mall. We now know that three of the five vehicles used in the attacks were purchased for cash from buyers in the Houston area. All transactions were initiated through an online classified ad site. We also know that the other two vehicles used in the attacks were purchased in Michigan several weeks after the Houston transactions. Again, the Michigan vehicles were purchased the same way.

Based on those findings, it is our assumption that all the warriors most likely staged in the Houston area before heading to Dearborn. We're surmising that the warriors were sent ahead of the leaders in order to make preparations. That's largely because we don't see how three weeks was sufficient time form Mumeet and al-Rasheed to surveil the targets and acquire the necessary weapons and materials."

"The sequence of their arrivals may be right, but they may have had other help. I think we need to also consider that people already in the country could have made some of the preparations, independent of the warriors and, later, the leaders," Carpenter said.

"PJ's right. We shouldn't jump to any conclusions. For one thing, we know Zafir Bahar was involved somehow," Patrick said. Bahar owned a mobile repair phone shop and the two homes used by the terrorists in Dearborn. There was evidence of a trip Bahar had taken to Washington DC found at one of those residences. The trip was likely a feint but most assuredly was directed by Mumeet. As further proof of Bahar's involvement, a car he owned was found at the Great American Mall. But Bahar had vanished and had been a dead end. "It's possible there could have been others besides Bahar who were not directly involved in the attacks."

"Both scenarios are potentially true," Ella Rock said. "Either way, the time from infiltration to attack was short, especially for attacks on that scale. And we think that was intentional. We believe Aziz is using an operational strategy of short lead times, where the leaders are inserted only after most, if not all, preparations have been made. This would reduce risk to the commanders, Aziz's most valued assets. He can always recruit warriors but capable leaders are harder to come by. It's a smart play."

Ella Rock's creative thinking, as much as her clear and concise analysis, was what distinguished her from other counterterrorism analysts Carpenter had worked with. Aziz had obviously not broadcasted his strategy, yet Rock was able to draw a sound conclusion from the different characteristics leading up to and during those attacks. It made sense to Carpenter. In his experience, the attacks in Minnesota were atypical and that pointed to a new operational strategy. Most often, the leader was the first inserted to the target area. This allowed the leader to conduct initial target surveillance and initiate logistical support before summoning the attack team. This process reduced the number of less-careful warriors in enemy territory during the initial phases of the operational planning stage of the attack cycle. From what they knew, the reverse process had been followed in Minnesota. On top of that, it was not uncommon for the leader to participate in the actual attack. Here, it was plain that Mumeet had planned for his escape. Carpenter suspected that must have been someone else's decision. For a zealot like Mumeet, there would have been no greater honor than martyrdom in an operation conducted on US soil. But, if Aziz and al Qaeda were committed to a return to jihad operations, it was shrewd to save Mumeet and his bomb-making and leadership skills for another day.

Al-Rasheed, on the other hand, was a different story. Unlike Mumeet, there was no evidence that al-Rasheed possessed any special skills. He was virtually an unknown until recently, and there was no apparent reason why he had escaped and not martyred himself. But, other than the questions about al-Rasheed, he found himself agreeing with Ella Rock's analysis. And Carpenter thought he might know the answer to the al-Rasheed riddle. "Why do you think al-Rasheed escaped?" he asked. "We can't know that he was told to escape but I think it points to that conclusion. I say that because, even if something went wrong, I would have expected that al-Rasheed would have tried to kill as many people as possible before we got him. But he didn't do that."

"Maybe he has a close relationship with Mumeet or Aziz, possibly both," Rock said.

"That's a rational explanation but planning for his escape was dangerous. Unlike Mumeet, al-Rasheed was involved in the actual attack. There was a good chance that we would catch him if we didn't kill him. If we caught him, he would have posed a security risk to Mumeet and Aziz's future plans. Why assume that risk when al-Rasheed doesn't seem to have any distinct talent, other than a personal connection to Aziz or Mumeet?"

"We hadn't really thought about it that way," Lane said.

"Let's go back to Aziz's two recent statements," Carpenter said. "Shortly after the attacks, he promised they 'were just the first in a renewed battle against the Crusaders.' Then, just before al-Rasheed was spotted in Tunisia, Aziz released that ambiguous statement through al Jazeera." Carpenter reached into his pocket and pulled out a copy of the statement before reading it aloud. "Aziz said, 'Brothers, the point of our sword is once again directed at the Western oppressors. The strong horse is favored over the weak one and ours will become mightier still as it feasts on every morsel, large and small, of the infidel. Prepare yourselves as your time at the table of Paradise approaches.' Taken together, what does everyone think the two statements mean?"

"I think we can all agree that Aziz is directing al Qaeda back to bin Laden's primary strategy of focusing on the 'far enemy'—the US and our allies rather than secular or apostate governments in Muslim-majority countries," Lane said. "But he doesn't need to carry out large-scale attacks in order to do that. Smaller attacks are easier to plan and execute. Al Qaeda is the 'strong horse' referenced in the statement. I think he is setting expectations by announcing that not every attack will be on the scale of those in Minnesota—the small morsels in his statement. By doing this, AQ can continue to build momentum without having to execute large-scale operations."

"Aziz might be positioning AQ for another reason," Rock said. "Although there hasn't been an attack of any kind since Minnesota, attacks like those can be an instigator for smaller-scale attacks. In many cases, they are carried out by people not associated with the party responsible for the initial attack. Aziz might be anticipating this and positioning AQ to get the credit for any random attacks to follow."

"I think you are both right, but I think there may be something more telling in the statement," Carpenter said. "If al Qaeda waits too long before its next attack, it risks the Islamic State or another terror group doing something to steal their mojo. It's possible AQ has another large attack ready to pop, but I think it's more likely it intends to bridge the gap between significant and complex operations with smaller attacks. And I think the latest statement means they are now ready to proceed with those smaller attacks."

"So, what does this have to do with al-Rasheed?" Patrick asked.

"I originally thought Mumeet and al-Rasheed were told to escape from the United States because AQ wanted to use them for another large-scale attack. I thought then and still think now that plans for at least one future attack were made before those two came here; probably when Aziz met them in the Rub Al Khali. Then Aziz comes out with the 'small morsel' announcement. Soon after that, we are told that al-Rasheed was spotted in Tunisia. There is no sign that Mumeet was with him in Tunisia. It's possible that al-Rasheed has since hooked up with Mumeet but the content and timing of Aziz's most recent statement got me thinking differently about al-Rasheed. While we doubt his ability to plan a sophisticated attack, we know from the attacks here that al-Rasheed is certainly capable of at least playing a key role in the execution of one. It stands to reason that al-Rasheed can lead one or more of the smaller momentum-building attacks. But for me, the timing of Aziz's statement is most significant. Aziz waited until he knew al-Rasheed was safely out of the US because al-Rasheed is going to lead an attack. Aziz was telling the others in the cell to get ready. That means we could be looking down the barrel of an imminent attack."

"You're thinking that the targets and dates have already been selected?" Patrick asked.

"If I am right, I do think al-Rasheed's target was selected when they met in the desert. But I don't see how a date could have been predetermined. There was too much uncertainty around al-Rasheed's availability. We're pretty confident al-Rasheed and Mumeet didn't jump on a flight out of here. Chances are they got out of the country the same way we think they got in—by slipping across the border into Mexico. But it's also possible they took some other circuitous route, maybe through Canada or aboard a ship leaving somewhere along one of the coasts. Whichever way they got out, it would've taken time, and spotting al-Rasheed in Tunisia shortly after Aziz's statement was released squares with my analysis.

"Once Aziz learned that al-Rasheed was safely out of the US, he gave notice to get ready. And al-Rasheed doesn't let any grass grow under his feet in Tunisia. Despite being in friendlier territory, he's out of there in a hurry and headed somewhere 'across the sea' according to our witness. Depending on where he went, al-Rasheed could be gearing up for the attack right now." Carpenter paused momentarily to let that sink in.

"Where did he go?" Patrick asked.

"He could be anywhere, though I doubt he circled and came back here. If the witness can be believed and al-Rasheed was stating his true intentions, the reference to 'across the sea' most logically means he is somewhere in Europe now," Carpenter said.

"Whoa, that's a lot to digest," Patrick said. "You take some pretty big leaps there."

"I do, but we're here trying to figure out al Qaeda's next move," Carpenter said. "Right now, we don't have any intelligence to give us insight so we're left to speculate. I'll admit what I said is nothing more than an educated guess. Does anyone have any other ideas?"

Initially, no one did. With Aziz in the mix, al Qaeda had shown a renewed ability. Not a person in the room was counting on AQ to retreat to the shadows; it was once again at the top of the threat chart. But Carpenter's analysis had put a sharper point on when those fears might be realized. It elevated the concern by making the threat more tangible and real. Yet, they still had no clue how to stop it.

"I think the way PJ is looking at this makes complete sense," Lane said. "But what we haven't acknowledged is Aziz's role."

"How do you mean?" Patrick asked. Before Samantha could answer, her colleague jumped in.

"I'll do a little spitballing," Ella Rock said. The counterterrorism analyst knew al Qaeda better than anyone. Ever since Aziz had entered the picture, Rock had spent her days and nights assessing Aziz and his role in the AQ organization. "Since the joint release a few days after the attacks, we heard nothing from al Qaeda until Aziz's recent statement. Normally, we would have heard from senior leadership, specifically al-Zawahiri. But he's been silent. That's unusual in and of itself. It's also a potential sign that al Qaeda senior leadership is either in the dark or made a knowing decision to cede control to Aziz. But I think it's more likely that Aziz is making his own power play; he's trying to take over AQ."

She looked around and noticed she had everyone's undivided attention. "We've already noted the change in operational strategy. This is a significant change, and one I think we have to attribute to Aziz. Now we're thinking Aziz gave instructions to Mumeet and al-Rasheed for not only for the attacks here in February, but for additional attacks. The silence from other senior leaders makes me think Aziz has cut them off. In that case, Aziz would have made those plans on his own volition. That would be another departure from the status quo. We know from their own statements in the past that senior leadership approves every single attack against the West. These are dramatic changes for an organization with strict controls. I think Aziz might be splitting from the senior leaders and is attempting to gain control of al Qaeda. Mumeet and al-Rasheed might be the means to that end. If they are party to Aziz's play, they could be all he has for loyal commanders who are capable of leading an attack. That dovetails with PJ's analysis for why they escaped instead of martyring themselves." As she waited for a response, Rock noticed the ponderous looks but she wasn't sure anyone else was buying her theory.

"I had just assumed Aziz was the new point man," Carpenter said, finally. "Maybe Aziz *is* attempting some kind of takeover of al Qaeda but there's another possibility. The appropriate analogy is al Qaeda in Iraq. When Abu Musab al-Zarqawi arrived on the scene, core al Qaeda thought it could control him. It could not. Zarqawi had his own plans to lead the jihad movement. He only aligned with al Qaeda when it suited his purposes. As he gained more notoriety, he became increasingly untethered from al Qaeda. By the time we killed him, al-Zarqawi had built an organization strong enough to survive him—it's now known as the Islamic State. It's possible that Aziz, like al-Zarqawi, is only working alongside al Qaeda until he can go it alone. But whether he is trying to wrest control of al Qaeda or is positioning to create his own separate terror group, Aziz has to have more help than just Mumeet and Fahd al-Rasheed."

"That's true," Patrick said. "He's got to have some trusted lieutenants to help with things like logistics and financing. Dalton," Patrick said to the targeting analyst, "how far back in Aziz's history have you scrutinized?"

"I've been looking at the relationships we know he's had since he sold his business," Jones said. "But there's not much to go on. We've cleared all of his known contacts."

"I want you to expand your inquiry of Aziz's relationships. Go back twenty years or more if you need to. Look at every person he worked with, spent time with, his lawyers, consultants to his firm, the whole shebang. See if any relationship patterns manifest themselves. And let me know the second you find someone suspicious."

"Yes sir," Jones said.

"In the meantime, we have al-Rasheed and Mumeet running around, probably preparing for more attacks as we speak. Now that we're thinking Aziz has carte blanche, does anybody have a different idea about potential targets and timing?" Patrick asked.

"If he's going out on his own, Aziz will need to prove he belongs in the jihadi hierarchy," Carpenter said. "This is pure speculation but I'd say it's more likely that we'll face attacks that are less sophisticated than what we experienced in Minnesota. Aziz needs more successes in order to build a following on the global order of al Qaeda or the Islamic State. We have to consider that objective in light of what we suspect is limited manpower. If I was Aziz, I'd be looking for some quick-hit wins, and I'd do it by deploying small teams to strike at high-profile targets where security isn't a real concern. That framework gives him plenty of options to be successful."

"I think that's right," Lane said. "I also think Aziz can earn greater credibility by showing that his organization has worldwide reach. Striking at multiple locations throughout the West would accomplish that."

This was a lot for Patrick to unpack. Gone was the assumption that Aziz was working with al Qaeda. The new thinking was that Aziz might be splitting from the terror group to form his own organization. "Let me get this straight," Patrick said. "We know al Qaeda carried out the attacks in Minnesota and, right after, Aziz was named a coleader of AQ. Now you say he is going out on his own. Was that his plan all along? To use al Qaeda to boost his own reputation?"

"I hadn't thought of it that way but, after listening to Sam and Ella, I think that is exactly what he did," Carpenter said. "He probably recognized that executing a coup was a long shot. To overthrow the shura, he would need a significant following. He'd have to spend a lot of time and money politicking to pull that off, and that would be a tough slog for someone who was relatively unknown until a few months ago. The faster way to power is by forming his own group, and now he can build off the acclaim he received for the Minnesota attacks to do it."

"Is there any doubt about Aziz's ability to carry out another large-scale attack?" Patrick asked.

"I would say no," Ella Rock said. "If he has Mumeet in his camp, we have to assume that Aziz fully intends to execute large-scale attacks. I think what we're all saying is that we expect him to conduct smaller attacks in the interim so that he can continue to build his own following."

Patrick was thinking how he was going to present this to the president without sounding alarmist. It was all conjecture but this unexpected twist to the threat matrix made an already frightening picture even gloomier. Adding to his angst was that his team knew almost nothing about Aziz's group. Beyond Aziz and likely collaborators Mumeet and Fahd al-Rasheed, they had no idea who else was working with them or where they might be planning to strike. But, as unsettling as this development was, it made sense. "We've got our work cut out for us," he said. "Let's do everything possible to find Aziz, al-Rasheed, and Mumeet before we hear from them."

Chapter 11
Istanbul, Turkey

Hamid Fahkoury stood outside the mosque, hidden among the mob of sightseers, and gazed southeast across the Bosporus Strait while waiting for the imam to call the faithful to prayer. Since his arrival in Istanbul, he had avoided going inside a mosque to attend services. Instead, he mostly prayed alone in the grungy apartment in the cluttered Old Town section of the ancient city. Occasionally, he found a spot outside a mosque where he could pray inconspicuously. The mosque here, in the shadows of the expansive Bosporus Bridge, was one such location. He had visited this spot twice before. It stood right next to a busy terminal for ferry passengers crossing the narrow waterway to and from the Asian continent on the other side. The heavy blend of tourists among the locals in the immediate area lessened the chance the mosque was under any kind of intense surveillance. Today, the crowd was especially large. An extended warm spell had settled over Istanbul and many people were out enjoying the unseasonable weather. His stay in Istanbul had been pleasant enough but now it was time to move forward with the plans he had made with Aziz.

Fahkoury had originally planned to travel to Istanbul only to hole up until it was time to move into position for the next attack he would lead. But now there was another reason he was there—an opportunity to kill the man who had interrupted his operation in America. And Aziz's plan to eliminate one of his prime adversaries would provide the opportunity. Aziz had originally intended to use another location to eliminate the main challenger to his rule, but Fahkoury had argued that he should use Istanbul instead. Fahkoury contended that the culturally diverse city of more than fifteen million was as good a place as any to do that. And Fahkoury proposed a way to entangle the Americans in the plot. Aziz was ultimately persuaded by the prospect of both using and harming the Americans. Fahkoury was grateful for the indulgence. While there was no guarantee, there was a chance the ploy would lure his adversary to Istanbul and a chance was all he wanted.

He had been consumed with vengeance since the day of the attacks in America. The coordinated attacks at the stadium and the mall had been greeted with critical acclaim by the believers, but Fahkoury was not interested in accolades. He expected perfect execution for every operation, and there had been some errors in Minnesota. The failures of his men to detonate the second car bomb at the Super Bowl and, later, to timely penetrate the mall and slaughter those inside were avoidable and, therefore, wholly unacceptable. The Americans had been saved a far worse fate than he had anticipated. But, as much as he should have faulted his men, Fahkoury reserved his ire for one particular man.

In addition to blaming the American for disrupting the attacks, Fahkoury also held him accountable for fouling up the escape plans he had with Fahd al-Rasheed. Immediately after the attacks in Minnesota, Fahkoury had headed to the Wisconsin border and the rendezvous location. He waited for al-Rasheed until the appointed time and not a minute longer. After driving through the night, he stopped outside Buffalo, New York to exchange the stolen Toyota Camry. The Vermont plates made the replacement vehicle easy enough to find among the cars in the ice rink parking lot. Inside the salt-streaked black Ford Fusion was a worn Canadian passport, with a picture bearing a reasonable enough facsimile to his rather ordinary appearance. He felt a pang of regret when he looked through the other passport that had been left for his brother, al-Rasheed. But Fahkoury quickly refocused. As long as he was smart and kept moving, he felt good about his chances. Despite being the most wanted man in America, Fahkoury's true identity remained unknown. Further aiding him was the fact that there was no quality photograph of him in circulation.

Dawn was breaking through low clouds when he left the ice rink and continued east across the state of New York. When he reached the capital, he guided the Ford sedan north along the banks of the Hudson River. Clearing skies and endless updates about the attacks on the radio lifted his spirits as he continued his journey. He arrived at the southern end of the Adirondack Park midafternoon and stopped for fuel and yogurt at a gas station just off the interstate. He overheard bits of conversation between the customers seated around several tables inside. Fahkoury reveled in their palpable fear and was forced to suppress a smile when he heard one woman warn her compatriots that terrorists could be anywhere in the country. Yet, for all their concern, not one of them even gave him a second look.

The reassuring experience stayed with him as he followed the rolling two-lane road that put him at the Vermont border less than an hour later. Once in Vermont, he followed a country highway that mirrored the eastern shore of Lake Champlain and wound its way north through the Green Mountain state. The rural backroad was probably the last place the Americans would expect to find him, but he made sure to adhere to the varying speed limits, especially on the few occasions when he passed through a small village. About two hours from the most worrisome point on his journey, he was pleasantly distracted by a spectacular sunset over the High Peaks region of the Adirondack Mountains towering above the western shore of Lake Champlain. Shortly after dark, he passed through Burlington, and approached the Canadian border a short time later.

It was just after 6:30 p.m. when he passed the small brick US Customs outpost at Morses Line. Less than fifteen hundred feet later, he was stopped at the guard post just inside the Canadian border. It was one of fifteen border crossings from Vermont, and one of the sleepiest. Fahkoury found it almost comical that anyone would think the lonely guard inside the booth-sized building was a sufficient deterrent against an incident with international implications. The secluded checkpoint sat among towering conifer trees at the end of a two-lane road. Killing the Canadian guard would not be a problem, if it became necessary. As he put the window down, Fahkoury calculated that he could probably be well into Canada by the time the US official a quarter mile away or anyone else realized there was a problem.

After an exchange of polite greetings, the guard asked Fahkoury his reason for visiting the United States. Fahkoury said he worked in Burlington and was going home to Quebec to visit his brother for a few days. When the guard asked why he was crossing at Morses Line instead of the main crossing just north of Burlington, Fahkoury said he had made a quick stop to see his girlfriend on the way. She lived in one of the small towns nearby. The guard looked at his Canadian passport again, this time seeming to study it more closely. Fahkoury steeled himself for trouble, but the guard looked up and smiled in mischievous understanding. He handed Fahkoury the passport and wished him a pleasant evening.

Fahkoury slowly pulled away from the guard booth and set his sights for Montreal, where the al Qaeda affiliate, Jabhat Fateh al-Sham, or JFS, had connections. Shortly after the Islamic State started to lose its grip on power in the Levant, three Canadian nationals had shown up at a JFS fortification in Aleppo. They said they wanted to join the al Qaeda affiliate. After a few rounds of what they would consider rather mild torture, the JFS leaders were convinced the men were not spies and welcomed them into the group. Having Westerners on the team was a real coup for JFS, and, when they learned of it, something al Qaeda brass encouraged its affiliate to exploit. The JFS leaders elevated all three men to the rank of lieutenant and kept two of them in Syria, while they sent the most capable man back home to Canada with specific instructions.

In no time, the jihadist was operating a recruiting station out of a mosque in Montreal. He was also building a modest real estate portfolio with financing from JFS. As they became available, funds were deposited in a money service business account in Dubai and were transferred to the terrorist's own account in Montreal through the bank's correspondent accounts in New York. JFS's Canadian jihadist had received more than one million five hundred thousand dollars through these channels, and he invested it in studio and one-bedroom apartments throughout the city. For each of the past fifteen months, the jihadist had been sending an average of two men and at least fifteen thousand dollars profit back to Syria.

It was in one of those portfolio studio apartments that Fahkoury had stayed for more than six weeks. He had no visitors to the flat off the Rue Saint Paul in the touristy Old Montreal section of the city. The local contact was under strict orders to avoid the apartment. As much as JFS assured him their man was clean, Aziz was unwilling to risk that the man was not being watched by Canadian intelligence authorities. Instead, Aziz arranged for money and information to be exchanged through a rented mailbox at a global logistics company store. For the first time in many years, Fahkoury was forced to live among the infidel. Other than to get food, he rarely left the apartment in the first weeks. But, over time, he gradually ventured out and began to assimilate into the freedom-loving culture. Recalling what al-Rasheed had said to him during their travels to the United States, he viewed the experience as an opportunity to burnish his clandestine skills. He purchased more fashionable clothing and ate most of his meals at many of the highly-rated restaurants lining the narrow streets in the cobblestoned district. He made the most of his time in Montreal, but he longed for a return to jihad. Finally, one day the confirmation number for a round-trip airline ticket, a credit card and a forged Turkish passport appeared in the rental mailbox. Two days later, he was bound for Istanbul on a non-stop flight, traveling aboard an Airbus A330 with one hundred fifty-nine fellow passengers and a crew of nine.

Now Fahkoury was in Istanbul looking down from the seawall, staring mindlessly at the garbage and oil slick floating on top of the rolling black water as he thought about his future. His thoughts were interrupted when the imam completed his incantations, and he began to prepare himself for prayer. But he first allowed the American to enter his thoughts one final time. The American's dramatic arrival at the mall in the helicopter played over in Fahkoury's mind yet once more. Based on the way he moved, and the quick end to the attack after his arrival, Fahkoury presumed the man was a highly-trained special operator. He had encountered such men in Afghanistan and Iraq. That there had been no mention of the man in the news in the aftermath furthered that conviction. It was clear the Americans wanted to keep his identity secret. Fahkoury had to assume the man was one of the best the Americans had. But no man was invincible. And Fahkoury had a plan to test his skills against his rival. He was convinced that dangling the prospect of getting Aziz in Istanbul would lure the American here. Then, he would have his revenge.

At the appropriate time, he looked toward Mecca and silently said his prayers. To any onlooker, he simply appeared to be mesmerized by the beauty and bustle of the strategic waterway, but he was fervently asking for the opportunity to redeem himself. When Fahkoury finished praying, he glanced furtively back at the mosque and then around the immediate area. Seeing no reason for alarm, he started walking toward the dock and the incoming ferry, shielded among the animated tourists packed along the seawall. While most of the horde was preoccupied with taking photographs of the busy channel, Fahkoury dodged between the people vacating spots on the railing and those rushing in to fill them. He continued toward the dock and the gathering crowd there, casually searching for any abnormal movement. As soon as the ferry docked, Fahkoury joined the group of disembarking passengers moving toward the Metro station. The busy time was his best opportunity to slip into the internet café a block away, without notice. It was time to initiate his plan.

Chapter 12
Langley

Three days later, Carpenter was toweling off after a fifteen-hundred-meter swim when his phone pinged. He walked over to the chair and saw it was a message from Patrick telling him to call immediately.

"What's up?" he asked.

Detecting an echo, Patrick asked, "Where are you?"

"I'm at the gym. I just finished my swim."

"It's four o'clock in the morning."

"Yeah, so? This place is open twenty-four hours. And, for the record, it's now closer to four-thirty. I assume you're not calling to check up on me."

"Not this time," Patrick said. "We've got some intel about a possible high-level AQ meeting going down in Istanbul."

"When?"

"In two days."

"How good is the intel?"

"Pretty solid we think. Ella and Sam will meet us and explain what they know. I'm going to jump in the shower and should be in the office by five-fifteen, five-thirty. Can you get there by then or do you need me to send a car to the gym?" Patrick knew Carpenter oftentimes combined his gym work with road work, choosing to run or bike to the gym instead of driving.

Carpenter checked the time. He had to change back into his running clothes and then run just over three and a half miles back to his apartment.

Once there, he had to shower and change before making the ten to fifteen-minute commute to headquarters. With just under an hour, it was going to be tight but he thought he'd be fine. "I'll be there no later than five-thirty," he said.

Carpenter walked into the conference room with two minutes to spare. Patrick was waiting for him with a twenty-ounce coffee. Samantha Lane and Ella Rock were also seated around the cluttered rectangular table. "Good morning," he said. The women smiled as Patrick slid the cardboard cup of piping hot coffee across the table.

"I'll get right to it," Lane said. "We have two pieces of corroborating intel that suggests one or more senior level al Qaeda leaders will be in Istanbul for a meeting of unknown purpose. The first piece of intelligence was a phone call NSA intercepted two nights ago. The call lasted seven seconds and was placed to an antique dealer in Rawalpindi. The dealer has been on our radar as a possible fence for the antiquities the Islamic State has been pilfering from Iraq and Syria. The caller said, 'My friend has agreed to the price. Send his packages to the gallery in Istanbul. Make sure they arrive in four days. Further details will be provided.' Taken alone, the message is obviously cryptic and plausibly concerns a legitimate transaction in artifacts. However, a report came in from Phil Buckley late last night and I've since spoken to him. One of his agents in Peshawar says there is going to be a high-level AQ meeting in Istanbul. He told Phil the rumors are that Mufakir will be in attendance."

The name "Mufakir" was potentially significant and immediately grabbed Carpenter's attention. Translated, it meant "the Thinker." Mufakir—whose real name was believed to be Abdullah Tahan—was reputed to be one of the members of al Qaeda's council of senior leaders, and someone who had risen in stature in recent years among the shura. Despite considerable efforts for many years, identifying the locations of Mufakir and the other senior al Qaeda leaders remained frustratingly elusive. As far as anyone knew, it was rare for any member of the shura to travel outside those secret confines, but it was not unprecedented. Unfortunately, whenever this kind of news surfaced in the past, it had always arrived too late to be of any benefit.

This was potentially different and, if true, a very big deal. But Carpenter knew that would all depend on the credibility of the intelligence. It certainly helped that Phil Buckley was involved. He was someone Carpenter respected. For starters, Buckley had been stationed in Pakistan for a dozen years and his network was extensive. Carpenter saw that firsthand on the several occasions they had worked together in Karachi. In Carpenter's view, Buckley was a sound case officer who had a very good bullshit filter. He appreciated that the veteran officer wouldn't report anything that didn't have at least a ring of truth. Still, Carpenter had a few questions. "How long has Phil worked with this agent?" he asked.

"For more than two years," Lane said.

"Is Phil paying him?" Carpenter asked.

"Yes. It's a retainer scenario. Phil now pays him a thousand dollars monthly. That is four times the amount they started with. He gets paid with the caveat that the first time he provides something that proves to be demonstrably false, he'll be cut off. Buckley says he's gotten good information from this guy on five prior occasions, including the tip that led to Bashir Halabi."

Until hearing this, Carpenter hadn't known the source of the intel behind the Halabi operation a year earlier. Halabi was one of the Islamic State leaders who was spearheading the terror group's expansion into Afghanistan. A drone had taken Halabi and his convoy out on their way back to Asadabad from a training facility in eastern Afghanistan. But that had involved an Islamic State leader. Now this agent was providing information about an al Qaeda meeting. As there was no love lost between the two competing terror organizations, it prompted Carpenter to ask, "How is this agent positioned to get information about both al Qaeda and the Islamic State? Was the Halabi operation a setup for us to do al Qaeda's dirty work?"

"It might have been a setup," Lane said. "It wouldn't have been the first time we were used in their internecine battle. But we got Halabi and we don't believe it was a setup, anyway. Buckley says the agent is an equal opportunity arms dealer in Peshawar with no apparent allegiance to any group. In fact, Buckley says most of his sales are now to the Taliban. He hears stuff from all sides and goes to Phil when he thinks it might be something that is both interesting and true. At least that's how Phil describes the relationship."

"What does Phil's agent say about timing for the meeting in Istanbul?" Patrick asked.

"Nothing other than his sense it will happen soon," Lane said.

"What does he base that on?" Patrick inquired further.

"The agent says that news this sensitive doesn't have a long shelf life. In his view, it's either a baseless rumor or it's about to happen. The agent wouldn't tell Phil how he learned this information but he said he believes it is real. We feel that the SIGNET and Buckley's report, taken together, cannot be discarded."

"What do you think Ella?" Carpenter asked.

"This news supports our analysis from the other day that Aziz is involved in a power struggle to take control of al Qaeda. If in fact Aziz is trying to accumulate power, it follows that at least some members of the shura would have something to say about it. Since al-Zawahiri released the statement naming Aziz al Qaeda's coleader, we have not heard from the shura. Maybe the shura is starting to have second thoughts and this meeting in Istanbul is an attempt to rein Aziz in."

"You think Aziz will be attending this meeting?" Patrick asked.

"If Mufakir is going to be there, we can assume it is a high-level meeting of some sort. The shura do not travel often and only for an important purpose. Even a meeting with a high-level person from an affiliate would likely not happen in a place like Istanbul. In the past, that person would go to the shura. I'm thinking Istanbul was selected in this case because it's neutral ground for a meeting of equals. So, unless this is another setup, there's a good chance Aziz will be there," Rock said.

"PJ?" Patrick asked.

"This smells like an offensive counterintelligence tactic. The information fell into our hands too easily. But to Sam's point about Halabi earlier, it really doesn't matter. It's a win-win for us if the meeting actually happens and we get a shot at Mufakir and maybe even Aziz. These opportunities don't come along often."

"In my mind, there's no question about it," Patrick said. "We definitely have to pursue it. I'll need to run it past Director Gonzalez and the president first, but I'm thinking we propose to go in quietly and small. The president has made it clear that he trusts no one, especially on the most sensitive matters. We saw that factor into his decision on Tunisia, and the rewards here are potentially far greater. Plus, I don't think we can risk inserting a full team into Istanbul. We need to limit the evidence that we were there. Our better option is to send in PJ alone."

Carpenter fully agreed. He'd been burned in the past when information was shared with the locals. He was convinced the Pakistanis had betrayed his operation to get another high-level al Qaeda leader a few years back. As a courtesy, the information was shared with the Pakistan's Inter-Services Intelligence. In return, the ISI demanded to lead the operation. The US had no choice but to accede and Carpenter was forced to hang back while an ISI team stormed the building. Yet, despite very credible intelligence, the raid was a complete failure. When Carpenter was finally allowed to enter the residence, there was no one there and the place had been completely sanitized. He thought it would be unwise to share this intelligence with the Turks, only to end up with the same result. And, besides the potential for leaks, he preferred a minimalist approach for covert action in urban settings. No matter the level of evasive measures taken, there were too many suspicious eyeballs for even just a handful of operators to fully escape. Raising the chances of detection was warranted only when absolutely necessary, and Carpenter felt that risk was not justified here. For starters, they didn't have any idea exactly where and when in sprawling Istanbul the meeting was scheduled to take place and they didn't have a lot of time to figure it out. Assuming they did learn those details, there wouldn't be enough time for a larger group to scout out and set up observation posts. Plus, more people complicated the exfil. Though he was certain the circumstances called for the smallest team possible, Carpenter knew he could not do this entirely alone. "That makes sense but I'm going to need at least some help," Carpenter said. "Is Railsey still in Istanbul?" Carpenter was asking about Pat Turley. Last he knew, Turley, who had once briefly served as chief of station in Istanbul, was back in the field.

"Yes, he's still there and crazier than ever," Patrick said. Turley had once been under his direct command and he knew that although Turley's ways were unconventional, his record was remarkable. "Turley being there is another reason I don't think we need to risk a full team of operators. I spoke with him as soon as the intel came in. He's already working his contacts. Nothing yet but I would be surprised if he doesn't come up with something."

"I like it," Carpenter said. In fact, Turley had been a mentor of sorts during Carpenter's first assignment with the Agency. At the time, Patrick was the chief of station in Beirut and had brought Turley over from Damascus for the specific purpose of tutoring Carpenter. Both Patrick and Turley put a premium on human intelligence and Patrick wanted someone in the field with his fresh recruit to teach him the finer skills. Carpenter often remarked that he had learned more during his three years with Turley in Beirut than he had the rest of his nearly two decades combined.

"Since we're all agreed, let me run this by Director Gonzalez and the president for their approval," Patrick said. "Sam, Ella, thank you. PJ, assume you're leaving in the next few hours. If this thing is going down, we have only two days to figure out exactly where and when and come up with a plan."

Chapter 13
Luxembourg City

Throughout each day and for more than a week, Prince Sadiq bin Aziz had dutifully checked for word from Fahkoury that he was ready to proceed with the scheme. It was two days after his most recent trip to the farmer's market that the message from Fahkoury finally arrived. The cryptic message was contained in a review on a popular travel and restaurant website for one of Istanbul's best restaurants. The review was posted by "Ben Around the World" and simply said, "Truly amazing food and stunning view of the city. Be sure to come here when you are ready for a great culinary experience." By the time Aziz saw the review thirty minutes later, there were already seventeen comments. Under the username "Hunger Games," Aziz replied, "Thanks for sharing, Ben. I'll be sure to bring my friends there when we arrive in five days. Very much looking forward to it!" The almost instantaneous "Like" from Ben Around the World confirmed that Fahkoury had received the message.

Aziz then swiftly dispatched Faraj, his longtime bodyguard, on the short drive across the border to Germany. When he arrived in the city of Trier, Faraj purchased a pre-paid phone and placed the call with the general time and place of the meeting. The contact in Pakistan related the message to the first in a series of couriers. A day later, it was delivered to Mufakir, the man who had been the number two man in al Qaeda's senior leadership circle before Aziz's ascension.

Although there was no guarantee the American would take the bait, Aziz was reasonably confident Mufakir would jump at the opportunity to meet with him in Istanbul. Over the past two months, Mufakir had been pushing for a meeting, reminding Aziz that the shura expected an update on his intentions. What at first were polite requests, most recently culminated in a demand that Aziz advise a time and place for the meeting. Aziz held off until Fahkoury was ready.

Now, three days after receiving Fahkoury's coded message, Aziz found himself pacing the first floor of his home. The wait was becoming unbearable and there were still more than forty-eight hours to go. Aziz harbored particular animus for Mufakir. In addition to eliminating a key ally of Aziz's putative coleader, Aziz would take particular pleasure in the pompous man's demise. But that satisfaction would not come for another two days when the plot was scheduled to unfold. And waiting patiently was not a virtue Aziz possessed.

To calm himself, Aziz walked over to the bar and placed two ice cubes into a balloon glass before pouring a generous amount of Frapin Cuvee 1888 Cognac. Beginning with the "first nose" sensation from an appropriately sophisticated distance, Aziz completed the requisite iterations of olfactory impressions. After allowing the combination of dried fruit and spicy scents to momentarily linger, Aziz lifted the glass and took the smallest of sips, allowing the expensive brandy to seize his palate. A few moments later, he consumed a slightly larger swallow, savoring the taste and the pleasant burning sensation at the back of his throat. To reinforce the sense of tranquility washing over him, he set off on his latest tour of the grand home.

It was only the third time he had stayed at the villa, and the first in nearly a decade, shortly after the stately home was purchased through a series of dummy corporations that all-but ensured that its true owner's identity would remain confidential. Situated on the banks of the River Alzette in the elegant Grund quarter of the Grand Duchy's capital, the largely unfurnished forty-six-hundred-square foot home was one of his favorites. It boasted colorful ancient ceramic wall and floor tiling on the first floor, which was complimented with exotic Brazilian tigerwood floors throughout the remainder of its three levels. But the real source of his fondness for the home hung on the wall above the broad mid-level landing on the elaborate staircase.

When he reached the landing, Aziz paused to admire the priceless piece of art. The painting—one of several masterpieces tastefully displayed in the multi-million-dollar dwelling—was thought to have been destroyed nearly four centuries ago, but Aziz had purchased Leonardo da Vinci's *Leda and the Swan* in a highly-discreet transaction shortly after purchasing this home. According to legend, the sensual painting had become a source of controversy in the French royal family, and it was ordered destroyed. Contrary to that belief, an enterprising servant had secretly removed the painting from Fontainebleau Palace and, for nearly four centuries, *Leda and the Swan* made the rounds through a series of secretive owners. Its dubious provenance and the previous owner's financial struggles allowed Aziz to purchase the Renaissance master's iconic painting for a song. But before he agreed to shell out the illicit arms dealer's asking price of five million dollars—which was ultimately paid in physical cash—Aziz had the painting authenticated. Using a high-resolution multi-spectral camera, the authenticator was first able to conclusively match the smudged fingerprint on a cloud in the painting's upper-left corner with that on another da Vinci painting hanging in Vatican City. Later, the art expert employed infrared reflectography, pigment testing, and carbon dating to cement his conclusion and earn Aziz's full satisfaction. When he accepted his five hundred-thousand-dollar fee, the shady authenticator suggested that he could arrange a sale that would net Aziz no less than fifty million dollars, after his commission, of course. But Aziz had no intention of parting with the masterpiece then or now. Like the expensive twice-distilled French beverage he was holding, the painting was a closet indulgence. And his fetishism for the curvaceous naked woman it portrayed, belied the puritanical fiber he purported to possess.

Although he was careful to conceal them, Aziz could afford such luxuries. When he sold his private equity firm in 2012, Aziz had a net worth that resided in the hundreds of millions of dollars. And since then, his portfolio—like *Leda and the Swan*—had appreciated considerably in value. Aziz had used his wealth and his influencing and business skills to wrest control of a failing organization and lead it back to prominence. The leadership co-sharing arrangement he had proposed was nothing more than an olive branch to the institution and its existing leader. When he made it, Aziz had no intentions of allowing old thinking to undermine his goals. His new strategy was a marked departure to the terror group's halfhearted practices in recent years. In his view, the shura was no longer capable of leading.

In fact, since he was named coleader, Aziz had rarely consulted with the council. Right after the attacks in America, the shura requested a meeting to celebrate and discuss future plans. Aziz respectfully declined, diplomatically reminding the myopic thinkers that convening so soon after an attack to discuss strategy, let alone to celebrate, was a sure way to disaster. On top of that, he had no desire to ever return to their third-world hideout. Undeterred, the shura persisted with additional requests for a meeting. Each time, Aziz ignored them. More recently, they had insisted on an opportunity to be heard. Aziz knew Mufakir was behind the demands. When Aziz had presented his plans to attack the Americans, Mufakir had been the most vociferous objector. And Mufakir's irritation spiked further when the shura agreed to name Aziz the organization's coleader. Apparently, al Qaeda's former number two was not going to be ignored. Fahkoury's ruse provided a cunning solution to that problem.

As Fahkoury predicted, Mufakir had jumped at the invitation to meet in Istanbul. Even though Aziz harbored concerns for Fahkoury's safety, he had to admit that the idea of using the Americans to do his bidding was genius. If they did not suspect already, the remaining members of the shura would know after the gambit in Istanbul that he had no intention of sharing power. And they were powerless to stop him. He had all the money and followers he needed to fend off any attempts they could mount to undermine him. If it became necessary, he would eliminate the rest of them after he took care of Mufakir. The shura would abide by his terms. It was his show now.

Aziz took one last sip of cognac and final admiring look at *Leda* before returning to the first floor. He had become very attached to his Luxembourg mansion. He had been living there since late January, but he knew it was unwise to stay in one place too long. The Americans were desperately looking for him and soon those efforts would be redoubled. But, for the time being, Aziz believed he was safe in the splendid capital of this tiny country. His opulent home and wealth were easily overlooked in one of the key financial centers in Europe. And the minimal, yet transformative plastic surgery further aided his namelessness.

He placed the empty balloon glass on the bar and gazed out at the river. As much as he wanted to believe his security here was assured, Aziz acknowledged there was a stronger reason he had no intentions of leaving just yet. The thrill of directing the organization from practically right under the noses of the enemy was undeniable. Aziz reflected that it would not be long before the next phase of his master plan was initiated. That thought, more than the brandy, sent a warm sensation throughout his entire body.

Chapter 14
Istanbul

It was a little before 6:00 a.m. local time the next morning when Carpenter sensed the private plane descending. Although Patrick had approval from Director Gonzalez and President Madden in no time, he had had trouble securing the aircraft for Carpenter's trip. All of the planes in the Central Intelligence Agency's fleet were accounted for or already being used, and none of the commercial flights were scheduled to leave until the following morning. Since they couldn't afford to lose any more time waiting, Patrick had decided to improvise. Fortunately, he knew who to call in a pinch.

The Agency had a long-standing contractual relationship with two Upstate New York businessmen who were more than happy to offer the use of their Gulfstream G650ER. In fact, under the terms of the contract, the entrepreneurs made several aircraft available to the Agency. And no matter how little lead time they were given, they had always come through, never demanding any concessions. They assured Patrick that getting a plane was no problem. But Patrick was also in need of two pilots for the ten-plus hour flight, so he pushed the request further. Afterward, he admitted to Carpenter that he was a little spooked by their enthusiastic response. Their excitement about actually participating in an Agency operation was obvious and a tad concerning. Even though Patrick knew how much these two men loved their country, he wasn't sure they were ready for this. But Patrick really had no other options. The two men assured him they fully understood the highly-classified nature of the flight and, less than two hours after the call ended, the luxury jet landed at the private jet terminal at Washington Dulles International. It was barely enough time for Patrick to arrange the landing rights with Turkish authorities.

As soon as Carpenter boarded the plane, he was greeted by the beaming faces of Jimmy Caffry and Rob Haas. While the plane was being refueled, its owners gave Carpenter a quick tour of the four-zone cabin, including the stateroom, complete with en suite bathroom, at the rear of the plane. At the end of the tour, Carpenter was shown the galley. Caffry apologized for the lack of variety, noting that due to the short notice, there were only some deli subs, several pre-made salads, and a cupboard full of snacks on board. However, Carpenter saw that the beverage choices were a bit more robust. Haas picked up on that and told Carpenter to drink whatever he wanted. Any other time, Carpenter would have been tempted by the several bottles of Chateau Lafite Rothschild Bordeaux residing in the onboard wine cellar system. But this was not one of those trips.

Carpenter had been on quite a few private jets in his day but this one stood out, as did the hospitality he was shown. And there was no question how excited Caffry and Haas were. Since Patrick had told him the men held security clearances, Carpenter decided to show his appreciation for the two patriots by sharing some stories. After the plane reached cruising altitude, Carpenter held court in the fore zone of the cabin for nearly four hours, telling and retelling stories about his earlier days in the Agency as the two men rotated piloting duties. The men lapped it up and Carpenter enjoyed it every bit as much. He felt slightly bad when he said he needed to get some rest. He was not planning on much, if any, sleep for the next couple days. So, with just under five hours of flight time remaining on the non-stop flight, Carpenter retreated to the stateroom. He had been sleeping soundly when he felt the plane start its descent to Istanbul's Ataturk Airport.

Now Carpenter rose from the comfortable double bed and entered the bathroom. After brushing his teeth, he stood under a hot shower and lathered up with soap for sixty seconds. Then he rinsed off under a steady stream of ice-cold water for another minute before exiting and changing into a new business suit and tie. After a quick call to headquarters, he walked forward to the galley where he had just enough time to savor an espresso before landing.

Almost as soon as the plane completed taxiing, a customs official was there to greet it. Caffry lowered the steps to allow the official onboard. Since he knew from the manifest that the plane was not staying other than to refuel, the customs official only asked to see the passenger's passport. Carpenter obliged, handing over the Swiss passport of Marcel Rochat. The official casually thumbed through the pages but not without noticing the stamp of Rochat's arrival in the United States five days previously. Before handing the passport back to Carpenter, the official said in flawless French, "I hope your time in America was enjoyable. Welcome back to the European Union, Monsieur Rochat." Caffry and Haas, sitting in the cockpit, overheard the exchange. After the official left, they moved back into the fuselage to see Carpenter off, wearing knowing grins on their faces. Carpenter shrugged in a "What can I do?" fashion and said goodbye. He thanked them and laughed when they said to call anytime he needed a ride.

At the bottom of the plane's steps to greet him was the old familiar face of Patrick Turley. Although their paths had crossed several times after Carpenter moved over to the Counterterrorism Center, it had been at least six years since Carpenter had seen his friend. Turley had been instrumental in gathering the intelligence for a last-minute operation in Manilla, and Carpenter was counting on him to do the same here. Carpenter considered it a stroke of fortune that Turley was currently stationed in Istanbul. Beyond their friendship, he knew Turley as a proven commodity. That was even more important here because it was just the two of them. Even though he expected things to get messy, Carpenter was confident he and Turley could get done what they needed to. But with the meeting supposed to take place tomorrow, they didn't have a lot of time to figure things out.

Carpenter stepped off the last step and took a moment to look his buddy over, finally focusing on Turley's patented shit-eating grin and the lanky body that had earned him his nickname. "You haven't changed one bit, Railsey," he said. "Except maybe for the hair. When's the last time you cut that mop?"

"It's all part of the game, bro," Turley said as he brushed his shoulder-length blonde hair behind his ears.

Turley appraised Carpenter for a moment. The pause was just long enough to be noticeable. Carpenter could tell Turley was winding up with some kind of smartass remark.

"Did you just come from a fashion show or something? I told 'em to send me a tough guy. I hope you're a lot tougher than you look," Turley added.

Turley was the quintessential ballbuster. And for as long as Carpenter had known him, Turley had incessantly needled him about his appearance and, despite his looks, Carpenter's natural awkwardness around women. But Carpenter could give it as well as he could take it. "Well, at least one of us doesn't look like he shops for clothes on skid row," he said.

"Yeah, I figured you'd want to be the good-looking guy on this operation so I dressed down."

"I think you might have overdone it."

The two men laughed heartily as they shared a warm embrace. But as much fun as they were having ripping one another, it was time to get down to business. Carpenter had a chance to briefly speak to Director Patrick before landing. There was no further intelligence on who might be in attendance, but he said Turley had been working his agents and might have a lead on where the high-value target meeting was to take place. Although there was no information about timing, Carpenter reasoned that as long as the intel was good, they had at least a day before the meeting started. But that did not give them much time for surveillance and planning if, that is, Turley was even on the right track. "So what have you been able to dig up?" Carpenter asked.

"I've got agents all over this city, including and especially shop owners. I've always found the shop owners know best what's going on in their neighborhoods. They know the regular flow and can easily spot outsiders and unusual activity. Based on what I'm hearing, we're going to focus on a building in the Old Town area, not too far from the Blue Mosque. Two of my guys independently told me about some questionable activity there. They've noticed some new faces cruising the street in the past twenty-four hours. According to them, these new men are Arabs and look to be pulling security detail. It was only last night that I learned this and, because all the shops close at seven and the streets get quiet, I only risked one rip through there.

But I saw some dudes on the street who looked out of place, so I think my agents might be on to something."

"Sounds like a great place to start. Should we head there now?" Carpenter asked.

"We should hold off until ten. There's almost always some flow, but the shops don't open until nine. The extra hour will ensure there will be optimal activity when we arrive at ten. Plus, you can't go walking around looking like a super model businessman. You look like you're teed up for some kind of hotshot merger negotiation in Levent or Maslak," Turley said, referring to the modern commercial sections of the city. "We've got to get you some new wears for where we're going. My apartment is about ten blocks from where we want to look around. We'll go there first. Depending on what you've got in that bag, you can wear some of my fine threads. And by the way, is that Armani you're wearing? Either way, feel free to leave that behind."

Chapter 15

On the walk to Turley's car, they talked about the weather. Although Carpenter knew Istanbul had a temperate climate, it was a bit cooler than he was expecting for April. Turley said the early mornings were normally this cool but it should warm into the sixties. He added that there had been a two-week spell of unusually warm days, when the highs were in the low eighties. He told Carpenter he missed it by only a couple days. After that brief meteorological seminar, Carpenter steered the conversation to their plans for the day. Turley suggested that before heading to his apartment, they drive past the assumed meeting place. Carpenter liked the idea. A single trip down the street in a car would give them a general sense of the environment without much risk of garnering attention. It was like a free pass to give the area a once-over. Unless, that is, Turley was driving something that was sure to stick out.

"Here she is," Turley said.

"What in hell is that thing?"

"This, my friend, is a Fiat Punto. Purrs like a kitten."

Carpenter didn't bother to ask the name of the reddish-brown color. It reminded him of dried blood. On top of that, dents pockmarked most of the hood and front panel on the passenger side and there were no hubcaps on the tires. "That kitten must be on its ninth life. Are you sure this piece of shit can make it into the city?"

"Get in cover boy, you'll still look pretty."

They left the airport and merged onto Kennedy Caddesi, following the avenue eastward along the southside of the peninsula and directly into the sun as it hastened its ascent over Asia. Since they had time, Turley suggested they take a more circuitous route so that Carpenter could take in some sights. Carpenter tried to find a comfortable position on the threadbare seat before he flipped the visor down to stem the blinding effects of the low sun. As he peered out the window, Turley prattled on about his latest sexual exploits. Carpenter was half listening while he gazed at the glistening waters of the inland Sea of Marmara, which he knew was named for the bountiful sources of marble on its islands.

When they were almost to the Bosporus, Turley turned off the wide avenue and steered the compact car north toward the center of the city. He noticed Carpenter ducking down to catch a glimpse of the iconic Byzantine-styled domed mosque as they passed the Little Hagia Sophia. He glanced over at Carpenter several more times as he wound the car through a series of cramped streets that would soon bring them near another stunning mosque.

"I forgot to ask, have you ever been to Istanbul?" Turley asked.

"Just once and I was a bit too busy to have a chance to do any sightseeing," Carpenter said.

"I'll give you the five-cent tour," Turley said. "Coming up out your window is the Sultan Ahmet Mosque, perhaps better known as The Blue Mosque for the tens of thousands of blue tiles decorating its interior." As Carpenter marveled at the cascading domed architecture of the beautiful mosque and its six towering minarets, Turley paused briefly. An appreciation for history and culture was a common bond between the two men and Turley wanted to make sure Carpenter had an opportunity to take in the view before continuing. "The mosque sits at the southern end of what once was a U-shaped hippodrome first built by the Romans just after the turn of the third century. This park is also named for Sultan Ahmet. This area is a big tourist attraction in the city, as is the Grand Bazaar a half-mile away. A lot of tourists walk between the two locations, browsing the traditional shops along the way. This regular pedestrian traffic flow will help us blend in since we're going to be hanging out only a few blocks from here."

At the northern end of the park, Turley turned onto a wider thoroughfare that headed back in a generally westerly direction. After a few blocks, he turned onto a narrower street. Each side was densely-packed with two and three-story buildings, each decorated with tired and mostly red-colored awnings. The sidewalks on either side of the street were busy with pedestrians, forcing some of them into the street and compromising what little room vehicles had to maneuver down the middle.

"You don't call this busy?" Carpenter asked.

"This is nothing like it will be later. Look out your window," Turley said.

Carpenter's eyes were instantly drawn to one of the more notable buildings on the block. Its dominant size captured his attention, causing him to initially overlook its grime-stained limestone façade. At three stories, it was one level taller than its nearest neighbor and nearly twice as wide. Although the more modern building standing on the far side of the mammoth building stood equally high, its lack of comparable girth detracted from its eminence. As they inched closer, Carpenter could see the mouth of a narrow passageway between the two taller buildings. When they were nearly abreast of the building, his gaze returned to the mass of people milling in front of it. He looked beyond them and into the arch at the center of the building's first level, and saw that it opened to an arcade that penetrated the entire length of the building. Shops lined both sides of the colonnade. He then glanced up at the second floor, stopping momentarily to study the ornate balcony jutting out over the arcade entrance. As he traced the balcony's decorative supports down the side of building, he noticed a slightly gaunt looking man in a bulky coat. The man was standing off to the side of the archway, shuffling his feet to ward off the forty-degree temperature. As much as his fixed position, his roaming eyes distinguished the man from the other people in the area. Just then, traffic halted, forcing Turley to stop. Careful not to look too obvious, Carpenter glanced back slightly and saw another dubious man at the edge of the crowd. He, too, appeared to be actively scanning the street and the passersby. Carpenter casually turned his head and stared at the cars in front of them before asking, "Are you thinking this is the place?"

"Yes. For obvious reasons, the locals call it the 'Kaya,' meaning rock. One of my agents, Mustafa, runs a shop on the far side of the arcade. You might have seen the bright orange flag that hangs above the entrance of his stall. He sells handmade soaps. I'm sure you noticed the two guys out front. They stick out like sore thumbs. Mustafa noticed them too, as did Baran, the other agent I told you about. Baran owns the jewelry shop up here on the left; the one with the gold awning," Turley said.

"What's on the upper two floors?" Carpenter asked.

"There are apartments on the second and third floors. They are only accessible from the central stairway that begins in the arcade and is secured by locked gate. On the backside of the building, there is a delivery alley. If we were to go around back, you'd see two more guys positioned there. At least that's what I saw last night."

"Any idea which apartment they might be using for the meeting?" Carpenter asked.

"None, but Mustafa says there are only four on each floor."

Carpenter thought those were decent odds, assuming this was the right building. He hoped his colleagues back at CTC could improve those odds while he and Turley tried to confirm they indeed had the right place. But first, he wanted to get the gear. "We need to grab the stuff I had sent in the diplomatic pouch. Do you have it at your place or do we need to go to consulate?"

"It's all at my place. It came in a few hours ago."

"Good. Let's head there."

Chapter 16

After leaving the Fiat in a car park, they made the short walk to Turley's apartment. It was on the second floor of a well-maintained white stucco rowhouse that was separated from the street by a narrow sidewalk decorated with pavers in a right-angle herringbone pattern. Carpenter was impressed. Turley unlocked the door and headed to the restroom, leaving Carpenter to look around.

He followed the short narrow hallway to a living area where Turley had a sofa, a recliner, coffee table, and television. A black and white photo of Maiden's Tower—the famous tower resting on the small islet at the southern entrance of the Bosporus Strait—hung on the wall over the sofa. Off to his left, and opening up to the living area, was the kitchen. It was relatively large for the size of the apartment. Beige tile adorned the back wall and contrasted nicely with the brown and black granite on the lone countertop. Rows of cabinets above and below featured white laminate, trimmed nicely with brown-stained wood. Carpenter was wondering if Turley actually lived there. Then he peeked inside the refrigerator and found only several takeout containers, some packaged condiments, and four bottles of Efes, a Turkish beer. *This is more like the Railsey I know*, he thought to himself.

"What do you think?" Turley asked.

"It's too nice for you. If I hadn't checked the refrigerator, I would have thought this place belonged to someone else."

"Ha!" Turley placed a large black duffel on the floor. "Here's your shit."

Because the Turkish authorities were inherently suspicious, there was a legitimate chance that luggage would be searched when Carpenter's plane landed at Ataturk International. Rather than potentially complicating Carpenter's arrival, Patrick had him provide a list of what he thought he might need in Istanbul. Before the plane departed even from Dulles, Patrick had the requested items assembled at Stuttgart Army Air Field in Germany. The duffel bag was swiftly delivered to the US consulate in Munich, placed inside a sealed container marked as a diplomatic pouch, and then flown to Istanbul and delivered to the US consulate there. It arrived four hours before Carpenter landed, giving Turley enough time to retrieve it and bring it to his apartment.

Carpenter opened the bag and reviewed the contents. Among the items inside were four semi-automatic, nine-millimeter pistols and plenty of ammunition, two tactical vests, several pairs of tactical gloves, and two KA-BAR knives. There was also the communications equipment Carpenter had requested as well as the MK 12 SPR rifle. Having now seen the target environment, Carpenter doubted he'd need the compact sniper rifle. It also meant he would not have to figure out where to sight it in, but he was glad to have it nonetheless. He replaced the rifle into the duffel and then grabbed the secure phones. The sturdy LTE handheld devices looked and functioned like regular smartphones but were equipped with micro encryption technology. He and Turley would have no problem maintaining secure communications, while blending in with the ubiquitous cellphone users that could be found on every urban street. He powered them on and was pleased to see both were fully charged.

"I'll be right back," Carpenter said. He grabbed his bag of clothes and retreated to the bathroom, which was accessed through the lone bedroom in the apartment. The bathroom floors and walls were covered in green and white tiles. A half-moon-shaped shower was positioned on the wall opposite the door. The toilet, located right next to the shower, was oddly tucked in the righthand corner at a forty-five-degree angle. Wedged in tight next to the toilet was a white pedestal sink. Because he didn't know how well sound carried through the apartment walls, Carpenter turned on the water in the sink and the shower before dialing Patrick. He didn't have any concerns about Turley. Rather, it was the neighbors who might be able to hear the conversation that made him take this precaution.

Patrick answered on the first ring. "Got anything yet?" he asked.

"First, I'll be using this number. Railsey will have the other one."

"I kind of figured that," Patrick said.

"Just making sure, Einstein. Anyway, I think Railsey may have found the building. We drove past it on the way from the airport. There were two guys posted out front. Railsey said he saw two others on the backside last night. They look the part, though they seem a little green."

"So, what are you thinking?"

Carpenter started by giving Patrick the address for the building. After Patrick read the address back to him, he told his boss what he knew so far. "The ground level is commercial, while the upper two are residential. Railsey thinks there are eight apartments in total. Assuming he has the right place, I'd like to narrow down the list of potential apartments. It's too early to say for sure, but it looks like we're going to have to go in to do this right. The location and layout call for an up-close operation, and we can't screw around knocking on doors. I need you to get as much information as you can about the building, its owner, and its occupants. Maybe we can figure out which apartment will be used for the meeting. And one more thing, see if you can find any record of a fire there. The dark stains on the exterior suggest there might have been."

The conversation then quickly moved to Carpenter's early assessment. The Kaya building was probably the right location, he said, but he wanted to do a closer inspection on foot. This would give him a sense of the security detail, their rotations, and their gear; information Carpenter would use to gauge any vulnerabilities. But he told Patrick he doubted there was much time before he would have to act. His gut told him the meeting was not too far off. In fact, based on the intel that the security detail had moved in during the past twenty-four hours, he thought it was possible the meeting could take place as soon as the early morning hours tomorrow. If that was the case, they might have less than twenty hours to prepare. This meant the best chance of putting together a strong plan of attack largely rested on what Patrick and the CTC analysts were able to find. The call ended with Patrick promising to get back to him shortly with whatever they could find out about the building.

Carpenter shut off the water and moved into the bedroom. After dropping his bag on the bed, he slid out of his suit and into a pair of dark jeans, a blue-checked shirt, and a pair of black Durashocks boots. He grabbed his black down sweater jacket and a gray beanie hat before heading back to the living area and Turley.

"That's better," Turley said. "Around here, we call that the 'Euro-touro' look. But you're still going to draw some stares. I'd be better off walking around with someone less good looking, like maybe Denzel Washington."

Carpenter flipped Turley off as he handed him one of the secure communications devices and then he set about organizing the pistols and ammunition. He checked to see that the magazine for each of the four Sig Sauer P226 pistols was full before tossing a pistol to Turley. "You still know how to use one of these?" he asked.

Turley smirked and took the jab in stride. As a former case officer himself, Carpenter knew Turley was not allowed to carry a gun. Although all case officers were trained with basic firearms, their primary role was to recruit assets. They had to rely exclusively on their wits to get themselves out of trouble. This situation called for an exception to that rule. Carpenter returned two of the pistols to the large duffel and, for good measure, grabbed two spare fifteen-round magazines. One pistol each and some extra ammo would be enough for today's surveillance work. "All right, since I wouldn't eat anything you keep here, let's find someplace to get some grub and then we'll go see what we see," he said.

Chapter 17

It was only a few minutes past nine when they walked out of the apartment, so they had time to be selective. Turley said he knew a place not far from the Kaya building, almost perfectly midway between here and there, he said. As they started their walk to the café, Carpenter huddled against the cold. A slight southerly breeze had picked up and the temperature had only crept into the low fifties. He was beginning to question Turley's promise of mid sixty-degree temperatures and his choice of the lighter jacket. But by the time they reached the café ten minutes later, Carpenter was running warm from the brisk walk and had shed the beanie.

They took a table inside and Turley ordered for them in the native tongue. Carpenter was on his second cup of Turkish coffee when the food arrived. Turley explained that it was called *menemen*, a traditional Turkish dish of eggs, tomato, green peppers, and pepper spices cooked with olive oil. For good measure, he had added *sucuk*, a dry spicy sausage, to Carpenter's serving. Carpenter wasted no time devouring the delicious food and was almost tempted to order another plate.

"You should be fat," Turley said. "Since I've known you, you've always eaten like a horse. You want the rest of mine?"

"No, it was the perfect amount. Let's get out of here."

A few minutes later, they were back on the street, heading toward the Kaya building and surrounding neighborhood. It was almost ten o'clock and the shops had been open close to an hour. The streets were buzzing with activity. As they moved closer, Carpenter suggested they take turns walking both sides of the building. Carpenter would walk down the street on the front side of the building and, after continuing for several blocks, circle back onto the delivery alley at the rear. Turley would take the opposite track. Beginning with Turley, the person traversing the alleyway would venture into the arcade running down the center of the building. Afterward, they would meet up back near the café to compare notes and decide plans for more surveillance. One block shy of the Kaya building, they split up.

As much as possible, Carpenter stayed on the sidewalk on the side of the street opposite the building. But good portions of the eight-foot-wide walkway had been appropriated by the shop owners to display their goods, and the browsers clogging the sidewalk often forced him to drop down into the street in order to keep moving. He eventually stopped in front of a travel agency and pretended to study the advertisements for various Mediterranean cruises. The garments hanging from the awning outside the clothing shop two stores down gave him cover to sneak several long looks at the front of the Kaya building. Just as he did in the drive-by earlier, he noticed a man positioned at each side of the entrance to the arcade. They were not the same two men from earlier but they were behaving similarly. For the most part, their attention was directed right in front of them, but they occasionally looked down opposite ends of the street. Their steadiness stood apart from the whimsical and carefree nature of the shoppers assembled near them. Carpenter moved on after a minute or so. Just after he passed by Baran's jewelry shop, an impromptu concert broke out on the sidewalk in front of him. Two men started strumming away on acoustic guitars, while a third man was pounding on some kind of wooden percussion instrument. Shortly after the music started, a fourth man, facing the band with his back to the street, began belting out what Carpenter assumed was a traditional folk song. It didn't take long before a crowd amassed around the band.

Carpenter edged closer to the gathering. He was now no more than fifty feet from the Kaya building and had an unobstructed view of the two guards out front. He settled in behind a group of Scandinavians, one of whom had a few inches on him. Carpenter used the Viking as a shield, alternately looking around either side of the man's head at the two guards. He had to assume they were armed, but he saw neither man holding a phone or any kind of communications device. Carpenter thought that was smart and also a sign that there were concerns about eavesdropping. Terrorists were well aware of the capabilities of US and other intelligence agencies to listen in on their communications. If one or more senior members of the group was in the area, it made sense to ban use of all communication devices. Instead, they would communicate face-to-face, a less efficient but far safer method. He briefly wondered if Americans would adopt similar strategies if they realized just how much information their government knew about them—from everywhere they went, everyone they interconnected with, and everything they searched for and bought—through the smartphone tracking devices they carried nearly every waking moment. Carpenter listened to the performers for several more minutes before moving on. He had seen enough. It was time to move around to the back of the building.

An hour later, Carpenter was back at the café waiting for Turley. The delivery alley had offered fewer opportunities to take in anything more than quick glances as the building came into view. So, as he drew closer, Carpenter hastened his pace and strode purposefully into the arcade, avoiding eye contact with the two scrawny men posted outside; the same ones he had seen when they drove by earlier. He penetrated the arcade to a point just shy of the central staircase, where he paused outside a pastry shop. As he watched two middle-aged women in the storefront window rolling dough into thin pizza-sized pieces with long, skinny wooden rollers, he stole a few looks at the heavily-bearded man slowly pacing at the bottom of the stairs. Unlike the guards posted outside, this man had a weathered, hardened face that suggested a trying existence, perhaps one resigned to the mountainous areas of Afghanistan and Pakistan. Carpenter had had close encounters with many such men countless times. During the minute or so that he spent outside the pastry shop, Carpenter noticed how the man's eyes darted toward the slightest abrupt movement and would linger on the offender until he was convinced there was no threat. Like the men outside, this man was wearing relatively new clothing. Carpenter realized each of them was wearing the same kind of hiking boot and same style khakis. The parkas were also the same, though the colors differed. But in contrast to the baggy garments on the other men, this man's clothes were too small. His pant legs stopped short of his ankles. Carpenter guessed the man stood about the same height as the Scandinavian he had used for cover on the street. He noticed how the man kept his right hand just inside the parka's front zipper. Carpenter strongly suspected the man was fingering a weapon of some sort, perhaps even a short-barreled rifle. Carpenter estimated the was probably in his mid-forties, while the others were no older than their late twenties or early thirties. Carpenter wondered if Turley had seen the menacing man last night, and made a mental note to ask him before turning and leaving the arcade through the back-alley entrance.

Now, Carpenter was sitting inside the café. Only a few minutes after he had sat down, Turley sauntered in. He asked Turley straightaway about the guard posted at the stairway. Turley was also struck by the man's foreboding look and said he was sure he had not seen him before. He also confirmed there was no guard at the bottom of the stairs when he walked through the arcade the previous night. Although Turley could not be certain, he said he believed all four men posted outside the building were there last night. That meant there were at least five guards, including the burly man now guarding the staircase, and Carpenter suspected there were more posted inside. But the appearance of a new, more seasoned soldier and his placement at the bottom of the stairs were very significant changes. He and Turley agreed there was a good chance at least one of the high-level target attendees had arrived. If that was true, the meeting was not far off and the most likely time frame was between midnight and dawn the next day. Just as they were discussing these implications, Carpenter's phone vibrated, announcing a message from Timothy Patrick. Almost immediately after, two more messages came in from Patrick, each of them with an attachment. Carpenter dialed his boss.

"I think we're in luck," Patrick said. He first gave Carpenter some background, explaining how Kevin Lingel, the CTC technology officer, was able to access Turkish real property tax records as well as those of the *Posta ve Telgraf Teşkilatı*, or Ptt, the national post and telegraph directorate of Turkey. Using that information, Lingel was able to identify the property owner and the names of everyone receiving mail at that address. "Lingel reported that the building belongs to a guy named Berat Yildiz. That is a common surname in Turkey, but it struck a chord with me. Then I recalled that the British had inquired about an Osman Yildiz not long ago, so I called Mornhinweg." Patrick was referring to Sir David Mornhinweg, the chief of the British Secret Intelligence Service, or MI6. "Sir David reminded me that the British are looking into Osman Yildiz. The name Yildiz popped up on the Brits' radar when MI6 questioned two men who were apprehended shortly after arriving back in England. Sir David said that although they are still trying to build a strong enough extradition case to present to the Turks, they are convinced Yildiz has been ushering Europeans through Turkey and into Syria to fight with al Qaeda."

"Okay, but that doesn't mean these guys are related. You said Yildiz is a common name," Carpenter said.

"I'm getting there. You might remember the data breach of Turkish citizenship records a few years back. Well, Lingel used those records to determine that the Yildiz boys are, indeed, related. Their fathers are brothers. The building owner is the cousin of Osman Yildiz, the same man suspected by MI6 of aiding al Qaeda. So I'd say there is an extremely good chance you guys have the right place."

"We were pretty sure we were on the right track and that information goes a long way to confirming it." Carpenter said. "But the problem is going to be identifying where in the building the meeting will take place. If we can't narrow that down, it's going to be loud and messy."

"We've got a pretty good idea about that too," Patrick said. "Yildiz, the owner, maintains an apartment on the third floor. As you look at the building from the street out front, it is located at the front left corner. I sent over the blueprints for the building. Check the first message with a document attached."

Carpenter opened the file and took a moment to mill over the blueprints. He saw that the stairway was located in the center of the building and set up in a half landing style. It opened up to a hallway on the second and third floors. The hallway bisected each floor lengthwise. On each floor, there were two larger apartments on the left side of the hallway and, because of the interrupting staircase, two smaller ones on the right side. On the third floor, apartment 3B—the one belonging to Yildiz—was at the front of the building, while unit 3D was located immediately behind it in the back-left corner. The two apartments affected by the stairway on the right side of the building, apartments 3A and 3C, were roughly twenty percent smaller. The second floor was laid out in the same fashion. He knew right away that using the stairs to reach apartment 3B would be problematic.

Based on their surveillance, Carpenter expected that any attempt to breach the building would be meet with stiff resistance. Although he wasn't too concerned about getting past the guards posted outside and at the bottom of the stairs, it was likely there would be even more as he moved up and onto the third-floor hallway. He couldn't afford a protracted firefight that allowed the Turkish authorities to intervene or the targets to escape. It had to be quick and clean. He was starting to think he may need the sniper rifle after all, assuming he could find a rooftop position across the street. The problem with that option was that he might only get one shot. Even if a target appeared in his scope, any others in the room might have a chance to take cover before he was able to get off another round. That was less than ideal. No, he decided, that wouldn't work. There was only one way to do this. It had to be up close and personal. "Even though we think we know the apartment, I'm going to be making a lot of noise getting up there. We can pretty much throw stealth out the window. Are you okay with that?" he asked.

"There might be another way," Patrick said. "We think the tenants right behind Yildiz might be away." Patrick explained that Lingel had also hacked into the public utility's database to examine each tenant's energy consumption. Initially, Lingel was only interested in changes in the apartment belonging to Yildiz. While there was nothing to indicate any drastic increase in usage in apartment 3B, Lingel did detect a significant decrease in the unit behind it—apartment 3D. According to the postal records, a man and a woman received mail at that address. Using the leaked citizenship records, Lingel discovered they were married and both in their forties. The dramatic reduction in energy consumption occurred nine days earlier and had remained constant since. "Our conclusion is that the man and wife are either both dead or have been gone for the past week plus," Patrick said.

Upon hearing that, Carpenter's plans changed. It was remarkable how these often-overlooked nuggets of intel proved invaluable. And he knew it would not have been discovered had Lingel not gone the extra mile. "Tell Kevin I said nice job," Carpenter said. As the new idea percolated in his mind, he remembered the other information he had requested. "Did you find anything about a fire there?" he asked.

"Yes, that's the last thing I wanted to mention. There's a newspaper article attached to the last message. It's all we've found so far. There was a fire in the building four years ago. No one was injured but there was significant damage done to the upper floors. According to the article, the building was in violation of recently adopted safety regulations. The fire chief told the reporter the extensive damage would have been far less had the building been properly fitted with the sprinkler system required by the updated code for mixed-purpose buildings. Why did you want to know about fires there?"

"Just a thought," he said. "Did any of the current tenants live there when the fire happened?" he asked.

"Let me check Lingel's report," Patrick said. It took him several moments to find what he was looking for. "Yes, three of the current tenants lived there at the time of the fire."

"Perfect. Thanks for the information. Call me if you learn anything more."

After he ended the call, Carpenter turned to Turley and outlined the plan he was developing. He said they would have to go back to the building to confirm a few things. While envisioning the plan in his mind, Carpenter scribbled out a list of what he expected he would need. When he finished, he turned to logistical considerations. Since they would be nosing around the building's perimeter, Carpenter didn't really want to use the car. Turley agreed that the lighter traffic during early evening hours increased the risk that it might be recognized from earlier in the day. It was settled; they'd come back for the car and hit the store later. Then Carpenter grabbed his duffel and told Turley to change clothes.

Five minutes later, they were heading to the Kaya building. This time they followed a different route that would allow them to approach it from the rear. During the walk, when they found themselves alone on a street, Carpenter brought up something that was nagging him. "Did you notice anyone following you when we walked around earlier?" he asked.

"No. Why, did you?"

"No, I didn't either, but I had an eerie feeling that I was being watched."

Both men were highly-skilled in detecting surveillance. They knew the behaviors to look for. While Carpenter was sure he wasn't being followed before, he had sensed someone was watching him. The feeling overcame him when he was listening to the concert. He glanced over at the restaurant across the street a couple times but didn't notice anything or anyone unusual. Still, he couldn't shake the sensation.

"If someone was watching us, they'd have to know we were going to be in the area," Turley said.

"I know and that's what's bothering me. Keep alert. That could change everything."

Chapter 18

Fahkoury finished one last bite of *yaprak sarma*. He had grown fond of the meal of wrapped vine leaves, stuffed with rice, onion, and spices during his stay in Turkey. Although he had been at this restaurant—his second of the day—for more than an hour, he had only eaten two of the five pieces served. It wasn't the first time that anticipation had left his appetite wanting. Even though it had been hours since he had spotted his quarry, his heart was still beating abnormally fast. But there was no guarantee the man from earlier in the day was actually the American. There was no way he could know absolutely. His previous and lone encounter with the man had been from a considerable distance. Still, it was the way the man had moved down the street that had Fahkoury convinced he was looking at the man who had foiled his plans in America.

Fahkoury first spotted him from inside a restaurant across the street—the first he had visited that day. He happened to be looking through the large front window when he noticed a black man step from behind a group of people camped on the sidewalk in front of a clothing store. Fahkoury had encountered few black people during his stay in Istanbul and the fact the man was alone further grabbed his attention. Although the man carried himself in a casual and carefree manner, he moved down the street with an athleticism that suggested lethality resided right beneath the surface. Fahkoury found himself staring at the man as he moved, ever alertly and closer to a musical group performing on the sidewalk. He shuddered when the man made the first of several deft glances in his direction. For an instant, Fahkoury thought he had been spotted. Each time the man looked again in in his direction, Fahkoury had to tell himself there was no way the man could notice him sitting at the table, three back from the window with the sun shining onto the glass. Besides, it was clear the man's real focus was on the building down the street. At least it appeared as if the man was peering at it through the concert audience. When the man stepped away from the musical performance, Fahkoury watched him for as long as he could. This time the man did not stop. As the man disappeared from his view, Fahkoury marveled at how he moved with an expert nonchalance, adjusting his rhythm and movements to the surroundings. Fahkoury was tempted to follow him but thought better of it. It was too perilous to follow this man, he concluded. He realized the encounter had shaken him, knowing that the situation would have been potentially disastrous had he run into the man out on the street. So he had spent the next two hours in the restaurant, calming himself until he considered it safe to leave.

After leaving the first restaurant, Fahkoury returned to the apartment. His ploy was working but he was having doubts he wanted it to. He needed to regain his composure so he laid down to rest. Several hours later, his fear yielded to rage. This was the encounter he had schemed for and he was determined to avenge his failures in America. He left the apartment and returned to the neighborhood surrounding the building. He knew the American would not have stayed too long in the area but he expected the man might return to conduct further surveillance. So Fahkoury found another restaurant close to the building and waited. But, despite sitting there picking at his meal for more than an hour, there had been no sign of him.

Now he decided it was time to leave. The shops would be closing at seven o'clock, leaving him slightly more than an hour to slip out of the neighborhood while the streets were still busy. After struggling to make sense of the waiter's hand-scribbled bill, he took a long sip of water, placed down a ten euro note, and headed toward the exit. Once out on the street, he took several breaths to help him embrace his tension and channel it toward the chance for redemption he expected in a few short hours. His concern about not giving the Americans enough information to identify the meeting location had been allayed. Aziz had fought him on that issue, telling him too much information too soon would heighten suspicion and push the Americans to conclude that a trap was being laid. They must be forced to work for it, Aziz said. And he had been right. The American was here and he had somehow found the meeting place. Now it was a matter of luring him into the apartment. And once he was certain the American was in there, Fahkoury would not hesitate to activate the powerful device he had planted in the back of the closet two days earlier.

Chapter 19

Carpenter walked across the narrow passageway and furtively looked up at the gap between the three-story buildings. He estimated the span was more or less twelve feet. Depending on the structure of the roofs above, jumping that distance would normally not be a problem. But he had to consider the gear he would be carrying as well as the noise he would make when he landed. He was going to have to land lightly. Otherwise, he risked alerting the entire third floor, and possibly the second, to his presence. It was going to have to work. The other options were not tenable.

Only moments before, he had walked past the back of the building for another look at the fire escape. But there was no way to use it without first subduing the guards positioned there. And doing that would abruptly end any element of surprise as soon as anyone came around to check on the guards. He had already dismissed the possibilities of accessing the Kaya building roof from the roof of the adjacent two-story structure on the other side. During the earlier reconnaissance, Carpenter had noticed the two gutters running down the side of the Kaya building and continuing down into the two-foot-wide space that separated it and the Kaya building. Originally, he thought he might be able to climb one of the gutters onto the roof. But as he studied them more, the rust stains around the brackets holding the gutters in place led him to abandon that idea. Instead of scaling the gutter, he had also considered throwing a grappling hook from the neighboring roof onto the Kaya building roof. But, without knowing where to throw it in order to gain purchase, he might have to try several times. The unnatural noise from a chunk of metal clanging around on the roof above the meeting place was an unacceptable risk. That left the Lygos apartment building he was sizing up now. The three-story Lygos building—so named as a tribute to the city's first name—was separated by a pedestrian walkway from the Kaya building, a space Carpenter had just estimated to be twelve feet. The next issue was figuring out how he was going to get up on the Lygos building roof.

He continued down the alley to the street, where some of the shop owners were already lowering the metal overhead doors. He checked his watch and saw that it was almost seven o'clock. He turned right and kept pace with the other pedestrians on the sidewalk. He pulled out his secure phone and punched in a message to Turley. The reply was immediate. It showed Turley's location on the left side of the Lygos building. A few seconds later, Carpenter rounded the corner and saw Turley holding a door open.

"We're in business," Turley said.

Carpenter walked through the threshold and saw the bottom of a metal staircase. On the far end of the adjacent short hallway, just beyond where the steps began, was another door. He assumed that led into the central lobby, located at the rear of the restaurant that occupied the street-facing section of the first floor.

"There's a roof hatch at the top of the stairs," Turley said. "It's locked, but it's a simple padlock."

While Carpenter was deciding whether to go up and check it out, his phone vibrated. The message was from Patrick. "Call me, ASAP!" it said. He wheeled to Turley. "Can you get us back in here?"

Turley dangled a key. "From my boy Baran—the jewelry shop owner. He lives on the second floor."

They started out for the parking ramp where Turley kept his car. Carpenter reminded Turley to watch for a tail. He was still bothered by the feeling of being watched earlier in the day. After a few blocks, they were out of the commercial area, walking on a nearly deserted street with the parking ramp coming into view. Carpenter pulled out the phone and dialed Patrick. "Sorry, I had to get to a quieter area. What's up?"

"NSA has been monitoring all the phones in your building. What do you call it again?"

"The locals call it the 'Kaya' building. It means rock."

"That's right. Anyway, Blake Palmer said there were two calls to the landline in Yildiz's apartment in the last thirty minutes. The first time, the phone rang just once. A few seconds later, a second call came in. This time the phone rang six times. The phone wasn't answered either time. Both calls originated in Frankfurt, Germany from a phone that wasn't used previously and hasn't been used since the calls to Yildiz's apartment. The two calls have been the only ones to that apartment since you gave me the address earlier. Seems like somebody is trying to get ahold of someone."

Carpenter took a moment to think it over. Patrick's was the most logical conclusion, but he was thinking in a different direction. "We know someone is up there, at least the activity outside the building suggests it. Because they didn't answer, I'm thinking the calls are some kind of code."

"Huh, that's interesting. Any ideas what it means?"

"Hold on a second." Carpenter paused momentarily so that he and Turley could get in the car and close the doors. He told Turley to remain parked before he resumed with Patrick. "Obviously, I'm just guessing but if I'm right, the calls denote the time of the meeting, and I can think of two possible interpretations. The first call—the one when the line rang only once—might have been a notice call, while the second call—when the phone rang six times—was to indicate timing. In that case, the six rings mean the meeting will start in six hours. The other scenario is that the first call served as both notice and the number of hours to deduct from the second series of rings, indicating that the meeting will start in five hours. I've used both methods myself, back before everyone had a cellphone and you had to call someone's home to reach them. If the calls came in thirty minutes ago, the meeting will start sometime between midnight and one o'clock. That timing lines up with what we know. Security has been in place for twenty-four hours at least. Long enough to set up, move some of the principals in, and gain confidence the place is secure, but probably not long enough for them to be concerned about attracting scrutiny. If Aziz will indeed be attending the meeting, he'd want to arrive in this window when everything's in place. This thing is about to go down."

"Are you ready?"

"For the most part. We need to pick up some things. Let me sign off. I'll call later when I have a chance."

He turned to look at Turley. "Drop me off at your place. While I'm getting ready, you head to the sports store and pick up the stuff on the list. You know what it all is, right?" Turley gave thumbs up to confirm. "How long will it take?"

"If traffic isn't too bad, maybe an hour and a half."

"All right, bust ass. Don't be any longer. We've got a lot to do."

Chapter 20

It was nearing eleven o'clock by the time Carpenter settled in behind the large rooftop heating and ventilation unit on top of the Lygos building. An accident on the Galata Bridge over the Golden Horn had delayed Turley's return from the outdoor sports store. He returned with all the requested items, but the rope required some modifications. The shortest ten-millimeter dry rope Turley could find was seventy meters in length, too long and heavy for Carpenter's purposes. Besides the unduly length and weight, the static rope was a light blue and gray weave. Carpenter was hoping for something darker, but Turley said the other options offered even bolder colors. They quickly unfolded the rope and Carpenter neatly cut off about twenty-five meters with his KA-BAR knife. While Carpenter was fusing the cut end with a lighter, Turley cut three six-foot sections from the spare piece of rope. When he was satisfied the critical end was properly fused, Carpenter tossed the lighter to Turley and began coiling the longer section of rope. By the time he was finished, Turley had the three shorter sections ready to go.

Carpenter arranged the various pieces of rope in his rucksack with the rest of the gear. He hefted the pack several times to get a sense of its weight. He estimated the extra seven or eight pounds of rope put the total weight to about fifteen pounds, an amount that equated to approximately eight percent of his bodyweight. More than doubling the load was out of the question, so he removed and tossed aside the tactical vest. He'd be nimbler without it, anyway. Still, he knew that the extra weight in the rucksack was going to impair his leaping ability. It was going to be a close call, but he was confident it would not be a terminal problem.

Now Carpenter was up on the roof of the Lygos building. He removed the backpack and looked around the HVAC unit at the Kaya building next door. He saw a small stairway penthouse in the center of the roof, with a single-bulb light fixture affixed to the side facing him. The light was bright enough to clearly illuminate the dented steel door below it but little else. Several paces to the left of the stairway penthouse was a collection of solar panels. He didn't notice any other assemblies on the rooftop. Fortunately, the solar panels lined up with apartment 3D, immediately below.

He stayed put behind the HVAC unit, waiting to see if there was anyone lurking in the shadows around the penthouse. While he waited, he examined the structure of the Kaya building roof. It appeared as if it was ringed with a two-foot-high parapet wall, much the same as the one on the Lygos building. He was glad the parapets were not taller. Having seen no signs of anybody next door, he kept low and moved over to inspect the parapet on the Lygos building roof.

The top of the parapet was flat and capped with a piece of metal. He looked in both directions for the best jumping point and noticed a short section that had been tarred. He crawled over to the area and tested the security of the metal cap and the tar lathered on top of it. There was no movement in the metal cap and the tar was cold and hard, but it still retained some of its stickiness. He looked behind him and saw there were no obstacles in his path. The landing point on the Kaya building looked clear too. He would launch himself from right here, he decided. He chanced a peak over the wall, and recognized that the gap he had estimated at twelve feet took on a greater dimension from this high up. Before slinking back to the HVAC unit, he tested the parapet one more time. He was going to have to hit it perfectly.

When he was back behind the HVAC unit, he checked in with Turley. "Where are you?" he asked. After dropping him at the side door, Turley had gone in search of a parking spot. Carpenter wanted him to park as close as possible but not within sight of either building.

"I'm walking back toward you. A spot finally opened up but the fucking guy took forever to pull out. It's parked right where you wanted it, a block away from the Lygos building."

"Good. Make a swing around the building and give me a sitrep. As soon as you give me the all clear, I'm heading over."

Chapter 21

Thirty-five minutes later, Carpenter was on his third set of pushups behind the HVAC unit. In between sets, he had been stretching his leg muscles. The exercises kept his muscles loose but, more importantly, gave him something to focus on while he waited for Turley. At the top of his thirtieth rep, he felt the phone vibrate in his pants rear pocket. He worked his way into a crouch and accepted the call.

"What's it look like?" he asked.

"Slight change," said Turley. "Still two dipshits out front and two more out back but this time there are two dudes at the bottom of the stairs. The same tough-looking bastard we saw earlier now has a twin buddy. Blinds are still down and the same lights are still on in the apartment. Didn't notice any silhouettes."

The stepped-up security was another sign the meeting was drawing closer. He checked his watch. It was 11:24 p.m. Time to go. "I'm grabbing my gear. Let me know when you're in a position where you can see the alley."

"You sure you can Carl Lewis that thing?" Turley asked.

"Only one way to find out."

They kept the line open while Carpenter slipped into the backpack and moved into position on the other side of the HVAC unit. He squatted down and bounced on the balls of his feet, waiting for a final update from Turley.

"Good to go," Turley said.

"Watch and learn, Railsey."

Without delay, Carpenter popped up and started running toward the roof's edge. It took him less than half the forty-foot runway to get up to full speed. When he was just past the halfway point, he adjusted his stride, innately calculating the necessary correction without losing any momentum. Six feet from the parapet he sprung off his right foot, sending his body slightly upward toward the top of the parapet wall. As soon as his left foot landed, he pushed off, up, and out toward the Kaya building. At the zenith of the jump, he knew he would make it. He landed on both feet, three feet clear of the wall, and instantaneously tumbled into a half roll to his left, keeping his chin tucked to his chest. The back of his left shoulder hardly touched the stony surface before he twisted through the remainder of the rotation and came to rest on his hands and knees. After a quick look around, he scanned his face and limbs for cuts and abrasions, finding none. The landing had been almost completely noiseless and he was fully intact. He pulled out the phone and called Turley.

"All good up here. How about down there?" While Carpenter waited for a response, he slipped the rucksack off and moved over to the solar panels.

"Other than seeing Spiderman bound between buildings, I've only seen a few cars pass on the street. The alley is still a ghost town but that can change in a heartbeat. And I shouldn't stick around here too much longer. You'd better get moving."

"Give me another minute," Carpenter said. By that time, he had already pulled out a six-foot section of rope and was wrapping it around one of the eight steel legs holding up the frame for the solar panels. When he finished with the double fisherman's knot, he rotated the short rope so that the knot was at the back of the leg and then attached one of the autolocking carabiners to the looped end. He tugged on the assembly to test its strength before slipping one end of the longer section of rope through the carabiner. A few moments later, after struggling with the climbing harness, he threaded that end of rope through the tie-in loop and secured it with a figure-eight retraced knot. Now holding the unsecured end of the long climbing rope in his right hand, he began backpedaling toward the edge of the roof. He peeked over the edge and didn't see anything. But his view was limited. "Still clear?" he asked.

"Alley is still empty," Turley said. He was across the street, opposite the alley, tucked into a store entrance. The vestibule was surrounded by storefront display windows, offering him a fairly unobstructed view through the glass as well as straight ahead. "And this side of the building is quiet. You're good to go."

Working quickly, Carpenter let out a few feet of slack and threaded the loose end of rope into the belay device. "Coming over," he said. While resting his stomach on the parapet, he pulled the rope through the belay device until the remaining slack disappeared. When that was done, he carefully slid off the parapet and began rappelling down the side of the building, landing on the small ornamental balcony outside apartment 3D seconds later. Up close, he now saw that the two window sections were designed to swing out. A piece of wood molding on one section covered the window joint. While examining the locking mechanism on the window, Turley's comment about the unusually warm weather popped into his head. *Worth a try.* He tugged on the outer window panel and it swung open. He pulled himself up and through the two-foot wide opening and into the apartment. "I'm in," he said.

He took a moment to listen. Hearing nothing, he untied one end of the rope and began pulling. Almost as soon as the rope dropped over the parapet and dropped below him, Turley's voice sounded in his ear.

"Somebody's walking down the street. He will be at the alley in a few more steps, and I can see thirty feet of rope dangling out the window!".

Carpenter feverishly dragged the rest of the rope into the room and gently closed the window.

"That was fucking close!" Turley said.

One disaster averted but he still had to clear the apartment. He removed the backpack and fished the small flashlight out of the side pocket. He was in the living room, only a couple steps from the wall separating this unit from Yildiz's apartment. The door to the hallway was straight ahead and above it, on the ceiling, was something he was hoping to see. Just off to the left of the door was an opening that appeared to lead to a kitchen. Beyond the opening was the beginning of a hallway.

Before moving deeper into the apartment, Carpenter checked his senses for any signs that he was not alone. There was a light musty smell, but he had no way of knowing if the smell was normal or the result of stale air from the apartment being untenanted for more than a week. He reached out and swiped his finger across the surface of the glass coffee table, disturbing a light and uniform covering of dust. Another sign the apartment was empty but, again, not definitive. Suddenly, he heard muffled voices. The sounds seemed to be coming from Yildiz's apartment. In an instant, there was silence again. He hesitated before finally moving closer. He pressed his ear to the wall and heard voices. Though he was unable to discern what was being said, at least he knew there was more than one occupant in the Yildiz apartment. How many, he could not be certain. With more time, he might be able to determine the number of distinct voices but further eavesdropping would have to wait until he checked out the rest of the apartment.

He walked in short, silent steps until he arrived at the kitchen entrance. The galley-style room was spotless. There were no dishes in the sink and no food on the narrow counter or on the small round table at the rear. He was unable to detect the faintest of odors that would indicate any food had been prepared in there recently. He moved on, down the hallway. It ended in a junction of three doors. He pushed open the door on the right and found an empty three-quarter bathroom. The center door turned out to be a linen closet. This meant the door on the left had to be the bedroom and the most likely place he would find someone at this time of night. He gently turned the knob and pushed the door until it creaked, causing him to freeze. A few soundless moments later, he shined the light into the room and glimpsed the near side of a neatly made queen bed. With his back against the hallway wall, he pushed the door the rest of the way open with his left hand. Nothing. He moved into the room and confirmed it was unoccupied. He was back in the hallway when he heard Turley's hushed voice.

"PJ?"

"Yeah, Railsey. All clear up here. What's up?" Carpenter whispered.

"I've got some activity out front. The goon we saw at the base of the stairs earlier just came outside. The two dipshits are there too, making it three total out front," Turley said, while retreating into the farthest recesses of the store's atrium. "The mean-looking bastard is looking up and down the street."

"At what?" Carpenter asked.

"I can't tell. Other than some light traffic, I haven't seen anyone in the past few minutes." Just then, a car stopped in front of the Kaya building. "Hold on," he said. Turley watched as two men exited the car. "Two more guys just got out of a car and went into the building with Mr. Mean."

While Turley was giving the play-by-play, Carpenter was processing the implications. It was clear the meeting was starting. There would be no time for further surveillance or planning. He would have to rely solely on his instincts, given what little he knew about what awaited him on the other side of the wall. But one element remained unchanged. It would have to be quick. He and Turley had estimated that once he initiated contact, he would have five to seven minutes to execute and get out. "Head back to the car as soon as you can. I'll be coming out of here hot so I need you and the car ready."

"You don't want me to stay here in case you need help?" Turley asked.

"If this goes like I'm thinking, I won't need any," he said. "I'll let you know when to pick me up or where to meet me. Get going."

As he did on the roof, Carpenter first looped a short section of rope around the balustrade on the balcony and then prepared the rest of the equipment for his descent. Once that was complete, he went to the kitchen and retrieved a large pot from the cupboard before snatching a towel from the linen closet. On the way back, he grabbed a magazine off the coffee table and began tearing it into pieces, placing each one into the pot. When he had nearly filled the pot with shredded paper, he heard a door close. Soon after, he heard voices coming through the wall, this time more distinctly. He stepped over and placed his ear to the wall. While the varied inflections prevented a full understanding of the conversation, he was able to get the gist of it from the bits and pieces he was hearing.

"Railsey?" he called out.

"Yeah, I'm here."

"Where are you?"

"Almost back to the car."

"Good. I can hear some conversation next door. Based on what I'm hearing, the two guys from the car are proxies for Aziz; he's not coming. One person is pissed about that. I was able to hear him shout, 'I'm not negotiating with you. I came here to speak with Aziz.' This meeting is going to end quickly. I'm going in now. You'd better hustle."

"I'm on it. Good luck."

In an almost seamless fashion, Carpenter removed the SRD9 suppressors from the rucksack, screwed them onto the two semi-automatic pistols, and tucked the weapons into the waistband of his Rip Stop BDU pants. He expected thirty rounds were more than enough, but for good measure he grabbed two more magazines and slid them into a side pocket. When he was finished, he threw on a dark flannel shirt, leaving it untucked to conceal the weapons, and then grabbed the pot and towel.

When the flames took to the magazine paper, he covered the pot with the towel, removing it momentarily several times to keep the fire going. Soon, smoke was billowing and beginning to fill the living room near the door. He lifted one of the nearby Bergère chairs and placed it underneath the sprinkler head for a stool. Using the corner of his phone, he delicately tapped the glass housing for the glycerin-based liquid until it broke. When the siren started bleating and the warning light began flashing, he channeled some feigned emotion and opened the door.

Chapter 22

On his most recent pass, Fahkoury ducked into a narrow gap between two buildings across the street. He peered around the corner and could see the entire face of the building. Although he could not see the left side or the rear of the building, he didn't expect he would have to. The reactions of the guards would let him know when his quarry arrived. And he did not dare get any closer. He wanted as much distance as possible between him and the blast. He was not there long when another guard joined the pair already outside, causing him to retreat further into the murky space. When a car pulled up to the front of the building seconds later, he carefully edged up closer and watched the newly arrived guard escort the two arrivals into the building. The two other guards remained in place out front.

I shouldn't have doubted Aziz, he thought. The plan was falling into place. Now it was just a matter of time before the American took the bait. Fahkoury slinked back into the narrow aperture and waited. Whether the American attempted to breach the building from the front or the rear alley, the resulting fracas would alert Fahkoury to his enemy's arrival. Assuming the guards didn't kill him first, he'd give the American a few minutes to reach the third floor. Then Fahkoury would trigger the explosion that would give him the revenge he longed for, while also clearing Aziz's path to absolute power.

Chapter 23

Carpenter burst out of the apartment and turned toward the stairwell, suddenly alerting the guard posted there. Holding the phone to his ear and wearing his best fearful expression, Carpenter said in Arabic, "Run brother, there is a fire in my apartment!"

The guard simultaneously drew a gun and moved toward him. He alternated between looking at Carpenter and the smoke billowing out the apartment door. He hesitated momentarily, deciding what to do before yelling, "You are not allowed here, *abeed*! Go back inside!"

The guard's hesitation allowed Carpenter to close the distance. Acting as if he was overcome with panic, he continued marching toward the stairs, all the while thinking the man's ethnic slur was only going to make this sweeter. As the gap between two men rapidly closed, Carpenter coolly rewrapped the secure LTE phone in the knuckles of his right hand. Just as the guard raised his gun and free arm to push Carpenter back toward the other end of the hallway, Carpenter turned slightly and delivered a vicious right hook to the man's chin. Almost before the guard's head snapped back from the punch, Carpenter was clutching the man's jacket in his left hand and plunging his knife into the soft tissue at the base of the man's skull. After he dragged the crumpled body into apartment 3D, he pulled the semi-automatic pistol from the front of his waistband and listened for signs of any other threats. A moment later, he continued down the hallway until he was outside the door to apartment 3B. He wrapped his knuckles on the door before taking a half step back.

A few seconds later, the door opened. Turley's Mr. Mean did not have a chance to utter a word before Carpenter fired two suppressed rounds into his forehead. Wasting no time, Carpenter stormed into the apartment, where he saw four men huddled near the far living room wall. The lone man standing against the far wall was the first to go down. He was instantly joined by the man foolishly rising from his seat. Out of the corner of his eye, Carpenter spotted a fifth man emerging from the kitchen. That man went down before he completed his next step. In the same instant, a bullet whizzed by Carpenter's ear. He ducked instinctively as a second round flew over his head. Carpenter turned back to the grouping of men along the living room wall. Before the shooter had time for another attempt, Carpenter dropped him with a burst to the heart, leaving one final breathing man gripping the arms of his chair in abject fear. Carpenter knew he was looking at Mufakir—the Thinker.

With one eye on Mufakir, he made a quick check of the kitchen, then remained at the mouth of the hallway, ensuring that he could see anyone coming out of the bathroom or bedroom. "Abdulla Tahan, you've got one chance and one second to save yourself. Where is Sadiq bin Aziz?" he asked.

"Fuck you, American!"

"Clever, but wrong answer," Carpenter said just before emptying the magazine. There was always a possibility the al Qaeda financier never intended to show up for the meeting. The pieces of conversation he had overheard through the wall pretty much confirmed it. Still, the question had to be asked. The exercise wasn't a complete was of time, however. At least Mufakir was dead.

Not bothering to check his watch, Carpenter estimated it had been less than two minutes since he dropped the guard in the hallway. If the sprinkler system in the building was linked up with the municipal fire alarm system as he expected, he might have less than five minutes to get out. But first he had to search the bodies and the rest of the apartment. After dragging Mr. Mean out of the doorway, Carpenter searched the man's pockets, finding nothing other than some wadded up Turkish Lira. Keeping one eye on the hallway, he took a picture of the man's face and moved on to the other stiffs. Except for the cellphone in the pocket of the man who had been sitting in the chair opposite Mufakir, none of them had anything on them worth taking. He tucked the phone in a side pocket and snapped some more pictures before heading down the hallway. Once he confirmed there was no one in the bathroom, he moved into the bedroom. He found it was also empty and began searching the closet for possible intel. While pushing aside the hanging clothes, he noticed a stack of three plastic bins. Inside the first, he found only shirts and sweaters. Tossing it aside, he started to remove the lid of the second container when he noticed something odd about the one below it. Unlike the others, the bottom container was taped shut. After quickly pawing through the clothes in the second container, he grabbed onto the bottom container and began pulling it out of the closet. It was much heavier than the first two. Using his knife, he carefully cut away the tape and removed the top. Inside, underneath a blanket, was a cellphone wired to eight smaller containers that were bundled together like bricks and bound with more tape. *Shit!*

Carpenter paused at the front door to call Turley. "Get your ass to the front of the Lygos building next door, but no closer. There's a fucking bomb in the bedroom closet. And it's wired to a mobile phone."

Carpenter had been trained in render safe procedures but he was no bomb expert. He took a few moments to study the device. He briefly considered trying to identify and cut the correct wire leading from the phone to the electrical firing circuit. But cutting the wrong one would be disastrous. Fortunately, he had another option.

In response to the proliferation of remote-controlled improvised explosive devices used by insurgents in Afghanistan and Iraq, the Department of Defense required all personnel to carry portable frequency jammers on their person. Recognizing that the potential benefit outweighed the minimal burden of carrying one, Carpenter had adopted the practice in certain environments. Now he was glad he had asked Patrick to include one in the supplies shipped from Germany. Still, it was not guaranteed to work. The problem was that several of the latest generation of jammers had been stolen from a supply room at a coalition base in downtown Kabul less than a year before. There was some concern that the top-secret gadgets could be reverse-engineered to create a counter-counter-measure which would either render them useless or, worse, trigger an explosion once activated. With time running out and no other options, he would have to put his faith in the portable all-frequencies jammer. "I can't carry the bomb with me and I'm not sure I can cut the detonation wire without arming it, so I'm going to have to use the frequency jammer and hope it works. Can you get us back into the building to retrieve the jammer when things calm down?"

"I'm sure I can. Remember, my agent lives on the second floor."

"Good. On your way over, call in a report of a bomb in this apartment. With any luck, I'll get there just after you do."

As he was ending the call, Carpenter looked through the peep hole in the door. Even though it offered a two-hundred-degree view, he was not taking any chances. He positioned himself against the wall and threw the door open. Seeing that everything was still clear, he peeked around the doorframe before moving into the hallway. He kept moving as he pulled the fire alarm on the wall, and he was inside apartment 3D when he heard the first running steps out in the hallway. He hoped the memories of the recent fire would cause the tenants to hastily flee the building. After hiding the jamming device underneath the bureau next to the wall separating the two apartments, he removed the bulky flannel shirt, slipped into the climbing harness and grabbed his rucksack. Seconds later, he was heading out the window.

Chapter 24

Why are all these people running out of the building? Fahkoury wondered. Shouts soon followed. Fahkoury, who did not speak Turkish, had no idea what was happening. He was not alone. The guards also appeared confused, until one of them ran into the building, dodging the flow of people rushing out. Fahkoury left his hiding place and walked into the street and toward the center of the building to get a more complete view of the unfolding chaos. Just before he heard the first wail of the emergency sirens, the other guard ran into the arcade and headed for the stairs.

Fahkoury stood in the middle of the street as a gathering crowd of onlookers surrounded him. He was beginning to think it was all a poorly-timed coincidence when he noticed a dark figure dash from the alleyway on the left side of the building. *The American!* He was no more than twenty yards away but already hopelessly too far. As the man continued sprinting down the street and farther beyond his reach, Fahkoury was tempted to initiate the explosion. The impulse was out of anger more than anything. The bomb could no longer serve as the weapon he intended. Besides, he was now dangerously close to the building. Even if he survived the blast, it was likely he would be incapacitated, a state that would almost certainly lead to his capture. And, by the time he moved to a safe distance, Mufakir might have escaped, anyway. That is, if the American had not killed him already.

He had no choice but to leave. But this fight was not over. The Americans had many skilled warriors but had sent this man for a reason. It was clear that his foe was heavily invested in this game. As he distanced himself from the pandemonium, Fahkoury clung to the thought that he would meet this American again. And soon.

Chapter 25

"No doubt about this being a setup," Carpenter said. The call to Patrick had been the second one he made after jumping into Turley's car. "After I cleared the apartment, I started searching for intel. Other than a cellphone, I didn't find anything. But I did find a pretty significant remote-controlled bomb tucked away in the bedroom closet."

"Are there any civilian casualties?" Patrick urgently asked.

"We're still in the area and, as yet, there has been no explosion. Right after I found it, Railsey made an anonymous call to the police to warn them about the bomb, and I made another one right before I called you. The cops and rescue teams are at the scene now, clearing everybody out of the nearby buildings. An EOD team is here too," he said, using the acronym for the explosive ordnance disposal team. "I placed a jamming device in the apartment next door. Sorry, but it was the best option. The battery life is about three hours, which should be enough time for the EOD team to disarm the bomb. We're going to have to go back and get the jamming device once things settle down."

"Thank goodness the bomb has not exploded. As far as the jamming device, it's not ideal if it's found, since it would all but confirm the professional nature of the hit. But it's not the end of the world. Besides the bomb, what are the authorities going to find inside Yildiz's apartment?" Patrick asked.

"Six bodies, including one belonging to Abdulla Tahan—Mufakir. If they get there before we do, they'll eventually find another one inside apartment three D, together with some climbing gear. If they look hard enough, they might find the jamming device too."

"What about the cellphone?" Patrick asked.

"It belonged to one of the two guys who showed up just before the meeting started."

"Bring it back with you and we'll see if there's anything on it. I'll talk to Andy about the jamming device." Patrick was referring to Andy Heck, CIA chief of station in Istanbul. "I'll have Andy send a team to retrieve it. Right now, you two get back to Railsey's place and stay there and out of sight. I'll get working on a plan to get you out of Istanbul later in the day when there will be some traffic. It would raise too many questions if I put you on a plane in the middle of the night."

Chapter 26
Luxembourg City

A few hours later, Sadiq bin Aziz was sitting in what had become his favorite recliner, watching the news from Istanbul. He had not moved from the comfortable leather chair since the story broke on the BBC. His initial disappointment upon realizing there had not been an explosion vanished hours later when the Turks held a press conference to report that Abdullah Tahan, a reputed member of al Qaeda's senior leadership group, was among the casualties. But he wondered what had gone wrong. The reporting said a bomb had been found inside the building. *Why didn't Fahkoury detonate the bomb?* Still, his primary objective was achieved. Although they were not stating it publicly, it was added satisfaction that the Turks had to be thinking the Americans were somehow involved. The resulting friction between the two uneasy allies would be a welcome development.

He finally alighted from the chair when the reporting started to repeat itself. He moved over to the desk and again revised the message he had been crafting over the past few days. After making adjustments for the lack of a destructive explosion, he copied the file to a thumb drive and summoned his trusted servant. Before sending Faraj on his latest mission, Aziz reiterated his explicit instructions on how to transmit the file to the news agency.

Very soon, he would deliver his ultimatum to the Americans and, in the process, stake his claim as the undisputed leader of global jihad. While he expected it would boost his own credibility with the believers, the taunt would do little to change the impressions of him held by the Americans and their Western allies. That was fine, as the true purpose of the statement was to unleash the next phase of his plan against the infidels. And, by the time it was done, they wouldn't know what to expect next.

Chapter 27
Langley

With the time difference countering much of the travel time, Carpenter's plane touched down in Virginia at 6:00 p.m. local time that same day. He could have been back sooner, but Patrick had delayed his departure from Istanbul to coincide with an uptick of scheduled flight activity in the early afternoon. Before he landed, Patrick had told him they would finish catching up the following morning. Until then, he suggested Carpenter should get some rest. Taking that advice, Carpenter deplaned and went straight to his apartment.

After sleeping soundly for almost eight hours, he arose at 4:00 a.m. To help shake off some lingering grogginess, he promptly drank two bottles of water and chased them down with an Americano from his treasured Nespresso machine. As he savored the last few sips of coffee, he prepared to head for the gym. Carpenter had found that exercise was the ultimate panacea for jetlag, especially when the interval between significant time changes was short. With temperatures expected in the upper-seventies, he decided to ride his bike. After changing into compression shorts and a tee-shirt, he stuffed some more gear into a small backpack before pedaling the first leg of a circuitous route to the gym. Once there, he spent forty-five minutes lifting, followed by ten intense laps of freestyle in the fifty-meter pool. Before his breathing fully restored, he was back on the bike. When he arrived back at his apartment, the app on his phone indicated he had ridden more than thirty miles to the gym and back. By the time he stepped out of the shower, the physical toll of the past three days had vanished. He ate the last of the grilled chicken he had picked up the night before and headed to the office.

Now it was past one o'clock and he was still waiting in Patrick's office. To keep himself occupied while he waited, Carpenter had been flipping through the magazines on the coffee table. He had a hard time believing the one he was looking at qualified as a news magazine, the claims of its editors notwithstanding. He tossed the magazine aside and turned on the radio behind Patrick's desk. He wasn't surprised when he heard Kent Busek's voice giving the starting lineup for the Washington Nationals. Among many shared interests, he and Patrick both loved baseball. And even though the Yankees were not playing, listening to a ballgame was a much better way to pass the time than reading a rag magazine. Plus, Carpenter really liked the National's play-by-play man. Like Vin Scully had during his sixty-seven seasons, Busek worked alone. And, now that Scully had retired, Carpenter considered Busek to be the best broadcaster in the game. Although he lacked Scully's tenure, Busek was the third-generation of broadcasters in his family, a history that began when his grandfather starting calling games for the Washington Senators in 1953. And Busek was able to call on the stories passed on by his father and grandfather to masterfully weave a few tidbits of baseball nostalgia into every broadcast.

As the broadcast went to a commercial break prior to the first pitch, Carpenter again wondered what was keeping Patrick. Although the ballgame would now make the wait much more tolerable, he was getting concerned. Earlier in the morning, Patrick had called and said that he would be heading to the doctor for a checkup after he and CIA director Melissa Gonzalez met with President Madden. The plan was to meet Carpenter around noon. Shortly after Carpenter arrived at headquarters, Patrick had called again, this time to say he was running late. He said he was about to leave the doctor's office that was near his home in Bethesda. Since it was typically a twenty-minute trip, Carpenter was concerned something had happened. He was thinking he should call him to make sure everything was okay. He knew Patrick had been under a lot of stress and he wasn't in the best physical condition to start with. It was impossible for him not to notice the toll the past few weeks had taken on his boss.

In truth, he considered Timothy Patrick more a friend than a boss. During the better part of two decades, he had worked closely with Patrick and come to greatly respect the man. Although Patrick tried to downplay it, he was the most intelligent and insightful person Carpenter knew. And, besides his keen intellect, Patrick was incredibly loyal. Carpenter realized there were times when he might have taken things too far but he could not recall one instance when Patrick did not have his back.

But, more than respect, it was Patrick's kind-hearted nature that had the greatest impact on Carpenter. Patrick's compassion had helped him through some of the darkest hours of his life. At age fourteen, he lost his mother. She was the only family he had and she was everything he cared about in this world. In her absence, there were no grandparents, aunts, uncles, or cousins to comfort him. The pain was so unbearable that he vowed he would never again love another person. He retreated emotionally and entered a rebellious stage, one often marked by bellicosity. Eventually, he got his act together and became a functioning member of civil society, but the detached nature stayed with him through his early years with the Agency.

That all changed when he met Lizzie Hewson. She was working at the embassy in Islamabad when they crossed paths. He happened to be at the embassy when the ambassador was hosting a staff appreciation event. Carpenter would not have attended the reception but Patrick had asked him to make an appearance as a show of goodwill. While drawing the attention of a beautiful woman was not an uncommon experience for Carpenter, he knew Lizzie was different the moment she introduced herself. That she was outgoing was readily apparent, but it was her unmistakably natural and authentic ease that eventually pierced his built-in guardedness. From that first encounter, things proceeded quickly. Time apart from her became unbearable. Carpenter realized he was falling deeply in love, an emotion reliably absent from his life since his mother's passing. Soon, they were making plans to move back to the States and get married. It was only a few weeks after they completed their wedding arrangements when Lizzie was killed by a car bomb. Forensics later determined the bomb had been the handiwork of Mumeet.

It was only through Patrick's tireless efforts that Carpenter was able to come to terms with his loss and regain some sense of normalcy. Over the intervening years he spent most of his free time with Patrick and his wife, Suzie. Their grace was something he would never forget and he considered them family. Now, as his wait for Patrick entered the second hour, Carpenter tried to convince himself that nothing was wrong. He thought of Suzie and, selfishly, how he was unprepared to deal with another painful loss. His concerns were allayed a moment later when he heard a familiar voice barking orders outside the door.

"Sorry, traffic was a mess," Patrick said when he opened the door. "I guess I was stupid to agree to a ten o'clock appointment when the doctor cancelled my appointment yesterday. I had to wait thirty minutes for the doctor and rush hour apparently never ends. Anyway, I digress. How are you doing? And why are you smiling?"

"I'm well; thanks for asking." Carpenter chose to ignore the other question. After looking him over, he noticed that Patrick either looked better than he had a few days ago, or he was getting used to his boss's new appearance. "You look a heck of a lot better than last time I saw you."

"Like I said the other day, I am feeling better. And the doc says everything looks good. Even my blood pressure was good today. Besides the blood pressure pills, I've been on a low dose of stress medicine for a few weeks now. I think it is actually helping me cope with this crap. Of course, she has no idea what I do for a living, but we've spent a lot of time talking about the adverse effects of obsessing over things beyond my control. You and I both know that's not possible in this business, but the perspective is a good one to bear in mind. You might give it a try yourself."

"You ever try meditating?"

"No, I couldn't do that. I can't sit still and don't have the time," Patrick said.

"You should give it a try. It's good for you."

"When do you ever have time to meditate?"

"I find time every day, even if for only a few minutes."

"The stuff I learn every day," Patrick mused. "I'll take it under advisement."

"Any fallout from your meeting with the president?" Carpenter asked.

"He's pleased with the outcome and said he'd do it again, even if there was no possibility Aziz would be there. Unlike with some of his predecessors, I'm finding this guy has no fear and you don't have to ask him twice to approve an op."

"Has he heard from the Turks?"

"They first called Secretary Christensen to express concern that the US might have conducted an operation on their soil. It was only after she denied any knowledge that they called the president. He denied it too, but he said he was glad someone in Turkey was taking the extremist threat seriously."

Carpenter appreciated the president's moxie. Although the interests of the two countries were not always aligned, the US and Turkey were allies and had been since the middle of the last century. But the conflict in Syria had tested the decades-long alliance. When the conflict broke out during the Arab Spring, the Turks had been quick to ally with anti-Assad forces in an effort to topple the regime—its primary objective in Syria. While the United States was no fan of Assad, it was more concerned about the emergence of jihadi groups, like the Islamic State, in the war-torn country. And, after years of indifferent efforts by the Turkish government to curb the flow of militants across its borders, the US decided that aligning itself with a Turkish antagonist was its best option to stop the spread of extremism in the region. The pick-your-poison decision to partner with the Kurdish militia group known as the People's Protection Unit, or YPG, was not without consequences, however. In particular, the strained relations had the potential to threaten the United States' use of Incirlik Air Base, an important strategic airfield for US Middle East operations. But, despite the long history of association and the strategic importance of Incirlik, President Madden put eliminating extremist groups at the top of his priorities. And, in the pursuit of that objective, he wasn't going to apologize to the Turks or anyone else.

"What's the bottom line? Have we created a problem with Turkey?"

"No, the feigned indignation is just posturing. In the end, this will amount to nothing. Turkey will come to heel. While we're on the subject, tell me more about Istanbul."

"Not much to add really. We got pretty much everything we could out of the operation," Carpenter said. "Although Aziz wasn't there, we got Mufakir. It's never a bad thing to take down a high-value target."

"Are you still convinced it was a setup and that you might have been a target too?"

"Given the way the intel fell into our lap, a setup was always a strong possibility. And I still think it's the likeliest scenario. I don't believe it was a coincidence that Aziz wasn't there. I'm pretty sure that was the plan all along. But I'm less certain about the intentions for the bomb. Of course, it could have been planted purely to take out Mufakir. On the other hand, if the whole thing was a plan for us to take him out, it's possible it was there as a backup plan in case we didn't show."

"Have you considered there is a third possibility?"

"That the bomb was intended to not only kill Mufakir but also whoever took the bait—in this case us and, more specifically, me?"

"Exactly."

"I told Railsey that I had a nagging feeling someone was watching me when we were surveilling the building. But I don't see how I could have been the target. There was no way they could have known I'd be the one to show up."

"I agree they could not have known that you would be the one sent to Istanbul, but we have to consider that there is a connection," Patrick said. "We have an asset inside the Turkish National Intelligence Organization. Andy Heck called earlier to tell me the Turks are almost sure the bomb was designed by Mumeet or someone who was trained by him."

"You're joking."

"I'm not."

Carpenter was now sure someone had been watching him. Still, the idea Mumeet was in Istanbul to get him seem farfetched. "Are you saying you think Mumeet was targeting me?"

"I think we have to consider the possibility. We have to assume Mumeet was there, but we can't know whether he knew you would be there. We just have to be aware of the possibility."

Carpenter thought what he might have done differently had he known the Bringer of Death was in Istanbul. He would not have left, that's for sure. "It doesn't change a thing," he said. "If he's coming after me, I say bring it on; I like my chances." He hardly needed extra motivation but he welcomed the increased stakes. He had been consumed with Mumeet for far too long and reveled in the thought the terrorist was having reciprocal feelings. The more Mumeet was worried about him, the greater the chances he'd screw up. Now that they suspected Mumeet was in Istanbul, it was even more important to understand the other players. "Do we know the identities of the other men?"

"Besides Mufakir, the Turks linked three others to al Qaeda. They don't have any idea about the other two, who are likely the two that showed up for the meeting. My guess is they are directly involved with Aziz. It appears the guards posted outside the building managed to evade the Turks, as there is no information about any captives."

Thinking out loud, Carpenter said, "Let's think about what Istanbul tells us. Mufakir went to Istanbul to meet Aziz. That tells us Aziz is not in physical proximity to the shura. It also tells us the shura are probably in the dark about his plans. We still don't know the level of collaboration leading up to and through the attacks in Minnesota, but things have clearly changed. If the other members of senior leadership wanted Mufakir out of the picture, there would have been easier and less elaborate ways to do it. So it's clear to me that Istanbul was an op designed by Aziz to take out one of the top people in senior leadership, whether he intended for us to do the work or not. If there wasn't a rift between Aziz and AQ leadership, there is now. The only people we know about in his orbit are Mumeet, al-Rasheed, and two stiffs in Istanbul. But moving Mumeet and al-Rasheed around the planet requires detailed planning and coordination. Aziz can't possibly do all of this by himself. Who is helping him?"

"We simply don't know."

"We had better figure that out fast because it feels like we're just sitting around waiting for a shoe to drop. Most concerning, this move in Istanbul tells me Aziz is setting the stage for something big, and we're not ready for it."

Patrick was following along up to the point about Aziz planning something big. He wasn't sure if Carpenter was merely venting about the lack of kinetic opportunities or if he was onto something. By all indications, they were dealing with a new group they knew very little about. That made developing a strategy to combat an elusive enemy even more difficult. "I agree that Aziz must be getting help from someone. But what makes you think he is planning something big?"

"Eliminating Mufakir was a message as much as clearing a path for himself," Carpenter said. "The message is intended for his followers and those who might be on the fence about throwing their hats in with him. Pulling that off demonstrates his independence. He's not only saying he doesn't need al Qaeda, he's saying he's moving on without them. We know he's smart and a careful planner. I don't believe he would have gone forward with Istanbul unless he was prepared to back it up."

It was tough to argue with that logic and it further added to the urgency to uncover Aziz's network. "He and his team can't keep a tight lid on their activities forever. There'll be a slipup we can take advantage of," Patrick said.

Carpenter thought that might be wishful thinking. Aziz was something altogether different and his plans had proven incredibly elusive. They had no insight into his thinking or the extent of his capabilities. The one thing they could expect was that Mumeet somehow factored in Aziz's plans. In his mind, the Bringer of Death had beaten him three times—nearly four if Mumeet had indeed been in Istanbul—and Carpenter hated losing. He thought again about the possibility that Mumeet had used and tried to kill him in Istanbul and it was really pissing him off. He told himself revenge would be his in due time but, right now, he needed to focus on a solution rather than the cause. His thoughts were then abruptly interrupted by the telephone on Patrick's desk.

"Yes?" Patrick asked. "PJ is with me now. Come on up." After he replaced the phone he said to Carpenter, "That was Samantha Lane. She says Aziz just released a statement through al Jazeera."

Chapter 28

Lane entered the office minutes later with several copies of the statement in hand. The look on her face foreshadowed the gravity of the news she was about to share. "This went up on the al Jazeera website thirteen minutes ago," she said as she handed them each a copy.

"What's he saying this time?" Carpenter asked.

"He's a clever bastard. You should read it."

Carpenter started reading. The release stated—

A statement from Sadiq bin Aziz: Yesterday, Abdullah Tahan, a beloved and dedicated leader of the al Qaeda organization and the jihad movement, was assassinated in Istanbul. Although no one has yet to take responsibility for this criminal act of aggression, one needs to look no further than the bloody hands of the United States. Once again, the Americans have violated the sovereignty of a Muslim nation. Regrettably, the loss of Brother Tahan has further incapacitated al Qaeda, and it is no longer positioned to lead our cause. We must move forward and not allow this tragedy to overcome us. Beginning today, we shall reorganize and be known as Al-Kalafa.

Believers, the time has arrived to finally end this oppression at the hands of the infidel. I call on every true Muslim to join forces with Al-Kalafa by declaring loyalty to Dar-al-Islam. Together, we will drive all traces of the United States and its Western allies from Muslim lands, while also channeling our righteous fury against the apostates occupying them. We will strike relentlessly at the oppressors with an unwavering commitment to violent jihad. As you heed the growing rhythm from the beat-beat-beat of the war drums, know that the climax will be the momentous victory that places us on the threshold of our objective of a global caliphate. As the leader of Al-Kalafa, it is my pledge that we will not rest until the day comes when only true believers occupy all four corners of the world.

When Patrick finished, he looked up at Lane and Carpenter. "Well, it seems pretty clear you two were right about him seizing power. Besides that, and the clear threat to the West, do either of you know what he's talking about?" he asked.

Carpenter collected his thoughts before answering. He used every opportunity to educate himself further about the issues and perspectives that guided his adversaries. In the process he had gleaned a deep understanding of the extremists' interpretation of Islam. "When he mentions Dar-al-Islam, he is referring to a binary state of the world. The centuries-old concept is not found in the Quran or *hadith*—the traditions or sayings of the Prophet Muhammad—but is the result of scholarly study of Islam. Historically, most scholars proposed a moderate definition of Dar-al-Islam. It means the 'house of peace' and was interpreted as an environment where a Muslim is secure to practice Islam. Most Western countries, particularly the United States, would be considered Dar-al-Islam under that traditional view. By contrast, *Dar-al-Harb*—the 'house of war'—is everyplace else; a hostile place where Muslims are not secure to pursue their faith. The more radical scholarly view, and the one Aziz is espousing, is that Dar-al-Islam can only exist in an Islamic state governed exclusively by Sharia, while the rest of the world would be considered Dar-al-Harb.

"Aziz is calling on all Muslims to pledge loyalty to the radical view of Dar-al-Islam. He's essentially saying that a house of peace does not exist anywhere in the world today, a warning not only to the West but also to secular governments in Muslim-majority countries. He also says that true believers must recognize they will exist in a house of war until they get what they want—a caliphate. But, unlike the caliphate that ISIS previously declared in Iraq and Syria, Aziz will not settle for anything short of a global caliphate."

"Does the name Al-Kalafa mean anything?" Patrick asked.

"It means 'the leader,'" Carpenter said. "I'd assume it's how he wants to be viewed as much as his new organization."

"How ingeniously original," Patrick said. "Sam, what are your thoughts?"

"I think we might have replaced one enemy with one even more dangerous," Lane said. "We're dealing with a cunning man of considerable wealth who is on the path to acquiring a powerful cult of personality. We thought the Istanbul op may have simply been a setup to remove an archrival, but it appears it was more than that. Aziz is shrewdly presenting it as an act of oppression, while portraying himself as the last line of defense against the West. He's building his own brand. After what happened in Istanbul, there's a good chance the other AQ senior leaders will be scared into silence, leaving his as the dominate voice in the terror group, if not all of global jihad. Now, to bolster his status, he is doubling down on his commitment for more attacks."

"Is he doing this with the blessing of al Qaeda?" Patrick asked.

"My quick assessment is that he alone is pulling the strings and controlling the message. He doesn't have to build consensus among the shura and, because of that, al Qaeda, Al-Kalafa, or whatever we're going to call it, is now a more agile adversary."

"On that point, is Al-Kalafa just a new name or does it represent a different organization altogether?" Patrick asked.

"I'd be inclined to say Aziz is breaking away from core al Qaeda," Lane said. "Al-Kalafa is independent from AQ; a distinct organization that only Aziz controls. And my guess is that he won't wait long to show he means business."

"I think Sam is right on both counts," Carpenter said. "Everything points to Aziz breaking off from al Qaeda with his own organization. I also agree he's not going to wait for someone else to step forward and challenge him. Momentum is on his side. To build on it, he's probably prepared to unleash one or more attacks."

"Does he have any resources, apart from those he took from al Qaeda?" Patrick asked. "And by that, I specifically mean personnel."

"It's possible that Aziz may incorporate elements of al Qaeda but it would be without the blessing of leadership. And I find it hard to imagine that this early on he would have already co-opted a significant number of al Qaeda members. No doubt some have been and will come to his side but that will not happen overnight. I'm guessing he filled out at least some of the Al-Kalafa roster before this announcement."

"Anything else in the statement jump out at you?" Patrick asked.

"That sentence about the drums is odd," Carpenter said. "Everything else is pretty clear but that language is goofy and almost intentionally awkward, as if to draw attention. I'm not sure if, by using that language, he's talking about the entire process or a particular aspect of his plans."

"Could it be both?" Patrick asked.

"It could but I'm leaning toward the latter. Going back to what we said before, he is in a tenuous position, whether he's trying to take over AQ or he just launched his own terror group. But either way, Aziz has to demonstrate that he's more than hot air. Because of that, I think the language about the drums climaxing in a momentous victory implies that something is coming soon."

"As if the statement wasn't ominous enough," Patrick mused. "In less than six months, this guy comes out of nowhere and is now probably the top threat we face. It makes me wonder how many other crazed bastards are out there with nine-figure bank accounts."

"It only takes one," Carpenter said.

Chapter 29
Paris, France

Less than eighteen hours later, Sophie Dubois was frantically going through her purse trying to locate her car keys. She was going to be late for work. She had checked her watch on the way out the door. It was 8:16 a.m. when she started down the two flights of stairs. As she scampered down the marble steps, she calculated that, in the best conditions, the drive from her two-bedroom apartment in Gros-Caillou to the parking garage in the modern La Défense business district required at least thirty minutes. Today, the conditions were less than ideal. The heavy rain would only worsen the extra congestion she had endured for the past week while repair crews fixed the damage caused by the most recent barge to strike the Pont de l'Alma.

When she finally located her keys, Sophie dashed out of her apartment building, covering her head with the Burberry leather attaché as she sprinted to her Renault Modus, parked several cars down on Avenue Bosquet. She threw the attaché and her purse onto the passenger seat, quickly slid in behind the wheel and slammed the door shut, finding momentary succor in the tranquility of the sealed space. On top of being late, there were few things she disliked more than the depressing sound of tires sloshing over wet pavement on a raw weekday morning. She closed her eyes and took a few deep breaths to calm herself. After one final slow and long exhale, she glanced into the mirror. *Oh, great!* Not only was she going to be late for the meeting, she looked like a hot mess. The eye makeup she had hastily applied only minutes earlier was smudged and had started to run down her cheeks. After she wiped off the worst of it, she pulled out her phone and shot a quick text to Marie, telling her colleague that she was probably going to be late. As an afterthought, she cryptically added that she had some big news to share.

Sophie and Marie had become very close friends while working in the strategy department for the largest bank in France for the past four years. In truth, neither was developing the skills required to be effective strategists. Their boss, a careerist whose vocabulary largely consisted of whatever corporate buzzwords were currently in fashion, was a glorified quant who had been kicked upstairs solely for the reason that she had been there so long. Eventually, the two young professionals resigned themselves to the hope that merely their job titles would be impressive enough to land a better job elsewhere, whether inside or outside the bank. In fact, Sophie was expecting an offer from a rival bank any day. The hiring manager all but told her the job was hers when she was interviewed by him last week. And Marie was interviewing too. Her second interview with a multinational transportation company was scheduled for the end of the week. But, until they each managed to escape, they had to feign contentedness while enduring the ennui of their current posts and their vapid manager.

Sophie was not looking forward to leading the presentation at today's meeting. Despite actively pursuing other opportunities, she and Marie remained committed to doing their very best. Yesterday, they pointed out the flaws of the underlying assumptions to their boss. Rather than showing interest in their reasoning and the potential problems to the proposed business case, the boss limited her comments to the color selections they had used in the PowerPoint slides. Sophie realized their critical analysis didn't matter; the decision by upper management to pursue the small acquisition was made before the strategy work had even started. It was all so pointless. As she started the car, Sophie reminded herself that the presentation was merely perfunctory. Management could wait a few minutes to hear what they had predestined. Feeling a bit relaxed after the little pep talk, Sophie allowed herself to smile. She wasn't going to let anything ruin last night.

She supposed there were better days to propose than on a Monday but the move fit Girard perfectly. Sophie met him last year after his band's performance in a neighborhood bar. She had seen the band perform there twice before, and the handsomeness of the lead singer more than made up for the band's musical shortcomings. After the band's last set, Girard jumped off the stage and headed straight for her. Some flirtatious small talk over a few drinks that early morning developed into a torrid romance and the two twenty-somethings had been inseparable since. Her father was especially slow to accept Girard, but the charms of the gladsome crooner had eventually won him over too. Sophie relished that her father had been particularly thrilled when she called her parents last night with the exciting news.

Now, thanks to Girard, she was going to be late for work. Earlier that morning Girard wouldn't let her get out of bed until they celebrated one more time. She wondered if he would ever grow up but quickly decided she did not want him to. His carefree attitude and whimsical lifestyle were the perfect compliments to her conformist professional life. However, as tedious as corporate life could sometimes be, she realized they were going need her income. Girard, at least for the time being, was not likely to be adding to the couple's coffers.

As Sophie pulled from the curb and began making her way north on Avenue Bosquet, she again considered giving up the apartment. Her new job—at least she hoped so—would be in the same office complex. The thought of continuing that commute had her thinking about moving closer to work. It would be much cheaper and more convenient for five mind-numbing days each week. But Sophie knew she was only fooling herself with such thoughts. She was the third generation of the Dubois family to live in the 7th Arrondissement and the beautiful aristocratic neighborhood, as much as anything or anyone, defined her.

Her thoughts shifted to the beloved figure in one of the world's other great romances as she edged closer to the Pont de l'Alma. Today, perhaps more than any other, she felt a powerful connection with Princess Diana. Sophie was a young girl when Diana died, but she remembered the tragic day vividly. As she matured and learned more about her, Sophie had come to deeply respect and appreciate Diana's unparalleled grace and altruism. Sophie even made it a habit to say hello to Diana each time she passed the

Flame of Liberty, the unofficial memorial to the still-adored former member of the British royal family. It was another reason not to move, she reflected. She recalled thinking last night how exquisite the gold-leafed monument looked, even in a dreary downpour.

Traffic had stopped again on Avenue Bosquet when she felt her phone vibrate. She looked down. It was a text from Marie. The senior executive had just pushed the meeting back thirty minutes, she wrote. And what is the news? she asked. Sophie laughed. She knew Marie suspected but would be going crazy until she had confirmation. As she approached the bridge, Sophie decided she would take a detour. She now had some extra time and this route was unlikely to get her to work much faster, anyway. She turned right onto Rue de l'Université, and headed for the Pont des Invalides. Today, she would honor Princess Diana by passing through the place where her heroine's life had come to a tragic end.

Chapter 30

At 8:34 a.m., Fahd al-Rasheed sat down on the cold metal chair and placed his espresso on the small circular, red-topped table. Besides offering shelter from the cold rain, the partially enclosed café was one of the few places he was able to enjoy a cigarette. Most important, it also offered an unimpeded view of the westbound entrance to the Pont de l'Alma tunnel. Wearing black Chelsea boots, matching colored jeans, and a slate mac over a blue-stripped Breton tee, al-Rasheed looked very much the chic Parisian as he lit his third Marlboro of the morning and waited for the festivities to begin.

Al-Rasheed considered it a blessing that he was there and things had come together so smoothly. He had finally escaped the United States after the attacks on the American heartland, but only narrowly. Unable to get to the rendezvous with his friend Hamid Fahkoury—the man known as "Mumeet," and the mastermind of those attacks—al-Rasheed was forced to improvise. Alone, and with only a few thousand dollars cash, his options were limited. Fortunately, his opportunity to escape came in the stampede of people that developed amid the escalating chaos at the Super Bowl. Immediately after the first car bomb, security personnel started directing people away from the stadium. Al-Rasheed used the directed exodus to slip from the parking ramp into a growing group of people, one that eventually swelled to the thousands on the heels of a subsequent, but failed bombing attempt. As the terrified mass stormed farther away from the epicenter of peril, al-Rasheed peeled off from the main group. His salvation arrived on a side street some fifteen blocks from the stadium. On his fifth attempt, he opened the unlocked door of a rusted-out SUV, only to find it would not start. He began to think he was going to be captured for the stupid reason that he could not manage the simple act of hotwiring a car. With his hands shaking with rage, al-Rasheed ducked down again under the steering column and realized his mistake. After using his knife to strip the covering from the actual starter wire, he touched it to the exposed power wire and the old engine roared to life. Rather than risk crossing the city to get to the designated meeting place, he headed west out of Minneapolis in the Jeep Cherokee.

He abandoned the stolen vehicle at a shopping center in Fayetteville, Arkansas two days later. He purchased some items, including new clothes and a cheap pair of vanity glasses, before adjourning to an out-of-the way restroom. There, he made quick use of electric clippers before applying what the package claimed was a "smoky gray" color to his freshly cropped hair. Using the money Fahkoury had given him just prior to the attacks, and wearing the faux glasses and a bright red, hooded sweatshirt that proudly proclaimed him an "Arkansas Dad," he paid cash for a one-way bus ticket to Memphis, Tennessee. For the next eleven days, he swapped out his attire and moved from one homeless shelter to the next in the Birthplace of Rock and Roll.

His stay in Memphis was merely to bide time until it was time to instigate the contingency plan in New Orleans. By the time he eventually reached the Crescent City, less than three hundred dollars remained in his pockets. The expenditures for fast food and thirty-three cab fares, needed over the course of two days to travel south from city to city, totaled more than a thousand dollars. With the aid of an ally to the cause, he secretly boarded an ocean carrier in the Port of New Orleans that was loaded with steel coils and bound for the Port of Tangier.

When the cargo ship docked in Morocco thirteen days later, al-Rasheed was met by representatives of the al Qaeda affiliate, Moroccan Islamic Combatant Group—GICM. Under the protection of GICM, he stayed in Tangiers a fortnight before his instructions from Sadiq bin Aziz finally arrived. He was to travel to Algiers, the instructions indicated. There he would meet part of his team and receive additional details for his next mission. Using a series of safe houses across the two North African nations, al-Rasheed arrived in the Algerian capital nine days later. Once there, he was placed in the care of another al Qaeda affiliate—al Qaeda in the Islamic Maghreb, or AQIM. Two men from AQIM drove him east to Annaba, the stunning city on the southern shores of the Mediterranean Sea established by the Phoenicians three thousand years earlier. Al-Rasheed arrived in the one-time home of Saint Augustine expecting to depart for France but discovered that the captain of the fishing vessel had just been detained by the authorities. His travel companions made other arrangements and quickly ushered him south to Tebessa, an ancient city reputed for its traditional Algerian rugs and a plausible destination for three men posing as traders. From there, the two AQIM soldiers led al-Rasheed on the dozen mile trek to the Tunisian border and deeper into the mountains before delivering him safely into the waiting arms of Hammad Dhib and Hafaza.

Dhib and his group had drifted apart from AQIM a year earlier. Weary of al Qaeda's desertion of jihad, Dhib had flirted with the Islamic State. But in the wake of the recent attacks on the American homeland, Dhib reaffirmed his allegiance to al Qaeda and, more particularly, to Sadiq bin Aziz. After spending a few days in the remote mountains with Hammad Dhib and Hafaza, al-Rasheed and his companions were confident they had not been followed. It was time to head back to the coast and hook up with their alternate transportation. After traveling by boat from Tunis to Marseille, al-Rasheed and his two companions continued on to Paris, where they linked up with Adel Shebani. Before knocking on the door of his dwelling, al-Rasheed knew nothing about his designated contact. He would learn that Shebani was a committed and experienced jihadist, one who had been commended to Aziz by a mutual friend in Shebani's native Libya.

△ △ △

Adel Shebani had been one of the first to join Ansar al-Sharia after the Salafist militia group formed during the Libyan Civil War. He was commended for his bravery throughout the conflict, especially during the Battle of Sirte, the final battle of the bloody civil war. Later, as Ansar al-Sharia turned its attention to the Sufi population, Shebani gained further acclaim for his participation in a series of attacks on Sufi shrines and peoples all across Libya. By the time a convoy of Ansar al-Sharia militants entered Benghazi to demand the imposition of Sharia law, Shebani's accolades had earned him a seat in one of the lead vehicles. A few months later, Shebani led one of the groups in the assault on the American diplomatic compound in Benghazi. That proved to be the pinnacle of his jihadist activities in his home country. Ten days after that attack, protesters stormed Ansar al-Sharia's headquarters, forcing Shebani and his comrades to flee. He stayed in Libya, hoping he would be able to keep a low-profile until the group was able to reestablish itself. But conditions did not improve and when non-Islamist forces launched a ground and air offensive against Ansar al-Sharia and other Islamist militia groups, the leaders of the organization scattered their fighters. Shebani was sent to France and told to remain there until it was safe to return.

No longer content to sit on the sidelines, Shebani had contacted his former commander a year earlier and told him that he wanted to return to Libya and rejoin the cause. The continuing political instability in Libya had opened the door for the Islamic State to make further inroads. When Shebani left Libya, the Islamic State of Iraq and the Levant was just beginning to exert its influence there. While many of his Ansar al-Sharia brothers joined ISIL, Shebani remained loyal to his group. As ISIL captured more territory and became the Islamic State, Shebani began to loathe the competing extremist group. He was determined to rid Libya of the Islamic State in favor of a purely Libyan Islamist group. His commander told him to stay in Paris, that there may be a more useful purpose for him there, one that would prove costly to both the infidel and the Islamic State.

Less than three weeks later, Aziz's man came calling. After Shebani heard the man's pitch, he swiftly pledged his loyalty to Sadiq bin Aziz. Armed with opportunity and cash, Shebani did not expect it would be difficult to recruit additional followers. But, after months of careful conversations, Shebani was only able to enlist two reliable men. He was relieved when Aziz's emissary said two trusted men would be sufficient. The man told Shebani that he would provide additional men when the time came. Shebani was given instructions to acquire certain materials. He was also told to expect another man to arrive in Paris with plans for an attack. That had been more than six months ago.

Since then, Shebani and his men had been living in the Paris banlieue of Sevran, among mostly Arab and African immigrants in one of the decaying cités—the massive concrete housing projects that blighted the former working-class neighborhood. The Parisian suburb had gained notoriety as one of the "no-go" neighborhoods that police entered only when absolutely necessary. In an area besieged by crime, violence, and high unemployment, most residents lived in near-constant states of fear and despair. These conditions resulted in a population that was increasingly withdrawn from society, which allowed Shebani and his men to go about their nefarious assignments without much concern. During their relatively short time in Sevran, they had quietly secured strategic assets and established a network of useful contacts, ones that would pay dividends in this attack and those still to come. When Aziz's man contacted him again several weeks ago, Shebani and his men were prepared. All they needed to do was await the arrival of their leader and the details of their assignment. Finally, Fahd al-Rasheed came knocking at their door.

△ △ △

When al-Rasheed had arrived in Paris days earlier, there was really little that he needed to do. Shebani had already acquired the necessary materials. At the recommendation of Aziz's man, the Zastava M70 machine guns were purchased weeks earlier from an arms dealer in Slovakia. Transporting them to Paris across the open borders of the Schengen Area was done without difficulty. And, with the help of a well-paid and sympathetic insider, Shebani had lined up two white box vans from a regional delivery company.

After meeting with Shebani, al-Rasheed kept a low profile. He continued to monitor the travel site for his cue. When it came, he told Shebani to execute his plans for the vans and assemble the men for a meeting. Later that evening, Shebani arrived with his two recruits and two brand new box vans. The vans were so new that they had yet to be adorned with the company's logo. With the vans secured, al-Rasheed had all the resources needed for the attack. The only remaining item was to go over the plan. It was a simple plan that Fahkoury had devised when he and al-Rasheed were with Aziz in the Arabian Desert. The plan was so straightforward that it required virtually no practice. After explaining the concept, the only thing al-Rasheed did to prepare his men was to drive the route with them, pointing out how and where the attack should unfold. Although perfect choreography was not necessarily critical to the plan's success, al-Rasheed explained how the timing of the second van would determine the scope of their victory.

In the end, al-Rasheed's most important contribution to the operation was choosing the men to drive the vans. Aziz had told him that Shebani was both trustworthy and capable and al-Rasheed had learned nothing to refute that view. In addition to Shebani, he selected Samir, one of the men he had traveled with from Africa, to drive the other van. It was an easy decision. He had seen enough of the other three members of the team to know he didn't trust them with the most important roles. They would only have to worry about killing, something the crazed look in their eyes told him they were more than willing to do.

All six men had assembled in the small auto repair shop in the wee hours that same morning. The cinder-block structure sat in the middle of a largely untenanted side street in an industrial section of Sevran. The mechanic who had operated the small business there had passed away almost a year before. He and his wife were occupants of the same cité where Shebani and his men had been residing. After learning of the mechanic's death, Shebani approached the sixty-eight-year-old widow with an offer. She readily agreed to rent the garage for a thousand euros per month, a sum that her late husband's business had provided them only rarely during the ten years he had operated the repair shop.

There was just enough room behind the garage's graffiti-painted metal overhead door to accommodate the two vans and their small arsenal. Al-Rasheed placed Samir outside while he and the rest of his team loaded the vans with the automatic rifles and twenty-liter Jerry cans filled with gasoline. After ten cans were loaded into each van, al-Rasheed connected a canon fuse to the burn cloths that stuck out of each metal container. When he finished just after 3:30 a.m., he called Samir inside and then reviewed the plan a final time. When he was convinced everyone knew their roles, he assigned Samir and his colleague from Tunisia to stay with the vans and sent Shebani and his men back to the housing project. Al-Rasheed hung around the garage for an hour to make sure there were no problems. If there was any suspicion about their activities, he expected the authorities would act on them quickly. With no sign of trouble, he changed clothes and then walked the streets until it was time to catch one of the first trains into Paris.

Now, a handful of hours later, he sat alone on the café patio, enjoying a cigarette and an espresso. He noticed that traffic was steady and moving slowly, both goods signs. A few minutes later, he was taking the last sip of still-warm espresso from the small ceramic cup when he noticed the first van. He casually placed the cup on the table and stood up from his seat. The operation was beginning.

Chapter 31

Just west of Rue Bayard, Sophie observed two cars swing around a slow moving white van. It was not until she got closer that she realized the van wasn't moving. Rather, it was standing along the side of Cours Albert 1er. She hesitated when she finally pulled up behind it, unsure if the driver was about to pull from the curb and head down into the tunnel. She waited a few seconds more. The van remained still, so she followed the lead of the other cars and swerved around it. She was not quite into the tunnel when she heard horns blaring behind her. She checked her mirror and saw the van was pulling into traffic, four cars behind her. *What is that guy doing?* she wondered as her car entered the five-hundred-foot long underpass.

△ △ △

Only seconds before, Shebani was approaching the halfway point of the tunnel in the first van when he radioed Samir in the second van to get moving. Traveling in the right-hand lane, Shebani slowed his pace further below the fifty kilometers per hour limit and waited for the large black sedan to pull alongside him. He could tell the sedan was moving briskly as it filled his side mirror. When the sedan was at his rear bumper, Shebani yanked the van into its path, slamming the sedan into a concrete pillar no more than fifty feet from the end of the tunnel. He slammed the brakes and then backed the van into an oncoming car in the right-hand lane, effectively closing off the exit. He quickly ordered the other two men out of the van as he ignited the eight-foot long cannon fuse. Once the fuse was lit, Shebani grabbed his M70 assault rifle and joined his brothers.

Immediately upon receiving Shebani's call, Samir had jerked the second van from the curb and began slowly moving toward the tunnel entrance, ignoring the loud protests of the cars in his wake. Traffic zipped past him in the left lane and several cars filled the expanding space in front of his van. When he saw the first brake lights flash in front of him, Samir was several car lengths into the tunnel. He allowed one more car to pass before he turned the van hard to the left. When it came to rest, the van was nearly perpendicular to traffic and almost evenly straddled the solid white line that separated the two lanes. He gestured to the wild-eyed man in the passenger seat next to him. Once Samir's comrade had the fuse burning, the two men jumped out of the sliding door, carrying their fully-loaded rifles and plenty of extra ammunition.

△ △ △

Sophie Dubois was not even halfway into the tunnel when she noticed the rapidly approaching sequence of red lights. She was forced to press hard on her brakes, barely stopping before plowing into the metallic blue BMW in front of her. *Just my luck!* she said to herself. Even with an extra half hour, she was still going to be late. The lorry that stopped next to the BMW's front bumper blocked her view to the end of the tunnel. Thinking there must be an accident up ahead, she grabbed her phone in anticipation of a traffic update. While she was waiting for the app to load, she heard a loud noise, immediately followed by a rapid series of bangs. She opened her window and thought it sounded eerily like gunfire she had heard on the news and in movies. She looked back and saw a white van. It was stopped at a right angle to the other vehicles in the tunnel. She estimated it was a dozen or so cars behind her. As she was about to look down at her phone, she glanced in the side mirror and saw two men emerge from the van. As they moved toward her, she saw one of the men raise a rifle. By the time she realized echoes of gunfire were coming from both ends of the tunnel, it was too late. She was trapped. As the harrowing sounds moved closer, Sophie grasped the inevitable. She closed her eyes and thought of her parents, Girard, Marie, and Princess Diana. And then she prayed to God to save her.

Chapter 32
Langley

"This can't be good," Carpenter said. It was 2:58 a.m. when he uttered those words into his phone.

"It's not," Patrick said. "Do you have a television in that place?"

"No."

"I figured as much. There was an attack in Paris in the last half hour. I just spoke very briefly with Pierre." Patrick was referring to Pierre Laurent, head of the Directorate-General for External Security, the French equivalent to the CIA. "Obviously, it's still early in the game, but from what is known so far, it appears two cargo vans entered the westbound tunnel under the Pont de l'Alma. The first van caused a crash that stopped traffic, while the trailing second van blocked off the other end of the tunnel. Multiple gunmen then worked their way into the tunnel from opposite ends, shooting the passengers in the stopped westbound cars, as well as those in the cars passing by in the eastbound lanes. Police arrived on scene within two minutes of the first reports of the accident. Not long after that, there were a series of explosions that seemed to start from each end of the tunnel and then triggered more as the fire engulfed additional vehicles."

"How many dead?"

"We don't know yet. The fires are still burning inside the tunnel. But it's going to be a lot." Neither man spoke for a moment. Patrick broke the silence. "Got any initial thoughts?"

"Despite what little you told me, my gut says it's Aziz. And he didn't waste any time."

"I know Aziz is top of mind for all of us right now but I don't want to rule out any others," Patrick said. "The Islamic State has pulled off attacks in France before. This could be them or some other group."

"I don't disagree but the level of coordination you described leads me to believe this was Aziz. Remember what Sam said about Aziz taking certain elements of al Qaeda and incorporating them into his Al-Kalafa group? I think this is an example of just that. Despite what Aziz calls the organization now, al Qaeda has the blueprint on synchronized attacks, and this fits their profile more than it does previous Islamic State ops which have used small arms or vehicles to run down pedestrians. The attack you described used multiple instruments and required precise timing."

"Explain that," Patrick said.

Carpenter paused a moment as he played out the scene in his mind. "First, they used the vans to create a concentrated killing field by trapping people inside the tunnel and blocking off the exits. This gave the gunmen opportunity to penetrate the tunnel from both ends and shoot up as many as possible. And I'm betting there was a third instrument used—the explosions. I think we'll find out the initial explosions were intentional and intended to take care of anyone who had not already been shot dead. And those initial explosions were probably triggered by some kind of timing device. Besides giving the gunmen an opportunity to kill, the delay was also designed to catch first responders. A tunnel is the perfect place for an attack like this. There is nowhere for people to run and hide. We should have seen something like this coming."

Patrick knew Carpenter was right, but this attack was just another example of how vulnerable they all were. And the endless supply of targets and scenarios made it nearly impossible to anticipate them. He was thinking this was just the first and was concerned about Aziz's known firepower. "If it is Aziz, do you think Mumeet led the attack?" Patrick asked.

"Is there any structural damage to the tunnel?"

"Pierre told me the tunnel appears to be intact but they won't know for sure about any structural damage until the fires are extinguished and they can get some engineers in there."

"Then, based on what you've told me, I doubt it was Mumeet. If I'm right about the explosions, it sounds like simple incendiary bombs were used. It was still a crafty plan, but I think Mumeet would have used more powerful explosive devices. He would have destroyed the tunnel. Besides that, Mumeet may have been in Istanbul two days ago. That's not enough time for him to get to Paris and plan this out. It had to be someone else. That person didn't need any special explosives skills to pull this off. Because we know so little about Aziz's network, I'd say al-Rasheed is more likely. This could be the news from 'across the sea' that Hammad Dhib would have been expecting if he wasn't rotting in a cave in Tunisia."

Patrick thought that over. As bad as it was shaping up to be, he agreed the attack would have been far more devastating had Mumeet been behind it. Al-Rasheed or someone else they didn't know about made more sense. As he ran it through his mind, he calculated that al-Rasheed would have been able to get from Tunisia and into France with plenty of time to make the final preparations and lead the attack. "That's probably right," he finally said.

"What else do the French know?" Carpenter asked.

"Right now, the DGSE doesn't know anything more than what I told you but they and the French National Police are fully mobilized. Their first priority will remain securing the area and the rest of the city. They're also canvassing witnesses and reviewing CCTV to try to piece things together, but so far, they don't have much."

"What are we going to do?"

"I'm heading into the office now."

"I'll meet you there," Carpenter said.

Chapter 33

Carpenter strode back into Patrick's office with his second cup of coffee of the morning. It was coming up on five hours that he and Patrick had been there, watching the news and getting periodic updates from Pierre Laurent, head of the French DGSE. By the latest count, sixty-two people were dead, most of them found in the westbound section of the tunnel. It was too soon to know whether the cause of death was gunshot wounds or the effects of the inferno that had consumed the tunnel. None of the survivors, including a young woman named Sophie Dubois, were able to identify any of the gunmen with any useful particularity. And the terrorists' charred bodies foreclosed the possibility of identification by other expedient means. DNA samples were gathered in the off chance a match could be found in any French or international database. Using the vehicle identification numbers, it was later discovered that the vans used in the attack had been previously reported as stolen by a regional delivery service.

"They want our help," Patrick said when Carpenter sat down with his coffee. "I think I'm going to send you over there."

Carpenter didn't say anything. He wasn't sure what to think. He knew that before he even left Tunisia, Patrick had called his counterparts in Europe, including Pierre Laurent, to give them a heads-up that al-Rasheed was on the move and possibly headed there. Even though the warning lacked any specificity, Patrick had told him that he was taken aback by Laurent's reaction. Without offering any substantiation, Laurent said the information was baseless, that the DGSE was not aware of any intelligence that remotely suggested an impending terrorist operation on French soil. Patrick urged him to reconsider and take the threat more seriously, but the DGSE director was dismissive and said France was choosing not to intervene in the brewing battle between the United States and the renewed al Qaeda. Carpenter was incensed when he heard Patrick's report of the conversation. He was pursuing one of the most-wanted terrorists in the world, someone who might be on the way to France and the French showed no interest in cooperation. But that episode was just the latest reason he was leery of working with them.

For starters, he was not as enamored with the new French president as the rest of the world seemed to be. The aristocratic young man hailed from one of France's wealthiest families and had entered politics four years earlier with a resume that was largely bereft of any real-world experiences. Rather, his reputation had been built on some high-profile philanthropy and the portfolio of supermodel girlfriends he paraded for the European gossip magazines. His case to the electorate was that France must claim its destiny in the new world order. He argued that other world powers, acting out of envy, had been relegating France to secondary status. And he made no effort to disguise the enmity he harbored for the United States, a nation he claimed was simultaneously jeopardizing world peace and the earth's fragile environment. His imprecise promises to remedy those perils and restore France to its former glory in the process were enough to distinguish him in an otherwise unimpressive field of candidates.

In short order, the new French president's pick to lead the security agency, Pierre Laurent, extended those antagonistic sensibilities to the DGSE. Laurent had spent his entire career in the DGSE and he took particular offense to France's non-inclusion in the intelligence alliance comprised of the US, Canada, New Zealand, Australia, and the UK. Known as the Five Eyes Group, the participants operated under a multilateral agreement that required all-source intelligence sharing. Several other countries, referred to as "associates" were parties to the alliance, but they did not always benefit from the compulsory intelligence sharing arrangement that existed between the principles. The fact France was not even an associate member riled Laurent even more, and he made no attempts to hide his disdain for the Five Eyes alliance and its members. And the tenuous relationship between the two countries had only worsened since the election of President Madden, someone the French president had publicly referred to as a jingoist and corporate opportunist during the American presidential campaign.

But Carpenter had viewed the French as a fickle ally long before the current French president took up residence at the Palais de l'Élysée. He was of the view that the French only offered their full cooperation when their economic and diplomatic interests were in perfect alignment with those of the United States. And that opinion was not an offhanded perspective; it was rooted in personal experience. The current situation was eerily reminiscent of his very first assignment with the Counterterrorism Center as a paramilitary officer. He had been given orders to kill an Iranian military officer who had amassed an extensive resumé of terrorist actions against US interests over the course of several decades. When Carpenter finally tracked him down in the City of Light, the Quds Force commander was under the protection of French authorities. France was negotiating with him for the release of six French citizens being held captive in Lebanon by Hezbollah. Diplomatic efforts to convince the French to turn the man over to the United States failed and, following the release of the French citizens, the man was allowed to leave France under heavy protection. The last Carpenter knew, the man was back in Iran and still deeply engaged with Islamist extremists the world over. Next to Mumeet, there was no other terrorist Carpenter wanted to kill more than the Iranian. And Carpenter had never forgiven the French for denying him the opportunity.

"You know what I think, but it's your call," Carpenter finally said.

For his part, Patrick considered the relationship to be, in the most diplomatic terms, complex. To put it mildly, the French were parsimonious with intelligence. Laurent, in particular, operated with a "you first" mindset and, even when his possession of intelligence was undeniable, he often withheld key pieces of information. Still, the DGSE was an exceptional intelligence service and Laurent had showed signs of warming, particularly since the November 2015 Paris attacks. Patrick also knew that a changing political climate in France was working in their favor. The French president was sliding in the polls at a time when he would soon be required to call for parliamentary elections. The unseemly prospect of governing with a prime minister from a party not his own—a situation known in French politics as cohabitation—was real. Perhaps recognizing this, the French president had been using some uncharacteristically hawkish language in the early hours after the attack. Patrick sensed a change in attitude and expected Carpenter might receive greater assistance than he was anticipating. "We'll take whatever help we can get," Patrick said. "Pierre is coming around and I think we can count on the French when it matters, as it does now."

"I'll take your word for it but, for the record, I think we have to handle this as if we're on our own. We are, and will remain, the top target. I worry about France's commitment, especially beyond its own borders. No matter where the trail leads us, I don't want to have to rely on anyone else, especially the French."

"Duly noted," Patrick said.

"Has Doc gotten anything out of Kashif Isawi?" Carpenter was asking about the prisoner who had been secreted out of Tunisia to a clandestine black site in Poland. In this case, the interrogation was being conducted by Tim Durkin, a master interrogator and one-time intelligence officer. Durkin had earned the sobriquet "Doc" for his preternatural ability to get information out of anyone. Durkin eschewed the more aggressive tactics Carpenter favored, arguing that such methods were often counterproductive. Despite his misgivings, Carpenter had seen enough to concede that Durkin's unorthodox methods were quite often effective. If Isawi had any valuable information, Carpenter trusted that Doc Durkin would extract it.

"I spoke to Doc yesterday," Patrick said. "He's convinced Isawi doesn't know anything useful."

"Did Isawi talk?"

"Not at first but then he wouldn't shut up."

Patrick went on to explain how Durkin ignored Isawi until late the second day. When the interrogation finally began, Isawi refused to answer even basic questions, egging Durkin to torture him instead, so he could prove his resilience. Durkin told Isawi that he was too smart for torture, that he reserved that method for simpler men. As the questioning advanced, Durkin continued to play to Isawi's vanity, but the terrorist still refused to share any information. The charade continued into the late evening. By the next morning, Isawi seemed convinced he was outmaneuvering Durkin. Feigning capitulation to Isawi's superior mind, Durkin deftly pivoted and suggested they take a break from business and enjoy a game of backgammon. After three straight losses, Durkin sensed that Isawi was beginning to doubt his mental superiority. But rather than embarrass Isawi further, Durkin professed luck had simply been on his side. Durkin then seamlessly reverted to the three men who had stayed with Isawi and his brethren in Tunisia. Perhaps showing appreciation for Durkin's humility or realizing he could not outwit his interrogator or both, Isawi began to tell Durkin everything he knew.

Isawi said only he and the group's leader, Hammad Dhib, spoke with their three guests. Isawi and Dhib were told only a few days before to expect the men. He claimed that one of the three guests introduced himself as Ali and said he was an al Qaeda recruiter based in Syria. Ali's two companions never offered any names and spoke only to Ali, always out of earshot. Ali said that Tunisia was the last stop on a successful recruiting trip across North Africa. While he was there, Ali shared a few stories of his time in the Levant, including one that Isawi related to Durkin in great detail. One day, Ali said he was leaving to meet a boat that would take him back to Syria. Before leaving, Ali thanked his hosts and said it would not be long before the new recruits would carry out attacks against the West.

"Doc is convinced Isawi is telling the truth. He doesn't believe Isawi could have made up a tale with as much detail as Isawi provided. Doc said he's not smart enough. Isawi truly believes al-Rasheed was a recruiter on his way back to Syria."

"Didn't the Saudis tell us they suspected al-Rasheed had spent some time in Syria recently?" Carpenter asked.

"They did. And besides providing a credible reason that Isawi was able to relate detailed stories to Doc, it's one more piece of corroboration that al-Rasheed was in Tunisia."

"And Isawi pretty much gave the same story the kid gave about al-Rasheed's time in Tunisia," Carpenter said.

"That's another reason to believe Isawi was being truthful with Doc."

"But it sounds like Isawi is a dead end," Carpenter said.

"That about sums it up," Patrick said. "Doc Durkin is convinced Isawi didn't know al-Rasheed's true identity and doesn't know anything about future operations."

"Back to chasing our tails."

"Unfortunately. So what do you make of today's attack? Do you think it was an isolated incident or part of something larger?" Patrick asked.

"Too soon to tell but we have no reason to doubt Aziz," Carpenter said. "If we take him at his word, that was just the first one. However, I am taking some comfort that there hasn't been another attack in Paris today."

Carpenter's assessment was a woeful reminder of the sequential attacks in Minnesota. But that was not much comfort in light of Aziz's repeated claims that he intended to strike the West repeatedly. Before his most recent statement, some in the intelligence community had started to question whether Aziz could back up those claims but Carpenter had not been among them. "We're in a different game," he said. "Aziz is a sly fox. It's clear he's learned from past mistakes and has adjusted the playbook. We haven't picked up any insightful human or signals intelligence about any attacks or his whereabouts. He's running a tight ship. But he has to have the ability to communicate with the terrorists carrying out the attacks. Again, that tells me that the plans for Paris might have been made before he was on our radar. The burning questions I have are: did he make plans for more than one attack and, if so, how much time do we have before the next one? And right now, we don't have a clue."

Both men were frustrated by the lack of intelligence that might otherwise allow them to get in front of the problem. Using the few names and scraps of information currently available, the analysts were trying to assemble Aziz's Al-Kalafa network. But they had no idea if it was comprised of some former al Qaeda members or an entirely different group of unknown jihadists. Patrick and his team needed to start turning over every rock they could find.

"I want you to head to Paris. See what you can find—a name, anything to point us in the right direction," Patrick said. "I'll call Pierre and let him know I'm sending you over. I'll also offer to send a forensics team to help sort through the carnage."

Chapter 34
Luxembourg City

Sadiq bin Aziz stood with his hands resting on the back of the chair, fixated with the coverage from Paris that was being shown on three televisions arranged on the far wall of the den. Despite the warmth of the fireplace filling the cozy space, he could sense the hair on his neck and arms rise each time live pictures of the scene were shown. From his secure location from a little more than two hundred-thirty miles away, he almost felt as if he were an eyewitness to the chaos. Although it was not without peril, the electrifying feeling coursing through his body told him that his decision to come here had been the right one. It was an ideal location for monitoring the next phase of operations.

Paris was just the beginning and the triumph in the French capital instilled confidence that the attacks to follow would meet with equal success. As with everything he did, Aziz had meticulously planned this series of attacks many months earlier. In fact, some of the planning began well before the shura approved his plans for the attack in America and named him a coleader of their decaying terrorist organization.

Nearly two years before, while Aziz was attempting to persuade al Qaeda's senior leaders to adopt his strategy, Aziz dispatched his most dependable associate with specific instructions. The younger man was the perfect envoy. Besides his intelligence, loyalty, and zeal, he was a European by birth and had cut formal ties to Aziz years earlier. What's more, the man was from a respected family. In his three decades before he committed himself to jihad, the man had traveled frequently throughout the world for both business and pleasure. Because of the man's peripatetic history, Aziz had no concerns about sending him to the four corners of the world to assemble a network of committed followers.

By the time the shura finally relented and gave him approval to strike the Americans, Aziz knew his future needs for al Qaeda and its infrastructure were limited. His associate had established a federation of jihadists that provided Aziz with multiple sleeper cells on every continent except Antarctica. Later, he had secured the allegiance of Hamid Fahkoury when they were together in the Arabian Desert. It was an added bonus when Fahd al-Rasheed immediately followed suit. Having the Bringer of Death and his trusted friend in the fold emboldened Aziz to move forward with his plans more quickly than he expected he would have been able to. The already solid foundation for his own organization was even stronger, and he knew that as long as he positioned himself properly, he would not need al Qaeda much longer.

Now, as he soaked in the news from Paris, he had done just that. Although he would not announce it for days, it was the first operation conducted solely by members of Al-Kalafa. Aziz could not have been more pleased. The attack had been executed flawlessly, and it appeared that al-Rasheed remained at large. Aziz had briefly considered pulling al-Rasheed from the operation. He was concerned when US intelligence accurately identified al-Rasheed as one of the perpetrators of the US attacks. But Aziz knew how important this first operation was to his new organization. Before appointing someone else to lead the Paris attack, he wanted to know that it was necessary. So he directed al-Rasheed to follow a circuitous route on his journey from Morocco. Those plans were nearly upended when the sea captain was arrested in Algeria. He again considered shelving al-Rasheed. Fortunately, the network his associate had helped establish came through with alternate plans. Seeing the devastation on the television, he was glad he had stuck with his original decision.

Aziz began to think about the next operations in this preliminary round of attacks. The series was designed to build credibility and momentum. Paris had things off to a brilliant start and it appeared he still retained his most valuable asset from that operation. And if al-Rasheed was indeed alive and free, he would be on his way to meet up again with Aziz's main weapon. Then, al-Rasheed and the Bringer of Death would deliver a shocking blow the West would never forget.

Chapter 35
Paris

Carpenter arrived in Paris early the next morning and went straight from Roissy Airport to the *Centre Administratif des Tourelles*, codenamed CAT and otherwise known as the headquarters for the Directorate General for External Security. He had been to DGSE headquarters on several occasions but none in the past few years. When he arrived outside the gates, he took note of how DGSE headquarters blended in seamlessly with its urban location on the eastern edge of the Paris city limits, just as the Agency's headquarters in Langley resembled a typical business park in the States. He also noticed that the complex seemed considerably larger than it was on his last visit. He recalled that plans to move the headquarters to a new location were scrapped due to a lack of funding and intense public opposition. Instead, the DGSE was provided additional premises in front of the *Piscine des Tourelles* belonging to the national swimming federation. As a result, the sprawling compound was now as often referred to as *La Piscine*—the swimming pool—as it was CAT.

Once he was through security and inside the compound, Carpenter recognized a familiar face alongside DGSE Director Pierre Laurent. He had worked with Chloe Pelletier in Libya in early 2011. They were there as part of a coalition assembled to support a group of rebels attempting to overthrow Muammar Gaddafi. Carpenter and Pelletier were two of the six coalition members embedded with the insurgents in the area around Misrata. While the coalition's primary objective was to offer training and support, on several occasions Carpenter's team directly engaged with Libyan forces. It was during one of those skirmishes that Chloe Pelletier made a lasting impression on him.

Carpenter had run out into the street to rescue an injured rebel. The man was hiding behind a burned-out car when Carpenter heard his cries for help. The Libyan forces had noticed him too and were almost on top of him. Carpenter hastily arranged for covering fire before dashing twenty yards to the man's side. Carpenter was just beginning to assess the man's injuries when he noticed a figure out of the corner of his eye. It was Chloe, bravely running toward them amid heavy fire. An instant later, she slid in behind the car next to them and looked up at Carpenter. Her soft brown eyes are what he most remembered most from that moment—remarkably captivating and fearless. But it was only after they had moved the man to safety that Carpenter glimpsed the completeness of her beauty.

Twenty-four hours later, Carpenter left Libya. At the time, he was still struggling to overcome Lizzie's death. Those painful memories and the demands of his profession conspired to swiftly push Chloe from his thoughts. But as time gradually dulled his agony, he found himself thinking more and more about Chloe Pelletier. He wondered if she had felt something that day, like he had. As the years passed, he eventually wrote those thoughts off to whimsical fantasies that had helped him cope during a time of loneliness and suffering. Besides, he told himself, it was unlikely their paths would ever cross again.

Now seeing her once more, those feelings came flooding back. He marveled at how truly gorgeous she was without days of desert sand and the grime of war veiling her. Her long, light-brown hair was pulled back in a ponytail, fully exposing her alluring eyes and the provocative curve forming from the smile on her full lips. Ignoring Laurent's extended hand, Carpenter marched straight over to Chloe and, having to bend only slightly, kissed her on both cheeks, before embracing her with a hug that revealed she was still incredibly fit.

"Mademoiselle Pelletier told me you two were acquainted," Laurent said.

"Yes, we are, Monsieur Laurent," Carpenter said as he turned to Laurent and finally shook his hand. "I am sorry to be here under these circumstances."

"We thank you for coming Monsieur Carpenter," Laurent said. "We are most grateful for your assistance. And please call me Pierre."

"I appreciate that. Please call me PJ."

"Thank you," Laurent said. "Shall we go to my office where we can speak more freely?"

A few minutes later they were in Laurent's office. As he entered through the doorway in the center of the room, Carpenter was struck by the size and tasteful design. The lavish space was painted in a gray color scheme and furnished with a mix of classic and modern, luxe-looking pieces of furniture. A large chandelier hung from the high ceiling in the center of the room. To his left, and opposite an antique wooden desk, was a seating area. Arranged on top of a large Persian rug, featuring red and blue hues with gray undertones, was a contemporary white leather sofa. Fronting the sofa was a rectangular glass-top coffee table, upon which a porcelain coffee service had been placed. On either end of the coffee table stood a bergère chair made of a mahogany frame and upholstered with a deep red fabric. Laurent led them over to the seating area and motioned for Carpenter to sit on the sofa.

After he poured coffee for everyone, Laurent locked eyes with Carpenter and began the discussion. "Since you seem to speak it so well, shall we continue our discussion in French or would you prefer we switch to English?"

"I would actually like it if we continued in French. I don't get to speak it often and I could use the practice," Carpenter said.

"Very good," Laurent said. "PJ, I spoke with Monsieur Patrick earlier. I understand you may have some reservations about our commitment to confront this threat. Our president wanted me to assure you that our countries are in this together and to pledge our full cooperation."

Carpenter had spoken with Patrick shortly before landing. While Patrick declined to tell him exactly what he said to Laurent, Carpenter got the gist of it. Though he wasn't happy his boss had shared his lack of enthusiasm for working with the French, Carpenter knew Patrick was merely trying to ensure things got off to a good start. Besides, there really was no harm as

Carpenter believed in getting everything out in the open, anyway. "Since we are speaking with candor, I was a bit reluctant to meet with you. This is a vicious enemy we are confronting and nothing short of a full commitment to eliminate it is good enough. It just so happens that our new president sees things the same way. President Madden—who I know is not viewed favorably here in France—has made it very clear that the United States will no longer try to appease this enemy with soft talk or indifference. Rather it will defend itself vigorously and actively confront this threat with lethal force at every opportunity. In my view, these broad and bold strictures are welcome changes form the policies implemented by his predecessors. During the last decade, we pulled back at times when we could have crushed al Qaeda and later failed to recognize the emerging threat from the Islamic State. So far, this president seems intent on not repeating those mistakes. But while I cannot speak for the president, you should know that I have absolutely no interest working with anyone who does not fully appreciate this threat and have the resolve to eradicate it." He studied Laurent's reaction to his remarks. The security chief didn't seem offended. Still, Carpenter couldn't be sure Laurent wasn't merely giving lip service to this renewed spirit of cooperation. As he did always, he would assess commitment by actions.

"Once again, I can assure you that France's resolve is steadfast. By the latest count, eighty-one of our fellow citizens are dead and dozens more are severely injured in this most recent attack," Laurent said. "We will stop at nothing to bring the people behind this heinous attack to justice. We also recognize the roots of this problem extend beyond France's borders. France can no longer treat this as a domestic issue. It must and will combat this problem everywhere. It is a threat to all people of good will."

"That is good to hear," Carpenter said.

With that fresh start, Carpenter spent a few minutes telling the two French security professionals what little the US knew about Sadiq bin Aziz and the men who had carried out the attacks in the United States. He knew Patrick had already shared this information but it was a good exercise to underscore his own cooperation. He also explained in somewhat greater detail the current thinking that Aziz was breaking away from core al Qaeda and establishing his own terrorist group. He confessed that the United States was increasingly concerned and frustrated it had been unable to crack Aziz's new organization. The coordination and secrecy of communications, movement, and planning were unprecedented, leaving everyone feeling like sitting ducks for the attacks expected to come. "We have to work this from the bottom up," he said. "That is our best way to find and eliminate those at the top of this new organization. I am hoping, for everyone's benefit, that we might be able to find something here that begins to point us in the right direction."

"Thank you, PJ. Director Patrick shared much of that with me previously, but it was most helpful to hear it from you. Chloe, would you please share with PJ what we have uncovered to date?"

Pelletier nodded confirmation and turned in her chair slightly so that she faced Carpenter. "As Pierre mentioned, the death toll is rising. By the early indications, most died from gunshot wounds, but a significant percentage died from burn injuries. Two primary explosions, originating from two stolen delivery vans at either end of the tunnel, subsequently triggered several uninvolved vehicle explosions. The accelerant for the primary explosions was basic automobile petrol, as it was for the succeeding explosions. The vans were completely destroyed, and there is also little left of the automobiles, or those inside them, that were closest to the original explosions. Fortunately, the most intense aspects of the fire did not penetrate the entire length of the tunnel. Although there were fatalities among those deeper inside, all of the survivors were positioned near the center of the tunnel. We have been able to take statements from several survivors. They all report the same version of events. Two white vans were involved in the attack. One stopped close to the tunnel exit and the other close to the westbound entrance. Men filed out of each van and began shooting with automatic rifles. All five terrorists perished in the fire. As of this moment, we still do not know the names of the men involved in the attack or the identities of anyone who may have been directing them."

Carpenter had come to France determined to find even the smallest opening into Aziz's network. Although appreciated, the information shared by Laurent and Pelletier did not add to what Carpenter already knew. He had been briefed by Patrick on largely the same information before he left. He was hoping the French had made some progress identifying the terrorists. It sounded like that would only be possible, if at all, through DNA testing, dental, and medical records. Right now, the terrorists who carried out the attack remained a blind alley to Aziz's network. But there were other possibilities. How they acquired the instruments used in the attack was one such avenue. By backtracking, they might be able to uncover a key link in the network that would lead them to Aziz. "How about the weapons? Have you been able to get any serial numbers or other identifiers?" he asked.

"Unfortunately, no. The markings were removed and, if the past is any guide, they were likely purchased in the Balkans or in Slovakia."

The weapons used in the attack were readily available on the black markets in those countries and untraceable. Another dead end. That left the vans and the one possibility that had interested Carpenter most. "Has anyone been back to speak with the delivery company since the vans were reported stolen?"

"No one from our office has yet to visit the delivery company. We only matched the vehicle identification numbers to the stolen vans last night, after business hours," Laurent said. "I did provide Director Patrick with a copy of the police report. Did he share it with you?"

"He did, but the report raises some issues."

"Chloe spoke with the investigating police officer last night and learned more information than is contained in the report. Chloe, would you please share that with PJ?"

"The vans were new additions to the fleet. They had yet to be put into use and were parked in an unsecured lot adjacent to the main facility, outside the range of the company's security cameras. There was no room to keep the new vans inside the company's fenced compound. The company is using its current fleet of vans until the end of this month when they will be sold in a pre-arranged transaction. The owner did not want to use the new vans until then in order to save on wear and tear. Utilizing the older vans also avoided the expense of carrying unneeded vehicles on the company's insurance policy."

Since Patrick had supplied him with a copy of the police report before he left Langley, Carpenter had been able to follow up on something in it that had intrigued him. What he learned added credence to his developing theory that there was a connection between the delivery company and Aziz. "Did I read on the report that the police recovered all the key fobs for the vans?" Carpenter asked.

"Yes, the police kept them for evidence."

"Do you know where the police found them?"

"All the fobs were still in the manager's office when the theft was reported," Pelletier said.

"Does the company have any suspects in mind?" Carpenter asked.

"According to the policeman, the owner has no idea who might have stolen the vans. Apparently, the business has had only one other crime incident. It occurred a few years ago when the office was broken into and some cash was taken, about two thousand euros."

"Did the policeman speak with the manager?"

"He said the same thing," Pelletier said. "He does not know how the vans were stolen."

"Have you checked out all the other employees? Do any of them have a criminal history?" Carpenter asked.

"Only minor traffic infractions," Pelletier said.

"Any on your watch list?"

"No and we have not found that any employee has a connection to any person on the watch list," Laurent said.

Carpenter was surprised by that answer. He knew the number of people on France's terrorism watch list approached twenty thousand, a number that surely included many with absolutely no connection to extremism. But it gave more weight to his theory. Aziz had proven himself a careful planner. Carpenter didn't believe in coincidences, and his gut told him there was a reason Aziz had chosen this particular delivery company. "I'd like to visit the delivery company. Can we do that?"

"Of course," Laurent said. "It is located near Roissy Airport. Chloe will take you there. Before you go, I must request that you keep things at a conversational level. If you find that circumstances may warrant law enforcement intervention, please coordinate with me so that I can arrange for the proper authorities to assist. We are treating this as a criminal matter as well as a security matter and we must take precautions to ensure that lines are not crossed."

That would not be an issue, Carpenter assured him. Based on the recap provided by Pelletier, he was confident the French authorities had asked all the right questions. The answers he wanted could only be learned by getting the lay of the land and making his own assessment of who he suspected might be the first new link to Aziz's network.

Chapter 36

The delivery company's headquarters were located less than a mile from Charles de Gaulle Airport, as Roissy Airport was otherwise known. Carpenter and Pelletier headed out in her Renault Zoe. The metallic gray interior of the compact car offered limited space, even for two physically-fit adults. And the proximity of the electric blue seats practically put them on top of one another, a situation that Carpenter did not find at all objectionable.

Along the way, they avoided topics relating to work and instead chatted about what they had each been up to since Libya. Outside of classified matters, there wasn't much for Carpenter to share so he kept the conversation focused on Chloe. He learned that she had recently divorced. The marriage had lasted less than two years. She had caught her ex-husband, an anesthesiologist, having an affair with two other women who worked at the same hospital. When Chloe confronted him, her ex-husband acted almost elated. The decision to end the marriage had not been difficult, she said. After Chloe finished recounting her marital troubles, the conversation meandered to less personal matters. They were lamenting the emerging popularity of US reality shows in France when Chloe guided the electric car into a visitor parking space.

Just before they opened the doors, Chloe turned slightly toward him and placed her right hand on the back of his left shoulder. "It is so good to see you again, PJ," she said. "I wondered what happened to you after Libya. I was hoping our paths would have crossed sooner."

As Chloe started speaking, Carpenter's eyes instinctively went to the developing breach in her blouse, exposing parts of a nude lace bra and the ample left breast contained in it. He nonchalantly raised his eyes as if they had not seen anything, let alone lingered for the time they had. When he finally met her gaze, she displayed a coquettish smile. He tried to hide his embarrassment as he scrambled to think of something to say. "Maybe we can grab a drink and catch up sometime after things quiet down." *Wow, that's the best you got?*

"I will hold you to that," Chloe said. She smiled and then lightly kissed him on the lips before getting out of the car.

The kiss discomfited him further. Still, he wasn't sure he was reading the situation correctly. As he alighted from the car, he did know for certain that the whole affair had caused him to lose focus, and he hoped the effects were not too obvious. He walked behind the car and paused long enough for Chloe to start toward the building. When her back was to him, he sheepishly glanced down to make sure he didn't need to make any further adjustments and then stepped from behind the car and followed her up the path.

Once inside, they were escorted to the office of Jacques Fabron, sole owner of the *Service Rapide* delivery company. After Chloe announced herself to Fabron, she introduced Carpenter as Monsieur Smith, a liaison from the United States. Fabron gripped Carpenter in a firm handshake and then invited his guests to sit down in the two plastic chairs in front of his disorderly metal desk. Fabron reminded Carpenter of Rich Uncle Pennybags of Monopoly fame. Even without the top hat, the resemblance was uncanny. The portly Fabron was on the shorter side of average and had the same white hair and bushy mustache as the board game's mascot. Fabron's secretary abruptly distracted Carpenter from those puerile thoughts when she returned with bottles of water for everyone.

When the secretary left and the door closed behind her, Fabron put on a serious look. With his elbows resting on the cluttered desk, he leaned forward in his chair and went into a lengthy expression of horror that vans belonging to his company had been used in the heinous attack, proceeding to condemn it and the perpetrators for several minutes. He followed up with an impassioned and enlightened argument against the government's misguided policies that resulted in a sense of hopelessness among a considerable portion of the population. Once he finished with his homily, Fabron pledged his full cooperation and asked how he could be of assistance.

When Fabron finally yielded the floor, Carpenter stuck to the investigation playbook. He started by asking Fabron some contextual questions. He learned the company had been in business for thirty-four years and currently had eighty-seven employees. Fabron explained his company provided delivery services throughout France, mostly for packages originating in the Paris metropolitan area. Fabron reiterated that none of his employees had a criminal record. He said a clean criminal record was a condition of employment, and he utilized a third party to vet every new hire. Fabron was proud to call Service Rapide a family business and said he fostered an environment that encouraged longevity. Turnover was extremely low, he claimed. In fact, the shortest tenure among his employees was more than two years.

When Fabron finished praising his employees, Carpenter was ready to fly a little closer to his target. He had homed in on the man before leaving the United States, the result of some research and consultation with an expert. Before leaving Langley, he had a chance to ask the CTC's resident technology expert, Kevin Lingel, about keyless technology. It was after hearing Lingel's explanation that Carpenter believed he was on the right track. But it was simply a working theory, and one he had chosen to keep to himself until it had more support. "When the vans are not being used, where are the keys kept," he asked.

"When they are not being used, the keys are kept in the manager's office. His name is Adam Alawi. The police also spoke to him the other day. Adam has been with us for eleven years. He is a good employee and a fine man," Fabron said.

Background on Alawi was some of the research Carpenter had gathered before leaving for Paris. That Alawi was of Moroccan descent was only of marginal interest. But it was a fact that could not be ignored. Although the French Republic considered ethnic and religious affiliation a private matter, it was estimated that more than six million of its residents—nearly ten percent of the total population—were from the Maghreb, a region in northern Africa with strong affiliations to extremism. Alawi's ethnicity took on greater relevance in light of his access to the keys for the fleet of vans, a fact Carpenter had gleaned from the police report. The two late-model vans in question were equipped with keyless ignition systems. He knew from

Lingel that hotwiring a keyless ignition automobile was possible but very difficult. The process required a high degree of technical proficiency and substantially more time than needed with older cars. These factors had combined to put Alawi in his crosshairs. Now he wanted to make sure he was on the right track before sharing his theory with Patrick and, possibly, the French. "Is Monsieur Alawi's office locked when he is not here?" he asked.

"Yes, at all times."

"Am I correct that only you and Monsieur Alawi have keys to his office?" Carpenter asked.

"Yes."

"Did Monsieur Alawi mention anything unusual about his office that morning? Perhaps some sign that someone might have broken into it?"

"He did not see any signs of a break in," Fabron said.

Carpenter paused, pretending he was hearing this information for the first time. "Would it be possible for me to speak with Monsieur Alawi?"

Fabron answered the question by picking up the phone and instructing his secretary to ask Alawi to report to his office. While they waited, Carpenter asked some stock questions about the delivery business. Fabron was explaining how technology was changing the competitive landscape when he motioned for someone to come in. Carpenter swiveled in his chair and saw a rail-thin, clean-cut man of about forty peering through the glass door. Alawi entered the cramped space and stood off to the side of Fabron's desk. He forced a smile when Fabron introduced him to Carpenter and Pelletier. Carpenter rose to greet him. Alawi quietly uttered hello as Carpenter maneuvered around the chair and extended his hand. He found Alawi's slender hand warm and clammy. He also noted the rapid blinking in Alawi's left eye.

As Carpenter prepared to engage with Alawi, he recognized that he needed Fabron's continued cooperation. Since the man clearly cared about his employees, there was a risk Fabron might put an end to what he perceived to be an interrogation. So he asked a few innocuous questions to put both Alawi and Fabron at ease. Alawi told the visitors he had not seen any suspicious characters in the days before the thefts. He also confirmed he had not noticed anything strange or disturbed in his office the morning he discovered that two new vans were missing. Alawi said everything looked as it had the night before when he locked up. "It is a real mystery," Carpenter offered. "I think the only other thing I would like to do is see where the keys are kept and where the vans were parked when they were stolen. Mr. Fabron, thank you for your time. We will let you return to your business if Mr. Alawi would show us around."

"As I said before Monsieur Smith, I am here to help. Adam will show you whatever you want to see," Fabron said.

Chapter 37

"Let's go to your office first," Carpenter said to Alawi as the trio walked down the hall away from Fabron's office. He wanted to examine the construction of the office and its proximity to the auxiliary lot where the new vans were stored. This information would tell him how much conviction to place with his doubts about Alawi.

According to the police report, the vans were equipped with keyless start technology, and the key fobs for the two vans were still in Alawi's office when the police conducted their initial investigation. The theory was that the thieves—that term was used as it was not certain that the terrorists had initially stolen the vans—used a so-called relay attack device to unlock the van doors and start the vehicles. Carpenter had learned from Kevin Lingel that the device was originally developed by a European company to provide auto manufactures with the ability to test the vulnerability of keyless ignition systems. The misuse had only manifested itself recently and no one knew how many different varieties of the relay attack device were out there. This meant that the full capabilities of the subversive technology were also unknown. But, after speaking with Lingel, Carpenter had a good sense of what was possible and what was myth.

Lingel had told him that keyless technology utilizes simple radio frequencies to transmit a signal from the key fob to the car. The keyless technology does not measure the distance of the fob from the car, rather it measures the strength of the signal. That signal can be amplified and captured—a "relay attack" in electronics jargon. Once captured, the signal is stored by the relay attack device and used to trick the car's keyless technology into thinking the actual key fob is nearby.

However, for this hack to work, the boxy device must first be able to acquire the key fob's signal. And that is especially difficult when the key fob is in some sort of Faraday cage. It was for that reason that some insurance companies were telling their insureds to hide idle key fobs in their freezers to thwart potential wrongdoers. This information added to Carpenter's suspicions about an inside job and a possible lead into Aziz's network. And what he had learned since he and Pelletier had arrived had only strengthened his hunch.

When he and Pelletier pulled into Service Rapide's offices, they drove through an opening in the fence that surrounded the three sides of the premises Carpenter was able to see. He estimated the building was approximately one hundred feet wide and stood back at least seventy feet from the fence at the entrance. The distance between the fence and either side of the building was not as great, perhaps thirty feet. Looking at the front of the building, he looked to his right and saw the supplemental lot where the new vans were being stored, just on the other side of the fence. Recalling what Lingel had told him, he deemed it possible that someone standing in the auxiliary lot would be well within the hundred-foot range necessary to capture a key fob signal with a relay attack device. But that was a clear-sight range, Lingel told him. The CTC technical expert said that any type of metal barrier would impede the device's ability to function. Carpenter assumed that limiting characteristic would also include the corrugated metal that covered the exterior of the building. That meant whoever captured the key fob signal likely had access to the building. Although all eighty-seven employees had that access, Carpenter remained focused on one of them.

Now that man was leading him and Pelletier down the hall to his office. Alawi led them to an enclosed space in the back two-thirds of the building. A wall separated the office area at the front of the building from the garage area in back. Alawi's office was located toward the center of the garage area, butted up against the separation wall. The small office was enclosed by sheetrock with the exception of the half-glass wall on the side overlooking the garage. Carpenter estimated that the location of Alawi's office put it at least eighty feet from the fence or close to the known range of a relay attack device.

"Where do you keep the keys for the van?" Carpenter asked.

"They are kept in this cabinet," Alawi said as he walked over to a metal locker and opened the door.

Carpenter saw dozens of regular keys hanging on hooks, underneath a label denoting the corresponding van's number. "None of these are key fobs," he said. "Where are the keys for the new vans?"

"They are in the box at the bottom of the cabinet," Alawi said.

"Have they always been stored inside the cabinet?"

"Yes, I placed them there when the vans arrived several weeks ago."

"Could anyone from the company come into your office without your knowledge?"

"No. I am required to lock my office when I leave."

"Have you had any visitors—not fellow employees—in your office since the new vans arrived?"

"Yes, a parts salesman was here yesterday."

"Anyone else?"

"Not that I recall."

Carpenter noticed that Alawi appeared to be very tense. For the most part, Alawi stood rigidly behind his desk and avoided eye contact with him and Pelletier. Although it was not uncommon for someone being questioned by the authorities, Alawi's behavior was telling. Adding to Carpenter's growing certainty was that the police's theory about a relay attack device was not holding water. Unless Lingel was not up on the latest technology—something Carpenter seriously doubted—he knew he had found a link to Aziz's network, but he wanted to keep Alawi thinking he was in the clear. They needed time to put surveillance in place before Alawi raised any alarm. "Thank you, Monsieur Alawi, you have been most helpful. Please let us know if you remember anything you think might be of interest. Mademoiselle Pelletier and I will see ourselves out and have a look at the auxiliary lot on the way to our car. Have a pleasant day."

He and Pelletier retraced their steps down the hallway toward the front of the building. They stopped at Fabron's office to extend their gratitude and say goodbye, but he was not there. That circumstance made Carpenter's gambit that much easier. He walked over the secretary and asked if Fabron had left. She confirmed he had and they continued toward the exit. When he reached the door, Carpenter spun around and turned to the secretary, as if just remembering something. "I am sorry, but I forgot to ask Monsieur Alawi for his phone number before he left to meet with one of the drivers. Would you be able to give it to me in case we have any more questions?"

"But of course," the secretary said.

A minute later, they were in Pelletier's car. After Carpenter shared his theory about Alawi, Pelletier was on the phone with Laurent. Carpenter had already sent a short note and Alawi's phone number in a text to Patrick by the time Pelletier ended the call.

"We cannot eavesdrop on Alawi's calls until we get permission from the select committee established to rule on those requests," Pelletier reported. She did not expect it to be a problem but, if it was denied, Laurent was prepared to take it to the president. "I was in a meeting with Laurent and the president yesterday. It is true what Laurent said about our commitment. The president told us to do what was necessary to get everyone responsible for the attack. It was long overdue, but I think this playboy is finally getting it," she said. "But Laurent said we can start searching the metadata right away. We can search the databases for all texts and phone calls Alawi has made from that number."

Carpenter knew France had beefed up its large-scale data competencies. While they fell short of US levels, France now ranked fifth in the world in terms of metadata collection. And the DGSE was the agency in charge of the program. The supercomputer intelligence center occupied three levels in the basement of DGSE headquarters and was capable of processing and storing dozens of petabytes of data collected from twenty or so interception sites located on national and overseas territory. While he welcomed the assistance, Carpenter did not expect to need it. He was confident the National Security Agency would find some hits in short order. And from there, Patrick and the team at CTC should be able to start building out Aziz's network.

Chapter 38
Langley

Following her meeting with Patrick and Carpenter to discuss the latest statement from Aziz, Samantha Lane had requested permission to add a member to the team. They had just agreed Al-Kalafa was almost certainly a new terror group, operating independently of al Qaeda and under Aziz's exclusive control. Up to that point, they had been under the assumption Aziz was working within the al Qaeda architecture, which was at least somewhat known to the US intelligence community. But they had no idea what the Al-Kalafa organizational chart looked like. That was something they had to figure out quickly. The top-down approach of hunting Aziz, Mumeet, and al-Rasheed was not getting them anywhere. Outside of the probable sighting of Fahd al-Rasheed in Tunisia, they hadn't been able to source any actionable intelligence. Lane agreed with Carpenter that they needed to shift gears and attack Aziz and Al-Kalafa from another angle. The hope was they could get to the people at the top by first building out the network from the ground up. So, when Lane later requested to onboard an expert in social networking analysis, Patrick gave her the greenlight.

Permission in hand, Lane immediately approached Leo Mezzrow for help. Mezzrow was a Deputy Director and head of the Agency's Directorate of Analysis, or DA in Agency parlance. Prior to joining the Agency almost two decades earlier, Director Mezzrow headed up the sociology department at the University of Pennsylvania. While there, he helped usher in a new era of network science. Mezzrow was regarded as one of the leading scholars on social network analysis, a mathematical method to map and measure complex, and sometimes covert, human groups and organizations. The origins of social network analysis, or SNA, drew on the work of Stanley Milgram, who famously conducted an experiment to understand the connections among random people. Milgram's ground-breaking research demonstrated that any two people could be connected by six or fewer acquaintances. Years later, Milgram's "six degrees of separation" concept was adopted for the parlor game "Six Degrees of Kevin Bacon," in which the actor could be linked to any other actor or actress through six or fewer films.

When social network analysis garnered the attention of the intelligence community following the 9/11 attacks, the Agency asked Mezzrow to come aboard. Out of his sense of duty and patriotism, Mezzrow promptly left his cushy job in academia. But he continued to teach part-time at Penn, and three years earlier, Mezzrow was able to convince one of his former and best students to leave a lucrative job in the private sector. It was not a difficult sale. Mezzrow was a legend and had been the man's favorite professor at Penn. The former student gladly accepted the opportunity to work with Mezzrow and the challenge of integrating SNA into the Agency's intelligence work. Consequently, when Lane approached him, Mezzrow knew exactly who to recommend for the job.

Shortly after Carpenter texted Patrick with Alawi's number, Lane gathered her team in the ancillary conference room. It was located across the hall from the one they had been using as an operations center since the days before the attacks in Minnesota. Other than eight wheeled office chairs backed up against the walls, the twelve-foot square room contained no other items or furniture. The small space was useless for anything other than meetings like this, but it offered the full team an opportunity to assemble without having to look around computers and through the phone and high-speed cable wires hanging from the ceiling in the operations center.

After the newest member arrived and began moving toward one of the two unoccupied chairs on the far wall, Lane closed the door and faced the team. "Now that everyone is here, let's get started," she said. "I first want to ask TimJoe Hanson, who joins us from the Directorate of Analysis to introduce himself. TimJoe?"

As Hanson sat down, the other members of the team shifted their attention from Lane to the newcomer taking a seat at the back of the room. There were all types working at the Agency and each person had an individual style of clothing, but most tended to favor one conventional look or another. While the striking duo of Samantha Lane and Ella Rock could preside over a high-powered corporate board meeting on a moment's notice, the original male members of the team had their own styles of business casual attire. CTC technology analyst Kevin Lingel preferred polyester pants and short-sleeved Oxford shirts. The choice of style seemed almost intentional, as if it was designed to conform to the technology geek stereotype, but the most physically fit member of the team somehow made it seem mainstream. In contrast, Blake Palmer of the NSA was an athleisure devotee and his wardrobe of functional fitness wear seemed to include every item ever made by the leading yoga clothing company. Targeting analyst Dalton Jones varied his sartorial ways, alternating widely between contractor chic and modern prepster.

Yet the new guy Hanson was clearly different. His spiked, platinum-blonde hair was an obvious differentiator, as was the mixture of philosophical and spiritual quote tattoos covering both arms, beginning at the wrists and extending underneath the short sleeves of the vintage rock band tee-shirt he was wearing. And Hanson pulled the look together with neon blue, thick-framed hipster eyeglasses and distressed black skinny jeans and white canvas high-top sneakers.

Even before Hanson arrived it was already an outwardly eclectic group, but each member possessed razor-sharp intellect and a fierce determination to defend their country. As they turned toward him, the original team members assumed Hanson was now part of the team for the same reasons.

"Thank you, Samantha," Hanson said. "I know my name might seem a bit unusual, so I usually get that out the way first. I was named after my daddy. My mamma started using my middle name to avoid confusion. I guess she tired of always saying 'Timothy Joseph' so she shortened it when I was about four years old and people have been using it since. The two names are combined into one word and both names are capitalized, if anyone is wondering. Anyway, I've been with the Directorate of Analysis for a little more than three years and I specialize in network science. I'll pause there until Sam asks me to explain how we will use social network analysis to get the guys you're after." He looked to Lane to indicate he was finished.

"Yes, we will get into that shortly. Thank you, TimJoe," Lane said.

"Where are you from TimJoe?" Dalton Jones asked. As the only Southerner in the group, the Georgian was intrigued by Hanson's accent.

"I'm from Purvis, Mississippi, a little town outside Hattiesburg. My parents were both professors at the state university," Hanson said.

"Well, it's good to have some more Southern hospitality on the team," Jones said.

"Thanks, it's good to be here," Hanson said.

"OK, let's get started, shall we?" Lane said to the group. "Until recently, we had assumed Sadiq bin Aziz was part of al Qaeda. Now we believe Aziz has separated from AQ and is moving forward with his own group of jihadists under the name of Al-Kalafa. We are pretty confident Aziz is working with Mumeet and his cohort Fahd al-Rasheed. Other than those three, we know nothing about the other members of Al-Kalafa. We also have no idea where Aziz is hiding or where Mumeet and al-Rasheed are planning to attack next. While we will continue to hunt those three down, we will be pursuing a parallel track to expose Aziz's Al-Kalafa network. If we can identify even low-level Al-Kalafa members, it might help us in our efforts to kill or capture Aziz and his two commanders. I asked TimJoe to join our team to help us put together an organizational chart for Al-Kalafa. As TimJoe mentioned, he specializes in network science and analysis. Okay TimJoe, please explain how SNA is going to help us on this project."

"Social network analysis is an emerging method to unlock the organizational structure of covert groups like intelligence agencies and terrorist groups," Hanson said. "At the outset, it might help your understanding if we compare it to a road system around a major city. Imagine being a first-time visitor to a large metropolitan area and being without a map to help you get around. Now imagine you are dropped off on a secondary road somewhere out in the boondocks, far from the city center. You know there is a downtown and you want to get there but you have no idea how you're going to do it. What do you do? Well, you have to figure out if that secondary road you're on will lead you to a main road that will lead you into downtown. That is the situation we have here.

"We now have a name to work with—Adam Alawi, manager with Service Rapide and a person with access to the key fobs for the stolen vans. We suspect that Alawi is somehow tied into Sadiq bin Aziz's new terror group, Al-Kalafa. Right now, we assume Alawi is a secondary road, perhaps one that connects to a main road, but we don't know for sure. We can determine his importance by uncovering and analyzing the strength of his personal contacts. Strength is assessed by how often he communicates or meets with his contacts. Some of his contacts may not have any connection to terrorism. We call those 'accidental contacts.' Others may be more suspicious, if not clearly associated with extremism. Those are 'intentional contacts.' As we discover Alawi's intentional contacts, we include them in the analysis. Then we probe each of Alawi's intentional contacts. As we repeat this process over and over, we add the intentional contacts of Alawi's intentional contacts until a picture of Al-Kalafa comes into focus.

"During this process, we will begin to see clusters of strong links emanating from certain people. We call those people 'connectors.' They are the main roads in our map analogy. The people around those connectors with weak links are secondary players; the secondary roads in our analogy. As more and more relationships are uncovered, we will see the relationships between connectors. The stronger the links a connector has, the closer that connector is to the top. This picture, or map, will ultimately lead us to Sadiq bin Aziz and his top commanders, including Mumeet and Fahd al-Rasheed."

"How do we keep track of all this information?" Ella Rock asked.

"I will plug the information we gather into software that I have specifically developed for this purpose," Hanson said. "The software will create and continuously update a chart that includes every person we uncover. On that chart, lines will link people who share a relationship. The stronger the ties, the thicker that line will be. People with a lot of thick lines linked to them are the connectors. The software will also allow us to monitor activity within the network. A spike in network activity may indicate that an attack is being planned or getting close to execution. It will also show us when new links are created within the network, potentially revealing plans for a new attack or some other key event."

"And we can start this with just Adam Alawi?" Kevin Lingel asked.

"Yes, now that we have the phone number of a suspected conspirator in the Paris attack, our first step will be to use all intelligence collection methods to identify Adam Alawi's known acquaintances. But the effectiveness of this process will be determined by the quality and quantity of the intelligence we gather." Hanson stopped briefly to allow the information to sink in. "Are there any more questions?"

When there were none, Lane said, "Thank you, TimJoe. Dalton has been working the top-down analysis, trying to determine who Aziz might be working with besides Mumeet and al-Rasheed, and he will continue that work. Beginning with Alawi and the contacts in his phone, TimJoe's methodology will allow the rest of us to work up from the bottom of the Al-Kalafa organization. Working those two paths in concert, we will be able to connect all the dots of the Al-Kalafa network. And, as each new person in the network is identified and located, Director Patrick will make a decision whether to kill that person or watch them further in hopes of discovering additional members of the Al-Kalafa organization. The expertise of everyone here will be needed. Ella understands terror groups and how they communicate and plan. That knowledge will help us distinguish patterns that are suggestive of hierarchy and attack planning. Kevin will help us recognize and tap into the Agency's technology capabilities, and Blake will use the information we gather to scour NSA's metadata and leverage its eavesdropping capabilities. TimJoe will assemble the emerging network with his software, while I make sure all of the information we gather, including whatever Dalton discovers, makes it into the social network analysis.

"Kevin and Blake, I want you guys to start with Alawi's phone. To start, identify all of his contacts and every number he has called during the past six months. Ella, you and I will use all open-source information to add any connections that Alawi might have outside those in his phone records. As we get information, we will feed it to TimJoe, who will plug it into the software he has created. Okay everyone, let's get to work."

Chapter 39
Alcoy, Spain

The next morning, the party atmosphere in this small industrial and university city in southeastern Spain was in full swing for the Festival of Moors and Christians. Of the many similar festivals that have taken place throughout Valencia since the end of the Reconquista, none were more popular and renowned than the one in this festal city that once stood at the border of Muslim-held territories. In a tradition dating to the sixteenth century, the festival was held around the Feast of Saint George, the city's patron saint whose miraculous appearance spurred the Christians to victory in the decisive battle that finally secured the city from Muslim control in 1276.

The highly-anticipated annual carnival is a sort of reconciliation but mostly a celebration of Valencia's Moorish roots and Christian heritage. The three-day party, which begins with a series of spectacular parades on the first day, special processions and masses honoring Saint George on the second and concludes on the third day with a reenactment of the famous battle seven centuries ago, dominates the social calendars of the city's inhabitants. The year-round preparations are testament to the event's cultural significance in Alcoy, and a key reason it has been recognized as a Fiesta of International Tourist Interest by the Spanish government. Unlike last year, glorious weather was forecasted, news that contributed to an expected record number of spectators to go along with the thousands of locals already participating in the ceremonies. Hopes were high that this year's festival would be among the best in memory.

The first day of the festival—*Dia de las Entradas*—had begun earlier that morning with *La Diana*—the military call to wake up the inhabitants and commence the first procession. Before darkness lifted on the clear eastern horizon, the first of nearly three dozen factions of Moors and Christians—known as *filaes*—began strolling through the ancient city, all decked out in extravagant Medieval costumes. In addition to the five thousand participants, a host of horses, camels, cows, geese, and even a few elephants added to the stirring pomp and majesty of the opening ceremony.

Shortly after the La Diana procession began, four men weaved along the outer fringes of the onlookers who were packed up against the orange-painted metal barricades that lined the narrow streets. Above them, as many more as could be accommodated filled the balconies and windows of the multiple-level buildings outlining the route. The gentle fluttering sounds in the pre-dawn breeze of thousands of white flags bearing the red cross of Saint George and an equal number of Baroque green pennants with the crescent moon of Islam were replaced by the constant beating of kettledrums, blaring of trumpets, and reports of harquebuses as each association passed by. To show their appreciation for each group and express their choices for the coveted best costume awards handed out at the end of the festival, the spectators cheered and unleashed a blizzard of confetti on the performers.

But these four men were not in Alcoy to celebrate. Their interest did not reside in a battle from seven hundred years ago, but rather, the one they were about to advance. They made their way along the parade route before taking up positions near the Plaza de España. From the back of the crowd, they shuffled their feet to ward off the brisk early morning temperature, and waited for La Diana to end. When the last of the *comparses* of Moor soldiers was out of sight and the smell of gunpowder was drifting away on the light breeze, the crowd began to thin. The men used the opportunity to take up assigned positions along the metal barricades, where they would patiently wait for the *Entradas* to begin.

After a brief interlude following the two-hour La Diana procession, the city was preparing to welcome the arrivals into the city of the Christian and

Moorish armies. In keeping with tradition, the Christian armies would be the first to enter the city. Right on schedule, music and gunshots were heard in the distance, followed by a deafening roar. The entrance of the Christians had begun.

The four men knew it would not be long now. As spectators began lining up, they held their positions along the temporary fence on Calle de San Nicolás, and steeled themselves for what was to come.

Chapter 40

Forty-five minutes later, the men were being pressed against the barricades as everyone maneuvered for position to see the captain of the Christian army leading his men in tight formation down Calle de San Nicolás and into Plaza de España. Each one of the imitation soldiers was wearing deep red velvet vests over light gray tunics and linen hosen, and carrying pointed gold-painted shields adorned with the black silhouette of a war eagle. In addition to the sword hanging from his waist, each soldier also carried a handheld weapon of choice. The soldiers maintained a momentary air of seriousness as they approached this momentous point in the parade. When the first few rows of the platoon had moved into the square, the captain halted the march. The foot soldiers remained perfectly still as the cavalry men moved to the head of the unit. A thunderous roar erupted from the crowd of onlookers. The soldiers broke their standstill and surrendered to elation, raising their faux swords, battle axes, and spears to the adoring crowd. The feverous pitch echoing down the street and around the square built even more as the governor slowly moved toward the captain and prepared to ceremoniously hand over the keys to the castle.

Amid this euphoria, the interlopers' leader subtlety signaled across the street to his two comrades posted there. The third man, standing near the leader but slightly closer to the plaza and behind the last row of the soldiers, also saw the signal. All four jihadists simultaneously jumped over the waist-high pedestrian barricades and rushed toward the rear of section of the mock military unit. The soldiers, who had been looking forward and skyward at the spectators, never saw the terrorists coming at them, or the six-inch combat knives each concealed at his side. Before anyone realized what was happening, the attackers started slashing the soldiers with the razor-sharp knives, moving systematically forward on opposite edges of the tightly-packed, unsuspecting group of role-playing actors. For the briefest instant, the nearby spectators assumed this was all part of the show, and they began cheering wildly. But at the first sight of blood, a collective gasp replaced cheering. Almost instantly, wails and shrieks filled the air. As other soldiers turned to check on the commotion behind them, the attackers continued their slaughter, stabbing them in the face, chest, and flailing arms. Several of the soldiers swung their blunted costume weaponry at their assailants, only to discover they were no deterrent to the determined madmen. As more soldiers fell to the ground, others began to run.

An elderly woman on one of the balconies watched in horror as one of the attackers grabbed a soldier from behind and ripped a knife across the actor's throat. She saw a second attacker on the far side of the street wildly swinging his knife in a semi-circle at the fleeing soldiers, while two other attackers followed more actors down the street and pounced on the wounded lying on the ground. The woman tried to scream a warning but found she could not make a sound. She was about to look away when she noticed one brave soul, and then other spectators, push through the barricade and surround the attacker immediately below her. Four men pummeled the assailant with feet, hands, and the soldiers' discarded ersatz weapons until the assailant was no longer moving. On the opposite side of the street, more bystanders knocked down the barricade and ambushed a second attacker. Further into the square, the soldiers had regrouped and initiated a counterattack on the final two assailants. More spectators rushed to their aid.

But when the massacre ended less than four minutes later, all the terrified woman could see through her tears was blood pooling on the cobblestones, oozing from too many motionless bodies for her to count.

Chapter 41
Hammond, Indiana

Shortly after noon on what was shaping up to be a glorious Saturday, Saleem Nasir was examining the seam he had just soldered onto a cone-shaped piece of copper. Satisfied that the integrity of the seam was strong enough to maintain the tapered shape of the pliable metal, Nasir began molding the explosive around its outer face. When he was finished, he placed the pointed end of the cone into the four-inch steel tube and packed the remaining four pounds of the white plastic explosive on top of it. He set the tube on its end and took a moment to admire his work as he wiped the oily substance from his hands. His wait would finally be over in a few hours.

Nasir had met Sadiq bin Aziz thirteen years earlier in London when interviewing for a position with the Saudi's investment firm. Much like the man who would become his new boss, Nasir had enjoyed a life of privilege. His family fortune traced back to an Algerian industrial conglomerate started by his great-grandfather with French backing during the first World War. Fearful that his two sons would not be willing to make the sacrifices necessary for the company's future success, Nasir's great-grandfather sold the company just as the drumbeat of the second World War was reaching a crescendo. When his great-grandfather passed away four years later, Nasir's grandfather and his great-uncle inherited an estate valued in excess of twenty million dollars. Shortly before Algeria gained its bloody independence from France in 1962, his father and grandparents emigrated to France and settled in Marseille. In an arranged marriage, his father later married an Algerian woman who bore him five children. Their youngest, Saleem Nasir—whose birthname was Claude Nebbou—was the most accomplished of the brood.

Nasir joined Aziz's firm right out of Harvard Business School. His matriculation in the esteemed school was cemented by a hefty donation from his father, whose net worth at the time had just eclipsed nine figures. It was during his two years in Boston that Nasir rediscovered his faith, a period that coincided with the war in Iraq. He came to despise the United States and committed himself to liberating Muslims from its imperiousness. During the recruiting process, Aziz was quick to recognize the potential in the bright and pious young man. Although he was careful to obscure his own views, Aziz discreetly probed Nasir's sentiments on certain sensitive matters. Trusting that Nasir was someone he could mold and eventually bring into his grand plans, Aziz offered him a job on the spot. Then he sat back and observed his new employee for signs that his instincts were correct.

Despite lacking any financial need to work, Nasir fully committed himself to the firm. He was determined to shun the gratuitous lifestyle his impious father had himself adopted and envisioned for his son. Strongly believing that laziness was immoral, Nasir was always the first to arrive and the last to leave the office, and he accepted every assignment, no matter how trivial or tedious. He labored tirelessly over every detail in an effort to meet Aziz's exacting standards. It was not long before Nasir had earned the respect of his mentor and Aziz named him a junior partner. But as much as he prized Nasir's financial prowess, Aziz was still unsure that the young man shared his own views.

To further test his instincts, Aziz began consulting with his protégé on every business decision, and the two often traveled together to inspect current and potential investments. Gradually, a friendship developed between the two unmarried men. Their free and open discussions eventually led to a sharing of their respective worldviews. At first, the conversations were superficial, but as each man became more comfortable, true feelings began to emerge. Aziz was reassured by the younger man's expressed loathing for Western values and culture. In point of fact, Nasir told him that he was troubled by the firm's success. He said he was only able to countenance that success because he knew it was causing harm and pain to competitors under infidel control. His true motivation, he told Aziz, was to one day use his skills and personal wealth for more virtuous causes. When Nasir explained his objectives, Aziz feigned disagreement on some of his protégé's more ambitious pursuits, while carefully encouraging others. He was impressed when Nasir refused to moderate his views on violent jihad. Over time, Aziz hinted more and more about his own passions, including his belief in the need for physical force against the infidel. Soon after, he was only slightly stunned when Nasir came to him with plans to leave the firm to join al Qaeda in Iraq. Aziz used the opportunity to fully share his frustrations with core al Qaeda's jihad efforts and his future plans to sell the firm and pursue his lifelong goal of leading the believers to victory over the Crusaders and Jews. Nasir immediately pledged his loyalty to Aziz and vowed to do whatever asked of him toward the noble cause.

After six years, Nasir suddenly left the firm and returned to his native France. His first undertaking was to secure a new identity. Citing his desire to express his heritage, Claude Nebbou petitioned the Minister of Justice to change his name. Saleem Nasir had been a famous general who, during the seventh century, led the Muslim conquest in the Maghreb and later in the Iberian Peninsula and southern France. Given his Algerian heritage and being someone who embraced similar ambitions, the selection of Saleem Nasir held particular meaning for Nebbou. As soon as the three-month publication period expired, the name change took effect, ending the recorded life of Claude Nebbou and instantly ushering in the existence of Saleem Nasir. A few weeks later, he received new identification documents, including a new French passport.

At Aziz's instruction, Nasir traveled extensively, including to the United States. Still possessed of family money, Nasir moved among the glitterati through the finest hotels and restaurants, all while leisurely establishing a future jihadist network and scouting potential targets around the world. When Aziz sold the firm two years later, he compensated his former junior partner by funneling eight million dollars to Saleem Nasir through a series of corporate transactions. Although Nasir did not need the money, he had earned it and the gesture further strengthened the union between the two men.

While he was globetrotting, Nasir also found time to keep abreast of current trends and investment opportunities for both his and Aziz's benefit. He was quick to realize the potential of cryptocurrencies for their collective future and he acquired several thousand of the first Bitcoins in circulation. Since then, the investment had appreciated in value more than eight hundred-fold. In addition to substantially increasing his personal net worth, the investment was providing a source of untraceable financing for the Al-Kalafa organization, including the needs related to Nasir's latest stay in America.

Nasir had been in the United States with his two Yemeni companions for nearly five months but their insertion was nearly foiled. They were apprehended in New Mexico while trying the cross the border. Although they were prepared with plans for such an eventuality, Nasir had concerns the other two could see them through. He knew from their training in Afghanistan that his companions were not the brightest of men, but they somehow managed to stick to the story about being Syrians seeking asylum from the vicious civil war there. Incredibly—and just as Aziz had predicted—the Americans accepted the tale. The three men were simply released with orders to return in two weeks for a court hearing, one they didn't bother to attend.

Nasir and his men had trained in Afghanistan with the warriors who would eventually carry out the attacks at the Super Bowl and the Great American Mall but they were never part of that campaign. In fact, they knew nothing about the operation in Minnesota. Indeed, Aziz did not share any of the details with Nasir. He told him only that attacks in the US were planned and they would be the first under his new strategy. Nasir was advised that his operation would be the final one in a string of subsequent attacks, a series that Nasir himself had helped organize.

Although there was no need for Nasir and his team to be in the United States so early, Aziz had anticipated that border security would tighten dramatically following the attacks the American media had since been referring to as "Bloody Sunday." For that reason, Aziz dispatched Nasir and his team in the same general timeframe during which the others had infiltrated the United States. Nasir had been given the name of a contact in Houston. The original plan was for Nasir and his team to live in one of the contact's several homes until it was time to move into position and prepare for their own attack. But their apprehension in New Mexico changed those plans. Aziz had given him contingency instructions in the event he and his small team posed even a remote risk to the other men. Potentially leading the Americans to the other brothers who were traveling through Houston around the same time was out of the question. So Nasir and his companions proceeded directly to Chicago.

Three days after being released by US Customs and Border Protection, Nasir and his men arrived in the Windy City. He was dumfounded the Americans had not searched them and found more than five thousand dollars he had hidden on his person. The money was not nearly enough for his needs, but it was more than adequate to get them to Chicago and settled, at least for a while. Once in Chicago, they checked into a hotel that charged by the hour and accepted cash, no questions asked. Eight hundred dollars secured them a room for two weeks. Over the course of the next eight weeks, the men remained together and moved from one fleabag hotel to the next, never spending more than two weeks in any one of them. From time to time, they would venture out for food or to a local mosque for prayers but, for the most part, the men stayed in whatever dingy room they occupied at the moment and watched the news.

In late January, Nasir made a decision to split up, one he deemed necessary when their pictures appeared on television as part of an alert from the US Department of Homeland Security about a potential terrorist attack. Even though Nasir felt assured by the measures the men had taken to alter their appearances, he deemed it safer that the three of them not be seen together. While he remained in Chicago, revisiting the circuit of seedy hotels they had used previously, he gave his companions the remainder of the cash and sent them south to Gary, Indiana. The places they stayed were not ones where anyone paid attention to anything other than the color of money. Everything was good if the rent was paid on time. All three men remained out of view and waited in their respective locations for the unspecified operation they knew was coming. The day after the attacks in Minnesota,

Nasir hopped on the South Shore train and joined his comrades in Gary to celebrate.

That celebration was not long-lived. The completion of the first major part of Aziz's masterplan signaled that it was time for Nasir to begin preparations for his very first jihad mission. His attack was to be the third in the series of the second wave. The target, weapon-delivery device, and general timing had all been established by Aziz before Nasir left for training in Afghanistan. The only open question was the composition of the weapon to be used. During his training, Nasir learned how to construct the precision-type bomb he would use in this attack, as well as the various explosives that could be employed. He knew that if the bomb was properly constructed, a readily available rifle-target compound could be used. A sufficient quantity of the ammonium nitrate and aluminum powder mixture could be purchased for less than three hundred dollars at most sporting goods stores, but its explosive power was merely one-third of another material that had captured Nasir's imagination.

During his networking travels, Nasir had come in contact with a weapons dealer in Eastern Europe. In addition to hand-held weapons, the man also trafficked in explosive materials. One particular material grabbed Nasir's attention and he was determined to use it in his own operation. He wanted to deliver the most lethal blow possible and, at the same time, underscore the message to the Americans about the renewed and far-reaching capabilities of their enemy. Although he did not know the exact date the second wave of attacks would begin, Nasir knew he still had weeks to prepare. He could always fall back on the less-potent rifle target mixture, but he had enough time to explore his preferred option. Even though obtaining his material of choice would be difficult and risky, he was determined to try.

Nasir knew one possible means of acquiring Composition C-4 was through the Dark Web. Nearly everything was available through the secretive fold within the Internet, including C-4. Accessing the untraceable Dark Web was no problem for Nasir, a master programmer and someone who had studied information technology during his undergraduate years. Shortly after arriving in Chicago, he had visited several of the virtual black-market sites and identified no fewer than two dozen sellers of the plastic explosive.

Although accessing the sites through the onion router program, or Tor, gave him reasonable assurances of anonymity, he was reminded that the proprietor of the notorious Silk Road website had somehow been identified and arrested by the FBI not long before. Clearly, the Americans were monitoring dubious transactions and had ways of exposing those involved. He ultimately deemed the matter of taking physical delivery, something typically done through the regular mail, was simply too great a risk. The Dark Web was a tempting method, but he ultimately decided on another avenue.

Nasir had discovered that there was an army ammunition depot not far from Gary. The depot served as the regional distribution point for all US Department of Defense conventional munitions, missiles, non-standard ammunition, and chemical defense equipment. All he had to do was compromise someone with access to the C-4 he wanted. Intermittently, over a period of six weeks, Nasir scouted the area around the depot, using public transportation for the twenty-two-mile trip from Gary. He visited the several diners and grungy bars around the small town until he eventually identified the establishments most frequented by personnel from the armory.

On a trip to the area less than two weeks before, he chatted up a pimple-faced private over a few drinks. Posing as a traveling machine parts salesman, Nasir learned that the young man worked security at the armory. The soldier mentioned that he was returning to a two-week stint on the graveyard shift the following week, something he was catching hell for from his new wife. He told Nasir his wife wanted him to leave the Army and get a better paying job, one with regular hours that would allow them to buy a house and start a family. Nasir affected sympathy for the man's plight and suggested that he might have an answer to the soldier's problems. He explained that his company had given just given him permission to hire an assistant at a starting salary that raised the young man's eyebrows. As the soldier asked more and more questions about the job, Nasir could tell he was fantasizing about a financially secure future. The hook was in. Two hours later, they parted ways with plans to meet again the following evening, the last before Nasir was scheduled to leave on the next leg of his sales trip.

The following evening, Nasir embellished his story of financial wellbeing by first ordering top-shelf whiskey in favor of the black label swill the private had been drinking the night before. To further draw the man in, Nasir told the earnest soldier about the ranch he had purchased in Montana. While showing his dullard new friend stock photos of mountain wilderness that he had downloaded to his phone, Nasir crowed how he had purchased the five-hundred-acre parcel as an investment or possibly for retirement. Nasir explained he would be heading back to Montana for vacation in a few weeks with plans to continue work on the horse pasture he was creating on the property. He explained how the pasture was inaccessible to heavy machinery and he was having difficulty removing numerous large tree stumps on the sloped ground. The dynamite, sold to him by a neighbor who was in the mining industry, was no match for the immovable stumps, he said. The soldier flippantly suggested that C-4 would work a lot better. Nasir pretended not to know anything about the explosive and excitedly asked, "Would it be cheaper than the fifteen thousand dollars I've already spent on dynamite?"

That sum grabbed the penniless soldier's attention. Nasir could almost see the him calculating the possibilities of a quick score. After some more back and forth on the subject, the young entrepreneur estimated Nasir would need no more than four pounds of the powerful explosive and suggested he might be able to get it for as little as ten thousand dollars. Nasir said that if what the solider was proposing was truly possible, he would swing back through the area in a week or so. The two men clinked glasses to consummate the transaction.

Eight days later, Nasir made a trip to Chicago where he sold more of the cryptocurrency through a Bitcoin ATM transaction. The transaction was not without risk, especially so close to the operation. It was the second time he had visited the vape shop in the hip Lincoln Park neighborhood in Chicago. But the repeat trip could not be avoided. The vape shop was one of the few locations that offered the Satoshi 2 machines where he could exchange bitcoins for cash. When he returned to Gary later that day, Nasir and his two companions, Zayeed and Tawfiq, stole a beat-up sedan from one of the commuter lots around Gary and headed out to meet the young private.

Carrying a simple black duffle bag, Nasir entered the bullet-shaped diner to meet his GI buddy for a quick bite, while his two companions waited in the car outside. After paying the bill and wishing the young man luck on the home front, Nasir grabbed a similar black bag from beneath table. He left the restaurant with four pounds of C-4, leaving behind the duffle bag with ten thousand dollars inside. He walked around the corner and joined his brothers in the stolen sedan. They shadowed the soldier home and then returned to Gary, parking the stolen car in a different commuter lot.

That had been two days ago. Since then, they had acquired a temperamental 2005 Ford F-150 pickup and a fifteen-year old Lund Classic 16 SS fishing boat, with trailer. In all, it cost Nasir less than thirteen thousand dollars in cash. Now that the explosive was packed tightly, Nasir climbed into the boat with the bomb to begin the process of hooking up the detonation device. As he was doing this, he thought briefly of the soldier.

Very early that same day, Zayeed and Tawfiq had returned to the private's residence in the Ford pickup. When the young man arrived home and stepped from his rusted-out Chevy Impala at 6:30 that morning, Tawfiq emerged from the corner of the tiny farmhouse style home and slammed a hammer into the man's skull, killing him instantly. He and Zayeed dragged the man's body into the house and placed him on the bed next to his dead wife. They found the duffle bag on the floor of the closet, with all ten thousand dollars still inside. Before they left, Zayeed sprinkled the two dead bodies with the money, just as Nasir had ordered.

Although killing the soldier and his wife had been necessary to close a loose end, Nasir also felt he was doing the man a favor. The authorities would quickly determine that C-4 had been used in the attack. Soon after, the explosive would be traced to the munitions depot and, ultimately, to the private. As Nasir saw it, he saved the man from a life of misery behind bars. His decision to leave the money behind potentially accelerated that discovery process. But he wanted there to be no doubt how it had all gone down. He wasn't particularly concerned, anyway. By the time the authorities finally pieced everything together, Nasir would be long gone.

Now Nasir shifted onto his knees on the boat's hull and finished installing the detonator. When done, he climbed out of the boat and motioned to his comrades. It was time to go, he told them. At a few minutes past two o'clock, Tawfiq pushed the opener for the overhead door to the small warehouse space Nasir had rented for one month three weeks earlier. Once it was open, Zayeed drove the truck and boat-loaded trailer out the door.

Chapter 42

Fifteen minutes later, Nasir and his men arrived at the marina. It was located on the southern shores of Lake Michigan, some sixteen nautical miles from downtown Chicago. The parking lot was nearly full with bicyclists, canoeists, boaters, and beachgoers seizing the opportunity to enjoy what had been the first forecasted beautiful weekend of the spring. For once, the meteorologists had not disappointed. Fueled by a southerly breeze and a spotless sky, the temperatures were expected to approach eighty degrees by late afternoon. At Nasir's instruction, Zayeed maneuvered the truck deeper into the parking lot toward the public boat launch. When they arrived at the wide expanse for the staging area, Zayeed swung the truck and trailer through a U-turn and positioned them third in line to use the launch.

When their turn finally arrived, Nasir and Tawfiq jumped out of the truck to help guide Zayeed down the concrete slope. Zayeed, who had been raised in Aden, was very familiar with boats but not the process of actually getting them into the water by this method. As he backed up, the trailer jackknifed, causing him to have to pull forward to straighten the hauling assembly. The second attempt ended in the same result. Suddenly, the curtain of the surrounding commotion was pulled back, exposing the men and their several failed attempts to launch the boat. The full attention of a growing crowd of onlookers was upon them. Nasir could see that Zayeed was panicking. He walked up to the driver window in an effort to calm him down.

"Breath, brother," Nasir said. "You have to relax."

"I cannot do this," Zayeed said.

"You must. We have come too far. Concentrate and do this!" To reassure his collaborator, Nasir reached inside the cab and gently patted Zayeed's head with an open hand. As he prepared to step away from the vehicle, he heard a voice behind him.

"You guys need some help?"

Nasir turned around to see a short chubby man in a baseball cap and large reflector sunglasses. Nasir glanced down and saw the shirtless man was wearing floral-pattern neon-orange board shorts that extended to well below his knees and flip flops. He was almost relieved at the comical character standing before him, thankful the man was not a cop, or at least didn't at all appear to be. "My friend is just nervous. This is the first time we have launched the boat," he replied.

"It can be a real bitch," the man said. "It takes a lot of practice before you get good. I can do it for you. I work here and have to help people all the time."

Nasir considered the offer. The line was beginning to swell behind them and everyone seemed to have taken notice of their troubles. "Thank you," he said, while motioning Zayeed to get out of the truck.

"One of you guys might want to get into the boat," the man said before jumping up into the cab. "You got to unhook it when I get the trailer in the water."

While the man was adjusting the seat and mirrors, Zayeed hopped onto the trailer and climbed inside the boat. When everyone was in position, the man gave thumbs up and then smoothly guided the trailer into the water on the first try. Zayeed unhooked the boat and freed it from the trailer.

After the man had pulled the truck and trailer back into the parking lot, he exited the vehicle and said to Nasir, "That's a good old fishing boat. I used to have a Lund. Are you guys fishing today?"

Nasir realized that on top of not being able to get the boat into the water, they had no fishing gear at all. In fact, there was nothing in either the boat or the truck that one would expect to find for a planned excursion on the water. Thinking quickly, he said, "No, today we are just going for a ride. As you can see, we need some practice using the boat."

"Sounds like a plan! But be careful out there, the waves are picking up and they can get pretty big if the wind blows any harder. I'd stick pretty close to shore until you guys figure it all out," the man said.

"We will do that. Thank you," Nasir said as he slid in behind the wheel of the pickup. Tawfiq joined him in the truck and the two of them drove out of the staging area in search of a parking space. They found two at the far end of the parking lot. Not wanting a repeat of their earlier dilemma, Tawfiq unhooked the trailer and simply pushed it into the space before Nasir nosed the pickup into the space alongside it.

On the walk back to the launch area, Nasir said to Tawfiq, "Make sure you are careful on the way. You have plenty of time. Do not go too fast and, until you move into position, stay away from other boats and do not do anything to draw attention." Tawfiq nodded his understanding.

Zayeed was idling out in the lake when he noticed them approach. When they were nearly at the short aluminum dock that accompanied the boat launch, he began moving toward shore. As soon as another boat vacated the space, Zayeed pulled the boat alongside the dock and grabbed hold of the metal upright to steady the craft so that Tawfiq could get in.

After Tawfiq was safely aboard, Nasir leaned down and said to his men, "I hope to see you in paradise one day my brothers. Praise be to Allah."

In return, both men quietly said, "*Allahu Akbar*," and then Zayeed slowly backed the boat away from the dock.

Nasir did not look back at the men as he walked to the truck. He had no personal connection to Tawfiq and Zayeed. They were merely two of a seemingly limitless pool of easily-manipulated fools. The two Yemenis told him they had initially been recruited for jihad while living on the streets in Aden. After years of experience setting up cells around the world, Nasir knew how the recruiters skillfully identified and lured lost souls like those two. There were many more like Tawfiq and Zayeed. *They are nothing special, that's for sure*, he said to himself. Since he had met them months before, Nasir had harbored doubts the two idiots would be able to pull this off. But it was too late now to make changes. As Nasir neared the truck, he was playing out the straightforward attack in his mind, trying to convince himself that they could execute the plan, when he heard a now familiar voice.

"Aren't you going for the ride?"

Nasir pivoted and saw the same short chubby man holding a case of beer in one hand and a fishing pole in the other. "I just realized I forgot my phone at the house," he said. "I'm going back to get it. I'll join them later."

"Sounds like a plan," the man said. "Be sure to put some sun block on. Even though we're both kinda dark, this is the first warm sun we've seen in months. Have a great day!"

Everything sounds like a plan to this dimwit. And I'd say pink is a better description for you than tanned. "You, too," Nasir managed to politely say. "Good luck fishing. I hope you have a blast." He turned and walked to the truck, smiling at his pun.

Chapter 43
Langley

Timothy Patrick was planning on having a late lunch with his wife. Over the past few days, he and Suzie had hardly seen each other. He was two blocks from his house when Samantha Lane called and asked if he could come back to the office. There had been some developments and she wanted to update him on her team's progress. Although she cautioned that it was still early stages, she said it was looking like Alawi's phone number was proving to be the break they were hoping for.

Twenty-five minutes later, Patrick was making his way into the underground parking garage. He was hoping Lane was about to shed some light on the Al-Kalafa organization. Besides Aziz, it was suspected that Mumeet and Fahd al-Rasheed were part of the nascent terror group. But who else was associated with Al-Kalafa beyond those three was a complete mystery. Lane had assured him she and her team could begin to assemble the picture as soon as they had traceable information about just one person with links to the group. Adam Alawi had been under surveillance since Carpenter relayed his name and telephone number. A team of operations officers from the Paris office were following him and the NSA was listening in on his phone calls and reviewing his emails and texts. Lane's update could not be related to that surveillance because he would have known about it. Besides that, he had not heard anything from either the Paris office or Carpenter, who remained on standby in Paris in case any actionable intelligence came to light. He assumed that Lane and her team must have instead found something else during their search of Alawi's phone records or through open source research. He hoped so because Lane's call was the first bit of positive news he had received. The attack in Spain two days earlier had considerably added to the urgent need for actionable intelligence.

When he stepped off the elevator and entered the lobby, he had to remind himself that it was a late Saturday afternoon. The usual activity during the weekdays typically abated over the weekends, but the two recent attacks in Europe had the place buzzing. As he turned down the hall, he noticed Lane standing outside the conference room door waiting for him. Patrick nodded hello and walked into the room. His eyes were immediately drawn to the large diagram projected on the wall. It appeared to contain scores, if not hundreds of names, with different color lines connecting them. A few of the names were highlighted in bold font. It reminded Patrick of some kind of elaborate spider web. He moved over to a seat opposite the projected image and waited for Lane to start.

"I think we are starting to piece together Aziz's network," Lane said. "Let me give you some background first." She provided an overview of the bottom-up, social network analysis they were pursuing with the assistance of TimJoe Hanson. While pointing to the visual display, she explained, in broad terms, the quantitative metrics they were using to investigate large amounts of data so as to create a picture of the Al-Kalafa network. "All we needed to start were two pieces of intelligence with some kind of link or ties between them. The stolen vans and Adam Alawi's phone records provided the initial seeds that got us started. By pulling his call records, we were able to build a grid of all numbers Alawi has called or that have called him. That process was repeated for every number in Alawi's web and so on. While we do this, we look for any connections or relationships between those telephone numbers. When we find one, we attempt to identify each person associated with the connected numbers. This process continues and this expanding lattice that you see on the screen derives from just Alawi's phone number. Does this make sense so far?"

"I'm following you," Patrick said.

"Good. I want to caution that this is coming together quickly and there is still a lot we have to confirm, but I believe we have identified a key person in the Al-Kalafa group. All we have right now is a name—Saleem—and we don't know if that is this person's actual name or an alias, but we think Saleem might be a key player in Aziz's network. I'll let Blake fill in some details."

"I initially started by pulling all of Alawi's phone records for the past six months," Palmer said. There are seventy-two distinct numbers that he either called or that called him during that time period. While those numbers were being plugged into the social network analysis software, I first ranked them according to frequency and then assigned a value to each call; basically, highest for most recent and lowest for the calls at the beginning of the six-month period. For example, a number appearing often in Alawi's records and more recently would rank higher than a number that appeared less frequently and earlier in the six-month period. As Sam said earlier, we followed the same process for every distinct telephone number in the grid that emanates from Alawi's number. Any questions about that?"

"No, I'm still with you," Patrick said.

"After applying the formula to Alawi's call records, we started digging into the phone numbers, beginning with those at the top of the list. For example, the phone number at the top turned out to be his apartment. Alawi is married so we assumed he was simply calling home to speak with his wife. The second-ranking number belongs to Service Rapide. This process of elimination continued until we came to the fourteenth number on my list. That number belongs to a man named Adel Shebani. Over the past six months, Shebani's number appears twelve times in Alawi's records, three of them within the past eight days. I received the recordings less than an hour ago," Palmer said.

Patrick fully understood how Palmer was able to do this. The rumors circulating in the press about the NSA's capability to record telephone calls were partially true. Inside the United States, the Constitution precluded the NSA from listening in on telephone conversations without court approval. However, this did not stop the agency from collecting metadata on those calls. In addition to providing a date, this information told the NSA who was a party to each communication, where they were when it took place, and how long they spoke. When collected in mass quantities, this was extremely valuable data and very few people appreciated the invasive insights one could glean from it. In fact, a former CIA director had once quipped, "We use metadata to kill people." Although gathering context from processed metadata was useful, eavesdropping was a swifter and surer way of capturing intelligence. Unlike the context metadata provided, eavesdropping produced content, allowing the listeners insight into the nature, if not the actual purpose of the conversation. And the NSA took full advantage of the rules regulating its conduct outside US territory. For the better part of a decade, the NSA had been recording every call made in almost every country on earth. The program worked on a thirty-day buffer that removed the oldest calls as new ones arrived. Every month, the NSA recorded billions of telephone calls, enabling it to rewind and review those conversations for situations like this.

"Here are the transcripts for the three recent calls Adam Alawi had with Adel Shebani," Lane said as she handed Patrick three sheets of paper. "The first is from three days before the Paris attack."

Patrick read the transcript on the first piece of paper. It said:

>Shebani: Are we set for tomorrow?
>
>Alawi: Yes, come by after seven o'clock.
>
>Shebani: See you then.

Flipping that sheet aside, Patrick read the second sheet, which was dated the day after the Paris attack. It said:

>Alawi: Call me when you get this.

The final page was the transcript of a call Alawi made earlier that day. It said:

>Alawi: Why did you not return my call? I know you said not to call but two people were here the other day. One of them, a man, was from the United States! He asked a lot of questions about the keys. I have been trying to stay calm, but I don't know what to do. You need to call me!

Patrick understood why he had not been told about the first two calls before now. Alone, they were meaningless. But the call Alawi made to Shebani earlier in the day provided context to the first two calls. Together they revealed that Shebani had a roll in the Paris attack and he had assistance from Alawi. "PJ was right about this being an inside job," Patrick said. "What do we know about Adel Shebani, besides the likelihood he is dead?"

"We have an address in Sevran and, to your point, we can confirm that his phone hasn't been used since the attack," Lane said.

Patrick made a note to share the information about Shebani and Alawi with Pierre Laurent. "I take it you also have the recordings of Shebani's calls in the past thirty days," he said.

"We do and we listened to all nine of them, which includes the ones with Adam Alawi," Lane said. "None of the other six appears in any way related to the attack."

From what Patrick was learning, Adam Alawi was probably just used for the vans. And Alawi might not have known how Shebani intended to use them. Laurent would get to the bottom of Alawi's role and what he knew but, for the time being, the trail had ended. Lane could have told him this over the phone. He assumed there had to be more. "How does this Saleem character you mentioned fit into this?" Patrick asked.

"That brings us to the other piece of news," Lane said. "And this is more interesting." She explained that they had expanded their search of Shebani's phone records to the past twenty-four months. One number kept showing up, first eighteen months earlier and, most recently, about seven months ago. In total, there were nineteen different calls between Shebani's phone and that number. And, during that eleven-month timeframe, it was the number that appeared most often in Adel Shebani's call records. "We believe the number belongs to this man Saleem," Lane said. "We'll get to why we think that in a second, but I first want to tell you that we have not been able to identify anyone in Aziz's past known as Saleem. None of his known associates has that given name or is called Saleem from what we've been able to uncover. And we can't trace the number to a person because the number is listed to a business, and that business is registered in the Bahamas," Lane said.

Patrick had been down this road before and understood the implications. Anonymous corporations were often used for illicit purposes, and they could be set up with a few clicks of a mouse and payment of a modest fee. Depending on the jurisdiction, the incorporator might only have to include the name of one director and the name of one shareholder. In the Bahamas, either a person or a corporation could be listed as the lone director and shareholder required under its laws. But it did not matter who was listed as a director or shareholder because Bahamian law prohibited the government from sharing any information about its corporations with any other country. And for the truly paranoid, there were other ways to secure one's anonymity. Using a process known as "layering," an initial corporation is established with an actual person listed as both the director and shareholder. After that first company is formed, a subsidiary company is created, listing the initial corporation as its lone shareholder and director. This process continues through several iterations, rendering it impossible to learn the true identity of the actual people associated with the chain of corporations. "Unless you somehow hacked into the Bahamian corporate registry records, how do you know the guy using that number is named Saleem?" he asked.

"The same way we discovered Adel Shebani's link to the Paris attack—phone records," Lane answered. "I'll explain why we think his name is Saleem and why we think he is central to the Al-Kalafa organization." She told Patrick there was only one common number that appeared in both Adel Shebani's and Saleem's phone records. It belonged to a boutique hotel near Bratislava, Slovakia. Shebani's records disclosed five different calls with the hotel, all made ten to thirteen weeks earlier and outside the thirty-day listening window. The phone number belonging to Saleem had just three calls with the hotel with the most recent occurring almost a year ago. But the boutique hotel was a different story. "There was a number in the hotel's records that also appeared in Saleem's records," Lane said. "The number belongs to a man named Taj Khan. Saleem was in regular contact with Khan until about seven months ago." Lane paused. "You might recall that time frame is also when his calls with Adel Shebani suddenly stopped. Twenty-three days ago, Khan made the first of two calls to the hotel. "Here is the transcript from the first call," Lane said.

Patrick took the piece of paper and began reading. It said:

    Khan: May I speak with Jozef Varga?

    Varga: This is Jozef. Who is this?

    Khan: I am Taj Khan, a friend of Mister Saleem. He recommended I contact you about rooms."

    Varga: Yes, I was expecting your call. When would you need the rooms?

Khan: Our plans are flexible. We can come anytime in the next two weeks.

Varga: Would you like access to all the amenities?

Khan: Yes.

Varga: Very good. Give me time to check our availability. Call me back in two days.

Khan: Thank you. Goodbye.

When Patrick looked up, Lane asked, "Does the name Jozef Varga ring any bells?"

"As soon as you said the hotel was in Slovakia, Varga entered my mind. There is a substantial black market for weapons there and we have suspected for quite some time that Jozef Varga is a key player in it," Patrick said.

"The second call took place ten days ago. Varga told Khan the rooms would be available the next day. Khan said he would be there. We have to assume Khan went there and picked up weapons for an attack," Lane said.

"I'm afraid you're probably right," Patrick said. "Do we know where Khan is now?"

"We don't, but we do know that he only used his phone in and around Brussels. There is one exception, however. Three days ago, his phone pinged a tower near Lille, France. The ping was from an incoming call that he didn't answer. The phone hasn't been on since."

Patrick stood up and prepared to leave. "I've got some calls to make," he said. In addition to calling Pierre Laurent, he planned to call the Agency heads in Paris and Bratislava. As he started for the doorway, he checked his watch and saw it was already six-thirty. He stopped and turned around to face his team. "Unless our luck changes and we get some intel on the whereabouts of Aziz, Mumeet, or al-Rasheed, Khan and Saleem are our best chance to stop another attack." He knew that every one of them had worked tirelessly, with very few days off, since the weeks before the Minnesota attacks, but there was no allowance for rest now. The orders he was about to give reminded him of the saying that no good deed goes unpunished. He just hoped his offer would soften the blow. "This is really good work you've all done. Thanks to you, we finally have something tangible to pursue. I'm sorry for this, but we have to use every minute we have. I was hoping at least some of you could enjoy part of the weekend but this can't wait until Monday. As a meager consolation, when you guys are ready, I'm buying dinner; whatever you want. Until then, I'll be upstairs in my office."

Chapter 44
Chicago, Illinois

"**Dad, you promised** that mom and I could do whatever we wanted. A deal's a deal."

In a bit of showmanship, Danish Jafari had mildly protested the idea, but he had entered into the bargain freely and now his daughter was calling in the chip. Danish looked at his seven-year old daughter and smiled. "Yes, Aminah, I did say that and if you really want to do this cruise, we will."

Although Danish doubted it would ever match the excitement of the last four hours, there was no way out of this bargain. Ever since going on a ride on the Des Moines River with friends back home, Aminah had become fascinated with boats. And, as enthusiastic as Aminah was about the excursion, he suspected his wife was even more so. An architect herself, Parisa was very much looking forward to cruising the Chicago River to take in the iconic architecture of downtown Chicago. Besides, enduring what he was expecting to be a boring river cruise was a small price to pay for their happiness. They had been good sports sitting in the hot sun earlier while he and his nine-year old son Ibrahim took in their very first major league baseball game together.

Danish Jafari had come to the United States in 1992 on an H-1B visa to work as a software engineer. He had been recruited by an American software company just after earning his master's from the National University of

Science & Technology in Islamabad. The decision to leave Pakistan had been agonizing. He had met Parisa only a month before and he already knew he wanted to marry her. Almost immediately after arriving in Seattle, he was thinking of returning to Pakistan. He was unfamiliar with the culture and didn't know anyone outside a few people at work. But he realized he had been given a wonderful opportunity, one that was unavailable elsewhere. He dedicated himself to work, determined to make a name for himself and to one day bring Parisa to America. For the most part, he spent what little free time he had alone. Over time, he began to cultivate relationships with his co-workers who were drawn in by his infectious personality. But his strong Islamic faith caused him to decline their invitations to after-work get togethers that all too often prominently featured alcohol. Danish did not at all begrudge his friends their lifestyles, rather he felt guilty for taking away from their fun. Eventually, his new friends caught on that his reluctance was faith-based, and they started offering up other activities, including baseball games. Danish soon found any desire to return home foolish. But he never relinquished his feelings for Parisa.

Three years after arriving in America, he was offered a position by a client in Des Moines. It came toward the end of a two-month long project for the nearly one-hundred-year-old privately-owned insurance carrier. Although he was deeply honored by the proposal, he was hesitant to accept it. He had just begun to feel settled in Seattle and did not want to leave what had become a very close-knit group of friends. His friends genuinely encouraged him to take the offer, that is if he could stand living in the Corn Belt. It was too good to pass up, they said. They were right. The company was solid and so too was the offer. It came with a salary and benefits far surpassing what he had in Seattle. The cost-of-living adjustment only made it sweeter. Plus, over the course of the two months he had worked on the project, he had become close with the ownership group. The men and women there treated him extremely well. Still, he was unsure. It was only when Parisa, who was still in Pakistan, counseled him to take the job, that he did.

As a condition to accepting the offer, he sheepishly asked that his new employers sponsor him for a green card. It was a prelude to earning US citizenship, an essential element of his goal. As soon as his requisite five years of permanent residency was completed, he filled out an application for naturalization. He had come to love the United States and its freedoms and could not imagine living anywhere else. A little more than a year later, he became a US citizen. Almost as soon as the party his employers had held in his honor was over, he went back to Pakistan and proposed to Parisa. They married immediately and promptly returned to Des Moines. Less than six years later, she, too, was a US citizen.

Danish excelled at work, earning greater responsibilities and bonuses. As content as he was, he started to realize there was a great need for his talents, one he could offer through his own business. His employers agreed and provided a seventy-five-thousand-dollar investment for Danish to launch his own consulting business. At the time, Parisa was just completing the requirements for a degree in architecture from the University of Iowa. In many ways, despite about to enter their mid-thirties, they were starting all over. Neither cared. It was an exciting time and, most importantly, they had each other.

Their resolve was tested even more when the recession hit a year later. Clients stopped calling and, worse, some stopped paying for services rendered. They were forced to sell the house Danish had purchased right after moving to Des Moines, and they moved into a small one-bedroom apartment. A few months later, the task became more daunting when Parisa, worried about their financial plight, tearfully announced that she was pregnant. Danish was beyond overjoyed when he heard the news and infinitely more so when Ibrahim was born. Unable to afford childcare, Parisa had to leave her job. In truth, the small design firm was preparing to close its doors, anyway. Despite their financial trials, the three of them persevered in the small apartment, thankful for their many blessings.

Danish juggled long days at work with the joys and responsibilities of being a father and husband, often sleeping no more than five hours a day. He was committed to providing the best for his family and his three employees, who he also considered family. Danish kept them on at full salary and never once missed payroll during the hard times, sacrificing for their benefit until things turned around. His employees picked up the pace, refusing to the take time off they had earned while the company was still struggling. Gradually, through their collective hard work and determination, things began to improve.

New business started to flow in and clients paid past balances in full. When Danish and his three loyal employees were unable to keep up with demand for the firm's services, he hired four part-time employees. Those four eventually became full-time employees and were soon joined by five more. To reward them for their loyalty and dedication, Danish gave each of his three original employees generous raises that more than compensated for their frozen salaries over the previous four years. Only after he was comfortable providing those arrangements for his employees did Danish and Parisa start looking for a new home. They ended up purchasing a modest home in Danish's old neighborhood shortly after Aminah was born. And, despite being able to afford a much larger and elegant home, the Jafaris still contentedly lived in the tidy three-bedroom prairie-style ranch.

The four-day vacation in Chicago was one of the more elaborate ones the Jafaris had ever taken. The Jafaris made plans to visit the city right after the Cubs won the World Series, ending a record one hundred eight-year championship drought. What the Jafaris lacked in generational lineage to the game was more than made up for by Ibrahim's passion for baseball and the Cubs. Danish and Parisa knew next to nothing about baseball when Ibrahim declared he wanted to play Little League. They were completely surprised by their then five-year old son's announcement. Ibrahim had been a very quiet and shy boy who had previously shown little interest in activities with other children. But right from the start, Ibrahim was a natural both on and off the field. By the fourth game of the season, he was hitting in the leadoff spot and playing shortstop. Even more impressive to his parents was the fact that Ibrahim was viewed by his peers and coaches as the leader of the team. They delighted in how Ibrahim's personality seemed to be blossoming right before their eyes. That first season, Ibrahim led the team in hitting and was named to the All-Star team. When the season ended, Ibrahim told his parents he was going to play in the major leagues one day. And his passion for the game had only deepened since.

Ibrahim and Danish started attending games of the Iowa Cubs, the top minor league affiliate of the parent team in Chicago. The Iowa Cubs' ballpark, situated downtown at the juncture of the Racoon and Des Moines Rivers, was one of the best in minor league baseball. For the past two seasons, Danish and Ibrahim had been season ticket holders. And they rarely missed a game. Ibrahim kept his official scoring from each game in a plastic bin in his closet. Posters of Cubs players who had passed through Des Moines on their way to the Big Leagues adorned his bedroom walls, and he religiously watched highlights from around the league on the MLB Network every night to keep up with his favorite team and players. And when he was not watching highlights, he was practicing the drills taught by his favorite MLB Network analysts, Harold Reynolds, Billy Ripken, and the hilarious Sean Casey.

But as much fun as the games were and as beautiful as the park was in Des Moines, Ibrahim and Danish had discovered earlier that day that the experience at home was no match for the history and splendor of a game at glorious Wrigley Field. The game had only added to the magnificence. The family arrived at the ballpark early so they could watch batting practice. After a stop at the souvenir stand, where Danish purchased jerseys bearing the name and number of Ibrahim's favorite player for himself and his son, the family headed down the gently-sloping steps to their seats eight rows behind the Cubs' dugout. Danish reveled in the look on his son's face as the players he had mostly only watched on television were warming up fifty feet away. After he began to accept it was all real and not a dream, Ibrahim turned to his father and said, "Dad, this is the best day of my life!" Danish grinned and hugged his son, cherishing the long embrace.

A short time later, the family of four stood and proudly sang the Star-Spangled Banner. Just before the game started, the couple sitting immediately behind them offered to take a picture. As soon as the young woman handed his phone back to him, Danish pulled up the picture. It was perfect—four smiling faces with a beautifully manicured baseball field and the iconic Wrigley scoreboard in the background. He asked Parisa if they could use it for their holiday card that year. But, as great as the pre-game experience was, Danish knew that the game itself would occupy a special place in his son's memory. Trailing by a run to their long-time rival Saint Louis Cardinals, the Cubs had come back in the bottom of the ninth inning with a dramatic two-out rally to win the game. To top it off, the man sitting two rows in front of them gave Ibrahim the foul ball he caught off the bat of Ibrahim's favorite player, just two pitches before he delivered the game-winning hit.

Now standing with his wife and children on Navy Pier with the gorgeous expanse of Lake Michigan in the background, Danish looked forward the making the next wonderful family memory. There was no price for the permanent smile that had been on Ibrahim's beaming face from the moment they entered Wrigley Field. Looking at his wife and daughter, Danish could tell that viewing the majesty of the Chicago skyline from the water would provide similar unbounded joy for Parisa and Aminah. As he was soaking this all in and chuckling at his lovely daughter's hutzpah, she stepped in front of him and defiantly stood arms akimbo.

"OK, Dad, enough monkeying around; it's our turn now," Aminah said. "Get your butt over there so we can get tickets for the next boat!"

Danish laughed heartily and moved into the ticket line for the architecture cruise. A man at the end of the line in a White Sox hat gave him some good-natured ribbing about the Cubs jersey he was wearing. Danish laughed some more and told the man about his family's first trip to Wrigley Field. The man shared his own first experience at a major league ballpark with his father, fifty years before. Danish listened in wonder as the man retold the experience from a half-century ago with incredible detail. As the two men exchanged more stories and shared their appreciation for the profound effects baseball clearly had on familial bonds, Danish realized he was truly living the American dream. He and his beloved wife had two beautiful children and lived in a wonderful home, surrounded by great friends and neighbors. His business was continuing to grow, with twenty-one employees and revenues that surpassed eight million dollars last year. Now they were making everlasting memories in one of the greatest cities in the greatest country in the world. He looked skyward to push back the tears that were forming in the corner of his eyes and thanked God.

Chapter 45

Saleem Nasir forced himself to slow down. He risked standing out from the other passengers making their way out of Millennium Station. He had failed to factor in potential problems when he gave Tawfiq and Zayeed the three-hour time period before leaving the marina. It should have been more than enough time for him to get into position. He had driven the pickup directly to the train station in Gary, but the train's departure was delayed almost sixty minutes because of a mechanical problem with the tracks. According to his phone, those three hours had just passed and he still had to cover three blocks from Millennium Station to the DuSable Bridge.

Once outside the station, Nasir sidestepped an elderly couple and settled in behind a group of teenagers, who were at least walking at a faster clip than the other tourists and shoppers clogging the sidewalk on Michigan Avenue. As he moved north on the bustling street, he clung to the promise that there was no set time for the attack. The three-hour window was merely a minimum interval before it was to begin. He had given Tawfiq and Zayeed three hours because he expected they would need close to that much time traveling by boat. He did not want to set an artificial time that they might have to rush to meet at the last minute. It was imperative they not draw attention to themselves at any point during the sixteen-mile trip form the marina in Indiana. Nasir had originally thought that his only problem would be trying to remain inconspicuous while he waited for them. Now there was a chance he might miss the spectacle.

His anxiety grew when he and the pack of teenagers were forced to wait for the light to change at Wacker Drive. He glanced at his phone and saw that three hours and seven minutes had elapsed since he left Tawfiq and Zayeed at the dock. He moved to the edge of the curb and craned his neck for any sight of the small fishing boat on the river, but the vantage point only offered a minimal view of the waterway. Once the light changed, he moved quickly across Wacker Drive and onto the stairway leading down to the river walk. He descended a few steps and, not seeing them to his left, ducked his head and peered under the bridge to his right. There was no sign of the boat. He pretended to adjust his shoe while he continued searching and breathed deeply to calm himself.

Once he was composed, he moved back up the stairs and onto the sidewalk. He crossed the bridge to the far side of the river and took up a position next to the tender house on the northwest corner. The location offered a clear view to and beyond the Irv Kupcinet Bridge at Wabash Avenue, the next bridge to the west. In addition to offering an ideal place to watch the attack, the Bedford stone of the bridge tender house would also provide much-needed protection from the blast he was expecting. He checked his phone again. It was 5:58 p.m.

Chapter 46

Danish Jafari leaned forward on the bench and sipped the last of his caffeine-free soda as he glanced over at his family again. Each time he had, including this one, Parisa was looking up at the buildings, captivated by the arresting architecture of the buildings towering above the Chicago River. Aminah and Ibrahim seemed to be equally captivated, spurred by their mother's descriptions of the designs and ornate features on the buildings. *This day couldn't be any better*, he said to himself. He almost wished the tour would continue for another hour but his stomach was beginning to protest.

He leaned back on the bench and recalled how everything had lined up perfectly the entire day, including the seats they had on the boat. He found it incredible how things had worked out in their favor. As they moved up the boarding line earlier, the usher put up his rope to count the number of passengers who had already boarded. When he returned, the usher allowed three more passengers onto the boat, leaving them first in line for the next cruise. Although it had cost them fifteen minutes, the Jafaris had their pick of seats when they boarded. They chose the bench on the top level of the sixty-five-foot vessel's bow, and the unimpeded view they enjoyed only added to what had already been a spellbinding tour. The short wait had indeed been well worth it.

Now, the tour was nearing completion. In another twenty minutes or so, the Jafaris and the other seventy-seven passengers onboard would be back at the dock at Navy Pier. Danish started to think about making dinner plans. It was nearing six o'clock and the last food they consumed had been at the ballpark. He was looking forward to some better fare. But those plans could wait. For now, he wanted to enjoy the last stretch of the boat ride. Besides, as well as the day had gone so far, he half expected they would luck into some kind of wonderful dinner. He tilted his head skyward, closed his eyes and listened to Parisa as she provided her own guided tour to the children.

"Do you see these two circular buildings?" Parisa asked the children. "These buildings are called Marina City." Parisa was referring to the identical sixty-five-story, mixed-used, residential-commercial building towers located just to the west of the Bataan-Corregidor Memorial Bridge at State Street. "These buildings were designed by Bertrand Goldberg and, at the time of their completion in nineteen sixty-eight, were the tallest reinforced concrete structures in the world. Remember earlier when I pointed out the tower cranes being used to build that skyscraper? Well, these buildings were the first ever to be constructed with tower cranes."

"Why can we see cars on the bottom floors?" Ibrahim asked.

"The bottom nineteen floors on each building serve as a parking ramp."

"That's so cool!" Ibrahim said.

"I wouldn't want to park my car there," Aminah said. "It could roll right out of the building!"

Danish smiled to himself as Parisa continued to amaze the children with more unique facts about Marina City. There had been something special about this day for everyone in the family, one they would each remember fondly forever. He was thinking that it just kept getting better by the minute when he was startled from his reverie by the man sitting next to him.

"What in the heck is that guy doing? the man asked.

Danish opened his eyes to see a small boat moving rapidly toward them.

Chapter 47

Nasir first spotted the fishing boat when it passed under the William P. Fahey Bridge at Columbus Drive. Zayeed was at the helm, with Tawfiq standing next to him. He continued to watch as the boat harmlessly approached the DuSable Bridge at the no-wake speed. As it drew closer, he slipped behind the tender house, not wanting to risk a knowing nod or gesture from one of the two men. A few seconds later, he looked down at the river and saw the boat slowly emerge on the west side of the bridge. After it had fully passed underneath, Zayeed slowed the boat to an idling pace and hovered near the seawall on the north side of the river bank.

Nasir kept his eyes focused to the west, squinting directly into the sun as it hastened its descent toward the horizon. Less than a minute later, when he saw the tour boat pass under the Bataan-Corregidor Bridge and turn slightly to the port side, he pulled his phone out and began recording. The tour boat continued its steady approach toward him and his brothers in the fishing boat below. As soon as the tour boat passed under the Irv Kupcinet Bridge at Wabash Avenue, he heard an engine roar to life below him. He looked down to see Zayeed turn the boat slightly away from the seawall and accelerate, putting it on a direct course to the tour boat, now less than five hundred feet away.

Tawfiq was on the floor with the detonator in his hand while Zayeed maintained the fishing boat's path directly at the bow of the cruise boat. The tubular improvised explosive device was secured in the front of the fishing boat, the tip of the copper cone inside it lined up precisely with the point of the bow. Nasir kept filming, capturing a panoramic of the fishing boat set against the skyline beyond as the vessel tracked rapidly toward its target.

Just before Zayeed was about to plow the fishing boat into the larger cruiser, there was a massive explosion. The shaped-charge improvised explosive device sent a concussive force at more than twenty-six thousand feet per second directly into the front of the tour boat, shredding it to pieces, and bringing Danish Jafari's American dream to a violent and sudden end.

Chapter 48
Langley

Looking around the conference room, Patrick could see the stress etched on the faces of his team. It was almost as if the intense pressure they all had been living under before yesterday's attack in Chicago was a walk in the park. The United States had been attacked a second time in the past three months and no one knew when the next one was coming. Like the coordinated attacks in Minnesota, there had been no intelligence about target or timing. The same was true for the attacks in the preceding days in Paris and Spain. What's more, the combination of pace, geographic dispersion, and the varying nature of the attacks was unprecedented. Although claims of responsibility had yet to be made for any of them, they were certain about the culprit. Sadiq bin Aziz had dramatically altered the few rules that previously existed in this war, and it was their job to adjust to the changing circumstances.

Without saying a word, Patrick walked over to an empty chair and sat down. After the attack in Chicago, they had all stayed until he sent them home, sometime in the early morning hours, for at least a few hours of rest. Words for a pep talk or an offer of reassurances eluded him. And he did not see any benefit either. As demoralized as they all felt, they knew they could not succumb to the agonizing weight of this latest setback. The ability to overcome adversity and cope with high-stress situations were two key requirements to working in the CTC. He had faith in the resolve of his team to find a way to get their backs off the wall. Each of them was highly intelligent and extremely competitive, none more so than the man whose voice he heard on the speakerphone as he sat down.

"I'm here," Carpenter said. He was still in Paris. He had wanted to go to Chicago, but Patrick told him to stay put until they had a better idea what was going on.

In the most confident and cheeriest voice he could muster, Patrick said, "Hello and good afternoon, PJ. And good morning to everyone here. I apologize for being a few minutes late." He stopped talking when he noticed someone was missing. "Where is Ella?"

"I spoke to her a few minutes ago," Samantha Lane said. "She said she is working on something at her desk."

"Any idea what it is?" Patrick said.

Rock had told Lane what she was doing but Lane decided it would be best not to raise anyone's hopes until Rock knew for sure. "She didn't say. She said it might be important though."

"Well, let's hope she's onto something. First off, I wanted to give you an update on Director Gonzalez's meeting with the NSC." Patrick was referring to the National Security Council, a forum of Cabinet-level principals that considered national security, military, and foreign policy matters. "I can't get into details but I am sure none of you will be surprised to learn that it wasn't pretty."

The NSC meeting had indeed been a highly contentious affair. An angry and bereaved president wasted no time before he started dressing down his top advisors. He told them that Chicago had been a systematic failure. The country was once again caught off guard, this time with absolutely no advance knowledge of the attack. He demanded to know from Director Forti how the FBI, with its considerable resources and extensive surveillance capabilities, had failed to discover that terrorists were in the country and plotting an attack. Included in his harsh words for the Department of Homeland Security was his disgust that nothing had been done to shore up the borders. The president said his fear was that the attack had been carried out by three men who had remained at large since the days leading up to the attacks in Minnesota. Those men, claiming to be Syrians, were detained at the border and later set free. He said decades of neglecting the security of the country's borders was political malpractice and that his administration would not be a part to it. From his first day in office, he had been calling on Congress to repeal the reckless "catch and release" policy implemented by the prior administration. He instructed Chief of Staff Bill Tackett and DHS Secretary Elizabeth Wilcox to plan on spending as much time as needed on Capitol Hill until Congress finally did. He also ordered them to make plain to every member of Congress who was holding up the repeal that he would make a point of calling them out if it was later learned that the people behind the attack had been beneficiaries of that senseless policy. And the president had not exempted the Central Intelligence Agency from his criticism. When pressed, Director Gonzalez could only say that the Agency believed Aziz was behind the attack. That it knew so little about Aziz and his organization was not a satisfactory answer to the president's question about why the Agency had been unable to discover so much as a hint that an attack was coming.

When he was finished with his rant, he let everyone in the room know that the next attack on the homeland would bring an immediate end to their time in his administration. The president concluded the meeting with what was technically a request, although everyone understood that denying it was not an option. And, with almost no deliberation, it was wholeheartedly granted by the remorseful NSC advisors.

With the exception of Carpenter, Patrick could not share any of this with his team. He would not, anyway. In situations like this, it was his job to insulate his team and frame the feedback in the most positive light possible. Everyone in the room felt responsible for the attack. There was no need to pile on. As Patrick shared what he could about the NSC meeting, he chose his words carefully. "The president rightly views this as an inexcusable failure, across the entire federal government. We simply must do better.

"But on the positive side, we now have absolute clarity for our mission. President Madden doesn't want to give Aziz the chance to build out his jihadist network. He is heeding the lesson learned from how the Islamic State was initially underestimated, and he does not intend to allow Aziz's Al-Kalafa to metastasize in similar fashion. He requested and received from the National Security Council more aggressive rules of engagement. Our orders are now crystal clear—no matter where they are, we are to find and kill Aziz and anyone with a demonstrable connection to the Al-Kalafa organization."

The president's assertiveness was welcome news to Carpenter. He knew that containment was not an effective strategy to combat extremism. It was a mistake to believe that whittling away at a terrorist organization's foothold would end the problem. Such a strategy would prove especially ineffective against Aziz and his Al-Kalafa organization. From what they knew, Aziz was adopting a different model. Rather than provide his adversaries with a location where they could focus their countermeasures, Aziz was mobilizing his forces. Carpenter also believed that unequivocal lethal force was far more effective than attempting to hold hardened terrorists accountable through the criminal justice system. Detention was not a deterrent. In fact, captured terrorists often used the rights conferred upon them to make a mockery of the judicial process. What's more, once in captivity, the terrorists rarely, if ever, gave up any valuable intelligence. No, Carpenter believed that short of killing them, having extremists constantly looking over the shoulder for a bullet or up at the sky for a Hellfire missile was a far more effective deterrent and method to win the war.

But the problem with the strategy laid out by the president was the dearth of knowledge about Aziz's network. "Is the president aware that, outside of Mumeet and al-Rasheed, we know nothing about the team of allies Aziz has assembled?" he asked. "Unless you guys have come up with something I don't know about, we don't have much. Adam Alawi is still in custody, but beyond admitting to helping Adel Shebani steal the vans, he's not offering much else. He claims he only dealt with Shebani and has no idea who else was involved. Shebani is almost certainly dead. That leaves Taj Khan, Jozef Varga, and the man you guys have been calling Saleem. Do we know anything more about them?"

"We're still trying to locate Taj Khan," Lane said. "His phone has not registered since it pinged the tower near Lille."

"I spoke with Pierre Laurent," Patrick said, referring to the head of France's DGSE. "He sent teams to check out the address we have for Adel Shebani in Sevran and to Lille in search of Taj Khan. So far, the DGSE has yet to turn up anything on either man."

"What about Jozef Varga?" Carpenter asked. "As far as we know, he's alive and we know where his hotel is located. I can get to Bratislava in two hours. Mick and I can get some quick answers." Carpenter was getting antsy and was pressing Patrick to let him meet up with Mick Richards, who served as chief of station in Bratislava. Richards was old school and unafraid to get his hands dirty, two qualities Carpenter admired. Carpenter argued it would be better that he was in Slovakia kicking ass with Richards than sitting on his own in Paris.

"Mick has already dispatched two of his people to search for Varga. He's in the wind. Apparently, the hotel is more like a bed and breakfast. Mick says it is pretty run down and doesn't look like it's entertained guests in years. Mick's people are keeping an eye on it in case Varga returns. There's no need for you to go there."

Patrick had just finished when the door opened, revealing a beaming Ella Rock. "Claude Nebbou!" she announced.

"Who?" Patrick asked.

"A French citizen by the name of Claude Nebbou once worked with Sadiq bin Aziz's investment firm," Dalton Jones said. "He popped up in my search yesterday. Nebbou was with Aziz for six years. He left about two years before Aziz sold the firm. Not long after he left, Nebbou seemed to disappear."

"And I know why," Rock said. "Not long before we got news of the Chicago attack, Dalton mentioned that he discovered this guy Claude Nebbou but was having trouble locating him. I started searching death records until we all became preoccupied with the events in Chicago. I didn't sleep well so I headed in early this morning, planning to continue searching the death records. On the way in, I listened to music instead of the news. A song by Prince came on and I started think about how he had changed his name to a symbol for a few years because of a contract dispute. That got me thinking that maybe Nebbou had changed his name.

"I found out French law requires that a proposed name change be published in the *Journal Officiel* and at least one newspaper that regularly publishes legal announcements. After I found the announcement buried in the Google search results, I called a colleague in France to confirm it. Claude Nebbou disappeared because he changed his name to Saleem Nasir—I'm sure he's the Saleem we're looking for."

Patrick bolted upright in his chair. "Any idea where is here now?" he asked.

"I came here as soon as I received confirmation, which was about a minute before I walked in."

"That is great work, Ella." Patrick looked her directly in the eyes to make sure the young analyst knew how much he appreciated what she had done. "Sam, you Ella, and Dalton try to find out everything you can about Saleem Nasir. He's our top target now. I'll call Pierre and get the French working on it too. PJ, sit tight; I'll call you as soon as we know something."

Chapter 49
Antwerp, Belgium

Hamid Fahkoury remained in his seat pretending to read the newspaper that was spread out on his lap. When only a few other passengers remained in his car, he rose and stepped off the train. After a few short paces, he paused and casually looked around the platform. Seeing nothing to concern him, he placed his feet on the escalator and began making his way up two levels toward the capacious entrance hall of Antwerp Central Station.

The stone clad train station was reputed for its eclectic fusion of architectural design styles and universally regarded as one of the most beautiful in the world. As he rode up the escalator, Fahkoury glanced skyward at the massive domed ceiling that scaled more than twelve stories at its peak, a height needed to accommodate the steam of locomotives when the station was built more than a century before. He was surprised that even on this densely overcast day, more than sufficient light penetrated the polycarbonate sheets bridging the burgundy-painted steel elements of the roof. When he arrived at the entrance hall, he made his way over to a newsstand and purchased a bottle of water. As he was about to hand money to the cashier, Fahkoury detected a man out of the corner of his eye who seemed to be giving him more than cursory interest.

△ △ △

Joe Hankinson was standing at the far side of the entrance hall when he first noticed the man. Wearing a lightweight overcoat over a dark business suit with no tie, the man was dressed like any number of men milling about the entrance hall. But the man's watchful manner grabbed Hankinson's attention. And, as the third-year operations officer scrutinized the man further, he realized that he just might be looking at Mumeet, otherwise known as the Bringer of Death. His dark hair and olive-colored skin were a match to the scant description the Agency had for Mumeet, but those characteristics were not particularly telling. Hankinson knew that there was a considerable Middle Eastern population in Antwerp, a city that was home to more than one hundred seventy nationalities and considered the second most multi-cultural center on the planet. The man's below-average height was another positive identifier but again, not dispositive. It was when Hankinson noticed that the man was wearing gloves that his interest truly piqued. He recalled that Mumeet was reported to have suffered a disfiguring hand injury many years before, and he thought it particularly odd that someone would be wearing gloves on a day when the temperature was hovering just on the low side of sixty degrees. While no single behavior or characteristic would positively identify the man as Mumeet, as a whole they were more convincing. But they were still not conclusive. And that was the essence of Hankinson's quandary.

For nearly a year, Hankinson had been assigned to a money-laundering operation. His team was gathering intelligence on a transnational criminal organization based in Russia that was using diamonds to launder the cash it was generating—primarily from drug and sex trafficking. Hankinson's target had touched down at Amsterdam Airport Schiphol an hour ago. While his colleague was keeping tabs on the train, Hankinson was supposed to follow Igor Popov when he arrived in Antwerp. And the train was due to arrive any minute from the Dutch capital.

It was the first time in months that Popov had been outside Russia and this promised to be the taskforce's first chance to identify the diamond dealers participating in the scheme. If Hankinson lost coverage, it might be many more months before he and his team had a second shot to unravel the syndicate. But as critical as it was to get eyes on and follow the target, grabbing Mumeet would top it. There was no easy answer and a decision needed to be made quickly. Hankinson called Tony Galvin, his boss and chief of station in Brussels. "Tony, it's Joe. I'm at Central Station waiting for Popov to arrive from Amsterdam. There's a guy here who just might be Mumeet."

"What? Are you sure?" Galvin asked.

"There's no way I could be; we don't have a definitive description of the guy. But based on what we have, this guy fits it." Hankinson explained what he had observed about the man and his behaviors.

"Damn it!" It was a tough call. In any other situation, Galvin would have Hankinson stay with Mumeet or, more accurately, who Hankinson thought might be him. But this was a key moment in the money-laundering operation, and there was no time to get someone else to Antwerp. Hankinson was it. "I don't have any intelligence that Mumeet might be in Belgium and we can't miss our chance with Popov. Keep an eye on that guy for as long as you can, but you've got to stick with Popov when he gets off that train. I'll call this in to Tim Patrick."

"Good timing since Popov's train is pulling into the station right now. If you're sure, I'm going to have to bail on the other guy so I can get into position for Popov."

Galvin hesitated. He hoped he was making the right call. "Yes, go with Popov," he said.

△ △ △

For the fifteen or so seconds required to complete the transaction, Fahkoury noticed that his watcher did not move from his position on the far side of the spacious entrance hall. Keeping the man in his peripheral vision, Fahkoury walked over to a nearby diamond shop. He stopped in front of the glass window and lingered before a display of loose diamonds, while examining the man in the reflection. Although the man was no longer looking directly at him, Fahkoury could see that he was on the phone. After taking a sip of water, Fahkoury turned and started walking along the storefront. When he reached the end, he slowly faced the entrance hall. The man was still on the phone and turning slightly away from him. Fahkoury kept his focus on the man's back while pretending to look from side to side, as if searching for more window-shopping opportunities. He set his sights on a clothing store located close to the escalators. As he walked calmly toward the escalators, he considered his options. There might have been others posted at the lower level of the station when he arrived. They could still be there waiting to move up the escalator on the man's signal. He considered going up instead. There was one level of tracks above but, unlike with the lower levels, he had no familiarity with the layout up there. At the last second, Fahkoury chose to go up rather than down. About one quarter of the way up, he looked over his shoulder and saw the man sliding the phone into his jacket pocket.

He walked the remainder of the single flight up the escalator, as if in a hurry to catch a train at the top level of the station. He moved toward the center of the open area and took a seat on one of the black stone benches resting beneath the station's famous decorative clock. Fahkoury waited nervously, partially hidden among eleven other people spread out on the large rectangular slab. He was anticipating the man to appear at the top of the escalator any second. He swiftly ran the possible moves through his head and realized he had few. The encounter was unnerving him and he was beginning to think that an elaborate trap was being laid. After several minutes, there was still no sign of the watchful man from the entrance hall.

Fahkoury rose from the bench and peered over the balcony at the levels below. He saw his watcher one level below the entrance hall, seated on a bench next to one of the tracks. As a train entered the station, the man rose from the bench and began moving toward the rear of the waiting area. Fahkoury had no idea what he was doing, but it no longer appeared the man was interested in him. Fahkoury headed back to the escalator. This time, he moved quickly as he crossed the entrance hall and exited the station through the north entrance. Once outside, he set his eyes on the park on the opposite side of the small plaza. There stood another man, although this one he was expecting. He marched over without delay.

"It is good to see you my brother," Fahkoury said.

"I can say the same to you," Fahd al-Rasheed said. "You are a sight for sore eyes. I was wondering if you had some trouble and whether I was going to see you again. Are you hungry? Would you like to get something to eat before we meet the other brothers?"

"I might have had some trouble. There was a man inside who seemed to be watching me."

"I did not see anyone follow you out."

"Maybe I am being paranoid. The last I saw him, he was waiting for a train on one of the lower levels. But I don't want to take any chances. Let's get away from the station and see if we are being watched. Our meeting with the brothers can wait until I am sure we are clear."

"Then let's take a walk. I know where we can go."

Chapter 50
Langley

Timothy Patrick was back in his office on the sixth floor when his assistant told him Samantha Lane and Ella Rock were on the line and asking to speak to him. It was a most urgent matter, they said. Patrick had left the first-floor conference room only minutes after Ella Rock had uncovered the identity of a person they now believed was a key figure in the Aziz and Al-Kalafa network. *This has to be about Saleem Nasir*, he told himself. "Please put the call through," he said to his assistant.

"Nasir was on a flight last night from O'Hare," Lane said, referring to O'Hare International Airport in Chicago. "It was a nonstop flight to Amsterdam, arriving just after two o'clock in the afternoon local time or about three hours ago."

"Son of a bitch!" Patrick said before quickly adding, "Please excuse my language." Patrick realized this meant that Nasir, in all likelihood, had been involved in the Chicago attack. It also more or less confirmed that Aziz and Al-Kalafa had been behind it. "What did he use to get out of the country?"

"He used his French passport," Lane said.

"How and when did he get into the US?"

"He claimed to have made a land border crossing from Canada sixty-two days ago."

"How do you know that?"

"He tendered the proper immigration form at the airport." Lane was referring to form I-94W. It was a paper document issued to people entering the country at a land port of entry under the Visa Waiver Program. "But Customs and Border Protection does not have a record of his entry."

"The form was a fake?"

"It looks that way."

"I wonder why he bothered to present it in the first place. Half the people never bother," Patrick said.

"Maybe he thinks it was better to offer it than to be asked; less likely to draw scrutiny. And he probably feels pretty confident we have no clue about his relationship with Aziz," Rock said.

That was true. Nasir had changed his name and used a bunch of corporate cutouts to conceal his communications with other suspected members of Al-Kalafa. Patrick knew how fortunate they were that Rock had been able to identify him when she did. Still, using a real passport was a calculated risk, as Aziz and Nasir must know that their relationship would eventually come to light. Their temerity pissed Patrick off even more. "What else do you have on Nasir?" he asked.

"We have his current passport photo and some older pictures from identification documents and a few financial publications," Rock said. "He wasn't particularly active on social media. We've only found an old LinkedIn profile. It was taken down eight years ago and there was no photo in the profile. We're searching for additional physical information to augment what can be gleaned from the photographs."

Patrick leaned back in his chair and placed his hands behind his head, a position he often found himself in when he was cogitating. He had to think about the strategic implications of this latest news. The pace of attacks was already unlike anything they had encountered previously, and he had no reason to expect it to slow down. Although Al-Kalafa had made no claims of responsibility for any of the recent attacks, its role was all but certain. Nasir had deliberately left a trail to flaunt his involvement in the Chicago attack. And given the sequential nature of all three attacks, it was looking more certain Al-Kalafa had carried out Paris and Alcoy. Aziz had declared an all-out war. If Patrick and his team were going to have any chance at stopping Al-Kalafa, they had to figure out what Aziz was planning next.

At that thought, something popped into his head. He suddenly understood something Aziz had said in his most recent statement. "I think I know what Aziz was saying when he said something about the rhythm of the drums. What was it he said? I can't remember the exact words."

"I have the full statement right here," Rock said. She scanned through the document until she came to the sentence she was looking for. "Aziz said, 'As you heed the growing rhythm from the beat-beat-beat of the war drums, know that the climax will be the momentous victory that places us on the threshold of our objective. As the leader of Al-Kalafa, it is my pledge that we will not rest until the day comes when only true believers occupy all four corners of the world.'"

"I think the beat of the drums are the rapid series of attacks we have just seen," Patrick said.

"I always thought it was strange how he repeated the word three times," Lane said. "At first, I wrote it off to awkward prose but the more I think about it, it's possible that the repetition was deliberate, like it was some kind of hidden message."

"If that's true," Rock said, "each beat of the drums could represent a particular attack. That would be three attacks leading up to a fourth—the 'climax.'"

"Then the questions we have to ask," Patrick said, "are how many attacks have there been so far and do we attribute all of them all to Al-Kalafa? I think we can safely assume Chicago, Alcoy, and Paris were all Al-Kalafa. But what about Istanbul? If we include that as an attack, that makes four, meaning Chicago was the climax."

"I don't think I'd include Istanbul," Lane said. "To me, that was an internal housecleaning matter. And, as horrific as it was, I am thinking Aziz is planning something more dramatic than Chicago for the climax."

Patrick briefly considered Lane's analysis and realized it squared with his own budding notion. "I'd agree with that," he said. "And based on Nasir's destination, I think I might know where he is planning to strike. The president is supposed to visit the Netherlands in four days for the Group of Twenty economic conference." This year, The Hague was hosting the annual G20 Economic Summit. President Madden and the leaders from the G20 countries, which included the European Union members, were scheduled to attend. "Aziz is going to hit the conference. The leaders of the most powerful countries will be in Holland for the conference. If he could kill them, or at least some of them, he could create tremendous destabilization around the globe and create a vacuum for him and Al-Kalafa." When there was no response, Patrick asked, "Are you guys still there?"

"We're here," Rock said. "Just thinking over what you said."

"That will be a very hard target," Lane said. "It will be the most secure site in the world for the three days of the conference."

"And it doesn't fit with the nature of the other targets," Rock said. "The security at the Super Bowl and the mall were nothing like it will be in The Hague. The attack in Chicago was on a soft target. So were the ones in Paris and Alcoy, again assuming Al-Kalafa carried those out. The Hague would be a pretty big change."

"But if you're right about Aziz wanting a showdown, he'd be hard pressed to find a better place than The Hague during a Group of Twenty gathering," Lane said.

"The more I think about it, there's another factor that supports The Hague being the target," Rock said. "Although it doesn't explain the one and most recent hit on his phone in Lille, Taj Khan primarily used his phone in and around Brussels. We know there is a connection between Khan and Saleem Nasir. Brussels is probably not much more than a hundred miles from The Hague."

"And we know Mumeet initially staged the Minnesota attacks from Dearborn, a distance that is five or six times farther," Lane said, picking up on Rock's thinking. "It's highly possible they could be setting up in or around Brussels. Saleem Nasir could get there from Amsterdam in under two hours."

"We'd know for sure if we had any idea where Mumeet was," Rock said. "I have a hard time believing that Saleem Nasir can pull off another attack so soon, especially one in The Hague. It would only give him a few days to surveil the target, plan, and prepare. From what we know, Nasir lacks the experience and skill to pull something like that off. To me, this screams Mumeet."

"And it wouldn't surprise me if Aziz intends to pair Mumeet with Fahd al-Rasheed again," Patrick said.

The three of them continued to brainstorm the various possibilities that could be extrapolated from the footprint Khan had established in Belgium and Nasir's escape to Amsterdam. The Hague or somewhere else in the Low Countries was the likeliest bet but it was far from certain the terrorists would stage there. Even though there was no record that Nasir had flown beyond Amsterdam, they had to accept that a car, train, or boat provided numerous options. With a three-hour head start, Nasir could be almost anywhere on the continent or in the United Kingdom. That realization opened the door to other possibilities for an attack. After talking it through, they agreed it would be dangerous to focus on The Hague at the expense of other potential targets. They were just beginning to assemble a schedule of all upcoming major events in Europe when Patrick's assistant knocked on his door.

"Director, Tony Galvin is on the line from Brussels. He says it's urgent."

"Please patch him into this call."

A moment later, Galvin was on the line. "Hello, Tim?"

"Hi Tony. I have Samantha Lane and Ella Rock on the line with me. What's up?" Patrick said.

"I'll get right to it. One of my guys thinks he may have just seen Mumeet at Antwerp Central," Galvin said. "He was there running a surveillance operation when he saw someone who fit the description we have for Mumeet." Galvin went on to explain what Joe Hankinson had told him only a few minutes before.

"Is Hankinson still watching the guy?"

"He's not. His target was arriving on a train when Joe and I were on the phone. It's the first time the target has been outside of Russia in nearly half a year and he's a key link in the money-laundering operation. It was a tough call, but I told Joe to stick with the target. And I didn't have anyone else even close to the area."

Patrick knew he would have done the same thing. Galvin was unaware of the information Patrick himself had only just learned and there was still no way to positively identify Mumeet. Patrick realized that if there had only been enough time for him to put out an alert that Nasir was in Amsterdam, things might have been different. "Tony, we just learned some information that suggests it may very well have been Mumeet that Hankinson saw." Patrick gave Galvin on overview of what they knew about Nasir.

"I'm really sorry, Tim," Galvin said.

"Don't beat yourself up, Tony. Under the circumstances, you made the right call. I would have done the same thing. Did Hankinson notice if Mumeet was with anyone else?"

"He said he was alone, and it appeared he was conducting countersurveillance more than looking for someone he expected."

"Thanks for getting this information to me so quickly, Tony. If you can spare some people to poke around Antwerp, it would be a big help. But be careful about using Joe Hankinson. Mumeet's been around this long because he's careful. I'd bet he memorizes every questionable face he encounters. I'll be sending a team into the area, so we'll be in touch. Thanks again, Tony."

Patrick disconnected Galvin's line and said to his two colleagues, "I think we just confirmed Aziz is targeting the Group of Twenty summit. For the first time, we have an edge, albeit a slight one. You guys keep digging on Nasir and Khan. They're going to lead us to the Bringer of Death and his buddy Fahd al-Rasheed. In the meantime, I'll call PJ and bring him up to speed."

Chapter 51
Antwerp

Al-Rasheed led Fahkoury into the busy *Grote Markt*, a large square in Antwerp's Old Town district. Rising before them through the throng of people and merchant booths, and stretching the length of the square, was the sixteenth century city hall, a magnificent structure that typified the Flemish Renaissance architecture prominently displayed throughout the central square. To their right was an equally stunning row of guildhalls, standing shoulder to shoulder on the northern end of the square. Al-Rasheed turned toward the southern end of the square and the numerous bars and restaurants situated there.

"I came here yesterday," he said, while pointing to one of the restaurants. "Apparently, this restaurant is famous for its pommes frites. They are very good."

They walked over and stood at the back of the line. Fahkoury glanced around for any more signs of surveillance. He had not seen the man from the train station or anyone else suspicious during their twenty-minute walk from Antwerp Central. As they moved up the line, he scrutinized the dress of the other men nearby and noticed they were dressed in very similar fashion to the clothes he and al-Rasheed were wearing. No one seemed to be paying them any particular attention. He chastised himself for having become paranoid back at the train station, but he could not escape the sinking feeling that the American would soon reenter his world. As they waited, he was having a hard time shaking off the feeling that the walls were closing in around him.

When it was time for al-Rasheed to place their order, he moved off to the side but kept his back to the activity in the square. He told himself to push the doubts aside. The operation was too important and it needed his full attention. He offered a silent prayer that he would have the opportunity to execute this one attack, then he would accept whatever fate was planned for him.

Minutes later, al-Rasheed handed him a bottle of water and a cone-shaped bag brimming with thick strips of fried potatoes. Al-Rasheed made a motion with his head and Fahkoury followed him into the square. When they had cleared the crowd at the restaurant, he said to al-Rasheed, "Where are we going?"

"Let's walk over to the river. There are benches along the shore where we can talk privately."

After a short walk, they selected one of the open benches and sat down on the banks of the River Scheldt, a key shipping route since the Middle Ages. The cloudy weather and a cool northerly breeze had considerably dampened interest for the leisurely viewing area, and they found themselves far removed from the nearest bystander.

"When did you arrive in Amsterdam," al-Rasheed asked.

"I arrived from Hamburg late last night." He told al-Rasheed he had been staying in Germany since leaving Istanbul, first in Berlin and then Hamburg for the past three days. "I spent the rest of the evening walking around the Red-Light District. It is worse than you can imagine."

Al-Rasheed laughed to himself at the thought of Fahkoury's revulsion at the carnival of vice going around him. He had been to the Red-Light District once, many years ago, and recalled the memories affectionately. He thought it best not to compare their experiences and moved onto a more germane topic. "Have you had a chance to see the convention center?"

"Earlier this morning. It is a very large building, bordered by a main street and a park on the east side and minor pathways on the others. There is no security in place yet, but I am expecting that the main street will be closed and armed men will be surrounding the building. If the brothers cannot get us inside, we will not be able to execute any kind of attack. What are your thoughts about the leader Nasir has chosen?"

"His name is Taj Khan. I met with him in Rotterdam. He seems fairly bright and capable. He told me he is thirty-one years old and has lived most of his life in Brussels. We conversed in French and Arabic; he is fluent in both. He said he also speaks Chinese. He is a Uyghur."

Fahkoury knew the Uyghurs well. Several members of the Turkistan Islamic Party had fought alongside him in Afghanistan. The jihadists from western China had proved to be very capable and brave fighters. "Did you get a sense he was expecting it would be you who showed up to meet him?"

"It was clear that he recognized me, but I think he was surprised."

"What does Khan say about the others?"

"The other brothers are his childhood friends from Molenbeek. I gather that none of them are educated, but Khan says they are all young and strong. He said he trusts them with his life and they are equally committed to the cause."

The competencies of Khan and his brothers was less important than their access to the building. In so far as the attack itself, Mumeet planned to use them as an imperfect secondary measure. The effectiveness of this operation relied upon Fahkoury's ability to strategically place the bomb. "Did you question Khan about access to the convention center?"

"It is his cousin, Jian Chong, who will give us access. Chong is in charge of building maintenance and security."

Using someone outside the organization was a risk, but Aziz had assured him that Saleem Nasir would choose someone who was sure to deliver. Fahkoury accepted that there was no other way. This plan was not possible without someone like Khan's cousin. He reflected back on the Yemeni hawaladar in Dearborn. Like Khan's cousin, Zahir Bahar was someone Aziz had found and recruited to assist. Bahar had lived up to Fahkoury's expectations. He would have to count on Khan's cousin to do the same. He cast those fleeting thoughts aside and returned his attention to the affairs he could control. "Does Khan have everything I asked for?"

"He tells me he does but we shall see."

"Let's go do that now," Fahkoury said.

Chapter 52
Langley/Paris

"Did you get the file?" Patrick asked. For the past hour, while he had been briefing Carpenter on the news about Saleem Nasir and Taj Khan, Samantha Lane and Ella Rock had put together a digital file on the two men.

"I'm opening it now," Carpenter answered. He had just returned to the US embassy in Paris when Patrick called. He looked over the photos and quickly scanned the biographical information the team had been able to gather so far. There was virtually nothing in Nasir's file following his departure from Aziz's firm. Khan's file was even thinner. The man was a ghost, with no work history in his profile. "At least the photographs are decent," he said. There was a recent passport photo for Nasir. Khan's photo, taken from the national identification card that all Belgians fifteen years and older were required to carry at all times, was of somewhat lesser quality, but still good enough to positively identify him. "You've shared these photos?"

"We have them out to all trusted intelligence agencies with the caveat to keep our interest quiet. We don't want to risk alerting either one of them that they're on our radar," Patrick said.

"And you've got our people looking for these guys and Mumeet?"

"The calls have been made. Every operations officer in the Low Countries is discreetly pressing their assets for information."

"Did you convince the president to hold off making a public announcement that he won't be attending the conference?" Carpenter knew his chances of taking down the terrorists would end once the president made the announcement. The rest of the world leaders would immediately follow suit, causing the terrorists to realize their plans had been discovered. As soon as that happened, they would scurry like the rats they were.

"He's not going to make any announcement—he's planning to attend the conference."

"What?" Carpenter did not agree with that decision. He knew Saleem Nasir had flown from Chicago to Amsterdam and he had just been told minutes before that Mumeet may have been seen in Antwerp. To top it off, a man named Taj Khan was linked to Nasir and believed to be living in Belgium. That meant all three men were within a stone's throw of the site for an important economic conference that was scheduled to begin in a matter of days. Carpenter could not imagine these matters were unrelated. This information unquestionably met the threshold of a credible threat, and it should have been enough to at least convince the president to recommend that the meeting be postponed. "Will he reconsider if we don't find these guys before he leaves for the conference?"

"I don't expect he will. Director Christie and his staff were waiting with the president when Director Gonzalez and I arrived to brief him." Doug Christie was one of the few holdovers from the previous administration and he continued to serve as the director of the US Secret Service under President Madden. "Christie was in his post when the Nuclear Security Summit was held at the same conference center, so he knows the landscape well. The current security measures will mimic those used five years ago. Christie and his staff are confident that security will not be an issue either at the hotel, along the route, or at the conference center. A two-block security perimeter will be implemented at the conference center, and no unauthorized persons or vehicles will be allowed inside. As an added precaution, Secret Service will bring additional personnel, and the Dutch have also pledged to contribute more resources. The president is confident that he and the conference will be more than adequately protected."

Carpenter knew that even the best security measures were imperfect. In fact, three years earlier there had been two notable breaches at the White

House, purportedly one of the most secure facilities in the world. One man had simply climbed over the perimeter fence and marched up to the front door with a gun in hand, while another man had flown a plane into the building. Fortunately, neither event had threatened the lives of the former president and those inside, but both revealed the vulnerabilities of any security system. "Did you and Director Gonzalez try to talk him out of going?" he asked.

"We did and the president is taking the threat seriously. He instructed Director Gonzalez to reach out to her counterparts in the countries whose leaders will be attending. He says the other leaders can make their own decisions, but he is going."

"Who are you sending me?"

"We're pretty limited right now. It's going to take a few days before I can get you some help," Patrick said. The opposition party controlled the upper chamber of Congress and the Senate was holding up President Madden's request to increase the CTC's annual budget. For the last six years, only inflation-adjusted increases had been authorized, putting a severe limitation on Patrick's ability to recruit new members to his team of paramilitary operators. Two recent retirements exacerbated the problem. "I've got one team in the Hindu Kush and another one in eastern Syria. Even if I pull those operations, it will take up to two days to get the teams out and to you. Until then, you're all I've got for operators. I can ask Secretary Fitzgibbons to send a Special Forces team, but again we might be looking at a turnaround of at least a few days."

Over the years, Carpenter had worked with every Special Forces unit in the military. In terms of lethality, the various units only competed amongst themselves. But this situation required a degree of finesse. Delta Force was perhaps most adept at clandestine work and certainly a possibility. But his preference was to use men he already knew well. Things ran smoother that way. "Send me some of our guys," he said. "I'll let you figure out logistics. In the meantime, send Tyler over." Carpenter was talking about Tyler Kennedy, the young man who had helped him at the Great American Mall.

"He's not ready," Patrick said. "He's still in training."

"I've seen what he can do under pressure and I need at least some help right away. I'll send him back when more help arrives."

Patrick didn't like the idea of sending a fresh recruit into harm's way, but Carpenter obviously needed some assistance and had confidence in Kennedy. "All right, I'll have him there by morning. But make sure you watch out for him."

"He's just going to be an extra set of eyes and ears."

Somehow Patrick doubted that. "Anything else?" he asked.

"No, I'm good. Just send me the kid as soon as possible."

Chapter 53
Antwerp

Following their sojourn at the River Scheldt, Fahkoury and al-Rasheed presented themselves at the small rowhouse, located several blocks east of the zoo. They were greeted at the door by Taj Khan. As al-Rasheed had said, he did not look Asian. Khan's long, wide nose and dark skin gave him the appearance of Arab descent rather than Chinese. Without saying a word, Khan ushered them up the narrow wooden staircase to the second floor, where the men had been assembled. Khan joined three others sitting on a scruffy couch in the center of the room.

Fahkoury silently studied the four men seated before him. At first glance, the men seemed rather ordinary. Like Khan, the other three men appeared to be in their late twenties or early thirties. They were all dressed in simple Western clothing, although it was more suitable for manual labor, and the boots each man wore were covered in a white dust. Their statures varied but each man looked capable of any physical demands he intended to place upon them. There was nothing about any of them that would garner a second look from a casual observer. But the look in their eyes suggested these were not ordinary men. Despite not knowing the details, these men knew they were about to participate in jihad. And Fahkoury anticipated their eager expressions would not fade when they learned it would be a martyr operation.

△ △ △

    Khan's heart was beating rapidly. He wondered if his brothers were having the same experience. He had only been told by Mr. Saleem that two men would arrive one day with plans for an operation. Mr. Saleem had not disclosed their identities but said the men were distinguished and respected members of the organization. Ever since the attacks in America, the thought that the revered man known as the Bringer of Death might be one of the two men lingered in the back of Khan's mind. Like many of his fellow believers, Khan had read the many social media posts about the attacks in the United States. Many of those posts and some of the more popular jihadist websites showed the same photos of Mumeet and Fahd al-Rasheed that were being circulated by the infidels. He became convinced the plans Mr. Saleem had for him would include the Bringer of Death.

    But, as the weeks passed by without any word, Khan began to think his time would not come. Then, two days ago, he found the note in his doorway that he was expecting. The next day, he traveled to Rotterdam for the meeting and immediately recognized Fahd al-Rasheed. After the brief encounter, he rushed home to tell his brothers. They were joyous with the very real possibility that the second man might well turn out to be the revered Mumeet. Khan and his brothers had been so excited by that prospect that none of them had slept.

    Now, even though neither one of the men had provided their names, there was no question in Khan's mind that the man standing before him now was the legendary Mumeet. As he looked up at the Bringer of Death, Khan suddenly realized this was no longer a fantasy. He was terrified as much as awestruck. He sensed there was a palpable resoluteness about this man, and mistakes would not be tolerated or forgiven. And the man's remorseless black eyes told him it was hatred, more than righteousness, that propelled the Bringer of Death.

△ △ △

    Fahkoury purposefully remained silent as he looked the men over. He suspected they all knew who he was. The blankness behind their stares told him these men were beginning to appreciate the seriousness of this matter. That they were clearly intimidated did not concern him. He would channel that fear to sharpen their focus. This operation would be his defining achievement, something he knew the moment Aziz broached it during their meeting in the desert just a few months earlier. This operation, more than the combined effects of all his previous work, would bring the believers closer to defeating the infidels and realizing a global caliphate. He would not be denied this opportunity and would not allow these men to fail him. Their attentiveness gave him some assurance they were prepared to learn their roles. Still to be determined, however, was whether they were prepared to accept the fate that awaited them.

When the designs for the attack were settled, Fahkoury had insisted that the men selected must be willing to martyr themselves for the cause. Although the assault he had planned for them had no bearing on the main attack, he intended to demonstrate the courage and dedication of the enemy that the West was facing. And, more selfishly, he didn't want anyone alive who might betray his anonymity. Although no special combat skills were necessary for this aspect of the operation, it was imperative that the men have experience in a particular trade, for that expertise would serve as the Trojan Horse for the prominent feature of his plan. Since the task of choosing these men had been given to Aziz's man, Saleem Nasir, Fahkoury was relying on Aziz's promise that those conditions had been met. But now that he was meeting the team for the first time, he would his own make his own appraisals.

"My brothers, each of you has been carefully chosen to participate in a most holy operation, one that will strike a blow at the mightiest oppressors of Islam," Fahkoury said. "Count your blessings for having been given this opportunity to rid the world of nonbelievers and prove your devotion to Allah." This opening declaration did not startle the men. Rather, they waited with rapt attention for him to continue. He thought he detected the faintest hint of anticipation on their faces, another positive sign they were ready to follow him without question. To be sure, he asked, "Are each of you prepared to martyr yourself in the name of Allah?"

The men erupted in chants of "Allahu Akbar!"

"Your place in paradise awaits you!" Fahkoury said, with equal enthusiasm. Before continuing, he considered the power he held over these men. It was intoxicating. With the assistance of Aziz's wealth and network, he believed he could not be stopped. Men like these would gladly give their lives at his instruction. And there was no shortage of them. For the first time, he truly believed the dream of a caliphate would be realized in his lifetime. But he quickly recognized that he was getting ahead of himself. He forced those thoughts aside and focused on the extremely important matter at hand. "When this blessed operation is over, the infidel will cower in submission. The West and the apostates ruling the lands of our brothers will fully understand the purity and power of our cause!"

"Allahu Akbar!" the men responded.

Fahkoury offered the slightest of smiles while he allowed the excitement to die down. When it had, he said, "Now, tell me how you have been spending your time in the land of the infidel."

The other three looked at Khan, who started by telling Fahkoury that he and his parents had emigrated from the Xinjiang region of China, where they were persecuted for their religious beliefs. He recounted a visit by his uncle when he was in his early teens. During that visit, his uncle tried to teach him the Prophet's ways, but he said he was not prepared to live them. However, his thinking began to change when he learned his uncle had been killed by the Chinese government. His uncle was accused of leading an attack that resulted in the deaths of nine off-duty police officers. He became angry when his parents condemned his uncle's actions and labeled him a terrorist. Khan, recalling his uncle's teachings on jihad, saw it differently. The very next day, he assaulted a female police officer. He was sent to prison, where he was quartered with a group of believers. It was there, Khan said, that he fully accepted the Prophet Muhammad's teachings on jihad.

His fellow inmates listened to his story and empathized with the oppression he and his parents had endured at the hands of the infidel. They also explained that his uncle would be celebrated as a revered martyr. By the time his incarceration ended, Khan had decided that he would become a jihadist to right the wrongs to his fellow believers and to honor the memory of his uncle. And when he was reunited with his three friends, he began to teach them the true way.

Khan then explained his relationship to his three brothers seated alongside him. They had known one another since childhood, each having been raised in the Molenbeek section of Brussels. None of them had completed his secondary education, confirming al-Rasheed's presumption. All four of them had spent time in prison for offenses ranging from vandalism to assault. Khan also explained that men with their limited skills had been lucky to find irregular work, mostly with low-paying jobs in the construction industry. In fact, Khan was the only of one them holding down a job when he was approached by a man almost two years earlier, someone Khan referred to as "Mr. Saleem." He met Mr. Saleem on three separate occasions, during which Khan answered many questions about himself and his immediate and extended family. Eventually, Mr. Saleem instructed him to identify three or four fellow believers who shared their views and could be trusted. That was easy, Khan told Saleem, he already had his team.

When Mr. Saleem was satisfied with the men, he helped Khan set up a restoration company. Khan was given money and instructions not to worry about the financial success of the company, only to learn the trade. He was told to focus on residential and small commercial projects where the customers were willing to pay cash in exchange for a discount. For the most part, the small company performed some work in Belgium but most of their jobs were across the border in Holland. The money Mr. Saleem provided was used to supplement their income and cover living expenses. Khan said he elected to rent the home in Antwerp because it was cheaper than the Netherlands and it offered a central location for the majority of their work. He neglected to say that his primary reason for selecting Antwerp rather than someplace in Holland was that he wanted to be closer to his girlfriend in Brussels.

As he listened to Khan, Fahkoury understood how these men had been open to recruitment for violent jihad. They faced bleak lives, given their lack of education and skills, especially living in a city and country with unemployment exceeding twenty percent. Those conditions would have made it that much easier for Aziz's man to recruit them. He also appreciated the appeal of the long-standing connection among the men. To a certain degree, he was counting on their relationships to help them suppress the doubts that would inevitably confront one or all of them as the time for action drew nearer. However, Fahkoury was less concerned with their resolve to see things though than he was their access to the target. And he knew that was the real reason Khan had been chosen by Saleem Nasir.

The value in Khan and his friends was Khan's connection to the convention center in The Hague. When Aziz shared the target and the occasion for the attack during their meeting in the Rub Al Khali, Fahkoury had dismissed it as fantasy. He said the security measures would be vigorous and more than adequate to stymie any attempts to assault the facility from its exterior. There was only one way to execute this operation, he told Aziz, and that required access to the building. Without it, the operation would be impossible. Aziz insisted that not only was it possible, but the necessary arrangements had, in fact, already been made. Fahkoury had thought it was too good to be true.

Now, he was about to find out. As Khan was finishing his story, Fahkoury studied each of the men. To this point in time, they had been living an adventurous dream. If they knew his true feelings, perhaps reality would reshape their perceptions. Beyond providing him access to the target facility, Khan and his men were worthless in his eyes. In all likelihood, they would all be gunned down before any of them was able to kill a single infidel. The carnage would all be done by his bomb, as long as he could get it inside. "Brother Khan, I understand it is your cousin who will grant us admission to the property," he said.

"Yes, he is a relation. A cousin, several times removed," Khan said. "But he is in charge of security and maintenance at the facility."

"And he is willing to do this for you and our cause?"

"He is. He said Mr. Saleem has secured his loyalty."

Fahkoury was aware of the arrangements Nasir had made. Although he distrusted anyone only willing to help for money, Aziz assured him that Nasir had vetted the cousin and was certain he would follow through on his end of the bargain. Still, Fahkoury had his doubts. It was an issue he would address when he met with Nasir. "How will your cousin contact you?"

"I gave him the number to the new phone I purchased yesterday, just like Mr. Saleem told me to do after I was contacted." Khan nodded toward al-Rasheed when he said this.

"Have you used this new phone?"

"Only once to call my cousin."

"Are there any other phones in this house?"

Fahkoury was pleased when all four of them shook their heads. He imposed strict communication protocols for his operations. He had given Aziz explicit instructions that only the team's leader was authorized to have a phone that was used for any aspect of this operation, and any such phone was not to be used to communicate with anyone else. He had also demanded that phones were to be discarded as soon as they were no longer needed. A lapse in communication protocol was the surest way for his plans to be compromised. That brought him to his biggest concern. Looking directly at Khan, he said, "Brother, I am aware the Mr. Saleem gave you a phone shortly after you met him. When is the last time you used that phone?"

"When I called the man to arrange pick up of the material and weapons. That was several weeks ago."

"And it has not been in use since?"

Khan summoned the most forceful voice he could manage. "No, sir," he said. "I destroyed it just as Mr. Saleem told me." Khan recalled how Mr. Saleem had waited outside the store while he purchased the prepaid phone. When he returned, Mr. Saleem warned him again that the number was reserved for calls between the two of them and to the contact in Slovakia. In a moment of weakness, Khan had given the number to his girlfriend when she moved from Molenbeek to Lille two months earlier. He told her not to call the phone unless there was an emergency. Perhaps due to the mounting stress he was feeling about the upcoming operation, they had argued the last night he spent with her in Lille. He left the following morning without saying goodbye. She called just as the train was leaving Lille. Because the phone was in his backpack, it took him several seconds to realize he had forgotten to destroy it and that it was her calling. He immediately pulled the SIM card, broke it into pieces with his fingers, and threw everything out the window. Although he had technically not violated Mr. Saleem's orders, Khan was sure the Bringer of Death would not agree.

Fahkoury sensed some equivocation in Khan's answer. He also detected that Khan's eyes cast downward when he gave his response. "Brother, it is best to be honest with me. If your answer was not truthful, tell me now. We can fix the problem."

"It is the truth," Khan said. This time with more conviction.

Fahkoury locked eyes with Khan, deciding what to do. If the man was lying, there was a grave risk to the operation. But there was no way to prove otherwise. His only choices were to believe the man or kill them all and scrap the operation. He mulled this over for a few moments but ultimately decided the opportunity was too compelling to pass up. "Very well," he finally said. "Do you have the blueprints?"

"Yes, they are in the basement."

"What about the material and weapons I requested?"

"It is all here, in the basement with the blueprints," Khan said. "Would you like to see?"

"Yes, please show me."

Chapter 54
Amsterdam, the Netherlands

Late the next morning, Carpenter stood outside the arrivals hall at Schiphol Airport and scanned the crowd of weary travelers in search of Tyler Kennedy. He was eager to get going after a day of disappointment. He had traveled to Brussels the previous day to meet with chief of station Tony Galvin and Joe Hankinson. The more he talked with Hankinson, the more Carpenter was certain the operations officer had indeed seen Mumeet at the train station in Antwerp. But, despite the efforts of Galvin and his team, there had been no further sightings of the Bringer of Death in or around Antwerp. Carpenter was hoping Khan might prove easier to find, but those efforts were also not bearing any fruit. So far, there were no leads to Khan's whereabouts. All they had been able to find for Khan was a years-old address in the Molenbeek section of the Belgian capital, and Khan was not known to have any association with Antwerp.

Still, Carpenter was convinced Mumeet had been in Antwerp for a reason. Although it was possible that Mumeet continued on elsewhere, there would have been no reason for Mumeet to be loitering inside the train station. Instead, he would have stayed on the train during the stopover rather than risk being seen. The most obvious reason for Mumeet to stop in Antwerp was to meet with someone, most likely Khan or Nasir, or possibly both. Khan could have easily made the twenty-five-mile trip from Brussels, and Nasir's trip via train from Amsterdam would have taken less than eighty minutes.

Above all, Antwerp was unnervingly close to The Hague. And those prospects lent further weight to the theory that Aziz was planning an attack in the City of Peace and Justice.

What's more, Al-Kalafa's role in the attacks in Paris, Alcoy, and Chicago was no longer in doubt. The newly-minted terror group had claimed responsibility for all three attacks shortly before Carpenter sat down in Brussels with Galvin and Hankinson. As proof, it released video footage of the Chicago attack and martyr videos of those who carried out the ones in Paris and Alcoy. Among those appearing in the videos was Adel Shebani, confirming the suspicions about him and amplifying the significance of his links to Saleem Nasir, who was also known to have been in contact with Taj Khan. The pieces were falling into place and they all pointed to the G20 Economic Summit in The Hague as the next big target on Aziz's radar.

Now Carpenter was waiting for help to arrive so that he could resume the hunt for Mumeet. A few minutes later, Carpenter's wait was over. He recognized Tyler Kennedy's gait before looking up and seeing his lively blue eyes and beaming face. Before moving toward the ground transportation exit, Carpenter surreptitiously motioned for Kennedy to follow. Once outside, Carpenter slowed his pace slightly to allow Kennedy to come alongside him. He glanced over at Kennedy, who at six-one was just a notch taller. Kennedy's dark, wavy hair was definitely longer and the Mediterranean skin he had inherited from his Italian mother had darkened from the early spring outdoor training exercises. "Welcome to Holland," he said. "Good to see you again."

"It's good to see you too," Kennedy said. "Thanks for asking Director Patrick to send me over. I've been getting pretty antsy sitting in classes all day."

As the two walked along, Carpenter noticed that Kennedy seemed to be a bit more chiseled than he remembered. The younger man was holding a navy suit jacket in his left hand and carrying a canvas duffel over his right shoulder. The position put added stress on Kennedy's white spread collar dress shirt, which already appeared two sizes too small, and the tailored suit pants clung to Kennedy's thick thighs and big ass, each a remnant of his hockey-playing days. Carpenter estimated Kennedy had put on at least ten pounds of muscle since the last time he saw him. "I hear you about the classwork," he said. "Some of it can be pretty tedious but it looks like they've been working you pretty hard outside the classroom."

"Nah, the workouts are pretty lame. But I've been able to do a little extra on the side. I haven't felt this good since I've was playing."

"Well, I wouldn't make any sudden moves in those clothes. They look like they're about to come apart at the seams."

"Ha! Aren't you the funny guy," Kennedy said. Patrick had told him to wear a suit on the flight over since Carpenter wanted to hit the ground running. But the only suit Kennedy owned was three years old. "Some of us don't have a personal tailor, Mr. GQ. And I didn't have time to get a new suit before I left. I guess I must have put on some muscle since my playing days."

"It'll work. We probably don't need them, but I didn't want us showing up at the convention center looking like we were on a covert op. Patrick called ahead for us and told the general manager that we're part of the president's advance security detail. This way, we'll look the part. Do you have a tie in that duffel?"

"I do, but it's got some beer stains on it."

Carpenter snickered and shook his head. "You obviously haven't gone through the 'how to dress' portion of training. It's a good thing I have a few extras in the car."

"No guarantees it goes back to you in the same condition," Kennedy said. That elicited more laughter. Kennedy hadn't seen Carpenter like this before. He had only seen him two other times, besides that day at the mall. Each of those times, Carpenter had seemed pretty reserved. This was a different experience. A joker himself, Kennedy enjoyed the give and take, and he was liking this new side of Carpenter. When Carpenter was done having his fun, he asked, "So what's the plan?"

Carpenter knew that Kennedy was briefed in by Patrick before he left the States. To fill in any holes, he told Kennedy what he had learned in Brussels the previous day, which wasn't much. Carpenter summed up the situation by saying that conventional wisdom still pointed to the G20 Economic Summit as the focal point for an Al-Kalafa attack, but there was no intelligence about method or timing. While Patrick was directing a furious effort to track down Mumeet, Saleem Nasir, and Taj Khan, it was their job to figure out where and how Al-Kalafa intended to strike. "Our first stop will be The Hague to check out the World Peace Convention Center. After that, we'll check out where the president will be staying, as well as the route to and from the convention center."

"Have you seen the security plans?" Kennedy asked.

"I've seen the one the Secret Service has as well as one prepared by the Dutch government. An assault on the convention center will be nearly impossible, but I still want to see it for myself to assess any potential vulnerabilities. My greatest concern is an attack along the route or at the hotel."

"I can't wait to get started. This is going to be way better than training."

"We have a little time before we get to it. Apparently, they're not quite ready for us at the convention center. Director Patrick called this morning to let them know we'd be stopping by. He told me the general manager who will be showing us around isn't available until midafternoon. Since we have some time, let's stop and grab some food on the way. I haven't eaten yet and I'm sure what you had on the plane was shit."

Chapter 55
The Hague, the Netherlands

A couple hours after leaving Schiphol, Carpenter was pulling the government-issued Ford Taurus off the A4 Motorway. They had stopped in Leiden for an early and unsatisfying lunch. Carpenter learned the Dutch were not elaborate lunch eaters, so he settled for a toasted ham and cheese sandwich, while Kennedy feasted on a *broodie bal*, a meatball on a soft white bun. Now they were winding through the city toward the World Peace Convention Center. "There it is," Carpenter said, as the building came into view.

The conference center was located at the northern end of a sprawling complex in the Statenkwartier district. The three-level meeting area and eight-story hotel rising from the center of its roof occupied slightly more than one-third of the facility's ten-acre footprint. A large, four-level parking ramp occupied the southern end of the campus and was linked to the conference center by an enclosed central walkway with outdoor garden patios on either side. A few moments later, Carpenter stopped the car underneath the covered loading area at the front entrance. "I'll do most of the talking, but if you have a question, go ahead and ask. But remember this guy has no clue about the potential threat, so be discreet."

They were greeted by a strong northerly wind when they exited the car, bringing with it a smell of sea air from the nearby North Sea. The gusts pushed at their backs as they entered the glass-enclosed foyer. Waiting for them was Liam Van den Berg, the general manager of the World Peace Convention Center. Carpenter walked up to the diminutive Van den Berg, whose handlebar moustache was exactly as Patrick had described. "Mr. Van den Berg, I'm PJ Carpenter and this is my colleague Tyler Kennedy. Thank you for showing us around today."

Even with the full benefit of his immaculately coifed blond hair, the rail-thin Van den Berg stood almost a half-foot shorter than the two muscled men standing before him. Their imposing presence only heightened his anxiety. Shortly after he had arrived that morning, the facility's head of security and maintenance, Jian Chong, had informed him of a leak in the storage room located behind the stage of the main auditorium. Apparently, it was a long-standing problem that finally manifested itself over the weekend. According to Chong, black mold was found on some of the ceiling panels. As if that were not troubling enough, a test cut on the wall separating the storage room and the auditorium confirmed the rot was not confined to a few ceiling panels. Van den Berg was humiliated that his facility had a potentially dangerous mold problem. He prided himself on running a world-class operation. He tried not to think about the shame he would feel if word of this crisis got out. And the timing could not have been worse. The world's leaders would be convening in his building in three days. Van den Berg authorized Chong to hire a remediation specialist and told him he wanted the repairs completed within forty-eight hours and a stipulated budget.

To make matter's worse, not more than two hours after Chong's terrible news, Van den Berg received a call and was told that two US Secret Service representatives would be arriving soon to inspect the property. Thinking quickly, he told the caller he would not be available for the meeting until midafternoon. Fortunately, the caller accepted the delay, as it would give Chong time to cover up the test cuts and at least replace the damaged tiles. Although it was unlikely that the Americans would venture into the storeroom, he could not take that chance. The unplanned visit also meant the remediation and remodeling work would have to be delayed. As much as he wanted the problem fixed right away, it was better that work not begin until the Americans had left. When he informed Chong about the change in plans, Van den Berg had no choice but to accept the man's request for more funding. Otherwise, there was a risk the work would not be finished before the attendees and the press began arriving.

Now, after a hectic morning, he had to put on a happy face and show these two men around the building. He wondered how many different inspections the US Secret Service intended to conduct prior to the G20 Economic Summit. This would be the second, following an in-depth, two-day visit slightly less than two weeks before. At least there had been no embarrassing issues then. Van den Berg was hoping this would be a less thorough examination and that he would be able to keep his guests away from the affected area. In that case, he would be able to get them on their way well before the remediation team arrived.

Van den Berg stepped forward and offered a welcoming smile as he extended his hand in greeting, only to experience successive bone-crushing handshakes with the two men. When the man named Kennedy mercifully released his hand, Van den Berg summoned the advice of his meditation specialist. He envisioned the tension draining from his shoulders and arms before surreptitiously taking one deep, cleansing breath. After the brief yet restoring exercise, he joyfully asked, "Shall we start the tour?"

Van den Berg proceeded from the lobby directly to the King George Auditorium, where the G20 Economic Summit would be held. He led them down the sloping central walkway to the foot of the stage. "The meeting will take place in this auditorium," he said. "The delegates from the participating countries will be seated on this level, while the press will occupy the balcony."

Carpenter turned and looked back at the auditorium. It was impressive. A sea of regal blue folding chairs was arrayed before him, separated into three sections which were parted by two red-carpeted walkways. Hardwood flooring covered the roomy surfaces between the rows of chairs. A similarly-decorated horseshoe-shaped balcony soared above them. The room was completed by an arching, black ceiling festooned with a sparkling constellation of small bright lights. Carpenter thought it was a fittingly regal setting for a convention of world leaders. "How many people can be seated in the auditorium," he asked.

"We have it set up to hold approximately twenty-five hundred people," Van den Berg said. "There is room for eighteen hundred on this level with the remainder in the balcony."

"How many entrances are there?" Kennedy asked.

"The only entrances are the five sets of doors we came in at the back of the auditorium and one on the left side of the stage." Van den Berg said as all three of them were facing the stage.

"Where does that exit lead to?" Carpenter asked.

"It opens onto a hallway that is lined with three smaller meeting rooms for breakout sessions. The hallway begins in the foyer and flows all the way to the back of the building."

"How will people attending the conference enter and exit the auditorium?" Carpenter asked.

"Everyone will use the doors we used when we entered from the lobby. Most of the attendees will be staying in the hotel on the property, which has been reserved for the exclusive use of conference participants and their staffs. Hotel guests will simply take one of the three elevators that open onto the lobby."

"What about people who are staying someplace other than the hotel here?" Kennedy asked.

"Some heads of state, like your president, have made different lodging arrangements. President Madden and those other leaders will enter the parking ramp beneath the complex and take the same set of elevators up to the lobby. In addition to the media, there are a number of unaffiliated guests that will be attending the conference. They all have offsite lodging arrangements and will arrive at the front doors, where you gentlemen arrived. All guests will be screened before they are allowed to enter the lobby."

"What about the stairs next to the lobby elevators?" Kennedy asked. "Will anyone be permitted to use them?"

"No, the stairwell will be guarded and closed off at all times."

"What did you say is at the back of the building?" Carpenter asked.

"On this level, there is only storage and our control center. At the upper two levels there are meeting rooms."

"And there is another elevator back there, correct?" Carpenter asked.

"Yes, I forgot to mention that there is a service elevator."

"That descends to the parking ramp as well?"

"It does, but your president and other leaders arriving through the parking ramp will use the main elevators that open onto the lobby."

Carpenter mulled over how an attack might take place. He knew from studying the architectural plans Director Doug Christie of the Secret Service had emailed that there were only two surface-level entrances to the conference center. One was at the rear of the building, providing access for the walkway from the main parking structure at the other end of the campus and the outdoor patios on either side of it. That entrance would be closed during the summit and heavily guarded. The other was the front entrance that they had come through and all the guests would use. The only other entrance was through the subterranean parking ramp. Access to the ramp was secured by steel overhead doors and guards would be posted both outside and inside the ramp.

Although security would be equally tight at the front entrance, Carpenter deemed it the more likely point of attack. He envisioned the possibilities when he and Kennedy had entered that way earlier. There would be a lot of commotion surrounding the arrivals and departures to serve as a distraction, and the glass windows enclosing the lobby could be more easily breached. In the event of an assault on the building during the conference, the Secret Service would usher the president through the exit at the side of the stage and into the service elevator at the back of the auditorium. If an assault occurred during a break when the president and others were in the lobby, he would be ushered down the stairs next to the main elevators. In either case, he would be taken to the steel-reinforced concrete parking ramp, where he would be safeguarded until reinforcements arrived and the threat was eliminated.

Although Carpenter was somewhat comfortable with the evacuation plans in the case of an external assault, the time necessary to implement them would be compromised in the event an attack was launched from inside the building. "Will any other parts of the building be in use during the Economic Summit?" he asked.

"Only this auditorium and the lobby will be used during the conference. Everything else will be closed off and locked."

"Will any food be served during the conference?" Kennedy asked.

"Yes, lunch and light hors d'oeuvres will be served in the hotel lobby."

"Just out of curiosity, besides the parking ramp, what's below, above, and around us?" Kennedy asked.

"The World Peace Conference Center is comprised of four levels. As I mentioned, the lowest level, which is immediately below us, contains the parking ramp, which covers the front half of the building. At the rear half of the basement, there is a mechanical room separated from several storage rooms by a central hallway. On this level, there is this auditorium. There is nothing above this entire auditorium. With the arched ceiling, it pretty much extends all the way to the roof. At the back of the building on this level are the storage and control center rooms I mentioned. And, to our left, the hallway and three meeting rooms I told you about. At the front of the building, above the foyer, is a much smaller auditorium on each of the upper two levels. The rest of the usable areas on the upper two levels consist of breakout meeting rooms."

As Van den Berg was finishing, Carpenter led them up onto the stage. It covered the entire width of the two-hundred-foot-wide auditorium. The surface was covered in gleaming hardwood, and it was at least seventy-five feet deep. A white curtain hung from the rafters at the back of the stage. Almost exactly in the center of the stage, a large wood and glass podium separated a row of tables that extended out fifty feet in either direction. Carpenter knew that the optimal moment for an attack would be when the world's leaders were assembled on this stage. He considered the possible ways to get to them, even if some of them stretched the bounds of credulity. A bomb or something solid and heavy could conceivably be dropped through the roof, assuming the helicopter or plane needed to carry it somehow avoided being shot down before it was in position. The drones used in Minnesota were another possibility to consider. He thought a more plausible scenario was to slip a chemical agent into the air system, but that required someone to be inside the maintenance room at the time of attack. And the mechanical room would be guarded and monitored continuously. A vehicle-borne improvised explosive device or a hand-held weapons assault team would have to penetrate what was expected to be a ring of steel around the building, comprised of heavily-armed forces and a fleet of armored combat support vehicles and armored personnel carriers. Even if an assault team was somehow able to penetrate that line of defense, a warning would be issued at the first sign of trouble. That should give the Secret Service enough time to get the president to the parking garage. But he knew that sometimes signs were missed and signals could get crossed. It was important that someone from the president's detail would be able to keep an eye on all areas of the building and coordinate a response. "Can we get to the operations control center by using the exit at the side of the stage?"

"Yes," Van den Berg said.

"Good. I'd like to see it."

Van den Berg had hoped to keep these men from this part of the building and the shameful disaster in the storage room. *Maybe they won't ask to see the store room*, he thought. In the four years he had been general manager, Van den Berg had always had a good working relationship with the security and maintenance chief, but in the last few months something had changed. Chong had become insolent, almost disdainful in their interactions. And two women on his staff had recently made complaints against Chong for similar treatment. For the past several weeks, Van den Berg had considered firing him. But he first wanted to give Chong an opportunity to explain his change in behavior. It was possible the man had a health or domestic problem and Van den Berg wanted to be considerate. Because of the upcoming G20 meeting, he had decided to wait to have that conversation. Now, in light of Chong's revelation about the maintenance problem, Van den Berg was beginning to rue his procrastination. *Chong, you better have covered up the mess.* He managed to smile at his guests and said, "Please follow me."

Van den Berg led them through the door at the side of the stage. It opened onto a broad hallway. He pointed out the doors leading to three meeting rooms on the far side of the corridor as he guided his guests toward the back of the building and a set of steel doors. The doors were closed and locked with a security swipe card system. Van den Berg used the security card hanging from the lanyard around his neck to open the door before leading his guests into another hallway, this one nearly twice as wide. After only a few steps, they arrived at the door for the operations control center, and Van den Berg followed the same process to open it. He was relieved to see that Chong was not inside, as he might have blurted out something about the storage room. Only the young technician was there, keeping an eye on two dozen screens displaying images from nearly four times as many security cameras dispersed throughout the complex. "We have a staff of twelve full-time security professionals who work eight-hour shifts around the clock. As you can see, in this room we monitor video footage from every area of the property."

"How long do you retain the footage?" Kennedy asked.

"It is stored for seven days before it is recorded over."

"Can he zoom in on the janitor on the second level?" Kennedy asked.

While Van den Berg related the request to the technician, Carpenter took a quick glance at the monitors on the wall. He noticed a few gaps in coverage on the building's exterior. He made a mental note to tell Secret Service Director Christie and the head of the president's security detail, Travis Keys, to make sure personnel were stationed in those blind spots. He turned his attention to the video from inside the building. As he looked from one monitor to the next, he saw that all areas of the conference center's interior were very well covered. He saw footage from the lobby, every auditorium, meeting room, and hallway. Anyone entering the building from the front and rear entrances would pass through multiple cameras outside and inside the doorways and all areas of the garage and the maintenance room in the basement were also under heavy video surveillance. His eyes settled on the screen showing the janitor. As the technician zoomed in on the subject, he was able to clearly see the man's face. Carpenter had seen enough to satisfy him that the Secret Service agents emplaced in this room would be able to keep tabs on all activities inside the building and nearly all those on the exterior. "Thank you," he said to the technician, before moving toward the door.

The others followed him into the hallway. Carpenter took a moment to look around. The far side of the hallway represented the building's exterior wall. Toward the center, there were three sets of glass double doors leading in from the walkway that served the parking ramp and the adjacent garden patios. Other than the doors for the rear entrance, there were no other doors or windows cut into the exterior wall's surface. On the interior wall, beyond the control center, and closer to the halfway point of the hallway, was another door. Carpenter assumed that door served the storage room Van den

Berg had mentioned, since the only other opening on the interior wall was the service elevator at the far end of the hall. "Can we check out the storage room," he asked.

Van den Berg felt a bead of sweat trickle from his left armpit down the side of his chest as he led his guests toward the storage room. His hand was shaking as he fumbled for the security badge hanging from his neck. Somehow, he willed his hand to stop trembling and managed to swipe the badge into the lock on the side of the wide, steel double door. He almost gasped audibly when the lock released, but he caught himself and casually pushed the door open to allow the two men inside.

As Van den Berg held the door open, Carpenter took two steps into the room. He took heed of the tables stacked neatly against the far wall and the rows of leather office chairs beginning along the left wall and filling most of the room's center. He assumed the comfortable executive chairs would be brought out to the dais for the conference. A line of shelves ran the length of the wall to his right. The shelves held a variety of items, as well as some spare parts and tools. He looked up at the ceiling and noticed that several of the ceiling tiles above the tables on the far wall looked newer than the rest. On the far wall, where the tables had been placed, was another metal double door, which he assumed opened onto the stage. He briefly considered trying to carve a circuitous pathway through the chairs to get to the stage door. By the way everything was arranged, it seemed almost designed to deter a full inspection of the chamber. Since he knew the Secret Service and other protection details would be taking another and closer look at all of the rooms immediately before and throughout the duration of the conference, he decided against a closer inspection. Instead, he was ready to move on. "I'd like to take the service elevator down to see the parking garage," he said.

"Of course," Van den Berg said, hoping he did not sound too liberated.

Once they were inside the roomy elevator car, Van den Berg scanned his security pass in front of the control panel and selected the basement level. The three men rode in silence for the few seconds needed to reach the building's lowest level. Van den Berg led them down the central hallway toward the parking garage. A large double door, ten feet in height, opened into the garage. Right next to the service door was the lone elevator that led to the lobby and the floors above, including those belonging to the hotel. The garage was relatively small, perhaps capable of holding forty vehicles on each side of a wide and straight path from the overhead doors at the far end. The parking spaces began approximately thirty feet from where they were standing. In between was a considerable space that delivery vehicles could use to turnaround and back up to the service door. Concrete pillars were spaced every fifteen or so feet along either side of the entrance path, providing support for the one-foot thick pre-formed concrete panels that comprised the ceiling sixteen feet above them. Except for a handful of cars, including one parked in front of a sign that read "General Manager," the ramp was empty.

"Thank you, Mr. Van den Berg, I think we have seen everything we wanted to," Carpenter said.

Van den Berg instantly felt a wave of relief wash over him. This time, he ushered his guests onto the lobby elevator. A few moments later, he accompanied them to the front doors, where they again thanked him for his time before saying goodbye. Van den Berg dutifully remained just inside the front entrance and watched his guests walk to their car. Seconds later, he saw a cargo van approaching. He cringed as it drove by, recognizing that it most certainly belonged to the restoration company Chong had hired.

Just as he opened the door, Carpenter had to step closer to the car to allow a white van to drive past him. He caught a glimpse of the green lettering on the side and watched as the van continued toward the entrance for the underground parking garage. He checked the time to confirm what his stomach was telling him. Before he even looked, he knew it was nearing dinner time. The disappointing lunch earlier had failed to put a dent in his appetite. As he climbed into the driver's seat, he found it odd that a work crew would be arriving so late in the day but he cast the thought aside. There was still a lot for him and Kennedy to accomplish and he had an idea about how they could increase their efficiency.

Looking at Kennedy across the roof of the car, he said, "We're going to drive the route the president will take to and from the conference. From what I've been told, the hotel he will be staying at is pretty swanky. I say we plan on having dinner there. Director Christie recommended it. He said it's right on the ocean and they serve lunch and dinner on a patio overlooking the

North Sea. And, since I haven't made any arrangements, we might as well stay there too."

"I'm in," Kennedy said. "Sounds nice, especially dinner on the patio. I'm starving and the sun is starting to peek out and the wind is dying down."

When the men finally got into their car and closed the doors, Van den Berg realized he had been holding his breath the entire time. As untimely as that episode had been, it might have been worse. If the work crew had arrived any earlier, he almost certainly would have had to explain the embarrassing problem to his visitors. As soon as the Americans pulled away, he reached for his phone to call Jian Chong. He wanted confirmation that Chong had made the arrangements to get the repair work done as quickly and quietly as possible. He no longer cared about the extra cost; he just wanted it done. With the G20 conference only days away, he feared another government's officials were going to want to inspect the property before the restoration work was completed.

Chapter 56

A few hours later, Hamid Fahkoury and Fahd al-Rasheed were getting off a train in Den Haag Centraal railway station. Fahkoury had decided they would stay in Antwerp the previous evening with Taj Khan and the rest of the cell members. For starters, it was late by the time he finished reviewing the blueprints and examining the materials. The disturbing episode at Antwerp Central earlier in the day was another factor in his decision. But the driving force was his need to know that things were proceeding according to plan.

Although he and al-Rasheed were scheduled to meet Saleem Nasir at the safehouse in The Hague, Fahkoury had some flexibility. In keeping with his practice, he had not agreed to a definitive day and time for the meeting. Instead, he gave Aziz a two-day window and told him to make sure Nasir was there. And, once he left Antwerp, he would not speak with Khan again until they reunited at the conference center. One of his inviolate operational protocols was to restrict communications with his operators to only face-to-face meetings, and he had no intention of making an exception in this case. So, before leaving, he had to make sure there were no problems with the prearranged timing. Until he knew that everything was in order, he and al-Rasheed were not going anywhere.

Very early that morning, Fahkoury had sent Khan to the train station to purchase one-way tickets to The Hague for him and al-Rasheed. Not long after Khan returned with the tickets, the prepaid phone rang. He stood nearby as Khan listened to his cousin on the other end. When the call ended seconds later, Khan advised the work had been authorized and could begin as soon as he and his team could get to the conference center. Khan told Fahkoury that he expected they should have their portion of the work done and be ready for him sometime the following morning. That was exactly what Fahkoury wanted to hear. After confirming some final details with Khan, he sent the men on their way to Holland and went down to the basement. He remained there for several hours, studying the blueprints and busying himself with the materials and the preliminary designs for the bomb. When it was nearing time for him and al-Rasheed to leave and catch their seven o'clock train to The Hague, he carefully arranged the supplies in the toolboxes so they would be ready for Khan to load them into the van the next morning.

Now, he and al-Rasheed were making their way through The Hauge's contemporary train station. As he searched for the subtlest sign of a tail, Fahkoury found himself distracted by the blues and yellows adorning the trains, turnstiles, and ticket machines. Ignoring them required a concerted effort, since the bright colors sharply contrasted the gray concrete and gleaming metal that otherwise dominated the airy hall. The bustle created by passengers from several concurrently arriving trains and those waiting for early-evening departures was a mixed blessing, as it provided a layer of concealment for both quarry and pursuer. Fortunately, there were no signs to indicate an encounter like the one he had in Antwerp the previous day. Once they were outside the boxy glass and steel structure, Fahkoury looked over at the line queuing up for taxis. Not wanting to stand around waiting and unnecessarily risk being identified, Fahkoury made the decision to keep moving. They would walk all the way to the home, rather than take a taxi part of the way.

Fahkoury ushered them into a nearby park where they gathered their bearings. Their destination was the Belgisch Park neighborhood in The Hague's Scheveningen district. After determining they needed to generally proceed in a northerly direction toward the sea, they continued through the park while keeping the setting sun just off their left shoulders as a guide. When they exited the park, they took their time, crisscrossing the streets and doubling back. In the end, they probably traveled half again what normally would have been a four-mile walk. But Fahkoury wasn't taking any chances.

It was dark when they finally arrived at the home two hours later. Fahkoury guided al-Rasheed to an open area across the street, where they settled into a reconnaissance position in a grouping of chestnut and Dutch linden trees. Fahkoury noticed the temperature had fallen considerably since they began their trek, and he felt a chill from the slight breeze that was blowing off the North Sea. Fahkoury took a few moments to study the home and its surroundings.

It sat on the edge of the neighborhood alongside several other expensive private residences. He found the location of the tony enclave ironic, since it was not more than a few hundred yards from Hague Penitentiary Institution and the ICC Detention Center that housed people awaiting trial before the International Criminal Court. Several lights were shining inside the home, providing a perspective of its considerable size. The area was quiet, save for the rustling leaves. They waited several minutes, watching for any unusual activity in or around the home.

When Fahkoury was assured, he whispered instructions to al-Rasheed. He hung in the shadows and observed, while al-Rasheed approached the front door. A few moments after the door opened, the outside light flickered. Fahkoury took one more glance around before he followed al-Rasheed's path.

Saleem Nasir greeted him at the door. Although he had heard much about him from Sadiq bin Aziz, it was the first time Fahkoury had set eyes on the man. Nasir was reputed to be extremely intelligent, resourceful, and loyal. Those were all admirable traits but they did not amount to a guarantee that this operation was on track. Nasir had two important roles, and the slightest lack of care on his part would be costly. Fahkoury was mindful of these matters as he and al-Rasheed followed Nasir into the kitchen. He hung back on the periphery and observed for a few moments, as Nasir put out some food and drinks. He noticed Nasir was taller than al-Rasheed, who stood almost half a foot taller than Fahkoury himself. Nasir was physically fit and, he guessed, probably close to thirty-five years old. His mannerisms and attire suggested a man of culture and means, a status Fahkoury once possessed in an earlier life. And the man's air of refinement was also reminiscent of Aziz. Fahkoury considered how it juxtaposed the lives of hardship he and al-Rasheed had willingly accepted and endured. But none of that mattered to Fahkoury. He cared only that Nasir was competent and trustworthy. And that determination would depend on the precautions the man had taken.

"This is a beautiful home," Fahkoury said. "I understand it is owned by Brother Aziz. How is it that we will be safe here?"

"This home is one of many owned by Sadiq bin Aziz," Nasir said. "Like all his homes, this one was purchased through a series of transactions, each involving a nameless corporation. The privacy laws of the jurisdictions where those companies were incorporated ensure that the identities of the shareholders are protected. Brother Aziz's name does not appear anywhere in the ownership records."

Fahkoury had little knowledge of the law, but what Nasir said sounded reassuring. The explanation helped him relax. The unsettledness he had experienced in Istanbul had returned after the incident at the Antwerp train station. He was having a hard time shaking the foreboding sense that his fate rested in enemy hands. He was not afraid of death. Rather, it was fear of being denied his destiny. With each operation he had led, he believed he had been chosen by Allah. That was particularly true this time. This plan was masterful and the consequences would alter the course of history. Because of that, nothing could be left to chance. And one man was a critical factor to his success. Fahkoury always preferred to handle important matters himself, but he was once again reliant on Nasir. "What is the status with Khan's cousin?" he asked.

"I met with Jian Chong late this morning to provide him with the final payment. He told me the reconstruction process will not begin until this evening. He had hoped to start earlier in the day so that your work could begin first thing tomorrow morning, but the general manager told Chong the work could not begin until he was finished with some visitors from the United States."

That unexpected news reenergized the anxiety Fahkoury was just beginning to push aside. When he parted company with Khan earlier that day, the work was scheduled to commence as soon as Khan and his men arrived at the conference center. There was no mention of any potential delay. He realized he was only learning this news now because of his strict communication protocols. Khan would have had to return to the home in

Antwerp to share the news. Yet he had not. Fahkoury had to assume Khan made the decision to stay close to the conference center and await word of the Americans' departure. While the delay was not welcome news, the visit by the Americans was even more troubling. "Does Chong know anything about the American visitors?"

"The general manager told him they were from the US Secret Service."

"Does he know whether this was a scheduled visit?"

"He was told that it was unexpected, that it had been requested at the last minute, sometime this morning. Evidently, the Americans examined the property two weeks ago. However, the general manager did tell Chong that the Americans also made several visits to the facility leading up to the nuclear summit that was held there a few years back. Chong said the general manager did not seem troubled by this second visit, other than his concern the mold problem could be exposed. He told Chong that if the word got out, the entire world would think he was overseeing a second-rate facility. Chong described him as a panicky type, always fretting about what people are thinking and saying about him and the conference center."

The only part of Nasir's statement that Fahkoury heard was the reference to the unexpected nature of the visit. He had been trying to convince himself that his sense of uneasiness was similar to what he felt during the lead up to every operation, but he could not shake the feeling that it was different this time. The news of the unscheduled visit by the Americans was yet another ominous sign for this operation. He began to wonder if it was doomed. "How long will we be delayed?"

"The delay actually works in our favor," Nasir said. "Because the general manager is so worried about news of the mold problem getting out, he does not want our men to stop working until the project is finished. Originally, the general manager did not want to pay the extra money to have the crew work overnight, but the visit by the Americans convinced him otherwise. When he found out the Americans were coming, he told Chong that he's willing to pay overtime charges and any extra costs to get the work done by end of business tomorrow. Instead of being ready for you in the morning, Khan will be ready for you tonight."

While it did not wash away all his concerns, that information restored his hope that everything was going to be okay. For at least a moment,

Fahkoury cast aside his worries and centered his thoughts on execution. "How will we meet up with Khan?"

"I gave Chong instructions to send his cousin to a prearranged pickup location. Khan is supposed to go there at midnight and, thereafter, on the hour every hour until you meet him. Assuming you are ready, we can meet Khan as early as midnight."

Using Chong as an intermediary was necessary but risky. Before the changes precipitated by the Americans' visit, only Khan and Nasir knew the pickup location. Now Chong was aware of that information and he could use it to double-cross not only Nasir, but Fahkoury himself. "How do you know you can trust Chong?"

"He knows that I recorded every conversation we had. As an extra precaution, I had one of my men pay him a visit after our meeting this morning. The man made it clear that any betrayal will be dealt with harshly. And that will include his wife and young daughter. Chong knows he is in this up to his neck and there is no way out."

Fahkoury was impressed with Nasir's brutishness as much as his thoroughness. So far, Nasir was living up to Aziz's portrayal. Fahkoury looked at the time on the microwave and confirmed it against the time showing on the stainless-steel stove beneath it. In roughly two hours, he could begin. "We will meet Khan at midnight," he said.

"Very well," Nasir said. "Now, let me show you around. And, until it is time to leave, please consider anything else you may need or want as I will be leaving Holland tonight."

Aziz had told him Nasir would not be sticking around. That was fine with Fahkoury. Nasir had fulfilled his duty by arranging access to the conference center and securing a base of operations for him and al-Rasheed. Fahkoury needed no further assistance from Nasir. Nor did Fahkoury want any of his input. The operation was now in his hands, just as he wanted. He gestured for Nasir to begin the tour and then fell in behind their host and al-Rasheed.

Chapter 57

As soon as the doors opened, Liam Van den Berg exited the elevator and began marching through the lobby toward the hallway. Jian Chong had not answered his call and he wanted an update before he left for the evening. It was nearly ten o'clock when he unlocked the steel door and entered the corridor behind the auditorium. He was greeted by an unsightly structure made of boards and clear plastic. The configuration was butted up against the interior wall and ominously placed in front of the storage room door. Peering around it, Van den Berg was able to see that the tables and chairs were neatly arranged further down the hallway against the exterior wall. Propped up against the wall at the far end of the hallway was the shelving from the storage room. Seeing this, he assumed the work was underway and cautiously made his way toward the storeroom to see for himself. As he passed the operations control center, the door opened and Chong stepped out.

"Mr. Van den Berg, what can I do for you?" Chong said.

Chong's sudden appearance startled him and he nearly jumped to the far side of the hallway. He quickly regained his composure and his irritation immediately returned. "Since you did not bother to answer or return my call, I am here for an update on the work."

"I'm sorry, sir. I left my phone in the operations center and just realized I had missed your call. As you can see, we have been very busy back here."

"Has the work started inside the storage room?"

"Yes, the restoration team should be getting ready to remove the affected debris now."

Just as Chong said that, Van den Berg heard a banging noise from inside the storage room. That was soon followed by a cacophony of similar sounds. "Do these men know what they are doing?" he asked.

"This company was highly recommended to me," Chong said.

As Chong was talking, Van den Berg glanced over his shoulder and saw someone dressed in a white, full-body protective suit. A respirator covered the person's face and a hard hat completed the ensemble. Van den Berg could not see any part of the person's body to know whether it was a man or a woman. The person looked as if reporting for duty at a nuclear disaster. As the person continued to approach the clear plastic enclosure with a gray polyethylene garbage cart, Van den Berg sensed himself retreating.

Chong looked over his shoulder and saw the reason for the frightened expression on Van den Berg's face. *Perfect timing.* "Sir, I think you might want to consider leaving this area. We have been instructed to keep out of the hallway until all of the hazardous material has been removed. It's especially dangerous during the demolition work that, as you can hear, just started."

"That is good advice," Van den Berg said. "I am going home now. Please provide me with an update in the morning. I will be in my office by eleven o'clock. Thank you, Mr. Chong and goodnight."

After Van den Berg left the area and closed the steel hallway door behind him, Chong wandered over to the storage room to speak to his cousin. He waited as Taj Khan stepped around the garbage cart and removed his respirator. "We are in the clear. That was the general manager. He just left for the night. I'll keep the security crew away from the garage and this area until you are done but don't waste time. If you don't want people poking around, get this room back in shape before the general manager comes back. You should have until midmorning."

Khan ran a quick calculation and determined he would have enough time, provided the other men were not unexpectedly held up. Chong had passed along instructions from Mr. Saleem, directing him to go to the pickup location every hour beginning at midnight. Since they were scheduled to leave Antwerp at seven o'clock, Khan assumed Mumeet and al-Rasheed were already in The Hague. "We can have our work done long before that," Khan said. "It's the other stuff I'm unsure about."

"Can you tell me who you're picking up?"

"I can't."

Nasir had withheld that same information earlier. Now his cousin refused to share it. Chong figured it was someone important but reasoned it was probably better he did not know, anyway. The knowledge would only give Nasir more reason to distrust him. "Well, if you're concerned about keeping identities secret, make sure whoever you're bringing here remains covered up at all times. For obvious reasons, I have permission to shut down the cameras in the storage room, but we have cameras all over the building."

"I'll make sure we are all covered up."

"Good. If you need me, I'll be in the operations room for another hour or so. Otherwise, I'll see you in the morning."

Chapter 58
Noordwijk, the Netherlands

Fifteen miles away, Carpenter and Kennedy were relaxing on the deck after finishing a delicious dinner at the hotel in Noordwijk. Carpenter had had a tinge of buyer's remorse when the waiter placed the plate of Black Angus rump steak, covered in teriyaki sauce and served with broccolini, macadamia nuts and udon noodles in front of Kennedy, but after his first bite of grilled wolfish in a zucchini cream sauce, he was more than pleased with his own choice. Beyond the quality food, the setting overlooking the North Sea was a good place for the men to catch up and for Carpenter to test one aspect of Kennedy's training. For most of the meal, the two men conversed in Arabic. Although Kennedy struggled at times to find the correct words and grammar, Carpenter was impressed with his progress.

Later, as they waited for the check to arrive, Carpenter retreated to his own thoughts. He reconsidered what he had learned since leaving the World Peace Conference Center earlier. They had followed the route the president would take each morning and evening between the conference center and the hotel in Noordwijk. The route was chiefly comprised of primary motorways that passed through an almost equal mix of urban and rural settings. Although the route would be lined with snipers and closed to traffic while the president was traveling to and from the G20 Summit, Carpenter fretted there was simply too much ground to cover. Even on their first pass, he had identified numerous locations from which to launch an attack.

While the rural areas offered a combination of dense tree coverage and clear lines of sight from open and flat fields, the urban areas offered attack positions from the homes and commercial buildings that had been consistently constructed only a few feet from the road. An improvised explosive device could be placed inside any of those structures, placing it mere steps from the center of the road and well within the lethal range of a powerful IED. On top of that, a shoulder-launched weapons attack could be launched from inside any of the structures. Worse still, a more powerful anti-tank guided missile could be deployed from the same location or from a greater distance in one of the many open spaces along the route. And that last frightening prospect was very real. Carpenter had read recent intelligence reports from the CIA and several allied agencies about caches of European and Russian ATGMs being captured in Syria by the Islamic State and the al Qaeda affiliate, Jabhat al-Nusrah. While some were being used against Bashar al-Assad's forces, there were rumors over the past several months that some of the weapons had made their way into Europe. It was entirely possible that someone with the wealth of Sadiq bin Aziz might have acquired them for this operation. And Carpenter was not certain "the Beast" could withstand a direct hit from such close range.

The president's limousine, affectionately known as "the Beast," provided a strong defense against most attacks. Inside it, the president was sheltered by eight inches of armored plating and five-inch thick bulletproof windows. Doors weighing as much as those on a jumbo plane closed with a perfect seal to guard against fire and chemical weapons. And the Beast ran on diesel fuel, which was more readily available than high-octane unleaded gasoline and had a lower volatility, thereby reducing the risk of explosion. But Carpenter recognized those security features were not infallible. Even if the integrity of the protective framework was able to withstand an isolated anti-tank missile attack, degradation could be expected during a sustained effort. And the limousine was not particularly agile. A well-coordinated attack might be able to disable the lead and rear vehicles in the convoy, effectively cutting off lines of escape before converging on limousine with a mobile force. And the Beast was not likely to win any races. At more than eleven tons, it was only capable of a top speed of sixty miles per hour.

Besides the problems along the route, the hotel presented its own host of perils. Though they were much the same as those at the convention center, the hotel added another wrinkle due to its proximity to the sea. While the beachfront would be guarded and the shoreline patrolled, boat traffic would continue offshore. The same anti-tank guided weapons that gave him the most concern along the motorcade route could as easily be deployed from the sea. Some had effective ranges of more than three miles, allowing for the missiles to be launched from well outside the planned patrol area. Beyond causing significant structural damage, a barrage of missiles from the sea could also provide cover for one or more assault teams to storm the hotel.

It was a lot to consider, especially knowing that there was credible information about an attack in The Hague. If it was his call, Carpenter would have the president stay home. If the president insisted on attending the conference, he would prefer for him to stay in the hotel at the convention center, since it would be much easier to protect the president if he was confined to one location. But the president was coming to The Hague and had refused to alter his plans to stay in Noordwijk. His predecessor had stayed there only a few years before, and President Madden saw no need to recreate the wheel. The hotel was known and a security plan was already in place. The president had vowed to make government more efficient and this was one small way to deliver on that pledge.

But Carpenter accepted those problems were not his or the CTC's primary concern. Rather, those security issues rested with the Secret Service and the Dutch military. He and his teammates at the CTC were tasked with finding and stopping the terrorists. Carpenter believed their best chances rested with Taj Khan and Saleem Nasir. If those men could be located, they would lead him to Mumeet. But there was no further news from headquarters about either Khan or Nasir. Until those two were located, Carpenter was left trying to anticipate where and how Mumeet was most likely to strike. In theory, it would give him an educated guess where to look for the Bringer of Death. Yet, after reviewing what he had seen and learned earlier, he still did not have a definitive feeling about where and how an attack was likely to go down. He adjusted his position in the cushioned wicker chair and reached for his glass of water.

Recognizing that Carpenter was in some kind of deep-thinking mode, Kennedy had kept himself occupied by working on his behavioral detection skills. He noticed that the dinner crowd had thinned considerably since they had arrived, leaving them mostly isolated in a corner of the dining area. Besides the diners scattered over six tables on the sprawling deck, there was a group of waitstaff hanging out near the outdoor bar, including one waitress who he found particularly worthy of scrutiny. He noticed the striking blonde was also quite popular with her colleagues. She appeared to be holding multiple conversations with several of the men, each vying for her undivided attention. Yet, she seemed more interested in the coquetry of a brunette mixologist who was equally attractive. Kennedy's intrigue was interrupted when he saw Carpenter shift in his chair. "What are you thinking about?" he asked.

"I'm trying to figure out what Mumeet is planning."

"Before we started eating, you were saying you didn't like the route the president would be traveling. You said the distance was too great and there were too many places to launch an attack."

"Those are undeniable problems but I'm just not convinced Aziz would try something like that. Think about it, it's kind of like robbing a stagecoach in the Wild West. You might know the route but you don't know the timing. The president's schedule will be a closely-guarded secret. He might get to the conference an hour early or just before a session is scheduled to begin. You'd have to move into position and wait. That greatly increases the chances of discovery, either by an observant citizen or a member of the security forces. Besides that, there's a reason no one has attempted to ambush a presidential motorcade. The limousine is basically a tank and the entourage will include highly-trained professionals who will be armed to the teeth. Mumeet would have to have nearly flawless execution and some pretty heavy-duty weaponry to have a chance. It would be a dramatic ploy but not one likely to end in triumph."

"So, if not during the motorcade, are you thinking here at the hotel or at the conference center is more likely?"

"This hotel does concern me. For one thing, there is no secure room to shield the president during an attack. There could be a massive firefight with an uncertain ending if a large enough group of terrorists was able to infiltrate the building. We've seen that scenario before in Mumbai and, more recently, in Kabul. Hotels are a prime target and the natural attrition of staff creates opportunities for terrorists to assimilate into the workforce, where they can plan and execute from the inside. While the president is here, the securities measures at this hotel will, of course, present steep challenges for an attack but it could happen." He paused for a moment, realizing he was doing all the talking. This was another opportunity to aid Kennedy's development. "How would you plan an attack on the hotel?" he asked.

Kennedy sat up in his chair. Beyond what he learned that unforgettable day at the mall, he had heard more about the lore of PJ Carpenter during training. Kennedy already looked up to Carpenter and spending the day with him had reinforced that respect. All day, he had been paying attention to what attracted Carpenter's attention and tried to glean his thinking from his statements and questions. It had been an illuminating experience, but now he was being asked to make his own assessment. He slid the chair closer and placed his elbows on the table as he leaned in. He knew Carpenter was challenging him and he welcomed it. "Are we assuming the terrorists have infiltrated the workforce at the hotel?" he asked.

"Sure, for this exercise we will."

"Okay." He gathered his final thoughts before continuing. "We're right on the beach and there are stretches of undeveloped land on either side of the hotel. I would have assault teams conduct diversionary attacks from either side of the hotel. Those teams would draw fire from the perimeter security before they got anywhere near the hotel, but those confrontations would lure some of the inside protection detail outside to assist, making it easier for an infiltration force to commandeer the hotel itself and move in on the president's location."

"That's good. How else could you do it?"

"Well, there's no way to get a vehicle close enough to the building to use an improvised explosive device. There's only one way in here and we had to go through two security checkpoints. Assuming I had people on the inside, I could try to have them hide suicide vests beforehand. I'd have to hope they weren't found and that my people could get close enough to the president." Kennedy abruptly ended there. The waiter was approaching with the check.

Carpenter took the bill from the waiter. After the waiter left, he filled in his room number, signed his name and placed it back in the leather folder. "Keep thinking about things. I like what I'm hearing. We have to think of every possibility, no matter how crazy it may seem to us. Otherwise, the one we miss will end up being the one that hurts. Give some more thought to the conference center too. I'm still inclined to think that is the target. Aziz has shown a proclivity for boldness, and the Economic Summit would be very appealing to him. The conference begins Thursday morning. That gives us a little more than two days to find the terrorists. If we don't, we will shadow the president's every move." He looked at his watch. "It's almost midnight. Let's get some rest and sleep on what we learned today."

Chapter 59
The Hague

Fahkoury and al-Rasheed ducked their heads and made their way into a concealed spot among the trees. After having parted ways with Saleem Nasir at the house twenty minutes earlier, they walked slightly more than a mile to the pickup location. The designated meeting place was a parking lot in the park adjacent to the World Peace Conference Center. The gravel parking area was accessible by a road that meandered through that section of the park and also provided access to a private tennis club. Besides the tennis club, the park was primarily used by walkers and bicyclists wishing to use the network of trails interwoven throughout two-hundred, heavily-wooded acres. Fahkoury halted their progress and they squatted down so that they were provided with a clearer view of the dark corridor through the forest. It was a few minutes before midnight.

After they settled in, Fahkoury noted the forest was noiseless. The gentle breeze that had been blowing earlier in the evening had vanished. The only remotely visible light came from the tennis clubhouse almost two hundred yards away. Under the circumstances, neither one of them spoke while they waited. A few minutes later, a vehicle entered the road from the north. As it approached the parking area, its lights flickered twice. Fahkoury watched as it rounded the subtle corner and passed by. It was a small cargo van, light in color. He and al-Rasheed remained in place as the van slowly continued down the lane to the east. When the tail lights were no longer visible,

Fahkoury tapped al-Rasheed on the shoulder and motioned for him to follow. He crept up through the trees and closer to the road. When he was nearly at the road's edge, he moved laterally a few feet to a spot where they would remain hidden by some low hanging branches. This time, they didn't have to wait long. Headlights approached them from the east. Once again, its lights flickered twice as it neared the parking area and the bend in the road. Fahkoury slithered through the branches and stood in the wash of the van's headlights. The van was less than fifty feet from him when it stopped. A few seconds later, a man emerged wearing a white coverall.

Al-Rasheed followed Fahkoury as they walked up to the van and Taj Khan. "Brother Khan," Fahkoury said, "thank you for being on time."

"It is my honor, sir. I thought there was a chance you would not be here until later."

"How are things proceeding?"

"Very well. We started the demolition work a few hours ago. The men were finishing up when I left. It should be ready for you when we get back there."

"There are no problems?"

"No, my cousin has kept everyone away from the room. We have been left alone to do our work."

"Are all the materials now inside?"

"Yes, everything should now be in the room, including the equipment."

This news pleased Fahkoury. As far as he was concerned, this was perhaps the most dangerous part of the operation. Unlike other attacks where one of many delivery methods could be employed, this one required him to place the destructive instrument inside the target. It was important that the materials and equipment were available and the space ready for him to commence work as soon as he arrived. He did not want to be on the property one minute longer than necessary. "Very good. Let's get moving."

"I have suits and protective gear for each of you in the van." Khan led them to the rear of the van and gave them each a Tyvek coverall with attached boots and hood. As they slid into the protective suits, he showed them how to place the respirator over their faces. "You do not need the respirators other than to hide your faces. Except inside the storage room, there are cameras throughout the building, so we need to wear them. But you can wait until we enter the parking garage before you put them on." He stayed by the door as the two men climbed into the back of the van. When they were clear of the door, he closed it and returned to the driver's seat.

It required a little more than two minutes to make the short drive to the World Peace Conference Center. Khan parked the van in the garage, next to the full-sized cargo van that bore the company's name. Sealed plastic bags containing the debris that had been removed from the storage room were stacked against the side of the larger van. Khan exited the van and opened the rear door. Seeing his passengers were fully dressed in their protective clothing, he said, "Please follow me."

Chapter 60

Khan led them from the garage through the large steel doors and down the broad hallway. As they neared the end, he suggested that Fahkoury and al-Rasheed don the hardhats he had given them in the garage. Chong had told him that workers were required to wear hardhats at all times in the construction area. Proceeding any further without them might elicit a rebuke in the off chance they came across someone from the facility. Although their bodies and faces were completely covered, Khan thought it in his best interests that they avoid any such encounters. After he led them through a second set of steel doors, the trio turned left toward the storage room.

Khan stepped aside and allowed Fahkoury and al-Rasheed to enter the plastic structure that encased the storage room door. Fahkoury was the first to enter the room. All the ceiling tiles and sheetrock against the stage wall had been removed, exposing the ceiling grid and metal wall studs. Two of the men were sweeping dust and smaller debris into dustpans before dumping them in wheeled containers lined with garbage bags. The third man was carefully placing the contents of a larger wheeled cart onto the freshly cleaned concrete floor.

Fahkoury motioned for Khan to come closer. "When the men are finished, place one man outside the entrance. Tell the other two men to wait in the garage. You will remain here to help."

When Khan went off to speak to the other men, Fahkoury and al-Rasheed removed their hardhats and respirators and placed them in a corner of the room. Fahkoury walked over to the neatly arranged materials. After assessing the arrangement, he stooped down and grabbed a tape measure. Then Fahkoury told the men it was time to get to work.

While al-Rasheed set up a workspace for the acetylene cutting torch, Fahkoury started measuring the distances between the metal wall studs. After he gave al-Rasheed a sheet of paper with the measurements written on it, Fahkoury began unwrapping and molding the plastic explosive. As al-Rasheed finished cutting the half-inch steel plates to size, Khan drilled holes in each of the smaller pieces that would serve as tops and bottoms for the boxes. When he was done, Khan placed the bottom pieces between the wall studs and secured them to the floor with concrete fasteners. Al-Rasheed kept busy by welding the rectangular sides to the larger square pieces that would become the fronts and backs of the five boxes he was forming. As he finished each one, al-Rasheed welded the form onto the bottom piece Khan had secured to the floor. When the steel had cooled, Fahkoury stuffed the malleable orange material into the steel chambers, leaving a narrow space on the side of the box facing the stage. Khan followed in his wake, filling the empty space with sheetrock screws.

Once all five boxes were filled with plastic explosive and shrapnel, al-Rasheed and Khan began moving sheetrock panels in from the hallway, leaving Fahkoury alone to work on the bombs. He began cutting and inserting pieces of electrical wire into the improvised explosive devices. He then took the loose ends of the wires and slid them through the holes Khan had previously drilled into the box tops. After placing the loose tops onto the steel boxes, he wove the wires through the metal studs until they converged near the detonator switch that he had fastened to a wall stud nearest the center of the arrayed bombs. When he finished, Fahkoury then stepped aside so that al-Rasheed could move in with the welder.

As al-Rasheed was fastening the top to the first IED, Fahkoury chuckled. Khan had jumped when al-Rasheed touched the electrical arc to the steel top. "Semtex will not explode when exposed to fire or heat," he said to Khan. "An explosion can only be initiated by a shock wave from a detonator. As you can see, the other end of the wire has yet to be attached to the detonator. And the detonator has to first be activated by a trigger. You can relax Brother Khan, you are safe for now."

When al-Rasheed was done welding the top of the last box, he and Kahn began hanging sheetrock on the wall. Starting in the left corner, they placed the sheets horizontally and attached them to the studs with sheet metal screws. While they were doing that, Fahkoury opened one of the Nokia 105 cellphones and removed the motor for the phone's vibrator function. After attaching the electrical wire to the vibrator circuit, he used duct tape to firmly secure the phone to the metal stud opposite the one to which the electric detonator switch was affixed. He then secured the wires protruding from the five steel boxes to the detonator. Then he moved back and waited until all al-Rasheed and Khan had placed all but the one piece of sheetrock that would cover the cellphone and detonator.

With the wall at that stage of completion, Fahkoury ordered al-Rasheed and Khan away from the area before he moved in. Working carefully, he attached the electrical wire from the phone to the detonator. Now that the device was active, there would be a slight risk of explosion. All three men delicately placed the final piece of sheetrock on the wall. Fahkoury and Khan held it in place while al-Rasheed screwed in the fasteners with a battery-powered drill. When the final screw was placed, Fahkoury stepped back and looked at the wall. There was nothing unusual to indicate the destructive force behind it. He believed the area would be unremarkable once it was taped and painted.

Fahkoury walked over to Khan. He gave him very explicit instructions to use extreme care when completing the remodeling work, warning him not to bang or slam into any of part of the wall, especially near the placement of the detonator switch. He also reviewed the orders he had given earlier, reminding Khan that after they finished with their work at the conference center, he and the men were to remain in the house in Antwerp until it was time to deploy for the attack. Fahkoury emphasized that there was to be no communication or interaction with outside parties. Once they were in position, Khan and his team were to wait for the explosion before initiating their part of the attack. After he finished going over the list of directives, Fahkoury said, "When we leave you, it will be the last time we speak or see each other. If you have questions or concerns, express them now."

"I understand what is expected of me and my team, and I do not have any questions," Kahn said.

"Good. Now take us back to the park so that you can return and finish the work here before anyone comes nosing around." Fahkoury checked the clock on the wall. They had been there slightly more than five hours.

All three men suited up in the protective gear and exited the storage room. On the way out, Khan told the man stationed outside the door to remain there and not allow anyone in the room until he returned. When the party arrived in the parking garage, Khan opened the rear door to the van to allow Fahkoury and al-Rasheed inside. Once they were settled, Khan closed the door and moved over to the full-sized cargo van. He wrapped his knuckles on the window to awaken the two men inside before telling them to prepare to resume work once he returned.

A few minutes later, Fahkoury sensed the van come to rest in the gravel parking area inside the park. Though it was still dark among the towering trees, the sun would be lifting over the eastern horizon very shortly. And with daylight, hikers and bicyclists would be descending on the park. Fahkoury wanted to hustle back to the house before the diurnal routines fully resumed in The Hague. By the time Khan opened the rear door, he and al-Rasheed were ready to go, having stripped out of their protective clothing during the short trip.

Fahkoury placed his hands on the sides of Khan's shoulders and looked him in the eye. "Brother, you have done well. Your contribution to our cause will be remembered and celebrated by all believers. For your reward, you will enter paradise. I pray that one day I will be worthy of joining you there. Praise be to Allah!"

Chapter 61
Noordwijk

Carpenter was just starting to pour himself a cup of coffee when Kennedy strode into the hotel lobby at a little past eight o'clock. Before parting ways after dinner, they had made plans to begin the day with a run on the beach. Promptly at six o'clock, Kennedy knocked on Carpenter's door. They were met with a stiff westerly breeze when they walked onto the sand. After stretching, they placed the wind at their backs and started down the wide and straight coastline toward the rising sun. Carpenter was impressed that Kennedy, despite his hulking physique, was matching him stride for stride. Carpenter pushed them to slightly more than three miles before they turned around. As they passed the halfway mark on the return leg, Kennedy began to lose a little steam. Carpenter accommodated by slowing the pace, but they still managed to finish in less than forty-one minutes. To cool down, they went to the hotel gym, where Kennedy more than countered any conditioning advantage Carpenter had held during the run. Now, Carpenter's arms and chest were screaming and he realized the foolishness of trying to keep up with his younger colleague.

"How are you feeling, PJ?" Kennedy asked, grinning like a Cheshire cat.

Carpenter handed him the fresh cup of coffee and began pouring another for himself. "I don't feel anything; I'm numb above the waist," he deadpanned. "But don't get too cocky, I'll get my revenge in the pool someday."

"I don't doubt that. I sink like a rock. What do you have planned for us today?"

"I think we'll take a closer look at the route from here to the conference center and try to pinpoint the likeliest places for an ambush. After that, we'll stop by the conference center again. Until we get something concrete, it's about all we can do."

"I forgot to ask if you had a chance to speak to Director Patrick last night."

"I did and he had nothing new to report. So far, they haven't found that Saleem Nasir or Aziz has any connection with the Netherlands. Same goes for Taj Khan. Patrick has been in regular contact with AIVD in Amsterdam." The General Intelligence and Security Service unit was commonly known as AIVD, the acronym for its Dutch language name, *Algemene Inlichtingen en Vieligheidsdienst*. "They have no information on any of them either."

"What about the Belgians?"

"We can't count on them," Carpenter said. "Their intelligence agencies are a mess." Belgium operated with two independently managed security agencies. While the State Security Service was under civilian control through the Ministry of Justice, its own General Intelligence and Security Service, also known as AIVD, functioned under the auspices of the Ministry of Defense. The lack of centralization was pegged as a primary reason Belgian intelligence services were universally regarded as the weak link in the European intelligence community. On top of the organizational dysfunction, each of the two agencies was severely underfunded and understaffed. "Patrick doesn't have a lot of faith in the Belgians. He believes we have better intelligence gathering in Belgium than the Belgians do. Despite that, he made some general inquiries. I wasn't surprised when he told me the Belgians have never heard of Taj Khan."

"Should we grab some food at the buffet before we get going?"

"Yeah, but I don't want to sit down. We'll be stopping at a few places along the route to The Hague. We can find somewhere to eat in one of those towns. For now, throw some of the cold meats, cheese, and fruit in a to-go box and we'll head out."

Chapter 62
Antwerp

Taj Khan made a second trip down the block, searching for a parking space near the apartment. Since they would have to load the weapons into it, he wanted the full-sized van as close to the apartment as possible. It did not matter where he parked his smaller van. Once again finding no spaces on either side of the narrow street, he decided to stay the course rather than looping around the block. Almost four blocks later, he finally found a space, and it was large enough to accommodate both vans. He motioned to the three men in the larger van behind him and pulled his van up to the curb.

He and the men had worked feverishly to finish up at the World Peace Conference Center. After applying a mesh tape to the seams, they used a quick-drying compound to cover it and the indentations created by the fastening screws. While the first application of compound was drying, they directed their attention to the ceiling tiles. Before they had finished installing the new ceiling tiles, two men dropped back and applied the second application of compound. Thirty minutes later, the ceiling tiles were finished and the compound had hardened and was ready for sanding. Two men sanded and cleaned the sheetrock, while Khan and another man followed with paint. An hour later, the storage room looked exactly as it had before, albeit an updated version. As the men were removing the remaining trash, as well as their tools and equipment, Khan searched out his cousin and asked for assistance. It was nearing the start of the work day and he wanted to be out of there before anyone came around to inspect their work. While Chong's security people moved the shelving, tables, and chairs back into the storeroom, Khan and his men loaded up the vans and headed back to Antwerp. After unloading the trash in a dumpster on the conference center property, they stopped for gas and sandwiches in Breda. It was shortly after ten o'clock when they finally parked the vans.

"We'll have to move your van later," Kahn said, after all of them were on the street. "Let's get inside. I'm exhausted and in need of a shower."

"What about food?" one of the men asked.

"We just ate," Kahn said.

"But we have nothing for the next two days. I think we should get food now."

"Our orders are to remain in the apartment," Kahn said. "We will have to make do with what we have. Let's go."

Chapter 63
Maaldrift, the Netherlands

A few hours after they left the hotel, Carpenter and Kennedy had only made it as far as the town of Maaldrift. It was the third layover on their journey back to The Hague. This time, they were stopped along the A44 Motorway to examine an area that had heightened Carpenter's senses when they drove through yesterday. That stretch of highway separated a commercial zone on the north side of the highway from a residential area on the south side and offered plenty of open spaces to the east and west of each. They were standing in one of those open spaces and Carpenter was pointing out a highly vulnerable position when his phone vibrated. He pulled it out of his back pocket and saw the call was from Tony Galvin, the chief of station in Brussels. "Hey Tony, what's up?"

"PJ, I think we know where Taj Kahn is living."

"Where?"

"It's a rowhouse in a rundown section of Antwerp, a few blocks east of the train station."

"How did you find it?"

"For the past two days, we've been working out from the train station, discreetly asking around about Mumeet and Taj Khan. A few minutes ago, one of my guys, Justin Gainsley, spoke with a Moroccan shop owner who recognized Khan's photo. His convenience store is at the end of the block on the same street. He said Khan and his buddies are in there all the time. He's pretty sure there are four of them. He keeps a close eye on them because he has suspected them of stealing on more than one occasion."

"Has Gainsley or anyone else on your team seen any sign of Khan or Mumeet?"

"We haven't."

"Are you watching the house?"

"I only got this information in the last fifteen minutes, but Gainsley has made a couple of passes down the street. He can't determine if there is anyone inside. Do you want us to knock on the door?"

"No, not yet," Carpenter said. Mumeet had been spotted in Antwerp, and it was very possible that he was staying with Khan. "We don't know what kind of arsenal they have, and I don't want to tip them off. For now, rotate your team members and have them keep an eye on the place from a safe distance. The summit starts in a little less than forty-eight hours, so we should have some time to set up more robust surveillance before they deploy. What's around there?"

"The street is packed with similar buildings—all three stories, very narrow and long. Gainsley said there are a lot of parked cars on the street but very little traffic and few pedestrians. Given the confines, I think it'll be risky to put a full surveillance team on the street. One of my other officers, Robin Barber, recalled seeing a place for rent on the next street over. It's directly across the courtyard at the back of Khan's place. She's talking to the landlord about a short-term lease as we speak."

"That's great work, Tony. We should be able to get there in ninety minutes. Text me the address for Khan's place and a location where we can meet, someplace nearby but not too close."

Carpenter hung up and looked over at Kennedy. "That was Tony Galvin. Khan is living in Antwerp."

Chapter 64
Antwerp

As soon as they were in the car, Carpenter called Director Patrick. In addition to telling him about Khan's residence, he asked for an update on the backup he had requested. It was just him and Kennedy and Carpenter did not want to rely on Galvin's inexperienced team if he decided it was necessary to enter Khan's house. While he had confidence that Galvin's people were capable spies and recruiters, he needed battle-tested operators to take down the terrorist cell. He also wanted a bomb specialist. If Mumeet was there, they could expect to find explosive devices inside. There was also a good chance the house was booby-trapped.

As Carpenter and Kennedy were approaching Antwerp, Patrick called back to say Mike Porter and Joe Gerardi were on the way. The two were former Delta Force operators and recent additions to the CTC. Acting on Carpenter's earlier request, Patrick had pulled them from Syria and was routing them to Europe through Malta. Patrick advised they were about to depart Malta and would be in Belgium in a few hours. Although Carpenter had not worked with either man before, he was glad for the help. In a stroke of fortune, Patrick had also secured the services of Jeb Morrison, an explosive ordinance disposal technician with the US Navy. Morrison happened to be in Cologne as part of an international team assembled to disable an unexploded three-ton bomb from the Second World War. The ordinance had been unearthed near the banks of the Rhine, where crews were digging the foundation for a new rail line at the main train station, Köhl Hauptbahnhof. The excavation site was also right next to the famous twin-spired Cologne Cathedral and the Ludwig Museum, which housed an impressive array of Expressionism and modern art, including one of Europe's largest Picasso collections. The Germans were not taking any chances and had called in support from around the globe. In order to get Morrison out of the assignment quietly, Patrick had had to take some liberties with the truth. As far as the Germans knew, Morrison was on his way back to the States to be by the side of his dying brother—one he did not have. As a final piece of information, Patrick said that Blake Palmer of the NSA was monitoring Khan's home for any telecommunications activity. Not surprisingly, Palmer had yet to detect any phone or email usage at the residence. The imposed silence was a classic sign that an operation was nearing execution.

Galvin was there to meet them when Carpenter and Kennedy pulled into a parking ramp near the train station. Carpenter was champing at the bit when he got out of the car and walked over to Galvin. "Tony, this is Tyler Kennedy." As Galvin and Kennedy started to shake hands, Carpenter asked, "What's the latest?"

"Nobody has left the house," Galvin said. "We have a laser listening device set up in our observation post that faces the back of Khan's house. We can hear a television and we've heard the toilet flush, but we have not heard any talking."

"How many people do you have watching the place?"

"Including me, there are three of us rotating and watching the front from the street. We have an unoccupied van parked on the opposite side of the street and toward the northern end of the block. We set up a camera in the van that is providing us a decent view of the front door. I also have one person manning the observation post."

"I like it," Carpenter said. "Since you've got things covered for now, I'd like to go to the OP first."

They headed out on foot for the short walk to the observation post. Kennedy struck up a conversation with Galvin, while Carpenter took in the surroundings. It was his first trip to the Belgian city, but he knew Antwerp was a key diamond center and was home to the second largest port in Europe. As they passed near the diamond district, the names on the storefronts were the first indications of the strong Jewish community in Antwerp. But he also encountered groups of Indians and Arabs on the street, reminding him that the diamond industry had long-standing roots in India and a nascent presence in Dubai. Signs that Islam was flourishing also abounded in Belgium's largest city. According to the latest unofficial data, Muslims represented nearly one out of every six of the city's residents. Antwerp was a good location for Mumeet to hole up. He noticed that the bustle lessened considerably as they moved further east and away from the diamond district and train station. A short time later, Carpenter followed when Galvin turned down a narrow street. Cars we parked along either side of the street, many of them encroaching on the sidewalk. They proceeded single file down the sidewalk until Galvin stopped walking.

"This is us," Galvin said.

Carpenter glanced up at the building that was serving as the observation post. Unexceptional was a charitable description for the tired-looking building. On the street level, grime-streaked limestone encased a wooden entrance doorway and, to the right, there was a metal overhead door. A bicycle leaned up against it, revealing that the opening was barely wide enough to accommodate a small vehicle. Red brick covered the exterior of the second and third levels. There were clear signs of rotting on the white wooden molding surrounding the two filthy windows on each of the upper floors. As Galvin wrestled with the lock, Carpenter looked up and down the street for any signs of life and saw none.

Galvin pushed the door aside so that he and Kennedy could enter the premises. Inside, there was a small entryway at the base of the stairs. After he locked the door, Galvin led them up the stairs to the third floor. There was a kitchen off to the side of the open space. Carpenter presumed it most likely served as the dining and living area when the home was occupied, while the bedrooms and bath were probably located on the second floor. Just to the left of the kitchen, a man was seated on a wobbly chair at the back of the building, peering through an open window that was covered with a curtain of translucent material. Carpenter recognized the camera-like device mounted on the tripod next to him. The laser listening device consisted of three main components: a laser transmitter, laser receiver, and amplifier with audio recorder. It utilized an invisible infrared laser beam to detect vibrations on window glass that were transmitted back to the receiver, where the vibrations were converted to electric signals, filtered, amplified, and fed into a dedicated recording unit. The operator could monitor the audio in real time, while simultaneously recording. And the machine had an effective range up to five hundred yards. The man turned around as Galvin led them deeper into the room.

"PJ Carpenter and Tyler Kennedy, meet Justin Gainsley," Galvin said.

After pleasantries were exchanged, Carpenter moved over and peered through the window. The device was aimed at another ramshackle building that Galvin confirmed was Khan's residence. Carpenter looked down onto an approximately sixty-foot-deep courtyard that separated their location from Khan's building. He did not see any gaps between the rowhouses on either side of the courtyard and concluded that the backdoor to Khan's building was an unlikely means of escape. Anyone wishing to leave the dwelling would have to use the front door or climb across rooftops. Carpenter retreated from the window and glanced down. On the floor, next to the listening device, was a laptop. The screen was focused on a door at the center of a tan brick building, which Galvin verified was the entrance for Khan's building. Carpenter liked what he was seeing. "Anything new, Justin?" he asked.

"Still quiet, other than a soccer match on the television," Gainsley answered.

"How about out front?"

"That's quiet too. No one has entered or left since we've been watching. But I know at least one person is inside. I've heard the toilet flush twice now and a couple of times I heard a door open and close. By the sounds of it, I think it might have been a refrigerator door."

"Tony, who's out on the street now?" Carpenter asked.

"Robin Barber and Joe Hankinson."

"Let them know Tyler and I will be coming out. Have them go buy some different shirts, jackets, and maybe some hats so that everyone can switch up wardrobes. We might be doing this awhile."

Chapter 65

Early that evening, Carpenter and Kennedy were reentering the observation post. Throughout the day, while two team members watched from inside the rented house, four others took turns patrolling the street in front of Khan's dwelling and the broader neighborhood. He and Kennedy had just concluded their second shift on the streets, which included a visit to the Moroccan's convenience store. Carpenter now felt he had a strong familiarity with the area and had already begun to assemble plans for either a snatch and grab on the street or a breach of the building.

When they reached the top of the stairs, Carpenter saw that Jeb Morrison was also there, chatting with Tony Galvin, while Robin Barber monitored the listening device and the footage from Khan's front door. After learning from Morrison that he had arrived from Cologne within the last hour, Galvin informed Carpenter that Mike Porter and Joe Gerardi had just touched down after flying in from Malta and would be there soon. The timing was perfect, as things were starting to heat up.

It was not until midafternoon that the first voices had been picked up by the listening device. The conversations were banal but the team was able to identify four distinct voices, speaking in French, over the din of the television. However, the increased activity inside was not matched at the front door, where no arrivals or departures had been noted. Beyond knowing at least four men were inside, the surveillance had yet to yield much actionable intelligence. Unless Khan and his men decided to leave, they were going to have to storm the building at some point. The economic summit would start in less than two days. If there were others involved in this plot beside those inside Khan's house, Carpenter needed to know that information sooner rather than later. He gathered everyone around Barber and the listening device to explain his plans. Carpenter was nearly finished when Barber raised her left hand to silence him. She had been listening to Carpenter with one ear, while the other was covered by the headphones.

"They are talking about going out to get food," Barber hurriedly said, as she pulled the headphone jack out of the device so that everyone was able to hear the audio.

A man's voice emanated from the speaker. "We have been over this; we are to stay inside."

"Are we supposed to eat stale bread and biscuits for the next day and a half?" another man asked.

"We cannot go into this operation starving," a third man said.

"All right, enough!" the first man said. "I still have to find a parking space closer to the building. After I do that, I will go to the market and pick up some food."

"I will come with you," the second man said.

"No, you will not. I will go alone," the first man said.

Carpenter had heard enough. The squabbling suggested there was no one really in charge. That all but ruled out the possibility that a high-value target like Mumeet was there. But the men inside were a link to whatever Mumeet and Aziz had planned. If they acted quickly, they could grab one of the men on the street and formulate a plan to storm the apartment. It would be a much safer option than entering without knowing what awaited them. Carpenter guessed they had no more than a few minutes to get into position. Unfortunately, Porter and Gerardi would not be there in time to assist. He handed Barber the headphones and directed her to resume monitoring the conversation across the courtyard. Then he handed out assignments.

"Tyler, you and I will be at opposite ends of Khan's block. Joe and Justin will back us up and be prepared to move in if we are compromised." Carpenter was referring to Joe Hankinson and Justin Gainsley who were still out on the streets. "Tony, I want you here coordinating and updating us on anything Robin hears. Jeb, how do you feel about driving the van?"

Morrison first acquired his demolition chops as a Navy SEAL and he had been on quite a few covert operations in his day. He sensed his pulse quickening with the prospect of returning to black ops after a number of years. "I'm game!" he said.

"Okay, let's go."

Chapter 66

"Comms check" Carpenter said. Everyone on the team was equipped with Motorola LEX L10 secure mobile devices. He and the rest of the team on the streets were using wireless earbuds and microphones that looked identical to those used with commercially available smartphones. One by one everyone checked in as Carpenter surveyed the scene.

From his position in front of the convenience store at the northern end of Khan's block, Carpenter could see Kennedy at the far end of the street, milling around the southeast corner of the intersection. Gainsley was half a block to the west of Kennedy on the intersecting street, and Hankinson was in a similar position from Carpenter, but to the east. The plan was to allow whoever emerged from Khan's house to get out of view from the dwelling before grabbing him, and the formation Carpenter designed would allow the team to move in any direction and leapfrog one another, if necessary, to avoid detection until the last moment. The final team member, Jeb Morrison, was hidden in the back of the black cargo van, which was positioned on Khan's street, in between him and Kennedy. When they were ready to grab the man, Morrison would move in with the van. Everyone on the street was ready. "Tony, do you copy?"

"Copy," Galvin said.

"Any update?" Carpenter asked.

"They have been compiling a list of items they want at the store. It seems one of them is getting ready to leave. Hold on." Galvin came back a few seconds later. "Robin said the guy is leaving now!"

"Heads up everyone," Carpenter said. "Target is coming out!"

Soon after, the front door swung inwardly and a man emerged from the building. Kennedy was marginally closer than Carpenter and he was the first to identify the man. "That's Taj Khan or his doppelganger," Kennedy said. "And it looks like he's coming my way."

"Keep a casual pace and move down the street in front of him," Carpenter reminded Kennedy. "Justin, be prepared for Khan to come onto your street. If he comes toward you, walk past him and Tyler will work around the block to intercept him. If he heads away from you, follow at a safe distance." He continued to watch as Khan strode purposefully down the quiet street, and Kennedy moved at a slower pace down the sidewalk in the same direction. A voice interrupted the silence.

"PJ, a car is approaching you. It's at the intersection and appears to be about to turn onto Khan's street," Hankinson said.

Carpenter adjusted his position and watched as the car turned onto Khan's street. As it approached Kahn, he moved closer to the sidewalk but did not slow down. The car continued down the street, toward Kennedy. Kahn followed the same path, albeit at a slower clip. As Khan neared the intersection, Carpenter signaled Gainsley to be ready. But Khan kept going through the intersection, unwittingly following Kennedy.

"Justin, he's staying the course. Let him get further down the next block before you come around the corner," Carpenter said. "Tyler, keep walking until Khan changes course. Joe, stay put in case Khan circles back. Jeb, I'm coming to you. Get ready to start rolling."

Carpenter was in the van with Morrison when Gainsley reported that Khan was passing through the next intersection, placing him two blocks from the residence. "Jeb, time to get moving," Carpenter said. As Morrison eased the van into the street, Carpenter issued new orders. "Tyler and Justin, keep Khan between you until Jeb and I are close."

Kennedy had had to increase his pace to avoid being overtaken by Khan. He was now through the next intersection and onto the fourth block from Khan's residence. "PJ, do you remember seeing a white cargo van at the conference center yesterday?" Kennedy asked.

"You mean the one that passed through as we were leaving?"

"Yeah, it had green lettering on the side."

"Yes, it said 'Crescent Construction.'"

"That's the one. It's just walked past it. It's parked on the street."

Chapter 67

Suddenly, it all came together. Carpenter's mind raced as he planned their next move. "Justin, we are coming up on you now. When we stop, get in. Tyler, slow your pace a bit. Let's see if Khan stops at the van or keeps going."

When he arrived at the next intersection, Kennedy stopped and pulled his phone from his pocket. While discreetly looking back in Khan's direction, he pretended he was speaking to someone on the phone. He saw Khan stop alongside the van out of the corner of his eye. "Do you want me to head back toward Khan?" he asked Carpenter.

"Hold off a second," Carpenter said. It was risky decision, as there might not be a better opportunity to grab Khan. In light of the conversation they had overheard, it was likely that Khan was preparing to move the van closer to his building, but there was also the possibility Khan was heading someplace else, maybe to see Saleem Nasir or even Mumeet. If Khan could lead him to either man, Carpenter was willing to take the risk of not grabbing him now. He motioned for Morrison to double-park, while saying to Kennedy, "Let's see where Taj Khan takes us."

Khan pulled the van away from the curb and immediately signaled for a left-hand turn. Carpenter, Morrison, and Gainsley followed. Kahn turned left again at the next intersection and began proceeding north. Carpenter realized if Khan was leaving the neighborhood, he would have not turned again. Instead, he would have continued east toward the main thoroughfare. "Joe," Carpenter called to Hankinson, "Kahn is heading back toward you and his house. Set up at the corner of his block. I want you there as a lookout when this goes down."

"I'll be there in seconds," Hankinson said.

"Tyler, start hightailing it back toward Khan's building," Carpenter said. "He's going back there to park the van."

While Carpenter and the van continued to follow Khan, Kennedy sprinted back up the street. He continued to receive updates as Khan's van proceeded north. He could see Hankinson posted at the other end of the block. Kennedy was almost to Khan's block when he heard Carpenter's voice.

"Tyler, he's heading back west, toward his street. Where are you?"

"I'm in position," Kennedy said.

"Okay, stay out of view until we're ready. And this is going to have to be quick. We can't have anyone inside Khan's place know what's going on. Wait for my cue."

"Got it."

As Khan approached the intersection with his street, he signaled left again. Carpenter could see Hankinson at the intersection, exactly where he wanted him. He had Morrison stop the van so that he could get out. As he hit the sidewalk, Carpenter saw Khan's van complete the turn. Khan would be in front of his building in a few seconds. "Tyler, do you have eyes on Khan?"

"I can see his van now," Kennedy said. He watched as it moved closer. "He's starting to pull up to the curb, almost in front of his house."

Carpenter rounded the corner in time to see Khan's van come to rest. "Tyler, stay on the sidewalk and start moving toward him," Carpenter said. "Jeb, double park at the end of the block until I tell you to move forward. Joe, start moving toward Tyler."

Khan exited the vehicle and started walking toward the back of his van. As he passed the rear bumper, he remained in the street, adhering to his earlier practice. Kennedy stayed on the sidewalk and started following him. Hankinson was also on the sidewalk, partially hidden by the parked cars and moving toward Khan. Carpenter was coming down the far side of the street, now less than fifty feet from Khan. Carpenter signaled to Morrison. Upon seeing the van move, Kennedy and Hankinson quickened their paces and closed in. Just before Morrison's black van was about to block his view of Khan, Carpenter waved his hands and called out, "Taj!"

Khan was startled at the sound of his name. He looked toward the other side of the street and saw a dark-skinned man waving his hand. As he was trying to decide whether he knew the man, he failed to notice the approaching van until it was almost on top of him. He stepped aside, closer to a parked car, to allow the van to pass, but it stopped right next to him. Just as the rear door slid open, he was slammed from behind and pushed into the cargo area. His raised his head long enough to see a fist smash his jaw. And then everything went dark.

Chapter 68

"**I didn't see** the hit, but I heard it," Carpenter said. He was in the passenger seat as Morrison guided the van through the neighborhood. "You learn that playing hockey?"

"I've slammed my share of people into the boards, but that was more like the football I played in high school," Kennedy said.

"How's your hand?" Morrison asked over his shoulder. "That was some punch. He's out cold."

"It's fine," said Hankinson. Before Khan's body stopped sliding across the van floor, Hankinson had delivered a vicious punch to the left side of Khan's face.

"I hope he won't be out for long," Carpenter said. "We need to interrogate him before his buddies expect him to be back."

"It wasn't much more than a jab," Hankinson said. "He should snap out of it pretty quickly."

"Well, bind his hands and feet and gag him. If there's anything to throw over his head, do that too. Jeb, just to be safe, let's drive around for a bit to disorient him."

Carpenter gestured for everyone to remain quiet and gave Morrison some hand directions. They drove around for a few more minutes before arriving at the observation post. As the van slowed to a stop, Khan was showing the first signs of recovery. He moaned something inaudible and struggled against the zip ties Hankinson had secured around his arms and legs. Gainsley held the hood over his head, while Kennedy and Hankinson held him down on the floor of the van. Carpenter got out and knocked on the door. Galvin opened it immediately. After he scanned up and down the street, Carpenter banged his hand on the side of the van. Gainsley slid the door open and Kennedy and Hankinson jumped out. They swiftly lifted Khan out of the van and carried him inside and up the stairs.

Galvin had set up a makeshift interrogation room in one of the empty bedrooms on the second floor. The lone window was covered with a blanket. The chair Barber had been previously using now sat in the middle of the room. Hankinson pushed Khan into the chair and Kennedy tied him to it with an electrical cord Galvin had found. After they finished, they left Khan alone in the bedroom.

Carpenter pulled Kennedy aside and they moved down the hallway, where it would be safe to talk. "Tony said there are weapons in the storeroom downstairs. We want to take the house as quietly as possible, but I want us prepared for anything. Choose accordingly. We're going in the front and back; teams of two at each entrance. Porter and Gerardi will be here any minute. Brief them when they get here. Any questions?"

"No."

"Give me five minutes with Khan, then I'll meet you guys downstairs."

After Kennedy left, Carpenter walked back to the bedroom and stood directly in front of Khan. He remained still for several seconds, without saying a word. Khan was leaning forward in the chair as far as the restraints would allow, and his chin was buried in his chest. Carpenter went over the questions in his head a final time. When he was ready, he ripped the hood off and pushed Khan's head back. He allowed Khan's eyes to focus on him before asking in French, "How many people are in your house?" he asked.

"I live alone," Khan said.

Carpenter slapped the side of Khan's head with an open palm. "If you lie to me again, that will feel like a kiss. Who are the other three men in your house right now?"

"They are coworkers."

"Are there any others?"

"No."

"How do you know those three men?"

"They are friends from Molenbeek. We grew up together."

"What were you doing at the World Peace Conference Center?"

How does this man know these things? Khan wondered. He decided he would have to answer truthfully, but maybe not fully. "We were doing a job."

Carpenter punched Khan in the stomach with two quick jabs. "Don't be cute with me Khan. When I ask you a question, you had better give me a complete answer. What kind of job?"

In between gasps, Khan said, "We were making repairs caused by water damage."

"Where in the conference center?"

"In a storage room. It is on the main level, behind the auditorium."

Carpenter recalled Van den Berg's uneasiness and how the room was arranged so as to dissuade anyone from venturing too far inside. He had felt there was something odd and he regretted not pressing Van den Berg about it. "Is that where you planted the bomb?"

"I do not know what you are talking about."

Carpenter slapped the side of his head again, this time with more force.

"Yes! The bomb is in the wall!" Khan said between whimpers.

"Who else helped you?" Khan did not immediately answer. "You have two seconds to answer me. Otherwise, I'm going to slit your throat and watch you bleed to death."

Khan began to sob as drops of blood dripped from his nose and mouth and onto his shirt. "He did not give his name but I am sure it was Mumeet," Khan said. Fearing another blow, he added, "And Fahd al-Rasheed was with him."

"Where are Mumeet and al-Rasheed now?" Carpenter demanded.

"I do not know; it is the truth, I swear!"

"When did you last see them?"

"Earlier today, just before sunrise."

"Where were you?"

"I dropped them off in a park near the conference center."

"What kind of bomb did Mumeet and al-Rasheed place in the storage room?"

"I do not know. They used orange material."

Semtex, no doubt procured from Jozef Varga in Slovakia. "Where were Mumeet and al-Rasheed going after you dropped them off in the park?"

"They did not say but when I offered to drive them to where they were staying, Mumeet said they preferred to walk."

That was a potentially significant piece of information. Mumeet was assuredly concerned about being spotted, something more likely during the light of day. If Khan did indeed drop them off just before sunrise, Mumeet and al-Rasheed would not have had much time to get to their safehouse under cover of semi-darkness. Their safehouse had to be nearby the drop off location. "What are you and the other three men supposed to do now?"

"We are supposed to wait for the explosion, then storm the building and shoot as many people as we can."

"When is that supposed to happen?"

"During the opening remarks for the conference."

"Do you have plans to see or speak to Mumeet again?"

"No. Mumeet said I would not see or hear from him again until we meet in paradise."

That gave Carpenter barely a day and a half to find Mumeet. But first, he had to take care of the men in Khan's house. And, after that, he had to disable the bomb. "Are there bombs and weapons in your house?"

"There are weapons but no bombs. All the explosives were used for the bomb at the conference center."

Carpenter asked some questions about the men and the layout of the home. Based on Khan's answers, he was confident the men inside the home, like Khan, were not hardened soldiers. Rather, they were merely playing a sacrificial role in Mumeet's grander plans. By that point, the interrogation had already passed the five-minute mark. Khan's men would begin to wonder what was taking him so long. It was time to deploy the team to raid the house, but there were a few questions that he still needed to ask. "Who hired you to do the work at the conference center?"

"My cousin. His name is Jian Chong. He is in charge of security and maintenance. He arranged the problem and hired us to do the repair work."

"Who is Saleem Nasir?"

"He is the man who recruited me and my friends."

"Where is Nasir now?"

"I have not seen or talked to him for many weeks. But my cousin saw him the other day. I am almost certain Mr. Saleem paid money to my cousin."

Khan would have kept talking but Carpenter didn't have time and he had enough to get going. "I'd better not find that you lied to me, Khan. In the meantime, spend some time thinking about your relationship with Allah. Despite what Mumeet told you, paradise was not in your future before we met. Murder is one of the seven greatest sins in Islam. If you want a chance at reaching paradise, you'd be wise to repent and ask Allah, the Most Merciful, for forgiveness."

Chapter 69

Carpenter left Khan to contemplate the choices he had made and what impact they would have on his uncertain future. Although the interrogation had lasted longer than anticipated, he had been able to gather valuable information. Things were finally moving in the right direction but they had a lot of work ahead to keep the momentum. But before storming Khan's house, he needed to get Director Patrick working on a few critical matters. He pulled out his phone and dialed his boss.

"I just finished interrogating Taj Khan," he said. "He's working with Mumeet and al-Rasheed. You won't be surprised to hear there's a bomb planted inside a storage room wall at the World Peace Conference Center. I'll explain more later. Right now, I need you to track down the general manager, Liam Van den Berg. Get me a home address and have Blake Palmer tap every phone and communication line Van den Berg is known to have. I'll send two of Galvin's guys to watch him until I get there."

Patrick decided to ignore Van den Berg for the moment. He homed in on something else Carpenter had said. "Are you sure Khan is working with Mumeet?"

"Based on what we already knew and the interrogation, yes. Besides, why would he lie about that?"

"Does he know where Mumeet is now?"

"The Hague, but he said he doesn't know exactly where and there are no plans for him to speak to Mumeet again. Khan and his brothers across the courtyard were supposed to assault the conference center after the bomb detonated, sometime during the opening remarks."

"What do you want with Van den Berg?"

"I'm going to find out what he knows. This is an inside job. Khan's cousin is a guy named Jian Chong, who happens to be the head of security and maintenance. That's how they got in to plant the bomb. Chong reports to Van den Berg. During our tour, Van den Berg seemed a bit unnerved when we looked at the storage room, so I want to talk to him. Plus, he's going to quietly get us into the building to disable the bomb."

"I can't authorize your detention and interrogation of a Dutch citizen. We have to get the Dutch involved."

"The president's directive was pretty clear."

"This is different. You don't know if Van den Berg was helping in any way. Besides, there is a live bomb inside an important building on Dutch soil. On top of that, the Dutch security service has been cooperating with us on this. I can't cut them off now."

"We can't make this into a big production! The Dutch will send in teams of people and create a huge spectacle. I've got one of the best explosive ordinance disposal technicians in the world with me. Jeb can handle this without alerting Mumeet that his plans are blown. This is our best shot at that son of a bitch!"

"I still can't have you running an operation inside Holland without approval. I'll speak with Director Gonzalez and the president and see if they can help put a lid on everything."

"Listen, I get it but the summit starts in less than thirty-six hours," Carpenter said. "I don't have time for a bunch of diplomatic bullshit."

Patrick took a deep breath before responding. Carpenter had a history of acting first and getting permission later, but that was not going to work this time. "I'll get you Van den Berg's address right away, but I'm going to tell Galvin that his men are not authorized to do anything more than get eyes on Van den Berg until you guys hear from me. It'll be my ass on the line before they get around to you. I will speak to Director Gonzalez and the president about your concerns and ask them to pressure the Dutch for a minimalist approach. I will speak to the head of the General Intelligence and Security Service. I've known him a long time. It will help if I can get him on our side. In the meantime, you worry about the men inside Khan's house. I have no plans to inform the Belgians. They are only likely to screw things up. Do we have an understanding?"

"Just make sure the Dutch don't show up at the conference center with an army. Since we will probably need help clearing the building, have them send an EOD team. That way, Jeb will have some assistance if he needs it. But tell them to wait for us to get there before they touch that bomb."

"Duly noted," Patrick said.

"I'll have Jeb text you what he needs."

"I'll get right on it when he does."

"Oh, I almost forgot. Put Palmer on Chong too. I'll call you when we're done at Khan's house."

Chapter 70

Carpenter put the phone away and walked over to speak with the rest of the team. The call with Patrick had not gone liked he had hoped. He conceded that he was asking for a lot and, despite not liking it, he had to respect Patrick's position. Everyone was gathered near Robin Barber, who was monitoring events at Khan's house. "What's going on over there?" he asked.

"So far, none of them are expressing any concern about Khan's absence, other than looking forward to his return with some food," Barber said.

"Are all three of them together?"

"As far as I can tell, they are all watching television. That's pretty much all they've been doing."

He looked at Galvin. "Where are Porter and Gerardi?"

"They just checked in. They're dealing with some traffic, but they should be here in the next few minutes," Galvin said.

That was disappointing news. Carpenter had a lot of balls in the air and too few hands to catch them. He briefly thought over his options, ultimately deciding it was better to be short-handed than delay his original plan. "Joe, you and Justin start out for The Hague. Director Patrick will be calling Tony with an address for Liam Van den Berg, the general manager of the World Peace Conference Center, and Jian Chong, head of maintenance and security. Find them and watch them until you hear from me or Director Patrick. I'm supposed to tell you not to detain either of them until the Dutch get there, but if either one shows any signs of running, cut him down if you have to. Get going." He then turned to Kennedy and Morrison. "It looks like it may be just us," he said. "Jeb, I didn't expect to bring you in on all this. Are you still good?"

"Hell yes! Absolutely, I am!" Morrison said.

"Awesome. Let's gear up."

Chapter 71
The Hague

"What do you know about Saleem Nasir?" al-Rasheed asked. "How do we know he didn't make a mistake that will jeopardize this operation? By the way he talks, he must be a lawyer or a businessman, but he's not an experienced jihadist. That much is clear by the men he selected. Taj Khan and his friends are stupid, more so than most men we have worked with in the past. And we don't know anything about Jian Chong."

"We can only rely on Aziz. Nasir is his man and it's clear that Nasir has earned his trust," Fahkoury said. "Otherwise, he would not have used him for such an important operation."

"Maybe so, but why did he leave?"

After making the final payment to Chong, Nasir had disappeared. He had not offered an explanation and Fahkoury did not ask for one. He did not really care. "Aziz must have other plans for him. We have no more need for him, anyway."

"Well, I don't like where he stuck us," al-Rasheed said. "This is not the kind of home a true believer would live in, and I don't like where it is. There is nothing around this place except other luxury homes. I feel like a caged animal."

It would not have been Fahkoury's first choice either. He believed in the virtuousness of hardship. This place evoked unpleasant memories of his childhood, when he was ignorant of his parents' evil ways. They shunned piety and instead wrapped themselves in the trappings of financial success. In many ways, he was ashamed of his upbringing and sought out privation in an effort to compensate. But he believed the temporary luxuries he and al-Rasheed were suffering would be forgiven by the damage they would soon wreak in Allah's service. And they would not have to bear the burdens much longer. The Economic Summit would get underway the morning after next and then they would be on their way. Nasir had left a car for them in the garage. The plan was to leave in the immediate aftermath of the attacks. The house was located a safe distance from the target and close to the main road they would follow to Germany. They would be in the Berlin safehouse before the infidel authorities had a chance to assess the damage and begin searching for the culprits. "Forget about the repugnance of this place. We will be gone soon. Besides, what would you have us do?" he asked.

"I'd rather be in a crowded section of the city. We might at least be able to venture outside without worrying about nosy neighbors. I get restless when I am confined to one place."

"We have no choice. This place was chosen for us and we will remain inside through the attack. We have to keep a low profile." Fahkoury was troubled by the fact the home had been vacant for years. Nasir was not sure Aziz had even visited the house. Signs of occupancy were sure to invite inquiries.

"Why don't we just leave? There is nothing more for us to do here."

"I want to remain here in case we are needed. Besides, I want to be close when the time comes."

"We are close but still far away. Don't you feel disconnected from the operation?"

"I do not," Fahkoury said. "The entire summit will be televised live on national television. We will be able to actually see the explosion inside and being here will give us a sense of the aftermath."

Al-Rasheed took measure of Fahkoury's perspective. "I guess it's waiting that is bothering me. Normally, we are very active at this stage. Everything is done; now there is nothing left to do."

"There is one important thing left to do. I will let you make the call to trigger the explosion, as long as you stop groaning about our situation here. Until then, go rest or read a book. Find something to do."

Chapter 72

A **couple hours** later, Carpenter, Kennedy, and Morrison were crossing the Hollands Diep on their way to The Hague and the World Peace Conference Center. While Kennedy drove, Morrison rode shotgun. Those two alternated between chatting about their backgrounds and trying to listen in on Carpenter's conversation with Director Patrick, one that had started shortly after the trio left Antwerp.

They were able to hear Carpenter explain how Porter and Gerardi had arrived just in time to help at Khan's house. While he and Kennedy moved into position to crash through the front door, Porter and Gerardi snuck across the courtyard to the rear entrance. In retrospect, that neither door was locked was a sign of how smooth the operation would prove to be. The television blared from the uppermost floor as they cleared the first level. While Carpenter and Kennedy kept watch on the stairs, Porter and Gerardi found a cache of weapons and ammunition in the basement, hidden behind a pile of boxes and concealed underneath a bed sheet. In capable hands, the collection of hand grenades and assault weapons could have inflicted catastrophic destruction on a large crowd of people. The two teams worked together as they silently moved up the stairway. Porter had no trouble restraining the man resting in bed on the second floor, and the two men on the third floor threw their hands in the air at the sight of Gerardi walking into the living area. Morrison was summoned and, while he and Porter searched for explosives, Gerardi and Kennedy separated the captives for interrogation. After just a few minutes, it was clear these men could not add anything to what Carpenter had already learned from Khan. For the time being, the prisoners, including Khan, were now in the basement of the observation post under the watchful eyes of Tony Galvin and Robin Barber.

Only the hum of the tires could be heard when Carpenter stopped talking and listened to Patrick's update. Kennedy and Morrison would later learn that while they were securing Khan's home, Patrick and CIA Director Melissa Gonzalez had had an intense call with President Madden and Secretary of State Julie Christensen. Only weeks before, the president had hosted the Dutch prime minister at the White House. As badly as he wanted Mumeet, the president was not prepared to allow Carpenter to even enter the Netherlands without approval from the Dutch government. Patrick was placed on hold, while the president's chief of staff Bill Tackett hastily arranged a conference call with the prime minister and the king. It was Tackett's voice that Patrick heard next, telling him Carpenter had approval to enter Holland with his team. Tackett relayed the president's order for Patrick to coordinate with the director-general of the Dutch General Intelligence and Security Service.

Patrick immediately reached out again to Director-General Theo Strous, a man he had known for decades and considered a good friend. The two had spoken before Patrick called Director Gonzalez and the president. By the time they reconnected, Director-General Strous had already dispatched two of his officers to assist Joe Hankinson and Justin Gainsley. Liam Van den Berg was said to have fainted when told there was a bomb planted inside the conference center. The first thing he wanted to know when he eventually came around was whether the horrible news would be shared with the press. Van den Berg was cooperating fully and had offered his suspicions about Jian Chong. Even before Van den Berg's accusation, Director-General Strous had sent a team to apprehend Chong, who was now in custody. Patrick told him he had sent Hankinson and Gainsley back to Antwerp to help Galvin and Barber. According to Patrick, President Madden was still deciding whether to turn the prisoners over to the Belgians or send them elsewhere. Given the Belgian's awful history in dealing with the extremist threat, the president was said to be leaning toward the latter. Either way, Patrick said, the decision would not be made until the situation in The Hague was fully resolved. Just as they were nearing the World Peace Conference center, Patrick added that a team of explosive ordinance disposal technicians would be at the World Peace Conference Center with Director-General Strous.

"That's all great news," Carpenter said. "but we're pulling up to the conference center now. I'll have to call you back when things are under control here. In the meantime, find Mumeet for me!" As he exited the car, a man stepped forward to greet him.

"Mr. Carpenter, I am Theo Strous."

"It's a pleasure to meet you Director-General. Director Patrick speaks very highly of you."

"I have known Timothy a long time," Strous said. "Besides being a consummate professional, I consider him a dear friend. Did he update you on Van den Berg and Jian Chong?"

"He did."

"Good. Van den Berg was here earlier to retrieve the personnel records for each member of Chong's staff. Since we do not know the identity of everyone involved, we are rounding up all of them. The four members who were on duty when we arrived and three others are currently being held at a secure location, and we are in the process of detaining the rest. Unlike Chong, the members of his team already in custody are cooperating and answering our questions. It is becoming apparent that they know nothing of Chong's involvement with terrorists. Finally, Van den Berg is with one of my officers at a different secure location."

As Strous was speaking, Kennedy and Morrison appeared by Carpenter's side. After introducing his colleagues, Carpenter asked, "Is there anyone inside the building?"

"Except for the four members of Chong's security team, the building was unoccupied when we arrived. I have a team of ordinance disposal technicians inside the building now."

"Has your EOD team located the bomb," Carpenter said.

"It's exactly where Taj Khan told you it would be, but my team has not done any work on the bomb. Director Patrick asked us to wait until Mr. Morrison arrived before any attempt to disable it is made. We did carefully move the tables and chairs away from the wall. My team is now searching the rest of the building."

"Were you able to get the equipment I requested?" Morrison asked.

"It is outside the storage room door," Strous said.

"Jeb, you ready for this?" Carpenter asked.

"I am and since the bomb is inside a wall, I think it would be best if I go in alone. Until the wall is removed sufficiently enough to expose the bomb, there will be a risk of triggering it. I'd rather not have anyone else jarring and banging around in there."

Strous was uncomfortable with the request. His concern was for Morrison's safety, rather than the usurpation of his team. But after challenging Morrison on the merits of the request, he agreed the danger would increase exponentially with each additional participant. And Strous was particularly impressed with Morrison's altruistic argument that it would be better to have one, rather than multiple casualties. As Morrison made his way into the building, Strous called his EOD team outside to safety.

While Morrison went inside to suit up, Carpenter used the momentary lull to work on his next objective. According to Khan, Mumeet was somewhere in The Hague. And something Patrick had said a few days earlier gave him an idea how they might pinpoint his location. The arrival at the conference center had caused him to forget to share it with Patrick. He stepped away and dialed his boss. "Hey, I've got a few minutes. Jeb is making his way in there now. I didn't have a chance to tell you an idea I had. You told me Saleem Nasir used a series of dummy corporations to buy a cell phone, so I'm thinking he might have done the same thing to purchase a safehouse for Mumeet and al-Rasheed."

"We had the same thought," Patrick said. "We're looking into it, but it's going to take some time. Without getting too far into the weeds, about one in three properties in the Netherlands is owned by a corporation. And those are just the title transfers that are recorded. One can purchase real estate in Holland without filing a transfer of title. The title records are maintained by the Land Registry Office. We started searching the records that the office makes publicly-available but the information and online search functions are not great. And the president wants us to seek cooperation from the Dutch before we hack into the database. We're trying to get it, but it's the middle of the night there."

"Keep pressing. It won't be long before the beginning of the conference will be measured in hours rather than days." He heard Morrison's voice. "Sorry, I've got to run. Jeb is calling me."

"PJ?" Morrison asked again.

Carpenter grabbed the hand-held radio. "Yeah, Jeb, I'm here."

"I'm geared up and heading into the storage room now."

"Okay, I'll stay on with you."

Morrison was dressed in the latest generation bomb suit. The full body ensemble was made of Kevlar and offered protection from blast heat and flame, overpressure, and fragmentation. He wore a helmet that was equipped with a mil-spec microphone and speakers, which utilized a very low radio frequency to minimize the risk of activating the cell phone hooked up to the improvised explosive device. In his hands, he held a FLIR hand-held infrared camera. He stopped a couple feet from the storage room wall and knelt down before he started running the camera over the area. A few moments passed before he said, "He's got it set up in a daisy chain. The bombs appear to be housed inside steel boxes, just as Khan said. And the detonator is wired to a cell phone that is affixed to a wall stud. This is going to take a bit of time, and I'm going to shut down the radio, just to be safe. If there's a problem, you'll hear it."

"Roger that," Carpenter said. "Good luck, Jeb."

Morrison began cutting sheetrock, starting with a hole several feet from the phone. Over the next hour, he gradually and meticulously enlarged the hole until the cell phone was fully exposed. He walked back into the hallway to calm his nerves and give Carpenter an update. "PJ, you copy?"

"I'm here, Jeb."

"I've got the phone and one of the bombs exposed. That son of a bitch knows what he's doing, but I think I know what he did. If something goes wrong, it will happen in the next few minutes."

Chapter 73

As the sun was coming up, Carpenter sat on a concrete bench with Kennedy outside the World Peace Conference Center. The bomb no longer posed a threat, and no other explosive devices had been found on the property. He took a sip of coffee and realized that neither of them had slept in the past twenty-four hours. He knew the same was true of Morrison, who was inside overseeing the removal of the last pieces of Semtex. Morrison estimated a lethal blast range of no less than two hundred feet, well within reach of the stage where President Madden and other world leaders would have been sitting. It was also possible that the bomb could have done structural damage to the exterior wall on the other side of the hallway from the storage room. Carpenter shook his head at what could have been. Aziz and his Al-Kalafa group had nearly pulled it off. If it was detonated during the opening remarks, as Khan claimed it was supposed to be, the death toll would have been high and the effect on global stability profound.

In a little more than twenty-four hours, the G-20 Economic Summit was scheduled to begin. He knew the Dutch and the White House were quietly sharing these unsettling developments with each member of the Group of Twenty. As of now, the conference had not been cancelled, but several leaders were reconsidering their participation. President Madden was not one of them. Despite his intimate knowledge of the details, President Madden had never wavered in his resolve to attend the meeting. Carpenter was unsure about the president's willpower. The Bringer of Death was likely somewhere in The Hague and might have plans beyond Khan's team and the bomb he planted inside the conference center. But as much as the president's determination concerned Carpenter, he appreciated how it helped his own cause. And he was liking his odds.

As far as anyone knew, the G20 Economic Summit was proceeding as planned. Carpenter had no reason to believe the man responsible for executing this attack had any idea his mission had been compromised. Carpenter assumed Mumeet would stick close by, just as he had in Minnesota. As long as there were no leaks about the discovery at the World Peace Conference Center, Mumeet was likely to remain in place. That gave Carpenter roughly one day to find and kill the Bringer of Death. After that, Mumeet would realize the jig was up and leave The Hague. As he wondered how he would do it, he looked up to see Strous venturing through the doors.

"Our friend Mr. Chong has decided to start talking," Strous said. "Besides confirming that he knew what his cousin was doing, he told us that he admitted to receiving two hundred fifty thousand US dollars for his troubles. He must have suspected that we found some of the cash at his home. Anyway, his services were retained by a man he calls 'Saleem.' He claims not to know the man's last name."

"We are pretty sure the man is Saleem Nasir, a former business associate of Sadiq bin Aziz," Carpenter said.

"That is good to know, as it provides some assurance that Mr. Chong is being forthright," Strous said. "Chong received the money in two installments, the latest yesterday. On both occasions, he met Mr. Nasir at the Scheveningen Pier. Chong also said he believes that Mr. Nasir walked to the beach for their last meeting. Chong was there early and watched Nasir approach from some distance. Out of curiosity, he followed Nasir after the exchange. He stayed with Nasir for almost half a mile before he decided he was pushing his luck. I hope that information may prove useful."

"What's the area by the pier like?"

"The beach and the pier are quite popular. There are several hotels in the area, as well as many businesses catering to the beachgoers."

"Are there any residential areas nearby?"

"Yes, there is a mix of single-family homes and apartments in that area. The closest true neighborhood to the pier is called Belgisch Park."

"How far is Belgisch Park from the park across the street?" Carpenter pointed to the east. "Would it be an easy walk?"

"The exact distance would depend on where in Belgisch Park one started from but, in any case, no more than two miles. And it would be a very leisurely walk through several other parks and quiet streets. Is that information somehow useful?"

"It is very helpful. Thank you, Director-General," Carpenter said. The puzzle was starting to come together. Khan said he thought Mumeet and al-Rasheed had walked to the pickup location. Now Chong was saying Saleem Nasir had walked to the pier for their most recent meeting. It was highly likely Nasir and Mumeet were using the same safehouse somewhere in Scheveningen, quite possibly, Belgisch Park. This information would narrow Patrick's search considerably. That raised the question of what he could do if and when Mumeet's location was discovered. "Did Director Patrick tell you the Bringer of Death may be in your country."

"He did."

Carpenter paused, expecting Strous to tell him the Dutch would be taking over the hunt. But Strous did not tell him to stand-down, giving him some hope that he would not be cut out of the picture when he was finally close to his target. "How do we work together?"

"Beginning later today, heads of state and their delegations will be arriving in Holland," Strous said. "Between our responsibilities protecting our guests throughout their stays and securing the conference center, our resources were already going to be stretched thinly. These developments have only heightened the threat to the world leaders who will be attending. I explained to our king and prime minister that we presently do not have the resources to allocate to a manhunt. Otherwise, we will compromise our primary duties of protection and security. Besides, you know far more about Mumeet than we do. It is my understanding that the king and prime minister have spoken with your President Madden, and they are prepared to let you handle this your way, provided you do not endanger innocent lives. Director Patrick will keep me apprised of your progress. Based on those reports, it will be up to me to recommend to the king and prime minister when, if, and how my team should intervene. In light of this arrangement, I am expecting that you will be thorough and candid with your director. Do I have your word on that?"

"You do. My main objective is to take Mumeet down. As much as I'd like to do it myself, I won't hesitate to call for help if we need it."

"Then we have a deal," Strous said. "Director Patrick explained your past with him. You will have my support to make sure it is our side that writes the history this time. Go find him. Godspeed."

Chapter 74

As morning turned to early afternoon, Carpenter and Kennedy were driving around Belgisch Park, trying to get a sense of where Mumeet may be hiding. Within seconds of getting the greenlight from Director-General Strous, Carpenter had called Patrick to tell him to focus on the seaside neighborhood. The information helped Samantha Lane, Ella Rock, and Dalton Jones, who had been struggling to use the dearth of public information available to narrow the search area. Conditions rapidly improved an hour later, when Secretary of State Julie Christensen secured an approved backchannel into the Land Registry Office's website. Blake Palmer of the NSA had the team up and running within minutes. Yet, there was still no indication where the terrorists were holed up and Carpenter was now starting to get irritated.

"This is a waste of time," he said. "We've driven around the entire area three times, and I can't get any sense where they might be. They could be in any of these apartments or private residences. But, even if a third of these properties are owned by corporations, that doesn't leave that many to investigate. What's taking them so long? At this rate, we might as well start banging on doors."

"I guess it would depend on the search functionality," Kennedy said. "They might only be able to search for corporate versus individual owner. In that case, they can probably only see the name of the corporation and not its domicile. Then they'd have to research where the corporation is registered and zero in that way."

"Well, tomorrow morning Mumeet will realize something went wrong and he won't stick around to find out why. We need to find him before that happens."

As they continued down the street, Kennedy recalled Strous telling them Belgisch Park was one of the more affluent sections of the city, with the nicer homes often selling for millions of dollars. It was their second pass down this street, one that served as the eastern-most boundary of the Belgisch Park neighborhood. He had to admit that the homes in this spot were certainly large and elegant but the location baffled him. Pointing to a large complex, he asked, "I still can't comprehend why anyone would buy a million-dollar plus home right next to that prison."

"Maybe because it doesn't look like a prison. The first time we went by it, we both thought it was a castle. Plus, with all the guards and cops around, it's a very secure area." Soon after he said that, they drove beyond the prison. Carpenter continued with his argument. "The homes in this area are all pretty nice, with a lot of space between them. Small parks and expanses of vacant land filled with nice trees add to the charm and privacy that you don't get in in the more densely populated streets closer to the beach. And it's not far from the ocean. At most, we're not much more than half a mile from the beach right here."

"Hey, if this gig doesn't work out, you might have a future in real estate," Kennedy said.

"My point is that this section of the neighborhood is precisely where terrorists would not be expected to be living. When we get to the International Criminal Court, turn around. I want to take another look along this street."

As the car approached the International Criminal Court, Carpenter's phone rang. "I hope you have good news," he said.

"I might," Patrick said. "While we have found dozens of homes in Belgisch Park owned by corporations, there are only a handful owned by corporations registered in secrecy jurisdictions and, of those, only one is registered in the Bahamas."

"Where is it?"

"Do you know where the prison is?"

"Yeah, we just passed it a minute ago. We're about to swing around in front of the ICC right now and head back toward the prison. Why?"

"After you go by the prison heading north, take a good look at the first house you come to. It'll be on your left, immediately after the wooded area. The house number is forty-seven," Patrick said.

"Hold on, we should be coming up to it now." He moved the phone away from his mouth and said, "Tyler, slow down just a bit when we get past this big group of trees. We want to get a look at the first house on the left. Number forty-seven."

As they approached the home from its southern exposure, its long, sloping red-tiled roof towered above the densely-packed deciduous trees that shaded that side of the house. As Kennedy drifted the car past the east-facing front, more sparsely-spaced trees impaired their view, but Carpenter was able to see enough of the tan brick façade to get a sense of its structure and size. The uppermost windows he was able to see began just beneath the bottom of a hipped roof. They were remarkably small, considering the home's grand size, and their placement indicated the home featured a third level of living space or, more likely, a capacious attic. The prominent chimney rising skyward from the base of the similarly pitched roof on the north side of the structure reminded him of the elongated neck of a prehistoric sea monster. The house was certainly distinctive yet they had failed to notice it on their earlier passes.

As they drove past the home, Carpenter looked back between it and its neighbor to the north. He saw that the back of the home was protected by another forest of trees. Somehow, they had to find out who, if anyone, was inside. But options for surveillance were few. The low dunes and trees across the street might offer surveillance options, but the trees fronting the home would block views of the upper levels and obscure a full look at the first floor. The gap between the home and its neighbor on the north side of the house offered a cleaner view, but there was no place to hide. And they would have to sneak to the very edge of the trees in order to get a clear view of the southern side of the house, something he deemed too risky during daylight hours. Speaking again into the phone, but also for the benefit of Kennedy, he said, "Reconnaissance is going to be tough. I'm not seeing a lot of options."

"I have a satellite image up now," Patrick said. "There is a large grove of trees behind the house, bisected by a road. On the far side of the road is a park."

"I noticed the trees behind the house, and we passed through the park earlier, but I couldn't see any homes. Let me call you back after we drive through the park again and take a closer look."

"Before you go, we need to be clear about something," Patrick said. "Right now, you only have permission to surveil the house and determine who's inside. We do not have authority for any kinetic action."

"What are the ROEs if we confirm Mumeet and al-Rasheed are inside and they start shooting or try to escape?"

"There are no established rules of engagement, at least not yet. Use your judgment. But any after action report had better not reveal that you caused either eventuality. We are guests of the Dutch. If things get out of hand, there will be fallout."

"I'll do my best but start laying the groundwork in the event we confirm we have the right place," Carpenter said. He put the phone away and turned to Kennedy, who was steering the car on a path that would take them on a wide loop around the neighborhood. "What did you think about the house?"

"Same as you," Kennedy said. "I think we can get eyes on it to watch any comings and goings, but it'll be tough to get close enough during daylight hours to actually see who is inside. We might have to wait for darkness." As Kennedy was saying that, something caught his attention and he started to pull over to the side of the street.

"What are you doing?" Carpenter asked.

"See that guy over there?" He pointed for Carpenter's benefit. "It didn't connect when I saw him earlier. What he's doing might be a way to get up close."

A casually-dressed young man, probably in his early twenties, was walking north along the sidewalk, holding some sort of packet at his side. Kennedy had seen the man when they were heading in the opposite direction, toward the prison and the International Criminal Court. On that earlier occasion, the guy had been walking down a front walk and Kennedy assumed he lived in the home. Now the same guy was approaching another house. As they got closer, Kennedy could now see the man was holding a clipboard and binder against his hip. Kennedy slowed the car and guided it toward the curb. He and Carpenter watched as the guy marched up to the front door and knocked. It was almost immediately opened by a middle-aged woman. Though they could not hear the conversation, it was clear that the young man was offering some sort of explanation. While the woman listened, the man removed a piece of paper from the binder and handed it to her. She appeared to quickly scan it over before accepting the clipboard and a pen from the man. The young man took the clipboard back from the woman and waved to her over his shoulder as he walked back toward the street.

"It looks like he's trying to get signatures for some kind of petition," Carpenter said.

"That's what I'm thinking, but there's only one way to find out." Kennedy abruptly got out of the car and met the young man on the sidewalk. "Good afternoon," he said.

The college-aged kid looked at him. "Hello, can I help you?"

"Are you trying to get signatures for a petition?"

"Yes, I am."

"What's the cause? I've done it many times myself," Kennedy said.

"We are objecting to the government's cut back on invalidity benefits." The man went into a lecture on how the Dutch government had enacted reforms to reduce the number of claimants receiving benefits during protracted periods of illness. The reforms reclassified the criteria used to determine a person's ability to work and, in this man's opinion, unfairly reduced the number of people receiving invalidity benefits.

"Are there pamphlets in that folder?" Kennedy asked.

"Would you like one?"

"Sure, I'll take a few if you can spare them, and I'll sign your petition too." After the guy handed him some leaflets, Kennedy took the clipboard. As he signed his name, he squeezed the clip and loosened one of the signature pages from the bottom of the stack. In one swift motion, he handed the clipboard back to his new friend, concealing a blank signature page underneath the pamphlets. "Good luck," he said.

"Thank you. Have a pleasant day," the young man said, as he moved on to the next house.

"You too," Kennedy said as he walked back to the car.

When Kennedy was back in the driver's seat, he proudly showed the swag to Carpenter. "Think you can manage to find us a clipboard and a pen?"

"You're becoming quite the wiseass."

Chapter 75

Mike Porter and Joe Gerardi were waiting at the US Embassy when Carpenter called and told them to head to Belgisch Park. They arrived at the staging area a short time later in an unmarked SUV with kit bags for each member of the team. Carpenter wasted no time placing his men in discreet observation posts around the property. Kennedy was shrouded in the small forest at the back of the house, while Gerardi hunkered down at the edge of the trees on the south side. Carpenter and Porter were hidden among some sand dunes across the street, where Carpenter set up the listening device he had transported from Antwerp. But Carpenter gave up on the listening device almost instantly. He struggled to find a clear line through the trees to shoot the laser and placing it anywhere else would have been even more conspicuous. So he packed the device and settled in with Porter to watch the front of the house.

For more than two hours, all four men scanned the windows for any movement inside or, more accurately, on the shades and curtains covering them. Eventually, exasperation led Carpenter to reassess his options. Time was slipping away. Although he was not crazy about Kennedy's idea, after hours of inactivity, he decided they had to give it a try. Telling Patrick was out the question, however. Patrick would immediately kibosh any scheme that would put Kennedy in harm's way. But Carpenter felt he was left with no other option. After he repositioned Gerardi to cover the back door, he left Porter in place and then met Kennedy back at the SUV.

Kennedy had already changed into some wrinkled khakis and a weathered polo shirt by the time Carpenter arrived. And Kennedy's wavy black hair was partially covered by a white baseball hat, emblazoned with an orange Dutch Lion. Other than his bulging arms, he looked like a typical college kid. "I still think this is too risky," he said. "Don't try to be a hero. If anyone answers the door, stick to your cover. Take in as much information as you can and then get the hell out of there."

"There won't be any problems," Kennedy said. "I actually have done some petitioning before, so my approach will seem natural and polished."

"Maybe so, but you don't speak Dutch," Carpenter said.

"No, but most Dutch people speak English."

"Don't start out in English. I don't want to raise any alarms. I'd rather you go with German or French, both of which are also fairly common here."

"How about I speak Arabic?"

"Don't be a smartass."

"Sorry but I couldn't resist. Anyway, my German is solid; my French, less so."

"Okay, start out speaking German, and if you get a blank stare, switch over to English. As a last resort, try French."

"I can do that."

"That's settled then. Be sure to keep your phone on so I can hear what's going on. Are you ready?"

"Absolutely."

Carpenter looked him over. Although Kennedy was brimming with confidence, Carpenter was still reluctant to send him on this mission. But they had no better options and they were running out of time. Sunset was now less than forty minutes away. If he dallied any longer, the occupants might wonder why a petitioner was knocking on their door after dark. "All right, you'd better get going. And remember, nothing stupid. This is not the time to be a hero. Just stick to the cover."

"I got this."

Kennedy, holding a clipboard and pen in his hand, starting walking toward the house. He had two full blocks to cover. Carpenter was chirping in his ear the entire time, telling him to watch for any indicators. At the last minute, Kennedy decided it would be smart to stop at the neighbor's house. It would temper suspicions in case anyone was watching from Aziz's place. Plus, it would give him a chance to practice his spiel.

Carpenter liked the idea. He was sitting in the SUV, just down the street and out of view of the target home, when Kennedy made his approach to the neighbor's house. He alerted Porter and Gerardi to the change in plans, then watched as Kennedy knocked on the front door. A well-dressed man answered and Kennedy immediately went into his pitch. In other circumstances, Carpenter would have laughed, but he was worried about the rookie. *Hell, he's not even a rookie yet*, he said to himself. Carpenter listened in as Kennedy went into his appeal. Despite Kennedy's convincing argument, the man just stood there and listened impassively. Carpenter was beginning to think the man was about to tell Kennedy to leave when he heard him say he would be happy to sign the petition. The man took the clipboard and scratched his name underneath several signatures he and Kennedy had previously scribbled on the form. *I'll be damned!*

"I think I could get a hundred signatures if I had to," Kennedy said when he was walking down the front walk.

"That was smooth but let's not get cocky," Carpenter said. "Mike and Joe, see anything going on?"

"Negative," both men said.

"Okay, hotshot, nothing's changed. Be careful!"

"Will do," Kennedy said.

Carpenter slid down in the seat and watched through a pair of binoculars as Kennedy approached the door to Aziz's house. *Please don't let anything happen to that kid.*

Chapter 76

There was another knock at the door, the second one that day. "Go see who it is," Fahkoury said.

Al-Rasheed got up from his seat at the kitchen counter and made his way down the hallway to the front of the house. The door was made of solid oak, so he went over to the window adjacent to it and pulled the curtain back, ever so slightly. He saw a hulking kid on the front steps, holding a clipboard with some papers on them. He turned to report his finding to Fahkoury, only to find him standing in the foyer with a pistol at his side.

"Who is it?" Fahkoury whispered.

Al-Rasheed tiptoed over to Fahkoury. "A kid with a clipboard."

"The same one from earlier?"

"No, definitely not. This one's not pasty-white like the first guy, and he looks like a rugby player. Should I answer?"

Fahkoury thought it over. Since they had ignored the previous caller, he supposed it was to be expected there would be another attempt during the evening hours when people were more likely to be home. His inclination was to ignore this person as well, but he was troubled by the possibility that these people might keep coming until someone finally answered the door. *Better to be done with them now, rather than tomorrow,* he thought. "Answer the door, but don't let him inside the house. If you have any doubts about his motives, signal me then move to your right and throw open the door. After I shoot him, quickly drag the body inside." Then there was another knock at the door, this time louder. "Go! Let's be done with this nonsense!" Fahkoury hissed.

Chapter 77

Kennedy did not hear anyone inside, but he saw the curtain move out of the corner of his eye. "Mike, did you see the curtain move?" he asked.

"I did," Porter said.

"Can you see anyone inside, Mike?" Carpenter asked.

"Negative," Porter said.

"Tyler, they are probably checking you out. Stay cool," Carpenter said. "And be prepared to dive off those steps if that door flies open. Mike, don't hesitate to take the shot if things go bad."

"Roger that," Porter said.

Several long seconds passed. "Tyler, knock again," Carpenter said.

Kennedy knocked loudly three times. He had just put his hand at his side when the door partially opened, revealing a thin man, about his height. The beard was gone and his hair was cut short, but Kennedy knew he was looking at Fahd al-Rasheed. "*Guten Abend*," he said.

"In English," al-Rasheed ordered.

"Very well. Good evening, sir. My name is Frits and I am collecting signatures to protest the government's refusal to pay benefits to sick and disabled workers. I am hoping to count on you to help us right this terrible injustice."

"Not interested," al-Rasheed said.

"But sir, I only seek your signature. I am not asking for money."

"Still not interested. Please leave now, I have things to do."

"Is there anyone else home I could speak with?"

"No, there is only me. Goodbye." Al-Rasheed slammed the door.

Kennedy made a show of waving a dismissive hand as he descended the three steps to the front walkway. Once he was halfway down the walk, he said, "I just met Fahd al-Rasheed."

"Are you sure?" Carpenter asked.

"Absolutely. He shaved his beard and his hair is shorter than in the photos we have, but it's definitely him."

"What else did you see?"

"Not much, al-Rasheed was blocking my view into the house. But I had a feeling someone else was standing behind the door."

"Any signs of an in-home security system?"

"I didn't see any."

That was good news and confirmed what Patrick had told him. "All right, head back up the street and keep walking past the SUV. I'll wait a minute or two before I head around the block and pick you up." Carpenter paused momentarily before adding, "Nice job, kid. That took balls."

Seconds later, Kennedy flashed a smile at Carpenter as he strode down the sidewalk past the SUV.

Chapter 78

"What's the hold up?" Kennedy asked.

Carpenter wondered the same thing. It had been four hours since Kennedy had confirmed that at least Fahd al-Rasheed was inside the house. Carpenter had expected to be rolling by now. It was past one-thirty, typically the beginning of the best window of opportunity for a raid. "I don't know but we're going in soon, whether we get the all-clear or not."

The first sign of trouble had come during the call he made to Director Patrick as soon as Kennedy was clear of the home. "We've got the bastards," he said. "Tyler says it was definitely al-Rasheed who answered the door. He didn't see Mumeet, but he thinks there was someone else hiding behind the door."

"What are you proposing?" Patrick asked.

"I'm going in after them."

"With just the four of you?"

"Who else?"

"The Dutch might want to have a say in this."

"Not a chance. Besides, it would take too much time to coordinate with the Dutch, even if we don't run into the usual pissing match. This needs to be stealthy and purposeful," Carpenter said. "If we start amassing a bunch of troops around their house, Mumeet and al-Rasheed are likely to catch on. On top of that, we don't want a standoff, and we don't know what else Mumeet might have up his sleeve. He could have the house rigged with explosives. Heck, he might have other bombs placed elsewhere in the city."

We were lucky to find the bomb at the conference center. That might have only been one of many. If they see us coming, Mumeet won't hesitate to use whatever he has. We need to take him out before he has that chance."

Patrick thought it over before responding. He was not sure about Carpenter's strategy but he made it his practice not to second-guess his people. That was especially true when it came to Carpenter. But he could not shake the feeling that Carpenter was setting this up to be a one-on-one showdown with Mumeet, and he hoped Carpenter's desire for revenge was not clouding his judgment. "I'll make the case for you, but I need you to stand down until I get this cleared with the president and the Dutch."

"Get whatever approval you need, just do it fast. This needs to happen while we still have the element of surprise."

Not happy about the delay but thinking approval was a mere formality, Carpenter had continued with preparations. He and Kennedy changed into dark clothing and, just as dusk was giving way to nightfall, headed out to join up with Porter and Gerardi, who had remained in place to ensure no one left or arrived at the house. All four men convened at Gerardi's original location in the trees on the south side of the property. After going over his plan, Carpenter dished out assignments. Porter and Gerardi would each be responsible for covering two sides of the house, while he and Kennedy waited in the trees out back. Porter set off for a clump of trees in the vacant land across the street that would put him in line with the northeast corner of the property. From there, he would be able to see the front door and the north side of the home. He placed Gerardi in the trees at the southwest corner, allowing him to cover the backside of the house as well as the entire south side. Between the two, all sides of the house would be covered. Gerardi would also be able to provide cover when he and Kennedy eventually approached the home from the back woods.

By eleven-thirty, everyone was in position. The temperature had fallen and there was a dampness to the air. Rain was forecast to come in sometime during the wee hours. While they waited for approval, Carpenter and his team watched the home and readied themselves for the opportunity to take down the Bringer of Death and Fahd al-Rasheed. Slightly more than an hour later, Patrick called back.

"I've got good news and bad news," Patrick said. "On the positive side, you have authority to conduct the raid. That was not easy. The prime minister was insisting on using the Dutch military to conduct the raid. With some input from Director-General Strous and some arm-twisting from the president, the king eventually overruled him. On the negative side, you're going to have to wait a bit longer. The Dutch are clearing the area. They want all occupants in a quarter-mile radius out of their homes. Director-General Strous is in charge, so I'm confident it will be done efficiently and discreetly."

"That's probably why Mike reported cars leaving some homes down the street," Carpenter said.

"I'm sure the events are related. As soon as everyone is out, Strous will have the cell phone signals blocked. Before you ask, I made sure that the jamming will not affect your radio frequencies. I'll call when I have the go-ahead. Hold tight; shouldn't be too long."

Now, another hour had passed and Carpenter was aggravated with the continued delay. The recurring thought that their quarry had somehow evaded them certainly was not helping matters. There had not been any signs during their vigil that the home was still occupied. Two sensor lights on either side of the back door that Gerardi had watched light up as darkness descended on The Hague remained on and continued to illuminate most of the backyard, rendering the night vision goggles he and Kennedy were holding in their hands useless. Porter had reported the same sequence and unchanged status about the light hanging over the front door. At least some of the interior lights visible to them earlier still shone inside the house, but their surveillance value was frustrated by the draperies and shades covering the windows. And he assumed Patrick would have called if Blake Palmer and the NSA intercepted any digital communications at the home. Despite the lack of any signs of occupancy, he told himself Mumeet and al-Rasheed had to still be inside the house. Except for the brief time the team assembled to go over his plans, they had the front and rear exits covered. But, with every passing minute of inactivity, the uncertainty was creeping in.

Carpenter decided they could not sit there forever. The G20 Economic Summit was scheduled to start at nine o'clock. If Mumeet had somehow slipped away, he wanted to know sooner than later so he might have another chance to track him down. The sound of the first drops of light rain striking the canopy above them only added to the urgency. He leaned closer to Kennedy and whispered, "The rain might be a problem. If it starts coming down heavy, we'll be dripping wet and sloshing around when we get inside." After a few moments, the pulse began to quicken and he felt some drops on the back of his neck. "Screw this," he said. He picked up the hand-held radio. "Mike and Joe, we're not waiting any longer. Get ready." As soon as the words left his mouth, he felt his phone vibrate. He accepted the call and said, "Please tell me we're good to go."

"You are," Patrick said. "The houses have been cleared in a quarter-mile radius. Strous left his men at that perimeter as your backup. Is there anything I should tell Strous?"

"Just that we're going in right now."

Chapter 79

Al-Rasheed was in pain. Nasir had left them with a refrigerator stocked with various types of food. After feasting earlier in the day on koftas, batata harra, and fattoush salad that Nasir had purchased from a Lebanese market, al-Rasheed decided to try some local fare. When Fahkoury went upstairs to sleep, he made himself a plate of gouda and crackers and settled in the den to watch BBC News. Finding the gouda delicious, he opened a package of Nagelkaas cheese, known as "nail cheese" for the resemblance between tiny nails and the cloves it contained. He had nearly eaten the entire block of the spicy cheese when he felt the first rumbles in his stomach. For the last hour, he had been hoping the pains would subside. Now he was keeled over on the couch.

He wished he could lay down, but his opportunity to rest would not arrive until three o'clock. Until then, he was supposed to keep alert for any signs of trouble. But the only thing he was focused on was the growing discomfort in his bowels. He was in no condition for sentry duty; it hurt to move. But he could not just lay on the couch looking at the television. It would not sit well with Fahkoury. The reprimand would be even worse if Fahkoury found that he was unable to move. He turned the television off before pushing himself up off the couch. The sudden movement brought on a sharp pain. After steadying himself, he limped down the hall to the closest bathroom, which was located off the foyer.

Al-Rasheed sat down without a second to spare. When he finished, he started to rise from the seat, only to find that he was not done. He had just resumed the position for the next round when he heard a noise at the window. It was light and sporadic at first, but it soon picked up in intensity. Rain had always had a calming effect on him. Al-Rasheed knew he wasn't going anywhere for at least the next few minutes, so he opened the window halfway to better hear the melody playing outside. Besides the soothing effect ushered in by the open window, it would alleviate the stench that was overwhelming the tiny space. He closed his eyes to concentrate on the rain and instantly felt some relief.

Chapter 80

"I'll move up to the edge of the trees first," Carpenter said. "When I'm in position, I'll signal you to move forward. Remember, one click means 'yes' or 'clear' and two means 'no' or 'trouble.' Then, after you're in position, you cover me as I move to the back of the house. Watch all the windows for any movement or signs that they know I am approaching. Stay in that spot until I call you in. And, like I told Mike and Joe, make sure it's not me before you shoot if somebody comes running out of the house."

"Doesn't it make more sense for me to go in with you?" Kennedy asked.

"No, it makes more sense for you to stay back until I'm inside. For starters, I don't know if he's got that place booby-trapped. Secondly, if I draw fire, I will need you to lay down cover fire. You'll have a better angle from back in the trees than Joe will. Got it?"

"Got it," Kennedy said.

"Once we get inside, don't be afraid to hit first, and when you do, hit hard. There are only bad dudes inside and none of them are coming out alive. You still sure you're up for this?" Although he had considered using one of the more seasoned operators for this job, he ultimately decided he wanted their marksmanship skills outside. He planned to do all the heavy lifting once they were inside, anyway. All Kennedy would be doing was protecting his six.

"I'm ready for this," Kennedy said. "In case you forgot, I didn't have any trouble at the mall. And I want these assholes too."

"I know what you can do; that's why you're here." He squeezed Kennedy's shoulder and said, "Thought I would just double-check. If you're ready, let's move in closer."

They were slinking toward the edge of the trees when Carpenter heard three clicks in his ear. "Yeah?"

"PJ, it's Joe. I've got some activity on the south side of the house," Gerardi said.

"What is it?"

"I've been watching a window since a light popped on a couple minutes ago. The window just slid halfway open. I can't hear anything because of the rain but I can see inside. It looks like it might be a bathroom and I think al-Rasheed is on the shitter."

"We're coming around now," Carpenter said. "If you can, move into a better position. Three clicks if anything changes; two to abort."

"Copy that," Gerardi said.

It would be risky, but it eliminated the chance of getting blown up trying to enter through a door. He pivoted toward Kennedy. "There might be another way in. When we get to the lawn, follow me and stick close to the trees until we make a beeline for the southwest corner of the house. We'll pause when we get there and then move down the side of the house. Be careful not to trip or make noise. Let's go."

Moments later, Kennedy was following Carpenter as they shuffled with their backs to the side of the house. Beyond Carpenter's head, he could see light shining through a small window. About fifteen feet from the window, Carpenter raised a closed fist. Kennedy leaned in so that his head was almost touching Carpenter's and listened as Carpenter whispered the instructions. When Carpenter finished, Kennedy gave him a thumbs-up. As he watched Carpenter crawl along the ground to the other side of the window, Kennedy slid down the wall until he was standing less than two feet from the opening.

When Carpenter was a few feet beyond the other side of the window, he stood up and looked at Kennedy. He opened his left hand and exposed some small stones in his palm, before closing his hand and mimicking a tossing motion. After Kennedy nodded his understanding, Carpenter tossed one of the pebbles against the window pane. For an instant, the clamor failed to draw a reaction, but then the curtain was slowly pulled to the side. When the curtain fell back into its original position, Carpenter tossed another pebble.

This time, Kennedy saw the top of a head emerge through the opening. He pressed himself against the wall and held his breath as the head protruded further. When al-Rasheed's neck breached the window sill, Kennedy grabbed the back of his head with his left hand and struck him at the same time with a right upper cut that crushed al-Rasheed's windpipe.

Carpenter was on al-Rasheed in an instant. While al-Rasheed was still staring at the ground and clutching at his throat, Carpenter reached over and wrapped al-Rasheed's jaw in his right hand and twisted violently. He released al-Rasheed's head and then pushed the window all the way open before he and Kennedy worked together to swiftly pull al-Rasheed's lifeless body through the opening.

When Kennedy was landing his punch, Gerardi had left his post in the trees fifty yards away. Despite sprinting the entire distance, he only arrived in time to help them lower the body to the ground. "Nice work," he said. "I assume there's been a change in plans."

"Go around and watch the back of the house," Carpenter said. "Have Mike move in on the front but make sure he can still see the far side. I don't want Mumeet slipping out of here." Gerardi left without a word. He turned to Kennedy and motioned toward the window. "Think you can squeeze through there?"

"It might be tight but I'll manage."

"Okay, after I'm in, I'll check outside the bathroom door to make sure it's clear. Then I'll come back to get you."

The window sill was about four feet off the ground. To mitigate noise, Carpenter used Kennedy's left thigh as a step and then slid through the window. He shut off the light and returned to the window a few moments later. "Hand me the guns and the goggles, then make it quick," he whispered.

Kennedy handed two Sig Sauer P226 semi-automatic pistols and two sets of night vision goggles to Carpenter before placing his palms on the sill. In one swift motion, he hoisted his torso through the opening, narrowly missing either side of the window frame. He rested on his stomach and kicked his legs straight, as Carpenter tugged him into the room. "I think we put him out of his misery," Kennedy said. "This place smells awful."

"Another reason to get out of here," Carpenter said. He handed Kennedy a gun and pair of NVGs. "Keep these handy but there's too much light on the first floor to use them, and there's a light on at the top of the stairs. Once we get outside the door, the foyer and front door are to the right. The stairs come down near the front door. There is a den or library off to the side of the foyer. As we move toward the back of the house, we'll come to a dining room first. I didn't venture beyond that but there's another light on in what I think is the kitchen. When we get out of here, we'll first recheck the library to be safe, then we'll work toward the back of the house. I'll go first and you watch our backs."

They moved out of the small bathroom into the hallway. While Kennedy kept his gun trained on the stairs, Carpenter crossed the foyer into the library. The area behind the desk was the only concealed spot in the room. After confirming there was no one there, he motioned Kennedy to follow him down the hallway. They proceeded back-to-back until Carpenter approached the opening for the dining room. After he crouched down and snuck a peek into the empty room, they resumed their formation and continued deeper into the house. After a few more steps, Carpenter saw a kitchen that opened onto a family room. Books lined the shelves on the far wall of the family room. In front of the shelves were two reclining chairs angled toward the center to the room. A large flat-screen television was affixed to the back wall. A long sofa stretched the better part of the room's width between where he was standing and the television wall. On the other side of the sofa was a square wooden coffee table upon which a plate of cheese and a drinking glass rested. The room was otherwise empty.

Carpenter rotated and faced the kitchen area again. Other than the far side of the island, he had been able to see the entire space when they first arrived. Beyond the kitchen, at the back of the house, was another eating area and beyond that was the rear door. He gestured for Kennedy to keep his eyes on the front of the house as he moved in on the island. When he confirmed there was no one hiding on the other side, he looked around. Some of the cabinets appeared large enough to possibly conceal a man but checking them would have to wait. They needed to clear the rest of the house before they started looking at every dubious hiding place. Besides, he had Porter and Gerardi positioned outside to cut down Mumeet or anyone else who tried to escape.

Kennedy was watching the stairs from the foyer when Carpenter met up with him. "He has to be on one of the upper levels," he said. Like nearly every home in Holland, where more than a quarter of the land was below sea level, there was no basement in this one. "And I'm betting he's not in the attic. He'd have limited options to get out of there. He's going to be someplace on the second floor. I'll take lead. When we come to a room, I'll enter first, then you buttonhook around the door." Kennedy nodded his understanding. "Stay close enough so that you can reach out and touch my back if you need to say something."

Carpenter led them up the stairs. He was mindful to keep at the edge of the six-foot wide staircase, where creaks were less likely. Kennedy was within two steps all the way up. At the top of the stairs, he paused to allow Kennedy to stand alongside him. He thought better of trying to extinguish the dim light at the far end of the hallway and then he motioned to the first door on the left. They crept silently down the hall until Carpenter was at the doorway. Without warning, he entered the room at a forty-five-degree angle. Kennedy swung around the near corner to cover the remainder of the room. The faint glow cast by an LED nightlight plugged into the wall revealed a queen-size bed, resting on an ornate Santiago frame in the center of the room and positioned between two windows. A large armoire stood against the wall to the left. Next to it was an open door, exposing a decently-sized and bare closet. On the opposite side of the room was another door. After Kennedy opened it and found an empty bathroom, Carpenter signaled toward the doorway.

The next doorway was on the right side of the hallway. They followed the same procedure into a second bedroom. The layout and furniture mirrored the first room, except this time there were two doors on the left wall. The door nearest them was slightly ajar. Carpenter headed for it and motioned for Kennedy to check out the far door. As he edged closer, Carpenter realized it led to a bathroom. He put up his palm, indicating for Kennedy to stay put. Carpenter moved back toward the center of the room while Kennedy took up a position between the two doors. He nodded to

Kennedy, who pulled open the far door, revealing the closet Carpenter was expecting. Like the one in the first bedroom, this closet contained nothing other than a few hangers. He turned and faced the bathroom door before signaling to Kennedy. Carpenter leveled his gun as Kennedy gently pulled the bathroom door open. The bathroom was unoccupied. But there was a door on the other side of the bathroom. Carpenter had a decision to make.

Chapter 81

Fahkoury was sleeping when he had heard a strange noise from the first floor. He rose from the bed and edged down the hallway toward the top of the stairs. As he stood there, he heard a commotion that sounded like it was coming from the bathroom. He was descending the stairs when he heard the bathroom door begin to open. It sounded like someone was opening it slowly and carefully. Realizing al-Rasheed had no reason to sneak around like that, he retreated to the top of the stairs and placed his back to the wall. As he peered around the corner, he saw a figure pass by the library and head toward the back of the house. A few moments later, he heard the bathroom door close. He moved as quickly as he could without making noise down the stairs and listened. He could hear two hushed voices from inside the bathroom. Although he could not make out what was being said, he was able to hear enough to know that English was being spoken. Images of the man from the mall in America and Istanbul came flooding back.

He briefly considered trying to leave the house but realized there was a good chance the men in the bathroom would hear the heavy front door open. Leaving through the back door meant he would have to pass by the bathroom. The risk was too great that the men inside would emerge at the very moment he was passing by. Besides, either of those options meant he would have to abandon the pre-programmed phone he needed to initiate the explosion. He had neglected to grab it off the table next to his bed before he made his way out of the room. His only choice was to stay and fight. He could not leave without the phone. Almost more than that was the opportunity to finally kill the American. The man had cheapened the success of his attacks in America and escaped his attempt at revenge in Istanbul. Now the American was trying to foil his greatest achievement. No, Fahkoury decided, he would end this contest here and now.

Fahkoury was frantically considering his next move. There were no weapons upstairs. If he retreated to one of the bedrooms or the attic he would be at a distinct disadvantage. The only weapon in the house was the pistol Nasir had left them. But it was in the kitchen. Someone he had to get past the intruders and retrieve the gun. He was at the bottom of the stairs when he heard the bathroom door knob twisting. As he was about to turn and head back up the stairs, he suddenly remembered the panic room underneath the stairway. He had been half-heartedly paying attention when Saleem Nasir showed them around the house. Nasir had not bothered to move the plotted plant in front of the secret entrance to the room but he did partially open the spring-loaded door. Now Fahkoury just had to find the doorway that was concealed in the ornate riven oak paneling.

He quickly took two steps along the staircase and began gently pressing on the wood in the area around the potted plant. On his third attempt, he felt a slight give in the square panel and applied more pressure to the raised trim until the door cracked open. He gently pulled the door outward so that it silently came to rest against the ceramic pot and then slithered inside. Just as he was closing the door, he heard the bathroom door begin to creak open. He held the door tightly against the door stop but did not allow the latch to clasp. Then he closed his eyes and waited.

It was only minutes but it seemed like an hour before he heard footsteps ascending the stairs above him. After the steps subsided, he waited several additional quiet moments before he opened the door and headed into the kitchen to get the pistol.

Chapter 82

Before entering the second bedroom, Carpenter had seen another doorway on the left side of the hallway. Since it was slightly narrower than the three other doorways off the second-floor hallway, he figured it led to the attic. And, unlike the others, it was closed. He had to decide whether to clear the attic before moving to the third bedroom at the far end of the Jack and Jill bathroom. But, if Mumeet was in the third bedroom as he suspected, clearing the attack would potentially create an opportunity for Mumeet to escape or launch a counterattack. He decided the attic would have to wait.

He guided Kennedy away from the bathroom and over near the doorway. From there, they would be able to see down the hallway as well as anyone coming through the bathroom door. "I want you to stand right here. Once I signal that I'm about to go inside the third bedroom, shift back toward the bathroom door to make sure no one tries to escape that way." Once Kennedy nodded his understanding, Carpenter added, "Don't hesitate if anyone besides me comes through that door. We have a clear kill order for anyone in this house." Kennedy gave him a thumbs up before Carpenter set off down the hallway.

He paused outside the door to the third bedroom and signaled to Kennedy. As soon as his partner disappeared into the other bedroom, Carpenter slid closer to the opening. After drawing a deep breath through his nose, he swung around the corner. He saw an unmade bed to his left and a nightstand next to it. On the wall to his right, were two doors, just as they had found in the second bedroom. He moved quickly to the far door. After confirming the closet was empty, he slowly opened the bathroom door, not wanting to alarm Kennedy. But when he peered into the opening, Kennedy was not where he expected him to be at the other end of the bathroom. He quickly backed out of the bathroom doorway and moved into the bedroom. When he sneaked through the doorway and into the hall, what he saw instilled an equal mix of searing rage and dread.

Carpenter made eye contact with Kennedy, who was standing in the hallway with empty hands held out in front of him. Carpenter noted that Kennedy's right shoulder and hip were in contact with the wall and his legs were squeezed together. The man behind Kennedy was nearly invisible but, in the space between his colleague's head and the wall, Carpenter could see the top of a head and a hand holding the business end of a gun against Kennedy's skull. A disembodied voice stiffened Carpenter's wrath.

"We finally meet," Fahkoury said from behind Kennedy. "Ever since I saw you run into that mall, I have been looking forward to this encounter."

"At least we have one thing in common." Carpenter shifted into a shooter's stance, hoping for an opportunity at the concealed target. "You have only one chance to get out of here alive, Mumeet. Drop the gun now!"

"That is not going to happen," Fahkoury said. "I have plans that cannot be broken. And, even if I believed you would not kill me, I have no intention of rotting in an American prison. No, I think it is best that we resolve our differences here. Unfortunately, you managed to slip away in Istanbul. But things will be different this time."

When Mumeet was not risking a quick glance over Kenney's shoulder, Carpenter could only see the very top of Mumeet's head. But there was not enough of it showing to line up a definitive shot. The bullet might only graze the top of his skull. If the round did not kill Mumeet, Kennedy was almost certainly dead. He could always fire a round through Kennedy's upper torso but that was even riskier. He had to keep Mumeet talking until he had a better angle. "I've always been curious about your real name."

"Ah, my name. It has been great enjoyment knowing my anonymity has been a source of frustration to you Western pigs. But my name is of no consequence. It does not define me and has not for many years. It is a remnant of a forgotten past. But, in light of that and the fact you will be dead very soon, I see no harm in telling you that my name is Hamid Fahkoury. Since we are sharing secrets, what do the infidels call you?"

"Preston James Carpenter."

"I seem to recall many years ago our sources in Pakistan's Inter-Services Intelligence mentioning an American named Carpenter. Apparently, this person was making threats to ISI officials and demanding information relating to an attack on an embassy in Islamabad. Could have that been you?"

Carpenter realized he was attempting to crush the gun with his right hand and forced himself to release some tension. He was not going to give Fahkoury even a mite of satisfaction from knowing he had killed his fiancée. And, as much as Carpenter was going to relish killing this asshole and avenging the loss of Lizzie Hanson, he would also be doing it for countless other innocent victims. "Doesn't ring a bell but I'm not a fan of the ISI, particularly because they've been known to protect pieces of shit like you. Besides, that has nothing to do with the here and now."

"Very well, Mister Preston James Carpenter, then I'd say it's time for you to make a decision. You can toss your gun into that bedroom and accept your fate or you can watch your friend's head explode before I kill you. If you are brave enough to die, I will let this young man live. Of course, I will shoot him in both knees so that he cannot follow me, but he would likely survive. What shall it be?"

As Fahkoury was talking, Carpenter gestured to Kennedy, angling his head to the side in an attempt to get Kennedy to squeeze in tighter to the wall. As much as possible, he wanted to force Mumeet into an even smaller area. By shrinking the target area, Carpenter could aim more precisely. Every millisecond was going to count. "It does not matter that he dies here," he said. He glanced at Kennedy after he said that. The "What the fuck?" expression on Kennedy's face was unmistakable. He gave Kennedy a wink and said, "It only matters that you do."

"Your false bravado humors me, Mister Carpenter. Unlike you, my brothers and I are not afraid to die for our cause. Your demonstrated cowardice is why you infidels will never defeat us."

"Yours is a lost cause, Fahkoury. And you're no brave warrior. All you do is hide in the shadows and send misguided fools to do your bidding." Carpenter saw that comment had aggravated Fahkoury, who was now pressing his gun harder against Kennedy's head. He lowered his left hand where he was sure it would be out of Fahkoury's vision and flashed three fingers before pointing at the floor. This time, Kennedy blinked twice to show his understanding. "You and the few *brothers* you claim to have are condemned by the entire world, including those faithfully practicing Islam. And it's my job to make sure you are a dying breed."

"There you are wrong again, Mister Carpenter. Our legion is strong and growing. Your futile attempts will fail under the wave of warriors who will continue to fight until there are only believers walking this earth."

The shrillness in his voice told Carpenter he was getting under Fahkoury's skin. He knew Fahkoury was now more focused on him, rather than Kennedy. The end was closing in but he needed to press his advantage further. "It's too bad you can't ask Fahd al-Rasheed what he thinks about my abilities." He saw Fahkoury's hand begin to shake at the mention of his fellow jihadist. Then the end of the gun shifted slightly across Kennedy's head and toward him. *Almost there.* While he leveled the gun in his right hand at Fahkoury's mostly concealed head, he shook three extended fingers on his left hand to warn Kennedy.

"Every brave warrior like Fahd al-Rasheed will be replaced by more who are equally committed to the cause. You are a fool to deny the fact we will keep coming for you. You are powerless to stop us!" Fahkoury shouted.

"That's where you're dead wrong, Fahkoury. I can and I will stop you and your asshole brothers," Carpenter said as his third finger folded.

Kennedy abruptly dropped to the floor, instantly exposing the priceless look of horror on Hamid Fahkoury's face before a dark hole materialized between his eyes.

"One bullet at a time."

EPILOGUE
Amsterdam

Several hours later, early risers on the East Coast of the United States were awakening to news that a major terrorist plot in The Hague had been thwarted. Details were sketchy, but rumors were that a high-value terrorist had been killed in an operation conducted by the Dutch General Intelligence and Security Service. More details were expected later in the morning when Director-General Theo Strous was scheduled to hold a press briefing. The major news networks were ruing decisions to largely ignore the G20 Economic Summit and scrambling to get reporters to The Netherlands.

Before news of the operation broke, Carpenter had been on a secure line with Director Timothy Patrick recounting the definitive events that had transpired since their previous conversation. After hearing his man out, Patrick forced Carpenter to listen as he expressed his own gratitude and that on behalf of a nation. Patrick then guided the conversation to an appropriate course of action to curb knowledge of US involvement in the operation. As soon as they were finished, Patrick was on the phone with Director-General Strous. A consummate professional, Strous was uneasy about taking credit for work not his own, but he ultimately came around to the idea. Having had seen Carpenter in action, Strous had an appreciation for Carpenter's skills and fully understood Patrick's desire to keep his most talented operator out of the limelight. Patrick hung up with Strous and called Carpenter, confirming implementation of the agreed-upon course of action and providing him with additional instructions. That call lasted less than fifteen seconds.

Now, Carpenter and Kennedy were among the small delegation awaiting arrival of the US President at Amsterdam Airport Schiphol. Beginning on the short drive from The Hague, Carpenter had had time to reflect on the significance of the past several hours. A quest that had largely fueled him for the better part of the last decade was over. Hamid Fahkoury, a man previously only known as Mumeet or the Bringer of Death was dead, as was his co-perpetrator in the recent US attacks, Fahd al-Rasheed. Carpenter had yet to come to terms with the impact of Fahkoury's death. While he derived satisfaction that Fahkoury would no longer pose a threat to innocent people in an ever-smaller and more complex world, Mumeet's demise had opened old wounds. Carpenter thought about Lizzie Hewson and what kind of life the two might have had together. He wondered if he would have been able to walk away from his job with the Counterterrorism Center like he and Lizzie had planned. While Lizzie's death had scarred him and left a huge void in his life, the passing of time since had also served to reaffirm who he was. His life's mission was to protect those who were unable to protect themselves. He admitted to himself that he possessed a unique set of skills that could be deployed in virtually any situation and circumstances to ensure no one else had to endure the pain he had.

As President Madden started to descend the stairs of Air Force One, Carpenter came to the realization that he had been doing what he was meant to be doing all along. While he might have stepped away for a short time, something would have pulled him back in. And he now knew that Mumeet's death was not the completion of his mission. It was merely a partial ending to a painful chapter. There was more work to be done and he fully intended to keep doing it for as long as he could. While the president exchanged pleasantries with the Dutch prime minister, Carpenter looked over at Tyler Kennedy, grateful to be working alongside dedicated people like the young man standing with him. An instant later, the president was standing before them. The president ushered Carpenter and Kennedy out of earshot of the gathering and huddled together with them.

"Gentlemen, you won't hear this publicly but I want you to know how much I appreciate what you've done for our country and the entire free world," President Madden said.

"Thank you, sir," Carpenter said, "but we had a lot of help."

"I appreciate your humility, PJ, but it doesn't change the significance of what you have done. You've avenged the loss of innocent life on our shores and beyond, as well as dealt a severe blow to Sadiq bin Aziz's Al-Kalafa terror network. I am absolutely certain that this would not have happened without PJ Carpenter."

"Thank you, Mr. President," Carpenter managed to say.

"You, young man," the president said to Kennedy. "I can't say I was all too pleased to learn that PJ pulled you out of training for this mission. But I have always been about results and they are undeniable here. That said, you and PJ may have managed to cause some angst in the intelligence community by undermining the integrity and sanctity of our training methodologies. Director Patrick tells me that PJ has requested that you forego additional training so that you can join his team fulltime. Perhaps against my better judgment, I will agree to PJ's request." Looking at both men, the president said, "Let's make sure we keep this a tightlipped arrangement."

The president waited for both men nodded their understanding before he continued. "Good. PJ, I know Director Patrick shared some new information with you earlier. There have been some updates. Now that young Mr. Kennedy is a full-fledged member of the team, I'll share the updates Director Melissa Gonzalez and Tim shared with me just before we landed. A plane we believe is tied to Iran's Quds Force landed in Luxembourg City late yesterday afternoon. Thus far, we have not been able to determine who was on board when it left or the aircraft's final destination. But we have since learned that Sadiq bin Aziz owned a home in Luxembourg. Director Gonzalez had an Agency team break into the home an hour ago. The home was vacant, but there is strong evidence it was recently occupied. She has operations officers working the city now in the expectation of confirming Aziz's recent presence there. I'm sure you'll agree that the conclusions are obvious. Despite a monumental victory here in Holland, the stakes appear to be rising. We hope to know more over the coming days. When we're ready to act, you two will be leading the charge. In the meantime, get some well-deserved rest. I have a feeling you're going to need it."

"We'll be ready and waiting for your call, Mr. President," Carpenter said.

"I know you will, PJ. And when you do, I know you'll see your way to delivering the same fate to Mr. Aziz."

"Looking forward to it, sir," Carpenter said.

With that, the president left their company and returned to the short greeting line. Carpenter looked at Kennedy. "Well, I guess we're on standby for the moment."

"Thankfully," Kennedy said. "I'm ready for some sleep."

"We can rest later," Carpenter said. "Right now, we're going to do a little training."

"You heard POTUS, he told us to get some 'well-deserved rest.' And he said I was done with training."

"Agency training but not mine. You'll learn that we've got to be prepared for anything, anytime. Your chance for rest will come but only after we do a little one-mile swim," Carpenter said.

"What? You looking for a rematch when I'm dog-assed tired?"

"Yup," Carpenter said grinning. "Just like the Bringer of Death did, you're about to find out that payback is a bitch."

COUNTER STRIKE

Made in the USA
San Bernardino, CA
14 February 2019